the Kissing Tree

FOUR NOVELLAS
ROOTED *in* TIMELESS LOVE

KAREN
WITEMEYER

REGINA
JENNINGS

AMANDA
DYKES

NICOLE
DEESE

BETHANYHOUSE
a division of Baker Publishing Group
Minneapolis, Minnesota

Published by Bethany House Publishers
11400 Hampshire Avenue South
Bloomington, Minnesota 55438
www.bethanyhouse.com

Bethany House Publishers is a division of
Baker Publishing Group, Grand Rapids, Michigan

Printed in the United States of America

ISBN 978-0-7642-3612-9 (paperback)
ISBN 978-0-7642-3781-2 (casebound)

Cover design by Brand Navigation

Karen Witemeyer and Amanda Dykes are represented by Books & Such Literary Agency.

Nicole Deese is represented by Kirkland Media Management.

20 21 22 23 24 25 26 7 6 5 4 3 2 1

Contents

Broken Limbs, Mended Hearts

REGINA JENNINGS

For girls who climb

One

1868
Oak Springs, Texas

Bella Eden had always known when it would happen—the day before her eighteenth birthday. A girl who commenced with kissing too young was bound for trouble. On the other hand, she couldn't wait until she was staring spinsterhood in the face either. A first kiss just before eighteen was reasonable, she reckoned. And she knew where it would happen. For years, she'd passed by a stately live oak on the way to and from school. Beneath the canopy of its spreading branches was the perfect place, and she'd spent many a walk home imagining exactly how it would occur.

The only thing she hadn't known was who.

But now all was clear.

"What's got you so tickled?" Jimmy Blaggart asked. "You're grinning up a storm."

Bella's heart was pounding like a steam engine. She pulled him away from the wagon trail and toward the oak. "I have a surprise for you," she said.

Today was the day, and Jimmy Blaggart was the man for

her. They'd grown up together, but only recently had he paid her any mind. Every day since April he'd walked her home, even staying and visiting for a spell afterward. That could only mean one thing.

The tree's majestic limbs stretched out in every direction, their farthest-flung tips nearly sweeping the ground when moved by the breeze. Jimmy paused as Bella ducked beneath them, and she pulled him inside the green cavern.

"It's like being beneath a colossal green parasol, isn't it?" Releasing him, she spun slowly, mesmerized as always by the unworldliness of her secret enclave.

"How would I know? I don't use a parasol."

If Jimmy wanted their marriage to prosper, he would have to develop an imagination. Bella looked at him again. He was decent enough. Caused no offense. His family was moving after he graduated, so this could be her last chance to make an impression.

She smiled. Tomorrow she would be eighteen, and in another week she'd be finished with school and able to devote more time to her sewing. Soon she would have enough customers to call herself a bona fide seamstress. This kiss was the next step to her future.

"My lands, would you look at this?" The canopy arched higher near the center, exposing the tree trunk. Bella had spent hours getting this spot ready, but it would be worth it. "Look at this. Someone has carved a heart in the tree." She leaned forward as if seeing it for the first time. "What's that inside the heart? *BE*? Why, those are my initials! How strange." She slipped her hand into her pocket and felt for the paring knife, glad she'd thought to stick the blade through a new potato so she wouldn't cut herself.

"Bella." Jimmy's passable face looked worried. "You're a nice girl. . . ."

Pushing the potato off with her thumb, she managed to get the knife free without slashing her pocket. "Look what I have."

His eyes widened. "What do you want me to do?"

"I want you to kiss me." She hadn't expected that she'd have to spell it out for him.

"You do? Right now? Right here?"

"Yes, I think it'll be real special."

He kept one hand extended between them. "And if I don't?"

"If you don't?" Bella looked at the tree where her initials were carved. In all her plans, she hadn't thought there needed to be a threat involved. "If you don't, I'm going to be heartbroken."

"But you aren't going to stab me, are you? Promise me you aren't going to stab me." His eyes never left the knife in her hand.

"Sweet potatoes! Are you joshing?" she cried. "This knife is for the tree. You're going to carve your initials in the heart above mine, and then you're going to kiss me. Why would I stab you?" Maybe Jimmy had more imagination than she'd credited him for.

Seeing that his epidermis was in no danger of being punctured, he simmered down. "Like I was saying, you're a nice girl."

She was not fond of the direction he was going. "You've walked me home every day for a month, Jimmy Blaggart. That's supposed to mean something."

"It means that I'm partial to those bird dog puppies of your pa's. I mean to buy one as soon as I get my hands on enough money. You know the one I want? The little speckled one?"

"I did not plan this encounter to talk about a speckled pup!" Bella stabbed the knife into the tree to free up her hands. Getting a kiss out of Jimmy might be more work than she'd figured. She flipped her honey-colored braid over her shoulder and wiped her hands on her skirt to calm herself. "Now, let's stop fighting," she said. "It's just a kiss. Tomorrow's my birthday, and—"

Something bounced off her head. She looked at the ground to find it. Probably an acorn. There were plenty of old ones from last fall scattered around. "What I was saying was—"

Thunk! And this one stung. Bella rubbed her head and looked above them. Something moved, and the leaves rustled.

"I'm going home," Jimmy said. "Tell your pa to save that puppy for me."

"You can't go home. Not yet."

"Happy birthday," he said, then ducked out from beneath the limbs and disappeared from sight.

Bella's hands clenched into fists. What was wrong with him? Weren't men supposed to be grateful for every kiss offered? She hadn't predicted this outcome.

"You can offer your thanks now."

Bella jumped. The voice had come from above her. "Who's that? Come out!"

The leaves rustled. Branches parted, and a face emerged. It was Adam Fisher, a classmate and rapscallion of the first order. And he had the audacity to be grinning at her.

"You should thank me," he said. "My well-timed missive stopped you from further embarrassing yourself."

Sweet potatoes, he'd heard the whole thing! "What are you doing up there, besides spying on me?"

"Where else would I go? It's not like I have a lot of friends."

Adam and his family had only moved to Oak Springs around Christmas. He was handsome enough, but Bella had already set her sights on Jimmy.

"It's no wonder," she yelled. "Who'd want a friend like you? Come down here this instant!"

"While you have a knife? No, thanks."

He was laughing at her. The most painful episode of her tragic life, and he was laughing at her. She'd make him pay.

"I'm coming up!" What she was going to do when she caught

him, Bella had no idea, but anything was better than standing around like a pitiful, scorned reject. She threw a leg over a low-lying branch and pulled herself upright. Straddling it, she could see Adam crouched on a limb closer to the trunk. "You're going to be sorry."

"Next time, just ask for an orange," he said. "That's a better birthday present than a kiss from Jimmy."

She got her feet on the limb and reached for another branch to steady herself. "I'm coming for you, Adam Fisher."

"Or maybe if you had traded him a speckled pup for a kiss, you would've had more luck. He sounded right taken with those pups."

Drat him. He didn't seem the least concerned that she was hunting him, but he'd learn.

She moved forward but couldn't reach the next limb up. She rose on her tiptoes. If she could just stretch a little farther . . .

"And just think, your poor initials are going to be all alone on that tree. What a pity," he crooned.

That was the last straw. She had to stop the horrible words coming out of his mouth. Then she spotted his foot hanging down from the branch above her. She'd show him. She'd drag him out of this tree if it was the last thing she did.

Bella lunged for his foot. The leather scraped against her fingertips, but she got no purchase because, at the last second, he yanked it away. Her weight shifted, and her foot slipped off the branch. The inside of her leg scraped against the limb as she sat down hard, but then she spun upside down, and suddenly she wasn't being hit by leaves anymore. There was only air.

She only had time to put out a hand to catch herself, but that was a mistake. The pain was immediate, bringing tears to her eyes and blurring the shocked face of the boy who'd mocked her.

Two

Three Years Later

From the seat atop his threshing machine, Adam Fisher stopped his four-horse team and studied the town of Oak Springs before him. He hadn't been back since he'd graduated from the one-room schoolhouse in the valley below. His parents had lived in the community for less than a year before moving on, but he planned on it being his home for the next few weeks, and maybe even longer.

"This is a likely spot." Dr. Paulson's black buggy pulled into the shade thrown by Adam's massive machine. "See how the land has a natural terrace down toward the creek bed? More than likely the soil has benefited from spring floods and silt deposits. I would expect that this would be a high-yield valley."

"You would expect correctly," Adam said, surveying the golden ripples of wheat interrupted by scattered homesteads. The heavy kernels bending toward the ground announced that he'd arrived just in time. "I lived here once. These farmers know what they're about."

A few more weeks of the farmers' toil, and then his thresher could be used to separate the yellow kernels from their stalks and husks. But would they hire him? Another payment was soon due on his equipment, and if he didn't stay busy, he'd never earn enough to make his payments through the winter.

Newfangled machines were more likely to be ridiculed than appreciated in rural Grimes County, and if a prophet had no honor in his own country, a student like Adam would be laughed out of the region. He rubbed his chin, the stubble barely chafing against his calloused fingers. When he'd left Oak Springs, he'd had no need for a straight razor. Amazing what changes three years wrought.

Dr. Paulson shook his reins, and his sharp carriage horse stepped lively. Adam roused his laden team, and they gamely followed. As the names of the local farmers came to mind, so did memories that he'd forgotten. That farm belonged to Mr. Granger, who'd hired him during harvest. The house by the road was the Bond family's. Mrs. Bond had quickly befriended his mother when they'd moved to town and always seemed to be in the Fishers' kitchen when he came home from school. And that farm east of town was Mr. Eden's.

There was one name he hadn't forgotten. Bella Eden. He'd always had a hankering for her. Her sweet, heart-shaped face and waves of light brown hair had caught his attention right off. Unfortunately, he hadn't caught *her* attention—not until he'd broken her wrist. After that, she'd given him the cold shoulder. But that had been years ago. What was she up to now? Probably sewing up a storm, like she'd always planned. If so, she might admire the gift he'd brought her—proof that he hadn't given up on her, no matter how long he'd been away.

Even though her family never had more funds than their neighbors, Bella had always dressed like a fine lady. It was due to her skilled needle, not any extravagant expense, or so Adam's sister had pointed out. Her dresses were the same aged cloth and worn cotton, but she managed to make them look like something special when she wore them. Adam had noticed that without his sister's help.

But Bella wasn't just pretty, she was spirited. He steeled himself for the possibility that someone had made her a wife by now. In a community like Oak Springs, he'd find out soon.

Dr. Paulson hailed the farmer with a scythe in the field next to the road. The small area of felled stalks around him showed he hadn't begun harvesting in earnest. Swinging the curved blade over his shoulder, he strode toward the road like a cheerful grim reaper, smiling from ear to ear.

"My lands, what is that behind your team?" he asked, not taking his eyes off the thresher. "It looks like one of those ironclads that dueled at Hampton Roads."

"That is not the *Merrimack* nor the *Monitor*," Dr. Paulson said, "but an innovation that will mean more to this country than either of those ships."

Adam saw the slight twitch of the eyebrow beneath the farmer's straw hat. Multiply that skeptical twitch over the three dozen farmers in the area, and he wouldn't be able to make the payment on his equipment.

"This is a threshing machine, Mr. Granger," Adam said. "I'm here to work the harvest."

Mr. Granger took a second look, and his cherry-spotted cheeks bunched up with his smile. "I'll be! I didn't recognize you, son. Never expected you to be riding in front of something that ponderous. How are your folks?"

Adam relaxed the reins. This was the welcome he'd hoped for. "They're doing well over in Brazos County. My sister married a Lawson boy this summer. From what I hear, they're doing fine too."

"And how are you doing?" Mr. Granger stepped back so that his question clearly included whatever nonsense Adam was hauling.

"Spectacular! As you might know, I spent a couple of years at the agricultural school, but when I saw one of these machines in action, I quit classes and headed north to learn more about them. I traveled with a threshing crew over the plains for a year, learned the business, and saved every dime so I could buy one of these marvels for myself. And now I'm here to show you what it can do for you."

He pushed his tongue against his teeth to dislodge the feeling that he was no better than the snake oil salesmen who traveled through. This was different. He'd seen the proof of it. He knew how hard these farmers worked during harvest, and this machine would revolutionize their toil, giving them better yields, more profit, and making him a pretty penny in the process.

Everyone would benefit, but he'd already learned the pain of being a true believer in a land of skeptics.

For now, they were friendly skeptics, but his former professor Dr. Paulson had a way of ruffling feathers that few could rival.

"Why don't you fire up that engine and show me how it works?" The grass crunched beneath Mr. Granger's boots as he inspected the thresher. "Is it steam-powered?"

"No, sir. Maybe next year I can afford a steam engine. For now, I have the horses. I hitch them to the gearbox on that treadmill, and they walk in circles. That turns the gears, which spins the tumbling rod, which activates the thresher. It's a sight to behold."

Adam knew that looking at the idle machine was like studying a hummingbird at rest. Not very impressive until you saw it in motion. He never tired of watching the belts and gears and wondering at how they transformed the slow steps of draft horses into rushing wind and motion and whirling parts.

Mr. Granger was more impressed with his horses. "Fine team you have there. I saw a steam pumper fire engine once in Galveston that looked as heavy as a mountain. It had a team like that tethered to it. Noble beasts, they were. Must have cost a strongbox of gold."

Just in case Adam forgot that he owed money on the horses too.

"I'd like to show you what this machine can do," Adam said.

"Go on, then," Granger replied with a smile.

"Not here. It takes some space to get it properly laid out. Then we need some cut wheat ready for separating. Also room for the horses—"

"Not asking for much, are you?" Mr. Granger's laughter died when he saw that neither Dr. Paulson nor Adam shared it. "Well, I'm sure there'd be plenty of folks around here that would cotton to some entertainment."

"How about tomorrow? I was thinking of that place by the big oak tree. If you could bring some cut wheat—"

"Hold on there, Adam. Why would I be giving you my cut wheat?"

"I'm going to separate it for you. You'll bring it to me on the stalk, and you'll go home with straw and grain separated. I won't even charge you."

"Charge me? The last time we paid for a show was that acrobat who came through town. He could juggle while standing on his head. Can you juggle while standing on your head?" Mr. Granger snorted. "I didn't think so. I'd better get back to work. You should've known that harvest was the wrong time to come. Nobody has time for diversions while there's wheat to bring in."

No time? They wouldn't believe how much time his machine could save them. Harvest was the only time that he could help. But the sinking feeling in his stomach was growing—that same sharp disappointment he'd met with in Anderson when no one else understood his dream. When no one gave him the chance to prove himself.

Dr. Paulson looked at Mr. Granger with a condescension that was impossible to miss. "In a few years, no one is going to winnow wheat anymore. Every community will wait with joyful anticipation for the threshing teams to come to town. You'll pay for the privilege of being the first in line to have your wheat processed. But it takes a man of vision to be the first. We'll find our man. Follow me, Adam. We won't accomplish anything else here."

Dr. Paulson had insisted on coming along so he could gather soil samples for his research. Adam wished he had offered to bring the soil back to the university and had made the trip without the professor.

"It was good to see you again," Adam said by way of amends. "Please send my regards to Mrs. Granger."

Mr. Granger spared him a pitying look. "Be careful, Adam. A man's known by the company he keeps."

But Adam wanted to be known for being innovative and intelligent. He had felt that the good ideas of the classrooms needed to come out to the farmers, and he wanted to be their ambassador. If he could convince the farmers to give his machine a chance, he could bring prosperity to Oak Springs while making the payments that would keep his dream alive.

And if he could find Bella Eden, then his joy would be complete.

Three

"You might think about bringing your students." Ben Eden stole a piece of bacon off her plate. "It could be quite the spectacle."

Bella looked up from her sewing to watch her father eat half her breakfast. Just as well. She liked to get some handiwork done in the mornings before school and before her wrist started aching. The last thing she needed was greasy fingers to spot the bodice of the gown she was reworking. She picked up her spoon, her thimble clinking against the handle, and took a bite of cinnamon-dusted oatmeal.

"Do you think it'd be worthwhile?" she mumbled. "The juggler was amusing, but he didn't help the students with their exams."

"I'll tell you one thing. If your students let their education turn them into a dunce like that professor, we might as well close the doors of the school right now. It takes a lot of study to figure out how to be as disagreeable as that man." Her father wore his dark hair longer than most men, but it was his glory, as untamed as a horse's mane.

"Maybe it'll spark some imagination," Bella said. "It's good for the kids to see the latest technology." Taking the thread between her teeth, she bit off the excess, wrapped it carefully around the spool for future use, then folded the dress and dropped it in her basket. "Time to go. That bell's not going to ring itself."

Her hand lingered atop her basket. All day she'd be thinking of the new cut that she was trying to emulate from *Harper's Bazar*. By the time she returned from school and helped her pa with chores, there wouldn't be enough light to continue. But the town needed a teacher, and ever since she'd fallen from that tree, she hadn't been able to do as fine a stitch as before. After a bit, her wrist started to hurt, and that was that.

Bella picked up her lunch pail. Teaching hadn't been her plan. She'd always been an eager learner but had never thought of herself as studious, mostly because of her poor performance under duress. Sitting in class, she soaked up the lessons that old Miss Hoyt had taught them, but when she looked down at the blank lines of the examination booklet, every fact simply vanished. She could no more produce the right information than she could create lace out of corn husks.

That was why she'd told the school board no when they asked if she'd be willing to replace the retiring teacher. But even after her wrist had healed, she found that the future she'd planned was unlikely. She might as well help the community, if that was what they needed. And as it turned out, teaching wasn't the same as testing. In fact, her struggles gave her patience with her less confident students, something that parents were generous to acknowledge.

Bella patted their bird dog as she walked out the door, leaving it propped open so her mother could catch the morning breezes as she put away the breakfast dishes. Her spirits were lifted by the thick golden sea that rippled around her. Harvest time. The early summer had been gentle. No droughts, no pestilence, no storms, no fires. With their typical pessimism, the local farmers refused to celebrate a good crop yet, but beneath their grumbling, one could hear the careful hope that this year would make up for several lean seasons. She hoped so. It would be good to see her students well-fed and unconcerned through the winter.

Something up ahead caught her attention. Was that the machine her father had spoken of? It had to be. Bigger than the saw at the mill and twice as ungainly, it blocked the road next to the oak tree. As she approached, the sun reflected off the machine's metal sides and warmed her face. The shape reminded her of a dragon. A dragon in armor. How fantastic would it be if it breathed fire while it worked? She put up a hand to shade her eyes, but even with that help she couldn't see anyone around. Surely the owner hadn't abandoned it.

Then, from beneath the dark canopy of the oak, she heard a man's voice projecting like he was doing oratory.

"This tree is remarkable, I'll grant you that, but there are hundreds of similar oaks in this part of the country. I'm afraid your admiration of this one is lost on me."

Pausing at the leafy edge of the tree's spread, Bella took another look at the machine behind her. She tended to avoid the tree. It was the scene of the grandest embarrassment of her life, and one with dire consequences. The only way she'd come within a stone's throw of the oak of shame was knowing that neither Jimmy Blaggart nor Adam Fisher had stepped foot within the boundaries of Grimes County since they'd finished school. Those were the only two people who knew what had happened that day. They were the only ones who could disclose her embarrassment.

She saw the tapered trouser legs first, then the suit coat with tails. The gentleman's eyes flew from her lunch pail to the books beneath her arm. He sighed.

"I beg your pardon." Bella would be polite due to his age, even if he'd dismissed her on account of hers. "Is this your machine? It looks very interesting."

His salt-and-pepper beard was trimmed to a sharp shovel's point, and when he talked, it looked like he was digging a hole. "The machine belongs to him." He motioned toward the tree. "He can tell you all about it."

The shovel stopped digging, and he walked toward town.

Bella took another look at the massive hunk of metal. However it operated, it probably wasn't as interesting as the armored dragon she'd imagined. Better to learn about it now than to interrupt lessons for no cause. Finding a gap in the limbs, she picked her way beneath the tree.

The cool, fresh air surprised her. Although she walked past it with every trip to town, she'd forgotten the magical beauty of this spot that had always enraptured her. It was so magical that she nearly forgot what she was doing there.

The second man had his back to her and was studying the trunk of the tree. She reached up to capture one of the extending branches. Her wrist twinged with pain, but it was expected and ignored as she rustled the branch to get his attention.

"Excuse me. I'm sorry to interrupt you, but your friend sent me to ask you a question."

He straightened at the sound of her voice. His cotton shirt stuck to the small of his back, showing the strength of the morning heat, but he answered without turning to face her.

"What's your question?"

Bella shivered in the damp air. It might be humid, but something about him gave her goose bumps. A sickly feeling of something being undone, of guilt, of a reckoning, made her lean more heavily on the branch. But she wasn't about to walk away. It was her town, and he was a stranger. He would answer to her.

"Your friend said that the harvesting machine is yours and that you could tell me about it."

He rested one hand against the trunk of the tree. Bella released the branch, suddenly and foolishly convinced that if they were both touching the same thing, then it was akin to touching each other. She looked to her feet. Did that include the ground? Sweet potatoes! Then she was touching everyone all the time, except for people who were jumping into the air, and she didn't think there were enough of those at any one moment for it to deserve her consideration.

But the short of it was that he hadn't answered.

"People are saying that you're doing a demonstration." She wrapped her left hand around her right wrist in a tight clasp that often stopped the aching. "If that's so, I'd like to know what your demonstration entails."

He took a deep breath, and she braced herself for an answer.

"Bella, how in the world have your initials gone unclaimed?"

She clutched her wrist against her stomach. It was Adam. Adam Fisher. And he was tracing her initials inside the heart with his finger.

"What are you doing here?" she gasped. And how were those initials still visible? She hadn't thought about them for years. She longed to stomp away, but her feet were as rooted to the ground as the old oak.

With the speed of a waterwheel, Adam turned, seemingly aware of the dramatic role he'd fallen into.

"It's my threshing machine," he said. "I came to Oak Springs to bring our town up to date. It's the 1870s. Progress needs to happen." He patted the inscription on the tree like it was a cherished pet. "But you haven't answered my question. What have you been up to, Bella Eden?"

Her greatest fear had been that either Jimmy or Adam would talk and word would spread of her embarrassing spectacle. As far as she knew, both had been gentlemen, but now Adam had returned, and it seemed he had no compunction against broaching the delicate subject.

With her lunch pail swinging, Bella hurried to the tree trunk.

"I'm going to take my penknife to that bark and scratch it bare. I'd completely forgotten."

"I hadn't, and don't you dare deface it. This is a piece of history." His eyes flickered to her wrist. "Are you all healed up now? It was pretty rough there for a spell."

It was so like him to remember that part too. After she'd fallen, it was Adam who'd taken her in his arms and tried to soothe her cries. Despite her anger at him, she'd been in too much pain to deny herself that comfort. When he'd seen the swelling in her wrist, he'd wanted to go fetch her parents, but she convinced him to help her home instead. She couldn't take the chance that they would see the tree trunk and wonder what she'd been up to. It was bad enough that he knew.

"That wasn't the worst of it." She turned away from the tree trunk. Seeing the empty space, unclaimed, above her initials hurt too much. Reminded her that *she* was unclaimed. And she couldn't place the blame for that at Adam's feet. "I'm fine. I've learned to live with it."

He was still handsome, with his inky lashes lining ice-blue eyes, and the way his upper lip widened when he smiled. "I brought you something," he said. He motioned to the machine. "It's some spools of thread. They're pretty colors. I remembered that you liked to sew, and whenever I saw a new color . . ." He shrugged. "They're in my bag. Give me a minute, and I'll fetch them."

"No." She shook her head. "I don't want them." He'd brought a gift for a seamstress, and she was a schoolteacher.

The sound of a school bell being enthusiastically but unevenly rung reached them beneath the boughs.

"I have to go," Bella said. She'd never been late for school before. Not so late that the students took it upon themselves to ring the bell. Then again, the last time she'd run into Adam Fisher beneath the oak tree, she hadn't made it to school for a week.

He followed her out into the sunshine. The golden fields around them spoke of a different world than the one beneath the tree. A world with seasons, students, and toil, but no time for romantic dreams and kisses on birthdays.

All fine and dandy, because Bella had no time for that either. And until Adam Fisher had made himself scarce, all she could do was fret over what trouble he would stir up next.

Four

Adam watched as Bella hurried off with a quick, stiff-legged stride toward town. He hadn't spent much on the thread, but she could have at least looked at it. And where was she going? Did she have an appointment with a client? A fitting scheduled? Oak Springs was changing from the sleepy village he'd known. It could be that Bella's business was thriving.

She was prettier than ever. He'd figured she would have changed a mite, but he must have forgotten how sweet her face was, or how tender her eyes. His daydreams were too filled with making his payments on the equipment to leave room for many romantic musings, but now that he'd returned, they all came back. How jealous he'd been of that rube, Jimmy Blaggart. How he'd waited to tell Bella, but by the time he had worked up his nerve, he'd ruined his chance. That was the way it went, sometimes. Too late to rewrite history, but there was nothing wrong with planning for the future.

And a big part of his future would be decided by his demonstration for the farmers.

After picking out the flattest spot that didn't block the road, Adam began to unload the gearbox, sweeps, and the tumbling rod. He used his two strongest pullers to get the treadmill situated and then measured the distance before settling the thresher in. Once the heavy pulling was done by the horses, he tethered them low so they could avail themselves of the tender grass before any more work was required of them. The assembling of the sweeps, the gearbox, and the traces all fell on him. The way the custom cutters he'd worked with operated, the farmer himself would pitch in when it was time to thresh his crops, but Adam could hardly ask that of anyone before they'd decided whether he was worth the trouble.

By the time he'd assembled the machinery, he only had a few minutes to munch on the cold chicken leg that the boardinghouse owner, Mrs. Doris, had given him for lunch. Taking the horses by their lead ropes, he pulled them so that they and he could practice for the trial to come. So much rode on this demonstration. True, there were other towns, but if he couldn't do it here, what hope was there?

The horses went willingly into their harnesses. They were well trained but hadn't worked the long hours of harvest that would be required of them—that *hopefully* would be required of them. Pulling the sweeps around in circles was still a game for them, not yet associated with boredom and monotony.

The last harness was the hardest to buckle down, but perhaps it was due more to Adam's nerves than the new leather and tight fit. He pulled the strap through the buckle, then yanked it tight. Wedging his fingers beneath the straps on the horse's back, he lifted and shook it, ensuring the best fit.

A crowd of men had gathered in town and were coming down the road. Dr. Paulson had done his job rounding up spectators.

"Here we go, then," Adam muttered to his team. And men weren't just coming from town. Over the ridge, he saw Mr. Eden and Mr. Granger in a wagon, coming from their farms, along with more of their neighbors on foot.

With a hand cupped to his mouth, Mr. Granger called out, "Where do you want the wagon?"

Adam directed him to the side of the thresher. As the wagon passed, he peered into the bed, and his heart sank. It was nearly empty. At the most, there were only five sheaves in the back. That was hardly enough to get the machine started up. Not worth the trouble. No way to show his prowess with this scant example.

"I told you I would do as much as you wanted." Adam tried to hide his disappointment. "If you want to get more—"

"I don't have any to spare," Mr. Granger said. "If I'm going to ruin some crops, this is more than enough."

Ruin his crops? How would this machine ruin them? It didn't eat them. Adam respected these men, but he'd underestimated how difficult it would be for them to make changes.

The men from town had arrived, Dr. Paulson among them. The professor's serene smile was appreciated, but what was wrong with the rest of the men? They hung back, as if unwilling to stand too close to him. Adam caught the glances they were sending one another. Something was awry. Had Dr. Paulson already offended them?

Leaving the townspeople behind, Dr. Paulson stepped up in the wagon and motioned the men together so he could better address them. An academic speaker like Dr. Paulson had experience in setting the stage and making himself heard, but maybe he didn't have experience in dealing with independent farmers like those of Grimes County. They never quite arranged themselves into a group that met Dr. Paulson's standards, but he began regardless.

"Gentlemen of Oak Springs and the surrounding farms, today you will witness a harbinger of your future. Today you will turn from the antiquated methods you and your forefathers used and become ambassadors for progress."

Unable to bear their scoffing looks, Adam focused on the buckles and tightened the harness again. He would have gladly gone unnoticed, but that was impossible when Dr. Paulson called him out by name.

"Many of you know my former student Adam Fisher. His work at the agricultural college has been a credit to this town, especially considering what a meager education he was given here. Adam and I have made it our mission to improve the yield and quality of your produce, and in so doing, to bring Texas up to the prosperity enjoyed by the more successful farmers of the Ohio River Valley."

Why'd he have to go and say that? The last thing these men wanted was to be compared unfavorably to a bunch of Yankee farmers.

Adam grabbed the side of the wagon and, with one foot bouncing off a spoke, vaulted up next to Dr. Paulson. He had to intervene.

"Howdy, folks. I'm right pleased to see you again. I'm Adam Fisher, if some of you don't remember me. My folks and I were only privileged to live here in Oak Springs for a year, but it's one of my favorite places on earth. Now, Dr. Paulson, he's very generous with his praise, but instead of believing him—who's a stranger to y'all and hasn't proved his worth—how about we fire this thing up so you can see for yourselves what it can do?"

Heads were nodding. Postures relaxing. While Adam recognized Dr. Paulson's genius, he wasn't surprised that it often went unappreciated.

"Now, what I have here is a machine that will cut your threshing time to a quarter of what it was. You know how you have to beat those stalks, or walk your cattle over them back and forth? And then you have to wait for a fine, windy day to toss your grain up in the air and hope the husks blow off? It's hard work, and it takes time. You could be using that time to finish the rest of your field, or to plow up more ground if you had a mind to. This machine cuts out all that middle mess. All you have to do is toss the wheat into this chute here, and then the belts, the fans, and the beaters will do the separating. But don't take my word for it. Let me show you."

Wiping the sweat from his hands against his britches, he walked a circle around the treadmill and checked the horses' harnesses again. With a prod from his whip, the big bay stepped forward, dragging the others along. Adam moved back to follow the workings of the gears and the pole above his head that meant the thresher's mechanics were engaged. The creaking sound behind him told him that the thresher was starting to move. All the gears were engaging correctly.

"Ain't you forgetting something?" Mr. Clovis laughed. "Or does this machine of yours make grain without any stalks put in it?"

He'd forgotten about Mr. Clovis, a farmer and beekeeper. His honey was sweet, but his temperament was not.

"In good time," Adam said. "I'm making sure the setup is right."

"I could've had three bushels of wheat winnowed by now," Mr. Eden chimed in. "And that's without the help of four draft horses."

"He was up here for pert near an hour getting this rig set up," Mr. Clovis volunteered. "With that kind of a head start—"

"I'm ready to begin." A group of farmers with fields nearly ready to harvest weren't as patient as agricultural students wasting class time. Adam lowered the tailgate of Mr. Granger's wagon and pulled the bound sheaves toward him. With his knife, he cut the bonds and loosened the stalks. Thankfully, Mr. Granger had brought a pitchfork as he'd requested. But by the time he'd gotten the sheaves freed, the horses had stopped, and the threshing machine's whirling ceased.

"That wasn't as good as the juggler," Mr. Eden said. "He stood on his head."

"Give the lad a chance," Dr. Paulson said. "You might learn something."

Adam was too busy to answer. When he raised his head, his eyes lit on Mr. Granger. "Mr. Granger, could I talk you into prodding these horses for me? Not too fast, just keep them going steady."

Granger readjusted his hat and tugged on the gelding's bridle. The threshing machine whirled back to life.

Adam couldn't help but look for signs that his audience was interested. They were, but maybe more interested in watching it fail.

Then they would be disappointed.

Standing at the back of the wagon, Adam took the pitchfork and tossed the first load of wheat into the hopper. To the new listener, the sound of the fans wouldn't be discernible from the sound of the beaters, but to Adam, it was as sweet as a whippoorwill's song. He pitched another bundle in, then another. The beaters were doing their work, but the evidence was hidden until . . . there! Straw was spitting out of the vent. Golden straw with no heads of grain. Mr. Garner lifted an eyebrow. Adam smiled. He'd impressed at least one, and there was even more to come.

The fan whistled inside the machine, and even though the work was hidden from their eyes, Adam knew the forced air was blowing across the grain and separating the kernel from the husk around it. And in just a moment . . .

The first clean grain dropped from the cleansing sieve. Like quickening raindrops, the kernels bounced faster and faster against the ground. Mr. Clovis swept off his hat and held it beneath the spout, catching the precious grain. "Whoo-ee, look at that. And all he had to do was toss the stalks in."

"After spending an hour or so setting up the machine, and

then it takes four strong horses and two men to keep it going." Mr. Eden wasn't going to admit defeat.

Adam pitched in the last of the wheat from the wagon. "But once it gets going, the man-hours are just a fraction—"

Uh-oh. What was that noise? Something inside the thresher had broken loose and was spinning free. The wheat had stopped feeding in, so it was probably the rasp-bar cylinder. Mr. Granger stopped the horses, and Adam waited until all the parts were still before peering down the chute.

"What's the matter?" said Mr. Clovis. "Did it break?"

Adam could see a string from the sheaves wrapped around the shaft. He should have been more careful. "Just a quick repair and then it'd be going again, but I think you all understand the process. How's that grain look, Mr. Granger?"

Mr. Granger plunged his hand into Clovis's hat and let his fingers trail through the kernels of wheat. "Amazing. That's really something!"

"Yes, it is," Dr. Paulson jumped in. There was a smidgen of respect in their eyes that hadn't been there before. "And while we wait for your fields to completely ripen, I'm here to do some research and finds ways that we might be able to improve agriculture in your area."

"Research what?" Mr. Eden stroked his glossy beard.

"I'll take soil samples from different areas for tests. It might be that we can find crops that are more suited to your land than what you're planting now. Also, I'll offer lectures on the latest farming techniques. The threshing machine is just one advancement that's been discovered recently. From looking at your primitive equipment, I'd say there are a lot of things you could learn from me."

Adam was proud of his association with Dr. Paulson. He was. But sometimes the professor didn't read a crowd as well as he read those scientific charts.

"Not meaning to be snide, sir," said young Calvert Ansel, who'd graduated the year after Adam, "but what makes you an expert on farming? You ain't a farmer. You're a teacher."

Dr. Paulson took the question with a grace that caught Adam off guard. "Excellent observation, young man. I've studied the subject and had educational opportunities that your local school can't provide. I was taught by the most highly regarded professors in my field. And what qualifications does your schoolmaster have here in Oak Springs?"

Adam instantly remembered old Miss Hoyt. For all intents and purposes, she'd retired about a decade before she'd stopped holding classes. Someone should have replaced her years ago. Was she still teaching?

"No qualifications that I know of," said Mr. Clovis. "Did she even take her teacher's exam?" He looked to Mr. Eden.

Mr. Eden's face grew hard. "I challenge this machine to a contest," he said in his quiet way. "Give me time for my crops to ripen, and then I wager that me and my crew can winnow a wagonload of wheat faster than this machine can."

Adam was stunned. This was what he wanted, wasn't it? He knew his thresher could beat a crew of men, but would beating a respected man like Mr. Eden help his cause, or would he be resented even further? And what would Bella think?

"I have an excellent idea," Dr. Paulson said. "I don't want to take advantage of your unfamiliarity with the process. We know that the machine will win, but we don't want you to pay the price. So I'll stand in the place of losing on both sides. Consider these terms—if Mr. Eden wins, then Adam and I will leave Oak Springs and never return. We'll never trouble you again. On the other hand, if Adam and his machine win, then the first obligation is that you gentlemen must guarantee Adam Fisher five hundred acres of crops to harvest. You'll be charged his customary rate of five percent of the product, which you will find is very reasonable. I don't doubt that you'll be soliciting him to do even more."

Dr. Paulson straightened for his next pronouncement, his suit coat stretching over his thin chest. "In addition to that, if we prevail, you'll allow me to send one of my teaching students from the college to teach at your school. I'll bear the expense for the first year, but I think you'll find the benefits of an educated teacher worth your future investment. That will be the obligation, unless you can provide a teacher with superior credentials."

Adam rocked on his heels. Everyone had to realize what a bargain that was. Even if they lost the contest, the town was going to gain from it.

But of everyone, Mr. Eden seemed the least pleased.

"I don't aim to lose," he said. "And while we have nary agin you coming back into town if you lose, if those are the terms you set, then I'm willing to abide them."

"Are you sure, Ben?" Mr. Granger looked unduly concerned. "You don't have to accept their terms."

Why would Mr. Eden worry about old Miss Hoyt? Surely he knew that his own daughter had a hard time passing her tests in school and that Miss Hoyt did nothing to help her.

Before Adam could puzzle it out, Ben Eden turned and stomped toward his farm. Just as well. Adam had a crowd of men gathering around the thresher, inspecting and exclaiming over the golden wheat in Mr. Granger's hat.

It had been a successful day after all.

Five

"All y'all who've finished your compositions may go. I'll stay put a mite longer if anyone has questions." Bella balanced her chalk on top of the blackboard and dusted off her hands. She didn't have the experience Miss Hoyt had possessed, but she worked hard to make sure her students understood their lessons. And if it was something that neither of them could figure out, she wasn't above recruiting a parent to explain it differently. If someone wanted to learn, there was always a way.

In a stampede of leather-soled boots and bare feet, the classroom emptied, leaving only a few students still toiling over their composition books.

Max Bresden raised his hand over his head, his forearm stretching past his too-short sleeve. "Miss Eden, may I make use of the dictionary?"

The boy was set to graduate this year. He was her brightest student, and she'd be sorry to see him go, but she had no doubt that he'd be successful in passing his entrance exams for college. Unlike his teacher, Max excelled when tested.

"Certainly, Max. Although I can't imagine what word you might need help with."

He pried himself out from between the little desk and chair. "I probably got it right, but it looked funny when I saw it written on the page."

A common enough occurrence. As Bella walked by Freda Longstreet, Freda covered the last page of her booklet with her hand. She still had a year before she would be finished with her schooling. By the time she was seventeen, she'd be doing work near or at Max's level. What did she not want Bella to see? Bella nudged the girl's arm over to find that the booklet was already full. She furrowed her forehead at Freda. If Freda was finished with her composition, why was she staying after class? Freda only shrugged in answer.

At first, Bella thought the shadow passing in front of the door was Max returning to his seat, but Max was already back at work, and it was school board member Hollis Woodward coming through the door.

"Miss Eden, I've got a question for you."

That was just like Mr. Woodward. He hadn't wasted any time making a name for himself in Oak Springs, and he wasted no time in conversation either.

"Mr. Woodward, how can I help you?"

"Have you passed your teaching exam?"

Bella's throat tightened. Max and Freda looked up from their work. "Why would you ask me that?" she choked out.

"There's been some discussion today that perhaps our community needs a better qualified teacher." He held up a hand. "Not that I'm questioning your ability, but I wanted to make sure that you have the credentials to answer the naysayers."

Credentials? She'd never needed credentials before. "The town begged me to replace Miss Hoyt. No one else wanted the job."

"That's not the answer I was looking for." He smiled kindly.

"I don't mean to meddle, but if you have a chance, you might go ahead and take that exam before anyone finds out."

Max's desk creaked as he turned to watch Mr. Woodward depart. Bella was shaken. Why should she feel ashamed? She hadn't tried to hide her lack of a certificate from anyone. She'd never planned to be a teacher. It was only after her dreams of being a seamstress were destroyed that she considered the job. And she'd definitely never planned to take the exam. Exams terrified her. No matter how well she knew her subject, her mind was wiped as clean as her blackboard when it came time for the test.

Mr. Woodward had already left the schoolyard before she could thank him for the warning.

What had brought about this concern? Was it because they'd reached the end of the school year? Were they looking at engaging a new schoolteacher for next year? Had she not done enough?

Max closed his composition notebook. Seeing him stand, Freda set hers aside also.

"I'll see you tomorrow." Max handed Bella the notebook. He looked like he wanted to say something but didn't quite have the courage.

Bella snapped the booklet out of his hand. She'd always thought he was sweet on her. Their ages weren't too dissimilar, but as his teacher, the most responsible thing to do was pair him up with Freda. "Thank you, Max. See you tomorrow." To Freda, she said, "And you're finished too? Maybe Max can walk you home."

Freda tossed her booklet on Bella's desk with a delight that proved her reason for staying late as she hurried to join Max.

At least Bella had ended the school day with a charitable deed, even if Mr. Woodward's visit had been unsettling. Part of her wanted to stay in town and see what Mr. Woodward had been talking about, but she was afraid. What if they insisted on her taking the exam? She would fail. Maybe the best course was to go home and ask her pa about it. Maybe he'd know something.

Bella had no more than stepped out of the schoolyard when Mrs. Clovis flagged her down by waving a pillowcase above her head. "Bella! Bella, dear, have you heard the news?" If anyone knew the town gossip, it would be Mrs. Clovis.

"I was hoping to see you." Bella stuffed the exam booklets into her satchel and reached for the pillowcase. Without asking, she flipped it to the opening and ran her fingers along the edge. Mrs. Clovis couldn't see well enough to do her own mending. Bella was grateful for the little jobs she offered.

"Lace here, I suppose," Bella said.

"The same lace as the others. I left a pillowcase under the iron and burned it, so I need a replacement."

"That should be easy enough." Then Bella added before she lost the nerve, "Have you heard anything about me taking a teaching exam?"

Mrs. Clovis nodded. "There's a wager going between the harvester and your pa. If your pa loses, we'll get a new teacher."

"What?" Bella's head popped up. "What does Pa have to do with it?"

"They made a wager over who could thresh the crops faster. If your father wins, then that Adam Fisher will never come back to the area. If Adam wins, then he'll provide us with a new teacher. You won't have the job anymore."

Bella couldn't breathe. Why would he do that? What did Adam have against her? She cradled her wrist as if she'd just felt it crushed again. First he'd ruined her dreams of being a seamstress, and now he was trying to get her dismissed as the teacher. Unbelievable.

"And here he comes," said Mrs. Clovis. "Doesn't he look proud of himself?"

Bella had nothing to say to Adam. With her head down, she bundled the pillowcase beneath her arm and hurried toward home.

Was that Bella in the schoolyard, talking to Mrs. Clovis? Adam's chest puffed out. No doubt she was hearing how miraculous his contraption was. No doubt she was awonder at his amazing machine. But as he approached the two ladies, he could tell something was wrong. Was Bella concerned about the wager with her father? Sure, Mr. Eden stood to have his pride hurt, but nothing beyond that. Dr. Paulson was so generous that the townspeople would gain even if they lost the contest.

As he drew near, Bella put her head down and angled away. She swung a wide arc around him before taking to the road that led back to her farm. He slid his hands into his pockets as he watched her walk past. He'd been looking forward to speaking to her again, but it was Mrs. Clovis who felt friendly.

"I didn't think it would bother her, this wager between you and her pa, but she lit out like her house was on fire when she saw you coming." Mrs. Clovis blinked her watery eyes. "I wonder what's amiss. I thought she'd be happy that we might get another teacher."

He looked at the empty schoolhouse, its door shut tight. What was wrong? Old Miss Hoyt would probably rejoice if they found a replacement for her.

"I don't understand," he said, but there was a better way to find out. Go to the source—especially if the source was Bella. "Excuse me, ma'am." He tipped his hat to Mrs. Clovis, then took out up the road. Bella might not be tickled to talk to him again, but in a town the size of Oak Springs, they could hardly avoid each other.

She chugged up the hill toward the giant oak tree, her skirts swishing beneath her trim waist. He thought of calling out but feared that might speed her steps. Instead he ran until he was at her side and could match her stride.

She lit into him right off the bat. "Why are you here? Haven't you done enough?"

"The wager with your pa wasn't my idea. He suggested it. And I thought Dr. Paulson's offer was most generous."

"Very generous indeed!" Her cheeks were flushed with anger.

Adam understood why she'd been mad at him for the Jimmy Blaggart incident, but he didn't deserve her ire over this. "I don't see how it matters. Even if your pa loses, he's not required to make any sort of payment. The whole town will benefit if Dr. Paulson brings in someone to replace Miss Hoyt."

Bella stopped. The way she stared made him feel that he'd left some breakfast stuck on his face.

"You don't know, do you?" she asked.

"Know what?"

An eyebrow arched. "Miss Hoyt retired. She doesn't teach anymore."

"Not that she did any teaching when we were in school." He grinned. "Who'd they get to replace her?"

Bella's hand went to her hip, and she tapped her foot. "Someone who was looking for work when an injury made her chosen profession impossible. Someone who never took her teacher's exam because she's a known failure at tests. Someone who was only a mediocre student but has found that she enjoys teaching."

Whoever this woman was, Bella was hopping mad on her account. An injured woman who was a mediocre student . . . ?

Adam's gut twisted like it had gone through a wringer. "Bella," he groaned. All the anguish he'd felt when he'd seen her in pain, all the shame he'd carried as he waited for her wrist to heal, came flooding back. "You're the teacher? What about your sewing?"

"Sewing?" She scoffed. "Try making those tiny stitches when your hand doesn't work as it should. Try to make a living when you can only hold a needle for half an hour before the ache becomes unbearable."

"It was an accident." He swallowed hard. That was why she didn't want the thread he'd brought.

"And now you're going to push me from another job," she continued. "Is that what you want, Adam? For me to stay out at the farm, trying to come up with work so I'm not a burden on Ma and Pa?"

While the wager with her father hadn't been his idea, he'd be blamed, sure as the world.

"I'll tell Dr. Paulson that there's no need for the teacher. If you're doing a good job and are willing to get your exam . . . ?"

She winced. Flinging her hand through the air, she turned to go up the road, parting the tall grass on either side of the wagon ruts.

Adam pursued. "I'm trying to make amends," he said. "I tried three years ago to help you, and I'll try again now."

"Your help brings great harm."

"If you have your certificate, then there's no reason for Dr. Paulson to bring a new teacher. The school board can easily refuse his offer."

"But I don't have it, and I can't get it."

"Why not? Aren't you healed enough to hold a pen now?"

"It's not about my injury. It's about the tests. I can't pass that exam. Any exam I've ever passed was only passed by the skin of my teeth. You wouldn't understand how nervous I get. It makes me sick just thinking—" She clutched at the bow on her collar. "Seamstresses don't have to take tests, but I'm not a seamstress, and thanks to you, I won't be a teacher either. The only way out of this is if Pa wins, and maybe he will."

"He won't." Now Adam knew what a doctor felt when telling a patient their dire diagnosis. "There's no way he can win, and even if he could, it wouldn't be good. If I lose, I can never come back to Oak Springs. I could never see—" His eyes flashed to her clear, honest face. "I couldn't see anyone from here again. No one, Bella. Besides, I need the work. The next payment on my machine is due in a few weeks. I don't have time to try another town. I need to start harvesting now."

"Then you have a choice to make," she said.

And those were her last words before she left him at the tree, wondering why God had chosen him to ruin her life yet again.

The words in the composition booklet blurred before her eyes. Bella dropped Freda's work on her kitchen table and looked out the window again. Where was her father? It was unlike him to be gone from home this late. She rubbed her bare foot on the bird dog beneath the table as she pondered her father's role. Why had he made this wager? Did he regret it? Or maybe Adam and this loathsome Dr. Paulson had underestimated her father. Perhaps she was bothered over nothing. Perhaps her father would win, and her fears would be put to naught.

The door opened, and her mother came in with a pail of milk from the evening milking. "He's coming through the east field," she said, not explaining how she knew that Bella was watching for him.

Bella bolted out of her seat and dashed out the door with the dog at her heels. Trailing his fingers through the wheat, Ben Eden walked with his back straight and his head high. They weren't in trouble. Adam Fisher might have caught them off guard, but the Edens wouldn't be shaken. Bella waited until her father reached the lawn before running to him and giving him a big hug.

"That's a nice surprise." He chuckled as he wrapped his lean arms around her. "Let me guess, you're concerned about the wager. Does your mother know?"

"I haven't said anything to her, but she's going to know."

"I challenged Adam over his threshing machine and nothing else, daughter. The clause about the teacher was added later, but don't you worry. You won't lose your job."

"I've done well by the students," she said. "The parents are pleased with their progress."

"But this know-it-all professor comes in and acts like we're ignorant country folk. He carries on like taking a test and getting a certificate makes you a good teacher. I'd rather have you at the front of a classroom than any fool he trained. To tell you the truth, I'm flummoxed by the Fisher boy. I'd always thought he was sweet on you."

Bella looked up at her father's face, certain she would spot a teasing smirk.

There was no smile. "You don't believe me?" he asked.

"It's impossible," she said. "He doesn't think of me at all." Or did he? Adam had been underfoot a lot since he'd come back to town. Bringing nothing but misery, but still . . . "At any rate, I doubt folks are taking him or his professor seriously."

"But they might." Pa tugged on his beard. "It wouldn't hurt for you to go ahead and get that exam done so you have your certificate. That'd show them that you were good enough all along."

Her arms dropped, and she stepped out of reach. "But you're going to win, and then I won't have to worry about it."

"Yes, I'm going to win. There's no way I'm letting that rascal get the best of me. Don't you worry. He'll soon be gone, and everything will be alright."

But everything wasn't alright. Adam Fisher was here, and she feared he wouldn't leave until everything was ruined.

Six

In the three days since he'd spoken to Bella, Adam had been looking for the right moment to get Dr. Paulson to change the terms of the wager. He reckoned that since Mr. Eden hadn't expected his proposal to threaten his daughter's employment, he would be agreeable to a renegotiation. Adam decided to broach the subject while he and Dr. Paulson took soil samples at Gabe Whitlock's farm.

"When the wheat is ready, we'll have that contest," Adam said to Gabe and Mr. Longstreet. "But I'm amenable to changing the terms. If my thresher is faster than Mr. Eden and his team, I'll have work, and that's all that matters. It's none of our concern who's teaching school in Oak Springs." He held out a watertight bag to accept the spadeful of soil from Dr. Paulson.

"Afraid you're going to lose?" Gabe dipped his neckerchief into a bucket of water, then slapped it on his neck.

Adam folded the flap of the bag closed. "No, but I don't see what business it is of ours who teaches in Oak Springs."

"We're sowing progress, Adam." Dr. Paulson cleaned his sample-collecting spade with a stiff brush. "Providing an educated teacher will bring the fruit."

"But Miss Eden has done well by my girl," Mr. Longstreet said. "She's learning up a storm."

"Bella is a good girl," said Gabe, "but put her up agin someone like Dr. Paulson here, and it ain't no contest."

"Dr. Paulson isn't going to teach at the school," Adam said. "The offer would be to send a student from the college. Most likely someone with no teaching experience. I don't see how it would be an improvement, honestly."

Dr. Paulson put a hand on Adam's shoulder. "He's being modest. Always afraid that people will think he's putting on airs, but the truth is that the years that Adam spent at the agricultural college expanded his options. An educated teacher could do the same for the students here at Oak Springs. I've had a hard time convincing him, but I think it's a gift that the townsfolk will appreciate."

"That's the truth of it," Gabe said. "Some of us were talking, and with the way the town is growing, we've got to start thinking about the future." He turned to Adam. "Don't you be changing the rules, though. Your rich friend here isn't weaseling out of this. He promised us a new teacher, and the only way you're getting out of it is if you lose the contest."

That hadn't worked as well as Adam had hoped. He'd have to try another approach, and that was to go straight to the victim herself.

He managed to send Dr. Paulson back to the boardinghouse without him so he could meet Bella after school. He waited in the shade of the smithy across the road until the students had stopped pouring out of the schoolroom, then headed to the schoolyard.

The door of the schoolhouse was open, but it wasn't until he stepped inside that he could see her at her desk. Her head was bent over a well-worn book. She held her wrist cradled in her hand as she leaned her forearms on the pages to prop the book open. It was a pose that was becoming familiar.

He shifted his weight until the loose board in the doorway squawked.

She raised her eyes, ready to politely address her interrupter, but then saw who it was. The cheerful tilt to her eyes evened, and she turned her attention back to the book.

Seeing that no invitation was forthcoming, Adam strolled inside. Hands in his pockets, he took a long look around the room. "You've made some improvements."

"No more smoking stove," she mumbled over her pages.

"But the board in the doorway still creaks."

"If I fix that, how will I know when someone is sneaking up on me?"

Grasping a desk in the front row, Adam squeezed his body into the seat normally reserved for the youngest of students. "I can't believe I ever fit into these seats."

"You didn't," she said. "When you came to town, you were already grown." She put her finger on the book and looked up. Her blue eyes flashed with annoyance. "Is there something I can help you with, or are you here to bedevil my last days in this position?"

"I'm here to help you."

"How?"

He shifted, and the whole desk moved. "I'm here to see how I can help you. I have a history of being a decent problem solver."

"You have a stronger history as a problem causer."

He dipped his head. "Fair enough. I caused this problem, so the least I can do is try to fix it." He leaned forward, the desk tipped, and he nearly toppled over. He shoved his legs forward to stop his fall and banged his knees against the desktop. The pain was worth the softening of her scowl. "Can you tell me what's keeping you from taking the exam and getting your certificate? Is there a fee?"

"I can pay it."

"Where do you have to go to take the test?"

"Anderson. That's not the problem."

Her desk was elevated on a platform, causing Adam to envy whoever had this chair. Old Miss Hoyt hadn't looked nearly as alluring at the front of the classroom.

He pried himself out of the desk and unfolded his body before approaching her. "Multiplication tables?" he said. Despite her attempt to cover the pages, the graph was easily seen. "Are you studying?"

"Yes, but it's pointless."

"I could help you. We could drill, and you'd get them soon enough."

"I know them. I've known them since I was eight years old. It's not that I can't learn them—it's that I can't take a test." She crossed her arms over her chest. "Don't you remember how I did on tests? I could write a composition without a mistake, but when I got up for the spelling bee, I'd go out the first round. I'd make the highest marks on my arithmetic assignments, but when doing a race at the blackboard, I couldn't do simple math. I'm like a racehorse that gets a cramp before every run."

Adam had never considered this complication before. He'd always excelled under pressure. He might be an average student, but when push came to shove, he'd pull out a bit of information or a new angle that he didn't know he had in him. He'd never considered that someone could perform less than they'd prepared. It didn't make sense, but he owed it to Bella to listen.

"But if you knew it was really important that you pass . . ."

She moaned. "That makes it even worse. The more important it is, the worse I perform. I'm so frustrated with myself. I should've taken the test as soon as my wrist had healed. It didn't really matter then whether I passed or not, but now, with everyone looking, I feel sick just thinking about it."

He called himself a problem solver, but he didn't know what he could do about this. Things that challenged him to work harder only paralyzed her. It was a conundrum.

With his hands spread wide and his elbows locked, Adam leaned over her desk as if her open arithmetic book offered the answers. He was too close for her to ignore, and too handsome for her not to notice, but Bella reminded herself that the gaudiest candy often gave you the worst stomachache. She diverted her gaze from his proximity and studied the picture of George Washington hanging over the pegboard.

Usually Bella was the one trying to help students overcome the stumbling blocks to their education. She wasn't accustomed to being the subject of intervention. From the set of his fine jaw—she was looking at him again—it was clear Adam wasn't going to let her beg off with excuses. She wanted to succeed, but accepting his help would most certainly mean disappointing him. For reasons she couldn't explain, failing him felt as painful as losing her job.

"You're under no obligation," she said. "I feel better now that I know you don't feel compelled to rob me of my livelihood."

"You can't be serious." Even in disbelief, he was as finely wrought as an archangel. Or at least what she imagined an archangel to look like.

She held up her hand to stop him. "It's been bad luck. The two of us should never meet. Nothing good can come of it."

"I disagree. I think something good can come. Maybe something neither of us expected."

Bella's head lifted. Had she imagined that change in tone? She was good at imagining, so she rarely trusted her instincts. Before she could decide if there had been any sentiment behind the comment, he'd walked to the blackboard, making it impossible to see his face.

He picked up the chalk and, going to the top corner of the board, wrote in crowded, slightly out-of-control penmanship:

I will not provoke Miss Eden.
I will not provoke Miss Eden.
I will not . . .

"Provoke me to what?" she asked.

"To anger? To despair?" He turned and set the chalk down with a grin. "You don't assign sentences, do you?"

"Of course. But not that one." Her eyes fell guiltily to the book on her desk. She should be studying, but Adam was once again interfering with her plans. "What do you propose?" She threw her shoulders back and braced herself for his suggestions. "I know the material. Studying doesn't seem to be the answer."

"We practice taking the test."

She shook her head. "As long as I know it's just practice, it's not going to work. There has to be a consequence for it."

"So you take a practice test, and if you fail, then something bad happens?" The corners of his mouth turned down as he thought it over.

"I don't know what would cause the most anxiety." She drummed her fingers against the desk. "I get anxious when I think of a flood wiping out our house, but since we live on a hill, that won't happen, and it seems a steep penalty for failing a practice exam. Measles—I worry about getting those too."

"I'm not going to give you measles. That's out of the question."

"Well, maybe I could pay you money if I fail. No, you probably wouldn't accept. I could give some money to someone. If there was a needy family . . ."

"Your donation could go to paying the new teacher's salary."

He held up his hands as she gaped. "Just pulling your leg. How about if you fail on this practice, you have to buy me a stick of peppermint candy?"

"A stick of candy?" Just thinking about failing was already making her skin feel clammy. Even the price of a stick of candy was enough to addle her. "Let's do it. The subjects I'll be tested on are spelling, arithmetic, geography, history, and English grammar."

"Since we haven't had any time to prepare, it sounds like spelling will be the easiest to start with." He picked up the dictionary that Max had consulted earlier. "Twenty words. You need to get fifteen right. Does that sound reasonable?"

Bella swiped her tablet of paper off her desk and went to the back of the room, where the chairs were larger and more comfortable.

She stretched her hand, dismayed that she could already feel the sweat forming between her fingers. *This is important. If I fail, I will lose my job, and everyone will know that I was unqualified from the beginning.* Her pulse quickened as she looked at the formidable blank page. Five words. She could only miss five words. Five out of twenty. It sounded impossible.

Adam flipped through the dictionary until he found a suitable word, and at his pronouncement, it was like her head had turned to stew. "Expiation."

How to spell that? As Bella slowed it down in her head, the syllables seemed to transform into something different. She sat up straight and took a deep breath. *Write it fast*, she told herself. *Stop thinking about it and write it down.*

Her fingers seemed to have the word already imprinted in their memory. Writing it felt good. It was the right thing. She relaxed. She could do this.

Adam read the next word—*pyrotic*. She knew what to do. Just let her fingers take control before she gave it too much consideration. But then something caught her eye. The first word she'd written didn't look right. How could she have made that mistake? How could she have come so close to missing it? She scratched through the word and rewrote it, switching the *a* and *i*. That didn't look any better, but she had to move on. Now, the second word, what was it again? She bit her lip, then wrote *pyrotism* just as Adam was reading the third word. Moving her mouth to form the second word, she had to admit that it didn't sound right, but he couldn't repeat it. Not now.

Her sinking stomach knew the results no matter how she tried to deny them. If Adam had thought she was exaggerating about her poor exam scores, he was about to find out that she spoke the truth.

Adam hadn't planned on administering a spelling test today, but it was worth trying. And from the frantic scribbling and re-scribbling that Bella was doing on her paper, it was clear her teacher's examination would be a disaster. By the time he'd made it through the list, she was pale, shaking, and continuing to edit words at the top of the paper.

"Time's up," Adam said.

"How much time do I get?" she asked.

"It doesn't matter. You've had too much time already. You've turned that paper into an alphabet explosion." He grimaced as he slid it out from beneath her hand and looked it over. "This is worse than I thought."

"Well, don't sugarcoat it," she said with an eye roll.

"In every case . . ." He paused to flip through the dictionary and double-check. "Yep, in nearly every case you wrote the word correctly the first time. When you went back to fix it, that's when you spelled it wrong."

She dropped her head into her hands. "See what I mean? There's no way I can pass that test before next Friday."

The same day as her father's challenge to his threshing machine. Would both she and her father be shamed? That had never been his intent.

Adam dropped to his knee next to her. "This is good news. If you had to learn how to spell, we'd be in trouble, but you don't. You just have to learn to take a test. In this case, always go with your first answer. That's going to be your rule for spelling." He couldn't tell if he was easing her trouble, but he'd keep trying. He had to keep trying.

He ripped the page of misspelled words off her tablet and started toward the trash bin.

"Don't throw it in there," she said. "I'd expire of embarrassment if my students saw it."

Adam folded the paper and stuffed it into his pocket. "I'll dispose of it elsewhere, then. Now, what's next? Geography? Do you have a book for the questions?"

She quirked her head. "If I fail the geography test, do I have to buy you two peppermint sticks?"

"No, you have to buy yourself one so that we can enjoy them together."

Bella groaned. "That's worse than the measles. You're in a contest against my father. I can't be seen spending time with you."

"Then you'd best pass this test." He put his hand over hers. A shock passed through him at the contact. He hadn't touched her since he'd carried her home three years ago. It had seemed the right action then, as it did now. "I'll get the book," he said and wondered if he was the one being tested.

Seven

"I did miserably." The peppermint made Bella's mouth feel cool and tingly. Her scores from her practice exams made her feel dreadful and heavy. Perhaps she'd learned to perform better on the tests, but would it be enough? Would she forget the strategies they'd discovered together just as easily as she'd forgotten the location of Crimea?

"We have two more weeks," Adam said. "Tomorrow we'll work on math—that might take a whole afternoon by itself—then on Thursday we can do grammar, although that's not my strong suit. You might want to find someone else to help you with that."

Bella grimaced. "What would people think about the teacher asking to be taught? You can't tell anyone what we're doing."

"Teachers have to learn too."

"At a normal school or a college. Not with a traveling harvester." She stopped before they came within sight of her house. "Adam?"

"Yes?"

"Why are you helping me? Win or lose, you're not staying in town. You'll be moving on after harvest, so it doesn't matter to you who is teaching. Is it out of guilt?" Guilt was the only motivation she could name. The thought that she ranked somewhere between Christian duty and charity to the poor was not flattering. But if she could have accomplished her goals without him, she would have.

"No, not guilt." He wrinkled his nose. "Maybe a little guilt at the beginning, but even without this exam looming, I would have looked for a reason to spend time with you."

Bella studied him. Not like she studied books, but studied past his fine features to the meaning behind. "Why? You haven't talked to me for years."

"I'm here now. Right back where I carried you."

He'd carried her this far when she'd broken her wrist, and for the first time she considered how he'd helped her instead of only blaming him for her predicament. Either way, she couldn't let him come any farther. "You should stop here. My parents wouldn't understand." How could they, when she didn't understand herself?

"You're probably right," he said. "I'll meet you after school tomorrow. Until then."

When he smiled at her like that, Bella didn't feel like a charity case.

The front door of her home was open to catch stray breezes. When she spotted Pa's unlaced work boots in the doorway, she knew something was amiss. It was harvest season. Why would he be idle?

Bella found him at the table, flipping and catching a coin. "Are you unwell?" She patted his shoulder and looked to her ma. Her ma paused in her churning, and the concern on her face was worrisome. "What's the matter?"

"Sit down, child," said her pa. "We've heard some distressing news."

Her neck tightened as she hung her hat on the peg, then took a seat on the bench opposite Pa. Ma settled the dasher, then joined them, wiping her hands on her apron as she stood behind Pa.

"Have you been consorting with Adam Fisher?" Pa asked.

Bella dropped her gaze. Word certainly did travel fast. She hadn't seen anyone coming or going from town, which meant someone had spied on them in the schoolhouse.

"Adam is helping me prepare for my teacher's exam," she said.

"Your exam?" Pa rolled his eyes. "If it weren't for Adam Fisher, you wouldn't have to take the exam at all. In fact, if it weren't for Adam Fisher, you wouldn't be teaching school in the first place."

She picked at a piece of skin next to her fingernail. Her parents had never gotten the full story out of her about what had happened beneath the oak tree. All they knew was that she'd fallen out of the tree and Adam had helped her home. Had he kept his mouth closed and not been heard apologizing to her, they wouldn't have suspected a thing. Naturally, she would never tell them what had happened, but the bulk of their suspicions fell on Adam.

Her mother sat next to her. "Why are you bothering with the test? Everyone knows that you're the best teacher we've had in years."

"Do they?" Bella asked. "From what I hear, some are eager to replace me."

"Poppycock. They don't know what's good for them. If they were to bring an arrogant college teacher here, they'd realize their mistake."

"There won't be any more college people here," her father said, "because I'm going to win the contest. Don't think for a moment that a lad and a pile of flinging belts and fans can do better than my harvesting team."

"Be wary, Bella," her mother said. "Adam can't really mean

to help you on the test. He's using that as an excuse to spend unchaperoned time with you."

Her mother was the second person to mention that possibility. Bella found it incredible. Adam Fisher of the sketches, machines, and experiments? Although confident and good-natured, he'd never seemed to be looking for a girl, but he'd just confessed that he was interested in her company. What did she think about that? Could she see past the embarrassment and hurt of years past? Was Adam someone worth knowing?

"Why are you smiling?" her father asked. "How can you even speak to him? Can a man serve two masters? Out of the same mouth proceeds blessing and cursing? What communion has light with darkness?"

"Love your neighbor," Bella said.

The room fell silent. Her mother covered her mouth while her father glared. "What was that?" he asked.

Bella didn't know where that comment had come from. She'd just been considering the possibility, and out popped Scripture. She stood and walked to the small square window looking toward town. "What if he does like me? It'd be horrible, wouldn't it? He's tied up in a challenge against my father, while wanting to court me? What a conundrum."

"Enough with your romantic notions," her father said. "Find a good man who loves God and can support a family. Not Adam Fisher. He owes the bank for that machine. If he doesn't get hired by some farmers, he's going to lose everything."

"If he loses to you, he'll lose everything?" Bella allowed this to sink in. It was her job or his. Unless she could pass the teacher's exam.

Putting on a brave face, she turned to her parents. "You've given me a lot to think about, particularly to wonder if Adam is besotted with me. Regardless, I don't see you have any worries about our studying together. He's a stern taskmaster."

Pa took a deep breath to answer, but before he found the words, her mother laid her hand flat on the table. "Be careful, Bella. You're such a sweet girl, it'd only be natural that he'd fall in love with you, but whatever you decide—"

"Whatever she decides?" Pa blustered. Then, pulling at his thick beard, he reconsidered. "I suppose it'd be in good taste to extend friendship. It'd show that I'm not going to enjoy beating the whelp at his game, yet at the same time, for us to be overly familiar with him will seem strange to our neighbors. My reputation . . ."

"You're not the one being courted by him, you old goat," her mother said. "I don't think there's any danger of you being overly familiar with him."

"The same better hold true for Bella," he said, his eyes pinning her with suspicion.

Overly familiar with Adam? Bella wasn't sure what they were warning her against, but her imagination came up with some intriguing possibilities.

The day had been profitable, Adam reasoned as he exercised his horses on the treadmill. None of the farmers in Grimes County would commit to hiring him yet. He couldn't blame them for waiting to see the results of Mr. Eden's challenge, but he was making inroads into the community. While most of them couldn't swallow Dr. Paulson's edicts from on high, they sought Adam out for private consultations to get his opinion on matters.

"Barley has always done well on my farm, but it's been six years. Should I keep with it, or give the soil a rest and switch to another grain?"

"What are they saying in town about the price of cotton? Will it stay this high until next season?"

"The wife has been deviled by potato bugs in our garden. How can she get rid of the critters?"

Often, Adam brought the questions straight to Dr. Paulson, then carried the answers back unaltered, but somehow they were more palatable coming from Adam.

These were the people he wanted to live among. When Adam was growing up, his father was convinced that prosperity could be found just over the next ridge, so they rarely stayed put for long. If he retraced his path, there wouldn't be many who remembered him growing up. Nowhere that would claim him. But Oak Springs hadn't been so long ago that his history had been erased. He had friends here. He had a start. This sun, this sky, this land—it was where he belonged, but he had yet to prove it to the townsfolk.

Even if he did succeed, he wouldn't be there year-round. To establish himself, he had to travel. Many families were in the same situation—soldiers, sailors, even the cowboys taking to the cattle trails every year. But not all women had the starch to handle a life apart from their husbands. Was Bella one of them?

Everything he'd seen since returning confirmed that she was.

Adam swished the whip over the horses' rumps to set the team moving again. Looking back, he could see that Bella had always fascinated him. Smart, determined, and as curious about the world as he was, but the time hadn't been right. She'd been nose-to-the-grindstone determined to lasso that Jimmy kid when Adam came to town. Just as well. Adam didn't have anything to offer her back then.

Did he have anything to offer now? Well, that depended a lot on beating her father at a contest and whether or not he could make the payment on his thresher. He had a lot of promise, but that promise might dry up like wheat in a drought if he couldn't make the payments.

Convinced that the horses had been exercised sufficiently,

Adam unharnessed them and set them loose in the pasture he was leasing from Mr. Longstreet. It was nearly time to meet Bella for more studying. So far, no one had remarked on their association. Maybe they thought it impossible that they'd be friends, considering the nature of the contest. Or maybe people had better things to worry about than the courting habits of their young folk.

No, it definitely wasn't that.

Coming toward town, he could see the students scattering out of the schoolyard, some running home, some dawdling with friends. He was right on time.

He'd thought the students were all gone by the time he entered the schoolhouse, but when he stepped onto the threshold, he heard a girl's voice.

"Miss Eden, is your given name Bertha?"

"No, Minnie. It's Bella. Why do you ask?"

There was some giggling coming from the corner. His eyes lit on a gaggle of girls in their pinafores.

"The reason I ask is because Mary said that those initials at the big oak were yours, and no one would put their initials in the heart with yours." Minnie's eyes went wide at the look on Bella's face. "I'm sorry, Miss Eden. I just wanted to know if it was true."

"Class dismissed," Adam said as he walked down the center aisle between the desks, keeping his gaze on Bella. "You girls hurry on home. Your parents will be looking for you."

They stepped back, giving him a wide berth before running outside.

Bella ducked her crimson face and rustled through a stack of exam booklets on her desk, pretending to be busy.

Adam rested his hand on the stack, demanding her attention. "How often does that happen?"

Her hands gripped the trapped papers. "About twice a year. Someone sees it and feels clever when they figure it out. At the most, I endure whispers for about a week, and then they settle down." She lifted one shoulder in resignation. "I'll never live down the oak of shame. What can I do? Kids are like that."

"Do you really regret not kissing Jimmy Blaggart?" he asked. "If you know where he's living now, I could send for him. I guarantee he's regretting that he missed his chance."

The pain around her eyes eased. She relinquished her hold on the exams. "You're a caution, teasing me over that. Shame on you. We have a test to study for."

Too bad, because Bella sure looked pretty when she was flustered. "Are you ready for the math portion of the test today?" he asked.

"I practiced last night, but it wasn't the same. If I'm not nervous, then I do fine."

"And that's why I'm here, to make you uneasy. Now, what's at stake?" He tapped his chin, pretending he hadn't been up half the night delighting in this idea. "How about, if you fail, you have to walk through town holding my hand?"

Her gaze sharpened. "Funny you should think of that."

And then something struck him that he should have thought of before. "Bella, when you're in these situations, do you ever think about what you have to gain, instead of focusing on what you have to lose?"

"I have nothing to gain by taking this exam, only disaster if I lose it."

"Nonsense. Instead of thinking of how you're going to be ashamed if you fail, why don't you tell yourself how much respect you'll gain when you succeed? Look forward to the exam as a chance to prove yourself. Think of rewards for when you pass it, instead of punishments if you fail."

Her eyes narrowed. "And what would my reward be if I pass the practice exam today?"

He grinned. "Don't you worry. We'll think of something."

Eight

Bella could tell that she was performing better. The question was if it was because she was learning how to take the exams, or because she couldn't be scared as long as Adam was in the room.

She bit her lip as she latched the schoolhouse door and then tied on her bonnet. She knew what was coming, and Adam, with his shining eyes, did too. Had she made a mistake in allowing this? Would he only hurt her again?

"I've never been so happy to see someone fail." He stepped forward and took her hand firmly in his. There was a pause, both of them waiting for a cosmic disaster to result from their shocking behavior, but when it was clear that the earth would continue spinning, he winked at her, and they started out through town.

Bella loved the fitting between them—how her fingers were surrounded by his hand, how her palm brushed so deliciously against his. If it were to be truly romantic in the proper sense, she reckoned they would both be wearing gloves, and she would have been escorted on his arm, but bare hands felt fine enough for a working day.

It was true, what her parents had said. Adam had courting

on his mind. If he was thinking along those lines, she needed him to clear up his intentions.

"I don't reckon I understand how your job works," she said. "You're going to follow the harvest, right? Are you going to do that every year?"

When he looked at her, he noticed that she was carrying her lunch pail. "Give me that," he said. "I'm supposed to do all the toting." She was afraid he'd forgotten to answer her question, but once they got past the mercantile, he commenced. "At first I'll travel. Harvest starts here in the middle of May, and I can follow it north as the crops ripen, all the way until November."

"Then what will you do?"

"Over the winter I'll make repairs on my equipment and maybe make some money working on whatever people need fixing in town. Eventually I'd like to settle down and have teams that do the harvesting for me. I'll train them and buy the equipment, but I'd be managing from a home office."

"And where is home?" she asked.

"If I lose this wager, home can't be here."

"Did you want it to be?"

"I had an idea that it'd be a nice place to live. There was this girl who lived here that I couldn't forget." Adam tugged on her hand.

Despite her sudden shyness, Bella met his gaze.

"Bella," he said, "when I started along this path, there was no guarantee that you would be here, no guarantee that you would want to see me, but I imagined this, just the same. If you had any idea—"

"Miss Eden, are you holding that man's hand?" Freda Longstreet called from behind the hardware store. Max Bresden leaned around her to get a peek for himself.

"This was her punishment for failing a test," Adam replied with a wink at Max.

Freda dissolved into giggles while sending Max a shy glance.

"Miss Eden wouldn't fail a test, but don't worry. We won't tell," Max said to Adam.

"The code among gentlemen," Adam responded as they continued up the road toward the oak tree.

"Now you've done it," Bella said. "Freda won't pass another exam for the rest of her days if it means keeping Max's attention."

"You're joshing me. No one would fail a test to catch a man."

"Not an important test," Bella said. Then, with a copious batting of her eyes, she added, "but maybe a practice test."

Adam stopped before the oak. "Bella Eden, are you telling me that you could've passed that test?"

She grinned. "I'm getting better. Surely you've noticed?"

"I was surprised you didn't succeed today."

"I did succeed." She lifted their joined hands. "I just changed the goal."

His chest rose with a quick, strong breath. "You . . . I . . ." He shook his head. "Pass your exam, Bella Eden. That's an order. Else I'm going to make the consequence that I won't hold your hand unless you succeed."

"Would you do that?"

"It'd be a trial, that's for sure," he said. He glanced at the tree. "You know, if it had been me three years ago, I wouldn't have refused to kiss you. I thought a lot of you then, and even more now."

"How so?" Bella spent all day, every day encouraging her students. She rarely got any encouragement back.

"Well, you taught yourself to sew. Then, when that wasn't possible, you taught yourself to teach. Now you're fighting to keep your place there. A lesser woman would've given up."

His hand slid from her hand to her wrist. Holding it out in front of them, he turned it side to side to study it. Even for a woman, her wrist was delicate. In his hand, it looked tiny. His grasp felt as strong and warm as the splint she'd worn until it was healed.

"My parents warned me that you were more interested in courting me than helping me keep my job," Bella said.

Adam turned her hand over and pressed his lips to the fine blue veins of her wrist. Her pulse jumped right along with her heart.

"Adam?" she breathed.

His blue eyes were solemn. "You would have to know, with me on the road half the year, that our lives wouldn't be a carefree paradise. There would be rough patches—missing each other, fearful for each other . . ."

"Sounds like now," Bella said. "Fearful for the future. Fearful that you won't be able to come back to Oak Springs."

"Fearful that I'll be the cause of you losing another position you love."

There was no denying the hardships before them if they chose this path. All they could do was pray for God to work His will on the matter.

Although the shade of the oak was nearby, Adam and Bella stood in the sun, knowing they hadn't earned the reprieve. Not yet. And after a shared smile, they continued on through the world of crops, tests, and conflict.

Nine

It was the last day of school, and the town planned to celebrate with a midday picnic, after which the children would go home and prepare for harvest. Bella took one end of a sawhorse while Freda took the other, and they toted it from the carpenter's shop to the schoolyard. Four more trips, and her wrist wasn't hurting yet. Not even a twinge. Looking over her shoulder as she walked backward, Bella dodged the kids rolling stumps that they were gathering to make benches.

Another wagon rolled up. Mrs. Whitlock climbed down with the weight of her cloth-covered basket digging into her arm. There would be plenty of food. Everyone was eager to get together to socialize. A last hurrah before they got down to the business of bringing in the wheat.

Bella kept a close eye on the road. Adam had said he was coming. It would be the first time he and her father would meet since the challenge had been made. Would her father behave himself? Would he even come? When she had left the house that morning, he'd been out in the fields with his two field hands, scything down his crops for harvest, even though the wheat for the contest tomorrow was already drying.

"Where are we putting the food?" Mrs. Whitlock asked.

"Inside the schoolhouse. Hopefully the flies won't be as bad in there."

Bella and Freda arranged the sawhorse, then lifted a board onto it to make another table. The younger students rolled stumps up to the table—switching them around until two the same height were matched—then dropped a plank over them.

The kids' excitement was contagious. Any time their parents had occasion to visit the schoolhouse, they thrashed about like eels in a barrel. Bella loved the pride they took in their classroom. She felt it too. But it wouldn't be her classroom much longer if she couldn't pass the exam. A stranger would sit at her desk and talk to her children. That room, where she would only be a visitor, would become foreign to her. She couldn't let it happen.

As she organized the parade of food coming in, she felt that old anxiety about the test rising up again. No, she couldn't do that. She stretched her back and followed the cursive alphabet that she'd painted over the top of the chalkboard until she calmed herself. *Think about good things*, she reminded herself. *How wonderful it'll be when I pass the test and am assured a place here as long as I want.*

But how long did she want to be here? According to the wager, Adam would be banned from Oak Springs if he lost. Was she willing to leave to be with him?

Oak Springs was her home. Teaching these children was what she was meant to do. But if she felt at home right now, why did she feel incomplete without Adam?

Seeing that everything was in place, Bella gave notice to the ladies, then went to ring the schoolhouse bell.

With the first pealing, heads turned her way. The kids scrambled like mad toward the school door, while most of the men returned to their conversations. She'd spotted Dr. Paulson first. His spotless gray suit and white hair made him difficult to miss in the group of men. They seemed to be hanging on his every word, but they weren't all farmers. There was Mr. Doris and Mr. Woodward. Neither had any interest in agriculture, but they were both school board members. In fact, that was the school board talking to him. Every single one of them.

Look for the positives, she reminded herself. Like the fact that Adam would be here soon. But where was he? She stepped out of the doorway and stood on her tiptoes as she scanned the schoolyard. Her father was coming down the road, but there was no sign of Adam.

"Looking for someone?" It was Adam, leaning against the corner of the schoolhouse. "You must be, the way you're craning your neck about."

Bella wanted to punch him and hug him at the same time. "I should be inside bragging on my students instead of waiting for some no-account man to show up."

"I'll watch for him," Adam offered, "and tell him you're riled he wasn't here sooner."

She found herself doing a sweeping take of him from head to toe. "Get yourself some food before it's all gone."

"I'll help serve first."

If her parents hadn't already known she was spending time with Adam after school, it would have been obvious from the way the students gathered around him. He'd often chewed the fat with them in the schoolyard while he waited for Bella to finish tutoring a struggling student. Bella smiled as Teddy pulled a frog out of his pocket to show Adam. Had that thing been in his pocket all morning? Probably, but it was the last day of school, and the boy had waited for his froggy entertainment as long as he could.

After conversing with his adoring throng, Adam came around the table and started handing out cornbread muffins to those in line.

"I need to talk to you," he said as he served. "Tomorrow is that contest, and if I lose, I'll be banned from stepping foot back in Oak Springs. If that happens . . ."

"Do you think it will?"

"Not a chance. It's impossible that a team of three men can do the work a thresher can do, but if by some miracle they did, I want to take you with me."

A jolt of happiness shot up Bella's backbone. The heavy spoon full of beans wobbled as she splatted the contents on the side of Max's plate, covering his thumb.

"I'm sorry." Bella grabbed a towel and handed it to the boy. "I wasn't paying attention."

Max took a rueful look at Adam. Then, remembering their gentlemen's agreement, he sighed. "I reckon you have other things on your mind. Thank you, Miss Eden."

Once the boy was out of earshot, she dropped the spoon on the table.

"What do you mean, take me with you?" she whispered to Adam. "Do you think I'd just pack up my things and run away?"

To her annoyance, he merely shrugged. "Would you?"

"What was the point of all this, then? All the studying and test practicing? I did that so I wouldn't lose my position, not so I could abandon it."

"I told you, Bella. My job will take me far from here every year. I won't be a man who is home before dark every night and leaves at first light every morning, but I want to be the man for you. That might not be what you want, and if not, I need to know. I need to know before tomorrow, because I can't leave this place without knowing if you'll follow."

"Would you want me even if I couldn't be with you all the time?" she whispered as she lowered a basket of chicken from the table so a little one could get another piece.

She couldn't look at him—couldn't bear to see the regret in

his eyes. Wiping her hands on her skirt, Bella straightened, but before she could turn to face him, Adam grasped her hand. His grip was iron. She stared straight ahead, aware that the parents and students visiting in the corner of the schoolhouse had no idea that her happiness hung in the balance as they gnawed on chicken drumsticks.

"Would I want you?" His voice strained. "Oh, Bella, getting a single day with you is worth months apart."

Their hands tangled in a desperate clasp. She laughed, and it was a low, throaty sound that surprised her. "In the summer, I could go with you," she said. "That is, if it isn't too much trouble to have me along."

"And I need a home to settle in over the winter. I was hoping for it to be here."

"But I won't hold you back. If you're willing to let me stay and teach . . ."

"We both have dreams." His eyes searched hers as he lifted her hand to cover it with both of his. "We'll pursue them together, even when we're apart."

With Adam's encouragement, everything seemed possible.

"My students." Against her wishes, Bella pulled away. "I'm supposed to be talking to the parents about the children. It's their party, after all."

Adam stepped out from behind the table to clear the way for her. "I'll be outside," he said with a hand on her back.

She sighed, then made her way to a grouping of parents. Most of them had already seen the report cards and knew their children's marks. There shouldn't be any surprises about the performance of their kids, but from the way the parents in this group were acting, you'd think they were dreading her appearance.

Bella smiled and made her way toward them regardless. It was her job to be welcoming, even if they were uncomfortable.

She'd just held out her hand when she caught the last line of the conversation from Mr. Whitlock.

"It's not as if we would've selected her over another teacher. She was the only one available."

Bella's smile vanished. Seeing her, Mrs. Longstreet cleared her throat and glared at Mr. Whitlock. The warning was obvious, but it was too late to spare Bella or anyone else in the group. She'd heard, and they all knew she'd heard.

Borrowing from Adam's show of courage, she addressed them. "I understand the sentiment," she said, "but do you have any suggestions on how I could be a better teacher? I'm capable of improving."

Mrs. Longstreet dabbed at her mouth with a napkin before answering. "You've done a fine job for someone in your circumstance. We aren't criticizing your efforts, but you don't have the qualifications that a new teacher might."

"I'm going to take my teacher's exam," Bella said. "I'm scheduled to take it tomorrow. If . . . when I pass it, I'll be just as qualified as any student straight from the college, and I have more experience, to boot."

Mrs. Longstreet's eyebrows rose. She shot a sideways glance at the others. "You're taking the test?" She spoke slowly, watching for the approval of her comrades. "That would be helpful. We don't mean to leave you without a job, but we want what's best for our children."

Bella kept her chin up and her back straight. Adam had been right. That piece of paper didn't change her teaching, but if it gave the community more faith in her, then it was worth it. All she had to do now was actually pass the test.

"Why would you listen to him anyway?" someone proclaimed from outside.

Bella cringed. The voice was her father's. She scrambled out the door to see him and Dr. Paulson standing among the long tables. Unfortunately, they had everyone's attention, and her father was making the most of it.

"This professor has made his living at a school. His time was spent in a classroom. If he has a theory that doesn't pan out, he still collects a salary." Her father turned and jabbed his chest with his thumb. "Me, on the other hand, I don't get paid for coming up with theories. I only get paid when those theories work. I've raised a family on what I've brought up from the ground. There wasn't anybody paying me money if I made a mistake. That's why I don't trust these theories from men with soft hands and proud ways. There's a lot of arrogance available when you haven't had to live on your theories. You can be sure about everything when it hasn't been tested. That's why I think I'll winnow my own crop this year. I don't have a year's worth of work I can gamble on the advice of an academic."

Bella wanted to grab Adam by the arm to stop him from getting involved, but she was too late.

"Mr. Eden, I respect your experience in farming," Adam said. "Everyone respects you, and you're right that you have more farming knowledge than we do. That's true. You know what weather to plant in, you know what seed does best on your farm, you know when the crops are ready to cut. You have all that knowledge. But my knowledge is in machinery." He paused to draw the eyes of the group. "I could learn a lot from all of you about farming, but mostly I wanted to find a machine that would help you so your farming wasn't so much toil. We're on the same side. We aren't in competition."

"Yes, you are," Mr. Clovis called out. "You're dueling it out tomorrow. Winner take all."

His exaggeration was appreciated by the crowd, but Bella fumed. It wasn't winner take all. No one was going to lose property, only their pride. But maybe that was worse than high-dollar stakes.

"I'll meet you at my farm in the morning," her father said. "And after that, I don't reckon we'll be seeing you in town again."

Bella looked at the sky. One day, and either Adam would be banned, or her job would be in jeopardy.

Ten

They hadn't set any particular time for the contest, but Adam was raring to go. Before the sun was up, he'd heard Mrs. Doris greeting people in the kitchen of the boardinghouse. Evidently no one was waiting for him to appear at Eden's farm. From the looks on their faces when he stepped into the crowded kitchen, they'd expected him to run away and miss the contest.

That was the last thing on Adam's mind. He had to have the money he'd make from these farmers. Turning down Mrs. Doris's offer of breakfast, he accepted a cup of coffee instead. No matter who won, there were going to be consequences. He only hoped Mr. Eden could lose with grace. He didn't want to embarrass the father of the woman he loved. Why had he allowed himself to get dragged into this event in the first place?

Hooking his team to the machine to pull it up the hill gave Adam time for his fears to grow. What was Bella thinking as she prepared for her father to stand against him? What was the attitude around her kitchen table this morning? But there was nothing he could do. He couldn't jeopardize his future success for her father's pride.

The men standing in the dim morning light had a lot to say about his getup, even though they offered no help getting his team harnessed. Those who'd seen it at work gave off an air of superiority as they described how the different gears worked. It would seem that he already had some believers here, but if he lost, they might be content to work their fields themselves.

The trip to Eden's farm was a parade. The womenfolk had had time to put away their breakfast dishes and had joined with their kids, who were boasting, speculating, and doubting with every breath.

Adam looked at Dr. Paulson, who gave him a tight nod.

"No fears, my boy. You know what this machine can do. Before dinnertime, this sleepy town will be thrust into the future. New machinery, a new teacher, and a new appreciation for progress. They will sing your praises for years."

He didn't want his praises sung. He wanted the money to pay for his thresher, and he wanted Bella to keep her job.

He'd thought that everyone in town was walking with him, but when he reached Eden's farm, he realized that wasn't the case. Just as many people were waiting at the edge of Eden's pasture. Two wagons sat side by side with enough wheat that it could be seen over the edges. With shirtsleeves rolled up to their elbows, two men Adam hadn't seen before stood nearby, looking buoyant and well rested. What had he expected? That Mr. Eden would enlist an elderly couple for the contest?

Adam set the brake and hopped off his threshing machine. He doffed his hat and stepped forward to shake hands with the two men, but his eyes were searching for Bella. She would be here, wouldn't she? Wouldn't she want to see his victory?

Perhaps not. Not when she had her exam later. Not at the expense of her father. Or had Mr. Eden forbidden her from being here at all?

"Step back, step back." Dr. Paulson lifted his hands toward

the crowd and tried to make space. "Adam needs some room to set up his equipment."

Adam went to the harness of his team. Unhooking them from the front of the machinery and re-harnessing them to the treadmill was the most time-consuming aspect of the process, but once everything was in place, they would rip through that wagon of wheat in a matter of minutes.

"Hold on there." The crowd parted as Mr. Eden stepped through. His worn cotton shirt was freshly laundered and his boots cleaned, but his hat was for work, make no mistake. "Since this contest is to determine which is faster, manpower or machine, we're not giving you a head start. You can't set up the machine until the contest begins."

Adam's eyes widened. "That's not a contest of the machine. It'd be a contest of how fast I can harness my team. That's not what we're disputing."

Mr. Eden shrugged. "If you have to set this machine up with every usage, the farmers need to figure in that time. Else they're waiting around for you to get ready instead of working."

Adam looked from the wagons full of wheat to the two men who would be working against him. It still was impossible for Mr. Eden to beat him. Threshing and winnowing wheat was backbreaking, hot, and dirty business. Once he got his horses harnessed, he'd be running through that wagon like wildfire, but it made the contest a little closer.

His nearest horse's ears perked. It stepped sideways, and he saw that Bella had come and was standing next to her mother in a perfectly fitted traveling suit. Today was the day of her exam. He should be done before she had to catch the stagecoach to Anderson. He'd talk to her then. It could be his last chance.

But Adam was going to win. He had to win for his future and hers. It looked like they were both going to be tested today.

He telegraphed her all the love he could across a field full of haymakers. Although troubled, she held his gaze bravely. Like him, unsure of the outcome of the day's events but determined to face them squarely.

"Let's get started, then," he said. "But at least clear a place before the clock starts ticking."

Mr. Eden had picked a good spot. The wind was brisk here, and stronger in the morning than it would be at noon. Adam positioned the treadmill, the sweeps, and the gearbox in a place where they wouldn't be obstructed, then directed his team that way. Eyeballing it one last time, he set the brake and climbed down. Dr. Paulson had already agreed to prod the team on the treadmill, but besides that, Adam was on his own. This was it.

Mr. Eden's helpers had pulled a large canvas forward into the field, and someone had handed them threshing flails. Adam's fear vanished. If he didn't believe in his machine, he wouldn't have signed the note to buy it. He would win. He only hoped Mr. Eden wouldn't hold a grudge in defeat.

Everyone was looking at one another, not sure what to do, but when there was a lack of leadership, Mr. Woodward naturally stepped forward. Holding his hand above his head, he waited until the crowd had stilled and then dropped his arm.

Adam sprang into action. Dr. Paulson had never assisted with the teams before, but he was doing what he could to free their harnesses while Adam hooked up the sweeps and gears that would power the big machine. Mr. Eden and his team lost no time in tossing the first sheaves onto the canvas and beating or threshing them with the hinged sticks.

Adam should have insisted on a larger sample for the contest. He should have thought to ask whether he'd be able to prepare his machinery, because those three men were beating at the crops with everything they were worth. Knowing that their labor would be over within an hour, they were holding nothing back.

Already Adam could see them gathering the beaten stalks and tossing them aside to make room for more sheaves from the wagon. The wheat was left on the canvas, but it wouldn't be for long.

Taking a rag from his back pocket, Adam wiped the grease from his hands as he turned toward the horses. Dr. Paulson had managed to get two unharnessed from the threshing machine, so Adam took them and started hooking them into their places on the treadmill.

From where he was working, he couldn't see the harvesters, but the crowd's excitement told him everything. They were making progress. So much progress that no one thought that he could catch up. But Adam knew better. Still, the bigger the win, the more impressed they'd be, and potentially the more who would become his customers.

The last horse was in place, and Eden's team was slowing on their threshing. A few more *thwacks* with their flails, and they must have felt that they'd gotten a respectable amount of grain off the stalks.

Adam climbed into the back of his full wagon. "Get 'em going," he called to Dr. Paulson. The professor didn't need the prod, because the horses knew their task and started around.

The machine began to whirl. Adam slashed the ties on the sheaves with his knife, then took up the pitchfork and tossed the first bunch into the feeder.

"Too late to start now," said Mr. Gleason. "They're all but done."

But they hadn't winnowed the chaff from the wheat. They had to remove the beaten stalks from atop the grain before they could begin tossing it in the air. Adam pitched in another load. All eyes were glued to the chute, but nothing was coming out, just noise. He lifted another load and threw it. Pieces of golden straw sputtered out the side. There was a murmur of appreciation as a yellow cloud of blown straw formed, but the opinion still favored the manual farmers.

They might be worried, but Adam wasn't. His worries vanished as he watched Eden's team toss the grain in the air. The wind caught the chaff, blowing it away, but they had a lot of work before everything was separated. All Adam had to do was finish shoveling in the wheat. The whirling machine would do the rest.

Already a mound of clean straw was forming at the mouth of the chute. In another few seconds . . . there. The sweet patter of clean grains of wheat hitting the bottom of the bucket could be heard above the whirling of the fan that was blowing the husks away.

"Look here." It was Bella's student—the one who thought she walked on water—pointing at the spout. "The grain is already cleaned."

Like a herd of hungry pigs gathering around a trough, the crowd pulled tight around the bucket. Adam lifted the last of the wheat and dropped it on the feeder. His work was done. All that was left was to watch the threshing machine do its job. That and celebrate with Bella.

She was supposed to be pleased that he'd succeeded. She was supposed to be proud of him and his work. What was the worry on her face? It was about her test, wasn't it? But when he looked again, he realized that wasn't what was worrying her.

She was hugging her arms tightly to her side, and her mouth was twisted and her neck tense, but this was more than worry for her job. She was watching her father.

Red-faced and sweating, Mr. Eden was shoveling furiously, throwing grain up before bending over to get another heavy shovelful. The breeze had died down, meaning that less chaff was separating with each toss, but he wasn't giving up. Even though defeat was unavoidable, he fought on like his honor depended on it.

And maybe it did.

Adam spared a thought for the older man—a man who was the best farmer in the area, respected for his knowledge and venerated for his wisdom. And here Adam came, a cocky upstart who told him that he was wrong. Who said he could beat him at his own livelihood on his own property, and then went about proving it. And if that wasn't bad enough, Adam wanted to take his daughter too. Mr. Eden had a lot to lose.

The sun glinted off Adam's beautiful machine as it continued effortlessly. What would happen if he walked away? What if he didn't make his payment and lost the machine? He was young. He could start again. But if he lost and couldn't come back to Oak Springs? Would they really enforce the rule? Would Bella leave with him? One look at her face, and Adam realized that her first priority was taking care of her family. She couldn't think past that.

He scraped his pitchfork into the corners of the wagon and caught the tangles of twine that had bound the sheaves. With everyone wondering at the falling kernels, no one was paying attention to him. No one but Bella.

It had been enough last time. Would it work again? He gave her a searing look, poured his heart out with no words, and prayed that she understood, because it just might be the last time he got to speak to her if she didn't. When she saw the pitchfork full of twine, she shook her head. But it was too late. He tossed it into the feeder before anyone else noticed.

The smooth whirling noise clacked. Adam winced at the sound of the gears dragging. It was the sound of his future being sacrificed for the love of Bella. His stomach turned as the gears jammed. He waved to Dr. Paulson to stop the horses. There was no sense in forcing the machine any further. With the twine jamming the feeder, it would do no good.

The pride he'd wanted to see on Bella's face was there now,

shining true and strong. Through tears she beamed, but he knew those tears were for the future they might have had together. Now, to choose him would mean leaving behind her family and her school and never returning. It would mean trusting a penniless man with no income to provide for her. It was too high a price.

"Look at that. The threshing machine can't get the job done after all."

"Never trust newfangled machines. They aren't reliable."

"Eden showed that professor a thing or two. We in Grimes County know farming. We don't need them to come in and tell us."

In the absence of the thresher's noise, the swish of the shovels against the canvas and the raining grain of Mr. Eden's team could be heard more clearly. Mr. Eden straightened. His field hands paused to see what he was doing.

His sweat-covered face wrinkled in confusion. "Are you finished already?" He leaned against his shovel, letting it support his weight as he caught his breath.

Adam swallowed to keep his composure. "It looks like some twine got caught in the machine. Gummed it up."

The shorter of Eden's field hands nudged the other. Seeing the miracle they needed, they scooped up more shovelfuls of grain and tossed them in the wind.

Mr. Eden hesitated, then turned to Adam. With a disapproving snarl, he handed his shovel to Bella. "Help them out, would you? This contest has to be decided one way or the other." Then he pushed up his sleeves, climbed on the side of the machine, and reached deep into the feeder, grabbing one end of the cord.

What could Adam do besides help? Rocking the belt of the feeder forward and back, he managed to free a strand. Mr. Eden pulled out the knotted rope and triumphantly threw it on the ground. With another turn of the gear, Adam could reach the last bundle he'd tossed in and extract it from the belt.

"Is that all of it?" Mr. Eden asked. "If you're set to rights, then I'm going to spell my daughter. I don't think her heart's in it." He lowered his voice. "And after seeing what you're about, maybe I'm not set on a victory either."

Bella let the heavy shovel rest against the ground. Looking down, she dropped it a little farther to her left, blocking the field hand from his next scoop.

"You'd better get this thing going again," said Mr. Eden. "She can't delay them for long."

He was letting Adam win? After Adam had tried to let him win? Adam yelped to Dr. Paulson, "Get those horses moving!"

The belt started to turn. All that was left was a few cranks. A few more kernels sputtered out of the chute, and the job was completed. Both teams had to stop.

Mr. Eden tossed a last scoop into the air, then stepped back. It didn't take long for the crowd to make the determination on Eden's crop. While he and his helpers had worked valiantly, the grain would profit from some more work before it was truly separated enough for the mill.

On the other hand, the bucket of Adam's wheat was as clean as any ever produced by their toil. And despite the delays in setting up the machinery and the mechanical trouble, there was no question of him acquiring customers from the crowd that day. He had prevailed, but more important than the contest, he'd won Mr. Eden's respect.

As the farmers crowded around, now comfortable inspecting the rig for themselves, Mr. Eden offered his hand.

"I know what you were up to," he said. "You didn't think Bella could pass that teacher's exam. You'd rather get beat in a contest than have her lose her job, but I've got news for you. Bella will pass that test and be teaching here next year, no matter what that professor of yours says."

Adam was taken aback. Mr. Eden thought he'd thrown the

contest for Bella's job? But, of course, his pride wouldn't let him imagine that Adam had done it for him. Adam would never tell.

"My stars, Ben Eden," said Mrs. Clovis. "I can't believe the show you put on. It was a close contest. I don't know how you kept it so close. Well done."

"I already have one field drying," said Mr. Granger. "By the time you get out to work on it, I should have the rest of the wheat knocked down. Put me on your list."

"Don't forget me." Mr. Clovis pushed to the front. "What do you charge? Five percent of the yield? I'll save that in waste alone. I'm getting in the field today to get started, so bring your rig to the farm early next week. I'll pay you some up front to secure my spot."

Adam nodded and shook hands, but the whole time he was searching past the men for the one congratulatory message he yearned for. She wouldn't leave without saying good-bye, would she?

Noticing his concern, Mr. Eden explained, "She had to catch the stagecoach, remember? She's going to take her test."

"I wanted to tell her good luck."

"She'll be back tomorrow. You could join us for supper to hear her news."

Where had this friendliness come from? Could it be that Mr. Eden suspected his real reason for throwing the contest? Could it be that he was grateful for the chance to save face?

"I'll come for supper, but could you do me a favor first? When Mrs. Eden and Bella get home from the station, could you send Bella . . ." Adam went on to explain his plan. Well, he didn't explain everything, just what Bella's father needed to know to do his part.

The rest was up to Adam.

Eleven

She'd passed the test.

Bella washed her face and neck to remove the dust from the stagecoach, then ran a brush through her hair. If what her father suspected was true, she wanted to look her best for the school board meeting that was to commence shortly. While she wouldn't have the test results back for a few weeks, she knew she'd performed well. Instead of worrying about the disaster that would befall her if she failed, she'd filled her mind with happy scenes. She'd remembered the days she felt helpful and knowledgeable in her classroom. She'd cherished the smiles and relationships she'd built with the kids and took pride in the older students who were a credit to Oak Springs. All of those things kept her calm while the exam was being administered, but mostly she was thinking about Adam.

Would he be at the schoolhouse? She'd been disappointed that he wasn't at her house, waiting for her to return, but when her pa explained about the school board meeting, she understood. Besides, Adam was probably too busy with work to be idling at her farm. He'd be able to make the payment on his threshing machine now. He'd stay here until harvest was complete, and then what? Would their courtship resume next summer when he came back?

She finished wrapping her hair into a roll and then dabbed some scent on her neck. They had to be impressed when she told them that she'd passed the exam. They had to believe that she would work harder for their kids than any outsider they could bring in.

Bella dropped a flat straw bonnet on her head and took to the road. The sun streamed its rays along the horizon, lighting up the gentle slopes of the fields and dancing atop the waving wheat, heavy for harvest. The road rose by the giant oak tree, and she could see town. There were no wagons in the schoolyard. No one was making their way to the schoolhouse. Instead of a contentious meeting, it looked like every other evening in Oak Springs. Perhaps the school board had already made their decision and had headed home?

She stopped and tugged at her ear. If no one was meeting tonight, why bother going to town? But maybe Adam was there somewhere. If he wasn't working in a field, there was a good chance—

The hairs on her arms tingled. Someone was standing in the corner of her sight. Someone she hadn't noticed before. He was nearly hidden in the branches of the oak tree, but there he was.

"Adam?"

The sun's rays hit beneath the boughs and washed him in gold. "It's me."

"What are you doing in there?" She didn't see his horses or machinery. No sign that he was doing anything other than loitering on the road.

"I'm waiting for you. How was the exam?"

"Wonderful. I did wonderful." She wished he'd come closer, wished he'd take her in his arms, but he seemed rooted to the spot, determined not to step away from the oak of shame.

"I'm proud of you. And you, no doubt, saw the conclusion of the threshing contest?"

"You could've beat Pa by a mile, but what you did was even better."

"And what he did was just as fine."

What was wrong with him? Why didn't he offer to walk her home, or walk her to town, or something? "I guess everything worked out satisfactorily."

"Not yet." His countenance fell. "Something has been bothering me for a spell, and I won't rest easy until it's fixed."

Bella arched her eyebrows. Had something happened that her parents hadn't told her about? Had the school board already determined to send for the student teacher?

But instead of allowing her to ask, Adam stepped back, holding one of the low limbs of the oak tree aside. "After you," he said with a bow.

What was he up to? Another jab at her past? Another reminder of her failures? No, they'd grown past that. It had to be something else.

"I have a school board meeting to attend," she said.

"There isn't a meeting, not with them. Just with me."

"But Pa said . . ." Then, seeing his smile, she said, "You put Pa up to that, didn't you? Alright. What do you want me to see?"

She stepped past the low-hanging branches and into the airy shelter beneath, and then Bella caught her breath. Beneath the canopy of green hung dozens of paper hearts suspended on strings. They spun with the leaves, fluttering like butterfly wings. She lifted one in her palm and laughed. It was covered in her penmanship. "Are these my practice tests?"

"I told you I wouldn't leave them for the students to find."

"You cut them all?" Her grin was so big her cheeks were getting sore. "And the thread . . ." She ran her fingers up the strand, then looked at the other hearts and the variety of colors that held them aloft. "I'm sorry for refusing your gift. The thread is beautiful, Adam. You created a true fairyland. Better than I could imagine."

"There's more." With his hands clasped behind his back, he leaned forward, his face full of eagerness.

"What? What are you hiding?" She grabbed his arm, thinking he was holding a present behind his back, but he spun around, and she found herself face-to-face with the trunk of the old oak.

The marks of three years ago were still there—the heart with her initials—but there was an addition. Bella pressed her finger into the first stroke of the *A*, then traced every inch of the carefully carved message.

"*AF & BE*," Adam said. "It took me long enough, but it's there for good. Nothing is going to erase the message that I love Bella Eden."

Bella's heart felt near to bursting. Adam was everything she'd been looking for, but God had waited until just the right time to remove the blinders from her eyes.

"There's only one thing lacking—that kiss you were hankering after. Now, I'm no Jimmy Blaggart—"

"Don't you ever say that name again," she warned.

"Yes, ma'am." His eyes held her warm and secure while paper hearts danced around them. "I'll just say your name, Bella, and I'll endeavor to have either you or your name on my lips as often as possible."

His fingers brushed her cheek, making her yearn for more. Before she could turn toward his touch, his mouth captured hers—sure, joyful, and more intoxicating than she'd imagined.

After a hearty kiss, Bella laid her head on his shoulder and watched the paper hearts spin in the breeze.

"It's this tree that brought us together," Adam said, "and I'm going to predict that our love will be as rooted and strong as it is."

"The oak of shame?" she asked.

"Oh no. That episode is forgotten. As of today, it'll have a new name." His gaze darkened as it met hers. "This oak is now known as the Kissing Tree."

Bella smiled. "Then it had better start living up to its name."

She didn't have to ask twice. He bent his head and kissed her again, like he'd never stop. But stop he must, for as fine as his kissing was, they had fields to harvest and a future to plan.

And Bella was already imagining what romantic adventures lay ahead.

Inn for a Surprise

KAREN WITEMEYER

To my editors, Dave Long and Jessica Barnes.
Your counsel is always worth hearkening unto.
Thank you for fine-tuning my romantic whimsy
with your practical insight. My inner Phoebe is always better
once your constructive Barnabas guidance comes alongside.
Thank you for sharing my vision, believing in my abilities,
and encouraging me every step of the way.
You are a blessing!

The way of a fool is right in his own eyes:
but he that hearkeneth unto counsel is wise.

Proverbs 12:15

One

1891
HUNTSVILLE, TEXAS

Illogical business proposals made Barnabas Ackerly's skin itch, but *this* one irritated like a hundred mosquito bites treated with a poison ivy poultice.

Barnabas eyed his employer warily. He'd been with Hollis Woodward for over five years, long enough to have earned his mentor's respect and trust. Yet as brilliant as Mr. Woodward was when it came to land development, he had a blind spot the size of a house when it came to his daughter.

Tread carefully. "Mr. Woodward, perhaps this isn't the best—"

"Don't give me that you-think-I've-got-a-screw-loose look, Ackerly." Hollis Woodward shoved up from the chair behind his imposing mahogany desk and braced his fingertips against the well-polished surface with enough force to turn his knuckles white. "I assure you, all of my mental hardware is fully fastened and functioning." He chuckled good-naturedly, but Barnabas wasn't fooled. The steel in Hollis Woodward's eyes wasn't the type to bend.

Barnabas rose from his seat and set the papers he'd just

examined atop the desk in front of him. "I respect what you're trying to do here, sir, but I wouldn't be doing my job if I didn't point out the flaws in this proposal. It's simply not a viable investment."

"Bah." Hollis pushed away from the desk and waved a dismissive hand through the air as he advanced around the corner and invaded Barnabas's territory. "I know this project is a bit afield of the usual work I assign you."

A *bit* afield? Apparently the moon was *a bit afield* of the earth.

"But you're the magician, Ackerly. You'll find a way to get the job done. You always do."

Magic had nothing to do with it. Yes, Barnabas had carved himself a place in the Woodward Land Development Company by cultivating the ability to sell the unsellable, but that came from long hours and hard-won experience. Not a wand covered in pixie dust or whatever concoction Hollis expected him to employ to transform this sow's ear of an idea into a silk purse. Barnabas might specialize in repurposing unwanted vacant properties into desirable real estate, but Merlin himself couldn't conjure a spell strong enough to turn this wisp of nonsensical whimsy into a profitable venture.

"Sir, I believe this endeavor is beyond my powers. A romantic rendezvous retreat? In *Oak Springs*? No offense, sir. I know it's your hometown, but no one outside a fifty-mile radius of the place is even aware it exists. And few, if any, within that radius would"—*waste their hard-earned money on such impractical lodgings*—"be interested in paying for a night at your daughter's inn when they could visit the, ah . . . what did she call it?" He glanced down at the first page of the proposal, where the inanely sentimental name smiled up at him, completely unaware of its own imbecility. "Ah, yes. The Kissing Tree. When they could simply visit the Kissing Tree of their own accord without staying at the inn."

Hollis crossed his arms. "I suggested we fence in the tree when we bought the acreage for just that reason, but Phoebe wouldn't hear of it. She said the tree belongs to everyone. The only reason she built the inn is to make it more accessible to outsiders."

"Built?" A boulder of dread sank in Barnabas's gut. "You've already built the inn?"

"Yep."

That didn't bode well. If Hollis had already invested funds, there would be no going back. Their only hope was to throw the lever and switch tracks before the entire train derailed. But what lever could he pull?

"Perhaps we can turn it into a . . . community center of sorts. Or a boardinghouse." Yes, a boardinghouse. Practical. Feasible. He'd just have to find a manager. A cook. Maybe a groundskeeper.

"Ma Granger already runs a boardinghouse in Oak Springs," Hollis said with a shake of his head, "and it's only full up around harvest time. We don't get many visitors."

"Exactly my point!" Could he not see the gaping holes in this plan?

Hollis unfolded his arms, pointed his right index finger, and deliberately prodded Barnabas in the hollow of his shoulder. "That, my boy, is precisely why I'm bringing you on board. You're a genius at finding ways to make the improbable possible. Besides, Phoebe will help. She has several ideas about how to bring in clientele."

Somehow Barnabas doubted a woman as out of touch with reality as Phoebe Woodward would be much help. Not that he would ever say so aloud. Hollis would sack anyone who disparaged his daughter. Besides, the young lady didn't deserve his censure. She was kind-natured and bookish, two qualities Barnabas generally admired. Not to mention that she possessed enough sense to avoid the grasping guests at her father's quarterly dinners at their home in Huntsville. Men clamored to strengthen business ties with the most successful developer in a dozen counties, and women hunted the wealthy widower for a more intimate connection. Few attended out of true friendship. Barnabas had run across Miss Woodward more than a time or two hiding in her father's study, a book in her lap. A definite mark in her favor. He'd passed many a pleasant hour reading in her company without the pretense of polite conversation while other guests entertained themselves with vapid parlor games.

Until today, he'd considered Miss Woodward a thoughtful, intelligent soul. Now he realized the truth. All that novel reading had rotted the poor lady's brain.

Barnabas cleared his throat and carefully weighed each word before letting it out of his mouth. "Even if she found a way to entice customers who possess the time, money, and inclination to travel to her inn, the logistics would create a barrier. The nearest rail stop is the Great Northern spur here in Huntsville. That would leave the clients twenty miles short of their final destination. I fear couples seeking a romantic getaway will be disillusioned by the realities of renting a buggy from the local livery and braving the unpredictable Texas weather for a four-hour trip to Oak Springs."

Hollis's expression hardened. "I guess you'll just have to find a way around that snag."

"Sir, I simply can't advise—"

"I'm not asking for your advice." Hollis's unyielding tone cut Barnabas off like a hatchet severing a tree limb. "I'm giving you an assignment."

Barnabas's pulse kicked so hard, he swore he could feel the vein in his neck knocking against his chin-high starched collar.

"You *will* find a way to make the Kissing Tree Inn work, Ackerly. I'll accept no less." The man Barnabas had long considered a mentor and friend clasped his shoulder with a firmness that communicated confidence, yet at the same time inspired a terrifying level of dread.

Disappointing Hollis Woodward was not an option. Not if Barnabas wanted to keep his position in the company. Woodward was fair, but he was first and foremost a man of business. Any employee who turned a profit and satisfied the customer was rewarded with more responsibility and a more lucrative clientele. Mediocre performance earned a loss of trust and, therefore, a loss of clients. Outright failure? Well, that tended to leave a fellow searching for a new position.

Barnabas wanted to believe that his excellent performance over the last several years would prevent one failure from costing him his career. But this was no ordinary project. No ordinary client. If Barnabas failed, so did Woodward's daughter. And that, he feared, would not be tolerated.

Oak Springs, Texas

Phoebe Woodward nibbled on the edge of her thumbnail as she waited for the verdict. She never mailed a story to her editor at *Lippincott's* without first getting her former teacher to look over her work. Mrs. Fisher was one of the few people who'd never counseled Phoebe to take her head out of her books and engage more fully with reality. Instead, from the time Phoebe was barely able to sound out her ABCs, Mrs. Fisher had encouraged her to delve even deeper into her stories and stretch her imagination.

When Phoebe's mother had died during her first year of school, it was the stories Mrs. Fisher read in class that offered an escape from the devastating loss handed to her by the real world. She'd been escaping into them ever since.

A tiny gasp from Mrs. Fisher cut through the silence of the Woodward parlor. Phoebe tensed, her hand falling back to her lap.

"Paper hearts?" Mrs. Fisher glanced up, a suspicious moisture gleaming in her eyes.

Phoebe's stomach cramped. "I'm sorry. I never should have taken such liberties. I can rewrite the ending, take them out." She tried to snatch the offending page back, but her friend proved too quick, dodging to the left and stretching her arm to keep it out of Phoebe's reach.

"Don't you dare take them out! They're as beautiful on this page as they were the day Adam proposed." Bella Fisher smiled even as she wiped a tear from her eye with the back of her hand. "To have a piece of our story immortalized in print . . . it's a gift, Phoebe. A beautiful, precious gift. I can't wait to show Adam and the children once it's published. Oh!" She suddenly straightened, her back thrusting away from the pale green upholstery of the chair. Her smile bloomed into a grin of pure delight. "I can order an extra issue and make *new* paper hearts. I can add the story hearts to the ones I kept from Adam's proposal and have them framed for our anniversary. Oh, Phoebe. It will be perfect!"

Relief untwisted the knot in Phoebe's stomach. "Are you sure? I changed the names and the entire plot of the story."

When she'd started penning stories for her Tales from the Kissing Tree quarterly column, Phoebe had made an unspoken vow to Oak Springs to protect the anonymity of its residents. While each of the romantic tales she wove featured real initials carved into the bark of the giant oak locals had taken to calling the Kissing Tree, she never used true names or circumstances. To do so felt too much like stealing. Love between a husband and wife was a sacred gift bestowed by God. The stories surrounding that love were sacred as well. Deeply personal and private. Phoebe would never intentionally profit from someone else's love story. Until now, her tales had been inspired by unidentified sets of initials and had been pure figments of her imagination. But when Mrs. Fisher had read her column and volunteered the details of her own personal Kissing Tree love story, Phoebe had been so enchanted that she had borrowed a few of the details.

"The story isn't *so* different." Mrs. Fisher winked. "Betina the seamstress—an occupation I planned to pursue until I injured my wrist—paired with Abram the blacksmith—a man familiar with mechanics and machinery? I can see the similarities. Though it was the paper hearts that gave it away."

"You truly don't mind?"

"Not at all." Mrs. Fisher returned the final page to the stack in her lap, then leaned forward to tidy the pile by tapping the edges on the tea table positioned between their chairs. "In fact, I insist you mail it off today."

Phoebe accepted the slender stack from her mentor, fighting the urge to clutch it to her bosom like a secret she wanted to hide from prying eyes. It made no logical sense to be shy about her work when hundreds, if not thousands, of subscribers would be reading it in a couple months' time. But those readers were strangers. Mrs. Fisher was a dear friend. As much as Phoebe trusted her former teacher, these encounters always left her feeling vulnerable and exposed. The stories might not be a part of her real life, but they were a real part of her soul.

"Now all we have to do is find you a love story of your own." Mrs. Fisher patted Phoebe's knee, then pushed to her feet.

Phoebe stifled a groan. She set the manuscript aside and fiddled with the wire rims of her spectacles to avoid making eye contact with her friend. She'd long ago learned it was better to say nothing and let the subject of beaus and marriage die a quick death. Refuting it only prolonged the torture.

Twenty-three-year-old spinsters who were plain of face and

odd in temperament did not attract suitors. A fact proven to Phoebe year after year as her schoolmates paired off and married while she remained unattached and largely ignored. Oh, a few hearty fellows had tried wooing her in a misguided effort to win her father's favor and advance their careers, but she'd developed a talent for ferreting out motives. Decades of watching life unfold from the sidelines taught a girl a thing or two about relationships. Which ones would last. Which ones would lead to heartache. Which had little to no emotion invested at all. Phoebe had always been a good student, and love was her favorite subject. It fascinated her. Lured her. Sparked her imagination.

Did she secretly crave a loving husband and babies of her own? She'd be lying if she said she didn't. But she wouldn't waste her days pining for what she could not have. She refused to become one of those dried-up spinsters who sucked the joy out of every room they entered. No, she would fuel her happiness by investing in the romance and love of others, encouraging *their* dreams and fostering their devotion to one another.

That was why her inn was so important. It was her way to make a difference in the real world, not just inside the framework of her own imagination. Her inn would be a tangible place to celebrate the rare and precious gift of emotional connection. A place that reminded couples of their love for each other, that reinvigorated older relationships and created memories for new relationships to build upon.

"You really should reconsider the pie social, Phoebe," Mrs. Fisher said as she rose and meandered toward the door. "It's a great way to meet people. *Male* people, to be specific."

As if the twinkle in her friend's eye hadn't made that point rather obvious. Phoebe joined her friend and made an effort to look as if she were considering her advice instead of mentally tossing it in the wastebasket.

Bella Fisher shook her head as if she saw right through the pretense. "It doesn't hurt to try, Phoebe."

Well, sometimes it did. Like the time Elliott Rayburn dropped a watermelon on her toe three years ago while trying to show off for one of the younger girls by carrying two melons at one time. Her foot had ached for a week.

"Eligible men aren't just going to line up at your front door, you know," Mrs. Fisher continued.

Oh, she knew.

Phoebe pulled open the door in question, but the good-bye perched on the edge of her tongue immediately glued itself to the back of her teeth. Barnabas Ackerly, in his perfectly pressed suit, stiff white collar, and black fedora, stood on her front stoop with his arm raised to knock. His blue eyes widened at her unexpected appearance, but his clean-shaven jaw never so much as twitched as he lowered his arm back to his side.

"Then again," Mrs. Fisher said softly out of the corner of her mouth, "I could be wrong."

Two

Barnabas quickly pulled his hat from his head, pivoted sideways to clear an exit route, then offered a bow to the older woman. “Pardon me, ma’am.”

The lady’s eyes met his, a puzzling sparkle dancing about her irises. Even more baffling was the smirk she tossed over her shoulder at Miss Woodward as she swept past. Phoebe Woodward had never struck him as the smirk-collecting type—the brand of female who whispered and giggled with her cronies until a man came within earshot, then traded gossip for telling glances and exaggerated expressions. She’d seemed a female of the more intellectual variety. Sensible. Quiet.

Then again, she’d proposed the Idiotic Inn of Tree Kissing that threatened his livelihood, so what did he know?

“Mr. Ackerly. I, uh . . .” Miss Woodward’s glance darted from her retreating friend’s back to his face to the ground. After an awkward pause, she straightened her shoulders and forced her chin up, connecting her gaze with his. “What brings you to Oak Springs? Surely you’re aware that my father is scheduled to be in Huntsville several more weeks.”

“I am.” Far too aware. Barnabas had just over a month before Hollis Woodward arrived to inspect his progress. Mere weeks to transform a disaster of an idea into a marketable commodity. It didn't help matters that his employer had apparently not informed his daughter of his intent to supply company assistance for her project. "Your father sent me, as a matter of fact. I'm to be your man."

Her brown doe eyes widened until they nearly matched the width of her spectacle lenses. "You're to be my *what*?" She braced her arm against the door as if doubting her ability to remain upright without it.

"Your man," he repeated, slowing down his speech and shortening his sentences to reduce the risk of misunderstanding. "Of business. To help with your inn."

She blinked once, very slowly.

Barnabas swallowed a sigh. "I'm here to ensure that the investment put forth by the Woodward Land Development Company on your behalf returns a profit."

Please, God. Even a small one.

Her gaze narrowed, the initial shock that seemed to have beset her at the outset giving way to something sharper. More focused. She pushed away from the door and straightened her posture. "I'm not in need of a man, Mr. Ackerly, *of business* or otherwise."

Only then did he realize how his initial pronouncement had been interpreted. Heat spread across his nape. He was a businessman, for heaven's sake, not some husband for hire. "I . . ." *I . . . don't have a clue what to say.*

It wasn't as if Phoebe Woodward didn't possess qualities a man less focused on building his career might appreciate. She had a fine figure, after all. Glossy hair the color of dark walnut wood. Fair complexion. Her nose might be a tad too large for her face, her neck a bit too long, and some fellows might be put off by the spectacles, but in his estimation, the imperfections made her more approachable.

Barnabas gave himself a mental shake. Good grief. He should *not* be cataloging her physical attributes. Especially when the lips he'd just fixated upon were pulling tight in displeasure.

"The Kissing Tree Inn is *my* project," she pronounced, "and I will proceed with it as I see fit. The building is already complete, and the decorating is under way. I plan to take out an ad in *Lippincott's Magazine* that will run beside my quarterly column once the inn is complete. So, as you can see, everything is under control. I'll let my father know that your services, while appreciated, will not be required."

Judging by her tone, his services were not at all appreciated, but he could let that pass. No one enjoyed having another person encroach on their territory. Besides, he was still reeling from the information she'd so nonchalantly dropped like an anvil on his toe about being a columnist for *Lippincott's*.

She wrote for a literary magazine? Hadn't Arthur Conan Doyle published his second Sherlock Holmes story in *Lippincott's* last year? Barnabas probably had a copy of that issue somewhere in the trunk that served as his periodical library. Yes, he was certain it had been *Lippincott's*. There'd been a short story by Nathaniel Hawthorne as well. If he dug out the magazine, would he find a piece by P. B. Woodward?

"Good day, Mr. Ackerly."

Her dismissal slapped him across the face and cleared his mind of all but the most urgent matter: preserving his livelihood.

He grabbed the door's edge, preventing her from closing it in his face. "Have you solved the transportation dilemma, then?"

Her brow furrowed. "What transportation dilemma?"

"How your guests will get from the depot in Huntsville to your lovely establishment here in Oak Springs."

She had no ready answer, so Barnabas capitalized on her hesitation by thrusting and parrying with every idea he could summon. He usually preferred a more strategic attack, but when one was backed into a corner, the most effective strategy often entailed swinging like a madman and praying at least one slash drew enough blood to drive his opponent backward.

"You have several options." And he'd weighed them all over the last few days. "One, you can simply leave that problem up to the clients to solve on their own. Of course, in my experience, wealthier clientele tend to prefer being catered to. Having to hire their own conveyance might leave them out of sorts. Especially if all they can rent from the local livery is a rustic open wagon that won't protect them from whatever unpredictable weather Texas decides to throw at them on the day they arrive.

"Option two consists of arranging transportation for them. We could contract with one of the liveries in Huntsville to be your regular supplier. You would pay his fees and roll the cost into the overall price charged to the client. I took the liberty of speaking to two different owners before I left town. Neither expected to make enough profit from the venture to promise that their best covered buggies would always be available for the inn's use. Therefore, if we choose to go that route, we will probably need to pay them in advance, which will mean a loss of income should the clients back out at the last minute.

"The final option—and the best, in my opinion—is for the inn to purchase its own carriage. A landau perhaps, since the hood can be raised in poor weather and lowered in pleasant conditions. It would provide ample passenger space, as well, in case more than one couple arrived on the same day. You would need to hire a driver, of course. Someone local would suffice. It is the most costly option, but it would allow you to control the client's experience, and that, my dear Miss Woodward, makes all the difference. You might have the most romantic retreat in the West, but all it takes is one grouchy liveryman to spoil the experience. Then, instead of raving about your inn to their friends, your clients will grumble about their inelegant ride to the train station."

Miss Woodward had returned to staring and blinking, the fire in her eyes currently banked. He'd had three days to work through these issues; she'd only had three minutes.

And he wasn't done yet. By the time he was finished flooding her with details, she would be begging him to stay.

Why wouldn't he just leave?

Phoebe's head throbbed. Carriages. Buggies. Wagons. Expenses passed on to clients. Clients who might not be as wealthy as Mr. Barnabas Ackerly and all his logistics seemed to have accounted for.

"My inn is to be accessible to couples from all economic walks of life," she insisted the moment he paused for breath. "I will not foist fees upon them for unnecessary extravagances." Though he had made a good point about the upper tier expecting a higher level of service. Until this moment, she hadn't considered the possible need to serve them *before* their arrival.

"Then perhaps we can offer varying price levels," he suggested without even having the decency to struggle over the problem for more than a heartbeat.

And he kept using the word *we*. It was *her* inn, not his. Definitely not *theirs*.

"Those who wish to purchase the most luxurious experience will pay a higher premium and will receive the benefits of inn-hosted transportation, maybe even a picnic lunch to tide them over during the journey. If the weather is fair, they could stop at some picturesque location along the way. I'm sure you could recommend a suitably idyllic spot, with all your travels between Oak Springs and Huntsville with your father."

He looked disgustingly smug at that bit of pandering, as if

expecting her romantic heart to melt into a puddle at his feet over a tepid compliment and the recommendation of a picnic. Just because the idea had merit didn't mean she'd be liquefying any time soon. She might go soft for a good love story, but she possessed backbone too. She wouldn't let some fast-talking salesman worm his way into taking control of *her* dream.

Phoebe opened her mouth to tell him exactly that, but he didn't give her the chance. As if her intent had been etched into the glass of her spectacles for him to read, he jumped into one discourse after another. Did the menu she planned to serve consist of fine dining items with decadent sauces and rich desserts? Or did she wish to capitalize on the novelty of the small-town lifestyle and serve more simple local fare? Would there be a schedule of events for guests to participate in, or would they be on their own for entertainment? If multiple guests booked the inn, would each couple be assigned a time to visit the Kissing Tree in private, or would the couples come and go as they pleased?

The barrage refused to relent. One question after another lifted from the ground to swirl around her head like fall leaves caught in a whirlwind. They blinded her. Dizzied her. Left her unsteady and not a bit charmed. Leaves were supposed to dance on the wind in magical fairy patterns, inspiring wonder and delight. But these closed in on her like a swarm of locusts, ready to devour her sanity.

All she wanted to do was provide a retreat for people so that they might write a special page in their own personal love stories. There was no need to make everything so complicated. Was there?

Phoebe staggered over to the porch railing. She turned, determined to keep the overwhelming Mr. Ackerly in sight as she leaned against the blessedly solid wooden support and clasped an arm around the pillar at her side. She didn't care if such a stance made her look weak. Having her knees give out would be a great deal worse, and she feared that was precisely what would happen if she released her grip on the column.

She would *not* fall at Barnabas Ackerly's feet. Not today. Or any day hereafter.

Thankfully, Mr. Ackerly proved himself a gentleman and ceased his interrogation. He stepped forward, tossing his fedora onto the seat of one of the nearby wicker chairs before standing directly before her.

"Forgive me for bombarding you in such relentless fashion," he said, his blue-gray eyes genuinely apologetic, "but I feared you would send me away before I could explain my value."

"If peppering women with verbal buckshot is a skill to value, sir, then you've indeed proven yourself a diamond of the first water."

He received her jab with a self-deprecating chuckle that took all the stodginess out of him. His smile reminded her why she'd always liked him best of her father's employees. Not the type to engage in insincere flattery or flagrant braggadocio, he'd always interacted with her in a straightforward manner free of both pretense and politics. And he knew how to let a person enjoy a book without filling a room with unwanted conversation—a diamond-worthy quality if ever there was one.

And his hair was never out of place. How did he do that? The wind was already tugging her tresses from the pins at her nape, yet his perfectly combed blond swoosh sat obediently atop his forehead without so much as a wiggle. Her father called him a magician for his skill in transforming properties, but she'd always thought the title better applied to the engineering of his hair.

"Look," he said, his voice growing softly serious after the breeze carried the last of his chuckle away, "for any new project to succeed, there must be both a vision and a plan. You, my dear Miss Woodward, have the vision. Let me help you devise a plan that will turn it into reality."

Three

Barnabas held his breath, willing Miss Woodward to choose sensibility over stubbornness.

Slowly, she unhooked her arm from around the porch column and straightened away from the railing. Lifting a hand to her glasses, she pushed them higher on the bridge of her nose, then met his gaze.

"Since my father sent you, he must believe you have something to offer." Though her expression made it clear *her* verdict was still out. "And since my father is the one financing this endeavor, I suppose I should abide by his wishes. To an extent." She stepped forward, closing the distance between them, the high neck of her lacy white blouse only accentuating the length of her throat as she jutted her chin upward. "It is still *my* inn, and I will have final say on every decision made. You will not order my workmen about, nor will you usurp my authority in any other matter. Is that clear?"

"Perfectly." Barnabas nodded, rigidly regulating his features into an expression of professional aplomb, despite the fact that his lips begged to grin. Apparently the reserved Miss Woodward had a suffragette's backbone beneath her bookish facade. "I am here in a consulting capacity only. All I ask is that you give my recommendations fair consideration."

He glanced down at his feet for a moment before raising his head to meet her gaze. "I hope you don't think me a braggart to say so, but I'm good at what I do, Miss Woodward. I understand the retail property market and have years of experience getting customers to open their pocketbooks and buy what I'm selling." He pushed his coat behind his hip and slid his hand into his trouser pocket. "I want your inn to succeed." No. He *needed* her inn to succeed. "And I promise you here and now that any suggestions I make will be solely motivated by the desire to achieve that end.

"I have nothing but respect for a woman striving to make a mark on the world. My mother did just that, all while rearing me on her own from the time I was four years of age. I admire her determination, fortitude, and creativity more than that of any other person I know. Including your father."

Everything he'd learned about survival and making oneself indispensable to one's employer came from his mother. Never once had they gone hungry. Never once had he gone without shoes. She stood tall beneath the shame others tried to heap on her after his perfidious father left them for a wealthy adventuress who enjoyed making lovers of other women's husbands. His mother made Barnabas feel safe and loved even as she taught him the value of hard work. He was the man he was today because of her.

And if his mother were here, faced with the daunting task of making the Kissing Tree Inn a successful romantic retreat, she'd be rolling up her sleeves and getting to work.

"So," Barnabas said, drawing his hand from his pocket and reaching for the hat he'd tossed aside earlier, "why don't you show me your inn?"

It took her a moment to answer. Those dark eyes peered at

him, weighing his words, his demeanor. His worth. Something he'd always measured by his achievements. Yet as much as he wanted to get busy achieving and proving his value, he forced himself to stand still beneath her perusal. She held the reins. Straining against the bit now would only sabotage his efforts.

"Very well, Mr. Ackerly." Phoebe Woodward marched a half circle around him, closed her front door, then marched the same orbital path back to the edge of the porch steps. With a glance over her shoulder, she tossed him a look of challenge. "This way, if you please."

Barnabas fit his fedora back onto his head and gave a sharp nod. "Yes, ma'am."

He'd expected the inn to be in town. Most rooming houses were, after all. But once they'd left Oak Springs behind, he realized he needed to adjust his expectations. Again.

Private. Romantic. Secluded.

That was how he'd need to describe the place. Give the isolated location a positive slant. Convince the client the inn would suit all his wooing needs. Ad copy bounced through Barnabas's mind as they walked, the swish of Phoebe's dark red skirt adding a rhythm to his thoughts as well as his steps.

Elegant lodging nestled in the quiet countryside. Take a walk down a country lane, hand in hand. Picnic by a stream. Surely there was a stream somewhere. *Woo your sweetheart beneath the branches of the world-famous Kissing Tree.* All right, it wasn't world-famous. It wasn't even state-famous. Barnabas tilted his head, his gaze ignoring the freshly plowed field on his right in favor of examining his thoughts more closely. *Beneath the branches of an ancient love tree?* No, that was drivel. *Beneath the arms of a chivalrous oaken knight?* Even worse.

Sentiment was not his forte. Maybe he could ask Miss Woodward to write something. He'd have to give her tight parameters—ad copy was a different animal from narrative prose—

but she obviously had literary skill. *Lippincott's* wouldn't have published her work otherwise.

A school bell rang nearby, bringing Barnabas out of his head long enough to take stock of his surroundings. A fortunate happenstance, as he nearly missed Miss Woodward turning down a narrow lane to their right. Barnabas lengthened his stride to make up for his lack of attention and nearly strode past his hostess when she slowed to gesture to something invisible on either side of the drive.

"I'm thinking of planting a pair of rosebushes here," she said, speaking for the first time since they'd left her home in town. "One on either side of the drive. To serve as a landmark of sorts, as well as to set a romantic tone for the guests' arrival to the inn."

A touch of charm that served a practical purpose. Impressive. Perhaps this Inn of Smooching Shrubbery wouldn't be the disaster he'd imagined. Barnabas grinned broadly. "I think that an excellent notion, Miss Woodward."

She blinked for a moment before a truly genuine smile blossomed across her face. An odd tightness closed around Barnabas's chest. That unguarded smile utterly changed her appearance. No longer was she the timid girl with downcast eyes who wished to be left alone to her reading. Nor did she resemble the feisty entrepreneur determined to protect her visionary masterpiece at all costs. This Phoebe Woodward was entirely new. Entirely . . . enchanting.

Barnabas's starched collar seemed to shrink against his throat. He swallowed roughly, forcing the sudden excess of saliva down his gullet as he jerked his attention away from the pretty blush that had scattered his focus. Well, that wasn't true. His focus was as sharp as ever, just aimed at the wrong target. His job was to attract customers to the Kissing Tree Inn, not to imagine kissing the attractive innkeeper beneath the nearest tree.

"You'll be able to see the inn and the Kissing Tree itself once we get past this line of trees." Her voice had lost its defensive edge, bubbling with excitement instead.

His own anticipation swelled in reaction.

"I have to admit, it still takes my breath away when it bursts into view," she said.

Barnabas smiled, intending to make a suitably polite statement about the value of dramatic impact, but the words prancing so smartly on his tongue did an abrupt about-face the moment he cleared the trees. They scrambled down his windpipe with astonishing speed, choking him in their hurry to disappear.

"Isn't it lovely?" she asked.

Barnabas stumbled to a halt.

Good heavens. It *wasn't* as bad as he'd imagined.

It was worse.

The Inn of Osculating Topiaries jutted up from the earth thirty yards down the lane—horrendously, garishly . . . pink.

Phoebe's heart pattered as if little cherub wings beat within her breast. As soon as the first coat of Valentine Pink had been applied earlier this week, she'd known at once it would be perfect. Nothing said romance like lacy, delicate valentines. And while the color was a bit bolder than *Comstock's Modern House Painting* recommended, she'd decided to be daring. It was important to create a memorable impression, after all.

"I selected a lighter fern-green shade for the gingerbread trim," she explained, waving her hand toward the inn as if holding a paintbrush herself. "The painter I hired assures me the result will be stunning."

"I'm stunned, all right."

Phoebe tore her gaze from her beloved inn to stare at the

gaping man beside her. His gaping didn't appear to stem from enraptured delight as hers did, however. This gaping was more of the fish-out-of-water-in-the-last-throes-of-death variety.

The prickles so recently soothed by his praise of her rosebush idea sprang back to thorny attention.

She folded her arms over her middle. "You're not the romantic sort, are you, Mr. Ackerly?"

The stuffy fellow didn't look a bit abashed by her accusation. "No, Miss Woodward. I am not. But I do recognize the role emotions play in the customer experience. *My* preference is not what matters."

Amen! Phoebe couldn't agree more.

Mr. Ackerly looked her directly in the eye, one brow raising slightly. "Just as *your* preference is not what matters."

Her preference? Of course her preference mattered. This was *her* inn.

"What truly matters," he continued, "is the *customer's* preference."

Phoebe's mouth, open to refute his claim about the insignificance of her opinion, snapped shut at his third pronouncement. Horsefeathers. He had a point.

But who was to say her preferences wouldn't match those of her customers? That cheerful thought returned a bit of starch to her spine. She was a romantic at heart. She'd been observing courting couples around the Kissing Tree since she was a child. Studying the carvings left in the bark. Dreaming up tales that delighted readers all over the country. She might be a spinster with little personal experience in romantic love, but she'd cultivated a base of knowledge that made her far more of an expert on the matter than Mr. Persnickety over there.

"I daresay my customers will have more in common with my sensibilities than with yours, sir. After all, the people who wish to reserve a room at the Kissing Tree Inn will be those looking for an atmosphere of love and romanticism. An atmosphere I intend to provide with or without your approval."

"You are, of course, correct. I am quite lacking in romantic sensibilities." Mr. Ackerly dipped his head in a shallow bow, yet his gaze was anything but conciliatory. "However, that doesn't mean I don't have other areas of expertise that could be of value. You might understand the intricacies of the heart, but I understand the intricacies of business. Both are necessary if this enterprise is to succeed."

She wanted to passionately defend her dream against the cold, unfeeling logic oozing from the man before her, but she knew instinctively that railing at him would change nothing. It would only make her look childish and histrionic. A man as stiff and stodgy as Barnabas Ackerly would not respect theatrics. Such behavior would simply lower his opinion of her.

An outcome, strangely enough, she found she wished to avoid, despite the fact that she found him rather irksome at the moment.

"Perhaps the interior will be more to your liking," she said, her jaw only partially clamped as she strode forward.

He fell into step beside her. "I look forward to seeing it."

"The furnishings are on order, so the building is empty, but that gives the paperers more space to work."

"You've already ordered wallpaper?"

Why did he sound like a man before a firing squad, asking if the bullets had been loaded?

"Samples." Phoebe took him around to the back of the inn and waved to the workman on a ladder who was brushing that beautiful pink paint along the second-story siding. "I intend to use a different pattern in each of the bedrooms, though I'm considering keeping things more consistent in the common areas downstairs."

She marched up the steps and let herself in through the back door.

"This is the kitchen." Sure to be his favorite room, with so many practical items on display. Cabinets. Stove. Sink. No irrational sentiment anywhere to be found. But that was all about to change.

Phoebe pushed through the swinging door into the dining room, where a pair of workmen were pasting sheets of wallpaper above the cherrywood wainscoting to help her envision which patterns she liked best. The blue-and-white one being affixed to the outside wall consisted of grapevines and frolicking cupids. The second sample, on the wall shared with the kitchen, offered subtle green and pink shades with lush floral bouquets and adorable little birds looking on from their garden perches.

A rough worktable in the middle of the room held a half dozen additional options, all handpicked for their fanciful designs and romantic overtones. Making a selection was going to be difficult, but once she could see them all on the wall, she knew the choice would become clear.

Mr. Ackerly crossed to the worktable in four strides, passed a quick glance over her painstakingly pared-down samples, then swept the entire collection into his arms, turned, and strode from the room.

Four

Hey!"

Barnabas ignored Miss Woodward's affronted call, not stopping until he stood outside in the fresh air. Well, fresh air doused in paint fumes. *Pink* paint fumes, which had to be the most toxic variety. Heaven knew his brain had been addled from their effect the moment he'd spied the Inn of Unfortunate Fuchsia-ness. Only one thought currently sparked in his fogged mind with any clarity—he had to stop the atrocities before the damage to the inn, and his future, became irreparable.

"What do you think you're doing? You can't just abscond with my wallpaper samples. That's thievery!" Phoebe Woodward lunged off the back porch and grabbed his arm.

"I'm not stealing your precious papers, madam," Barnabas objected. "I'm merely holding them hostage temporarily so we might negotiate a few terms."

She harrumphed as she released his arm and crossed hers over her chest. "Kidnapping carries more prison time than theft, I'll have you know."

Barnabas nearly smiled. Miss Woodward might have atrocious taste in inn décor, but her verbal sparring skills were on point. He couldn't recall the last time he'd been so invigorated by a conversational adversary—male or female.

"Rest assured, all captives will be returned in good health as soon as negotiations are complete." He glanced around. "Is there someplace nearby we can speak privately?" He didn't want to question her authority in front of the workmen.

Miss Woodward exhaled heavily, then uncrossed her arms and strode north. "This way."

He followed, straightening the wallpaper samples as he went, until he realized where they were heading. He'd been so focused on the inn, he'd failed to notice the tree for which it had been named.

An ancient live oak stood before him in stately grandeur. Barnabas's steps slowed as his gaze climbed from the ground to the leafy, neck-crimping top. The gentle giant had to be at least thirty feet tall. Maybe more. And the width of the canopy . . . he couldn't even estimate. Seventy feet in diameter? Eighty? It was the most magnificent tree he'd ever seen.

"This is amazing."

The awe in his voice must have caught Miss Woodward's attention, for she ceased stomping through the dirt and grass and turned to face him. The pique that had lined her face softened into a fondness no one could deny.

"Yes, it is," she said. "But it gets better." She actually smiled, as if his appreciation of her tree made him less a villain. "Come see."

She pushed a group of thin branches upward and gestured for him to enter her sanctuary. He hesitated, the place feeling a bit too sacred for the argument he knew to be in store. But curiosity drove him forward. This tree had not only inspired the inn he'd been tasked with turning into a success, but it inspired the woman before him. A woman, he suspected, who was much more complex than her superficial affinity for overblown floral patterns and pink cupids would suggest.

Ducking his head, Barnabas stepped beneath the canopy. His breath stilled. Branches wider than his shoulders stretched above his head, then reached down like a grandfather's loving arms.

"It's magical," he said.

"Isn't it?" Miss Woodward slipped her hand through his elbow and drew him forward.

The touch surprised him so much that he nearly dropped his wallpaper plunder. Her hand felt alarmingly wonderful in the crook of his arm. And with the way she glanced over her shoulder at him, her eyes filled with delight and secrets begging to be shared, he nearly forgot his purpose was confrontation, not courtship.

It was unfair, really. Taking a man unawares like that. Letting filtered sunlight dance over oneself like fairy dust. Smiling at him as if she were no longer cross. More than that—as if she actually desired his company. It stole a man's sense. And apparently his vocabulary, for Barnabas could think of nothing to say as she drew him toward the massive trunk at the heart of the tree.

"This is where the true magic lies," she said, her voice reverent as she released his arm and traced a set of scarred letters visible in the bark. "These are the oldest initials, carved a generation ago by a couple who found love under these very branches."

A heart enclosed the letters *AF* and *BE* at a spot slightly below eye level. But other pairs of initials surrounded that first carving. Dozens, by the look of it.

"Kids started calling it the Kissing Tree, and before long nearly every courting couple in town found their way here, either before or after the wedding. According to local legend, Freda Bresden refused to accept her husband's proposal until he'd carved their initials here." A soft laugh escaped Miss Woodward as she traced a nearby *FL* and *MB*. "She dragged poor Max all the way from her front parlor to this tree, then made him dig out his pocketknife and engrave a forever symbol of their love before she gave him her answer."

Miss Woodward glanced at him, a smile in her eyes. "Freda believed that once a couple's initials were carved into the Kissing Tree, the lovers were guaranteed to remain dedicated to each other until death." She turned away, a melancholy dimness dousing some of the light in her eyes. "For some, that dedication lasts even beyond the grave."

She backed away from the trunk and turned to follow the path of a large limb that stretched above her head. As the branch gradually sloped toward the ground, she placed her hand against the bark, running her fingers lightly over the surface. When it came even with her face, she ducked beneath the limb and followed its downward progression until it was level with her waist. There her hand stilled, and her gaze fixed on a spot Barnabas could not see.

Rolling the wallpaper samples into a tight cylinder and tucking them loosely under his arm, Barnabas ducked under the branch and circled around behind his contemplative companion. A pair of initials were etched into the branch, the only initials on this section of the tree. *HW* and *LW*.

"My parents," Miss Woodward said as she traced the heart that bound the two sets of letters together. "Hollis and Laurel. As far as I know, they're the only couple to add their initials to the tree after being married for several years. I was five years old when they brought me here to make a memory. The most treasured memory I have of the two of them together."

She glanced at him, and there was such a tender tranquility about her that Barnabas swallowed the words of sympathy springing to his tongue. Polite platitudes would ring hollow in a place rife with such personal significance. So he said nothing, just held her gaze and waited.

"It was their eighth anniversary." She turned around and leaned her back against the limb that held a sacred piece of her family history. "Mama had suffered a fever a few months before, and it left her with a weakened heart. I was too young to realize what her growing frailty signified, but Father must have known the end was near. He came home early that afternoon, bundled the two of us up in the buggy, then drove us out here. He carried Mama in his arms and set her on the stone bench he'd arranged to have placed here before he commenced with the carving." She gestured with a tip of her head to a white marble bench that had been hidden behind the large drooping branches of the oak.

"Father made a production of it." Her face lit with fond reminiscence. "He stopped every few minutes to tell stories about how he and Mama met. How he knew right away that she was the one for him. Then, whenever he returned to carving, Mama would share tales about their courtship. Like the time Father rented a buggy and took her for a drive, only to have rain pour down on them. Their buggy wheel mired in the mud, and they had to ride one of the horses back to town. They arrived bedraggled, Mama's dress utterly ruined. But it had been worth it, she said, to snuggle up against Father's back as they rode. Arms around his waist. Cheek lying against his shoulder. She realized she could rely on him to see her through any hardship they might face together."

As she spoke, pictures swirled in Barnabas's mind. A pale, thin woman wrapped in blankets and wreathed in smiles. A little girl on the bench beside her, legs swinging as she thirstily absorbed the stories of her parents' romance. A man determined to fill his wife's last days with joy, not only out of an unwavering love for her, but to plant seeds of happy memories in the tender heart of the daughter they both cherished.

Barnabas had always respected his employer for his keen

mind and no-nonsense leadership style, but seeing him through his daughter's eyes gave him an entirely different picture of Hollis Woodward—one of a man ultimately motivated by love, not profit.

It also painted a clearer picture of Miss Phoebe Woodward. This inn wasn't just an unrealistic exercise in romanticism dreamt up by a naïve young woman who read too many novels. It was a preservation of the abiding love her parents had shared. Yet instead of hoarding the magic for herself, she sought a way to share it with others. Rather remarkable, that.

"He's never looked at another woman since," Miss Woodward continued. "Even when everyone urged him to remarry for practicality, if not for love. *'A girl needs a mother,'* they said. But he refused to let another woman step into that role, and I was glad for it."

She pushed away from the limb, wandered over to the bench, and sat down. "Sometimes I wondered if I was selfish by not encouraging him to look for a new love. But when I asked him a few years ago if he ever thought about marrying again, he said he'd only consider it if he met a woman who made his heart skip a beat the way my mother had." She shrugged. "I guess that hasn't happened."

Barnabas wondered if the lady herself was waiting for the same lightning to strike.

"But this wasn't what you wanted to discuss with me in private," she said, sitting up a bit straighter as she packed away the softness brought on by family memories and prepared to resume matters of business. "I believe you were going to explain why you pilfered my wallpaper samples."

Barnabas slid the rolled samples out from under his arm and tapped the end against his palm. "Right." He strode over to the bench and gestured to the unoccupied section to her left. "May I?"

He didn't want to tower over her while they talked. To do so felt disrespectful, as if he were looking down on her and her ideas, which was far from the truth. After this glimpse into Phoebe Woodward's soul, not only had his respect for her grown, but the constant itch beneath his skin that had plagued him since inheriting this project had subsided. He was beginning to see the value in what she proposed, even if the manner in which she was going about it made him cringe.

Something had happened beneath the leaves of this mighty oak. He no longer wanted this inn to succeed for the sake of his employment. He wanted it to succeed for her.

With a dip of her chin and a wave of her hand, she invited him to join her on the bench. She scooted over as he took his seat, yet as he swiveled to face her, his knees brushed hers. A touch of pink flared on her cheeks, which caused an unsettling ferocity to afflict the beating of his heart.

Hollis Woodward's comment about meeting a woman who made his heart skip a beat echoed in Barnabas's mind, but he shoved it aside. Distraction led to mistakes, and he couldn't afford to be careless.

He cleared his throat. "Before I speak to the wallpaper issue, may I ask why you selected such a . . . vibrant shade of pink for the exterior of the inn?"

Her shoulders stiffened. "Pink and red are the colors of love. Of romance and valentines. The perfect color for a couples' retreat."

He'd have to choose his words with care if he hoped to navigate those raised hackles without getting pricked. "Tell me, what is the most important element for this retreat? The inn or the Kissing Tree?"

He held his breath, praying he'd gambled correctly.

She hesitated only a moment. "There would be no Kissing Tree Inn without the Kissing Tree."

Barnabas nodded, the tension in his neck loosening just a touch. "A logical answer. Yet when the inn first came into view today as we walked down the lane, I missed the tree completely." He gestured to the massive spread of branches and leaves surrounding them. "As large and majestic as this beauty is, I didn't see it. All I could see was pink. While there is nothing wrong with having a pink inn, a color that vivid is certain to provoke strong reactions from those who see it for the first time. Some will no doubt find it charming, the symbol of romance you intended. But others will find it shocking. Perhaps even off-putting."

Her brows lifted. "As you did?"

He tipped his head in silent confession. "In my years of property management, I have learned that the key to fetching a good price lies in making the property as attractive as possible to as many people as possible. This means making selections based not only on what the majority of people find pleasing but on what is least likely to *displease* potential customers. Neutral shades, simple patterns, uncluttered room arrangements. Those tend to generate maximum interest."

Miss Woodward fiddled with her glasses, then glanced to the samples in his hand. "I assume you find my choice of paper similarly off-putting?"

He did, but the tinge of hurt in her voice made him loath to admit it. "Let's just say I find these samples excessively . . . feminine."

"What's wrong with feminine designs?" Her eyes flashed, zeroing in on his again. The spark that had temporarily gone missing reemerged with a vengeance.

Barnabas fought a smile. "Absolutely nothing. But being the non-romantic, stodgy nag of practicality that I am, I think it important to point out that you are designing this inn for *couples*. As such, half of the people you are designing for are men. Even more significant is the fact that in the majority of cases, it is the male half who will be footing the bill. While these men will undoubtedly wish to please their wives, if you hope to secure their return business, it would be wise to cater as much to them as to the ladies on their arms."

Her brow furrowed. "But I was given to believe that men care nothing about design. That they actually prefer their wives, daughters, or sisters to handle the decorating details for them. Even my father, who is not shy about sharing his opinions, as you know, has never shown any interest in such things."

"Not about the public areas of the home, perhaps. But what about the rooms he spends the majority of his time in? I've been in his Huntsville home. I've seen his study. I imagine his private chambers are much the same. Lots of wood paneling. Darker colors. Artwork featuring rugged landscapes. Maybe even some antlers or a mounted deer head from a prize hunt. No flowers. No lovebirds. Definitely no cupids."

Miss Woodward leapt from the bench and flung her arms wide. "But none of what you describe is *romantic*!"

"Correct." Barnabas set the samples aside and slowly pushed to his feet. "But it *is* what makes a man feel comfortable."

He took a step closer to her and started reaching for her hand. He caught himself a few inches away, fisted his fingers, and dropped his hand to his side.

Good heavens. What kind of reckless impulse had that been? This was a professional partnership, not a personal one. *Keep your head about you, man.*

"I'm not advising that we turn your inn into a rustic hunting lodge, Miss Woodward. However, what I *am* advising is that you give equal consideration to attracting male customers as you give to female ones. Perhaps switch the color palette for the exterior from pink with fern-green trim to fern green with pink trim. Not only would the more neutral shade be less likely to provoke polarizing reactions from your guests, but it will more easily direct their attention to the main attraction—this magnificent tree."

"And the wallpaper?" Her tone challenged, but her posture had softened. He might just be getting through to her.

"I propose an experiment. Before any decisions are made about the décor in the public spaces downstairs, let's collect some scientific data. We'll each take an upstairs bedroom and decorate it in the style we believe most conducive to romance. Then, in exchange for a free night at the inn during the off-season, say January or February next year, we'll ask several local couples to view the rooms as soon as we have completed them and share their honest opinions on an anonymous ballot. We can ask three questions. Which room would they most like to stay in? Which element did they find most welcoming in each room? And if they could change one thing about each room, what would they change? Once we analyze the data, we can use it to inform our choices for the rest of the inn. What do you think?"

A half grin quirked her mouth. "What I think, Mr. Ackerly, is that your room won't stand a chance at winning."

Five

Two weeks later, Phoebe stole up the inn's staircase, cracked open the door to her competitor's room, and peeked inside. Her stomach clenched. It was worse than she'd thought. Barnabas Ackerly might actually *win*.

Glancing behind her to ensure the coast was clear, she inched across the threshold and surveyed the cozy scene her nemesis had created. How had the self-proclaimed stodgy nag of practicality created such an inviting space?

He'd obviously taken inspiration from the Kissing Tree, for the walls were papered with a subtle green oak-leaf pattern that spread like a canopy up from the oak wainscoting she'd had installed in all the bedrooms. He'd used the oak furnishings she'd purchased—bed, wardrobe, dresser, and washstand—but he'd added some of his own pieces as well. A natural wood hat stand that looked as if it had been taken directly from the tree outside. A love seat upholstered in fabric resembling the red, gold, and brown leaves of fall that matched the elegant gold hue of the bed's coverlet and dark red throw pillows. He'd added a decorative wood onlay of leaves and acorns to the molding above the two windows. The lighter stain of the onlay made the acorn details stand out in dramatic fashion.

The color palette was definitely darker and more masculine than what she had selected for her chamber, but the room had a rustic charm that lent it a cozy air.

She moved deeper inside the room, her gaze examining everything from floor to ceiling. There were no carpets on the floor, no little decorative boxes on the chest of drawers to hold a lady's hairpins, no mirror beyond the small one above the washstand for a lady to check her appearance before going out.

Apparently the perfect Mr. Ackerly had missed a few things. A little zing of triumph surged through Phoebe's chest. Though it didn't really feel like victory. More like . . . affirmation. The man with the perfect hair and the perfect business instincts and the perfect understanding of masculine clientele just might need a lady's help—a lady with a fondness for shocking shades of pink, frolicking cupids, and romantic novels.

Not that said lady would be helping him today. The judging couples were visiting in less than an hour, and she wanted as many imperfections on display as possible. Not very charitable of her, perhaps, but for once she'd like to get the upper hand against the man her father called a magician. Barnabas Ackerly had the incredibly annoying habit of being right far too often.

She'd already received dozens of compliments about the new exterior color scheme of her inn. The soft green was such an elegant choice, they said. Like a natural extension of the Kissing Tree. How clever she'd been to switch the pink to an accent color.

Only she hadn't been clever at all. Barnabas Ackerly had been. Yet he never corrected anyone's assumptions. In fact, she'd overheard him praise her outright to Adam Fisher, telling him that she had a wonderful vision for the inn. He'd said he was simply there to offer the occasional bit of advice and assist with logistics.

The *occasional* bit of advice? Phoebe snorted softly as she ran her fingers over the edge of the bed's coverlet. Only on those *occasions* when the sun rose from the eastern horizon.

No. That wasn't fair. Barnabas really had been very collaborative in the days following the wallpaper pilferage. He listened to her ideas. Offered suggestions. Even sought her opinion on areas of operation like menus, entertainment, transportation . . . just not in matters of decorating. He still quailed at the mention of floral patterns and chubby cherubs. Which was precisely why she brought them up on a regular basis. The little flashes of panic that widened his eyes were just too delightful. He needed his composure rattled every now and then. It was only fair, with how often he rattled hers.

Phoebe grinned as she wrapped her fingers around the short newel post on the footboard. Swinging herself toward the curtainless window—which she happily added to her list of imperfections—she caught a movement out of the corner of her eye.

Sucking in a gasp, she spun toward the door as a male hip finished bumping it open.

"Phoebe! I . . . I mean, Miss Woodward." Mr. Ackerly shifted his parcels, as if more concerned over what she might see than the fact that he'd caught her trespassing. "What are you doing in here?"

She fingered the wire rim of her spectacles and bit guiltily at her lip. There was nothing for it. She'd have to make a full confession.

"I'm sorry, Mr. Ackerly. I know we agreed to keep the rooms secret from each other until they were complete, but with the judging almost upon us, I succumbed to temptation. I promise I haven't been inside your room before this moment. I've held to the spirit of our bargain, if not to the strictest letter. Please say you'll forgive me."

He set aside what appeared to be two framed pieces of art—

one smaller, one larger—leaning them against the side of the bureau, then crossed the room to stand in front of her. He didn't look terribly angry or affronted. In fact, a small smile curved his lips.

"I'll forgive you on one condition."

Was it her imagination, or were his eyes bluer than usual today? And why was she noticing that *now*, of all times? He already had her at enough of a disadvantage. She didn't need to get all fluttery over his eyes. Though it was rather hard not to, when they looked as tender and teasing as they did now.

Get yourself together, Phoebe. He's here under orders from your father, not out of any kind of affection for you. It's just business to him.

"First larceny and kidnapping, now extortion? You're accumulating quite a list of felonies, Mr. Ackerly."

Good heavens. Had she just flirted with him? She'd intended to spear him with a dose of prudishness and thereby reestablish their boundaries, but her tone had emerged far more playful than prim.

"Shocking, isn't it?" His grin widened. "I've always been such a law-abiding citizen too. I guess you bring out the unexpected in me."

Double good heavens. Had he just flirted back?

Phoebe had read countless romantic stories with heroines who experienced heart palpitations when the hero rode to their rescue or slayed a dragon or swept them up in strong arms, but here she was, experiencing unmistakable palpitations over nothing more than a witty rejoinder and a teasing smile.

Dipping her lashes, she stared at her shoes, hoping the view of sensible black leather would restore her brain to proper, unfanciful functioning. "So, what is this condition of yours?"

Probably something to do with gaining her promise to forgo all cupid adornments.

"I'd like you to call me by my given name."

Phoebe's head shot up. A touch of red darkened his face, and his gaze lacked the confidence she was so accustomed to seeing. The always composed, always correct Mr. Ackerly was nervous. The realization turned her insides to butter.

Clearing a throat that seemed intent upon throbbing in time with her pulse, Phoebe managed a nod. "I agree to your terms, Barnabas. As long as you call me Phoebe in return."

He dipped his chin in a small bow. "'Twould be my honor."

So gallant.

So dangerous.

A stuffy, insufferable wallpaper thief should not set her pulse flittering like a hummingbird's wings. Even if he was rather dapper, exceedingly intelligent, and possessed of the nicest smile she'd ever seen. One he happened to be aiming in her direction at that very moment.

Get ahold of yourself, Phoebe. He'll be leaving as soon as the inn is finished. This isn't one of your novels.

Forcing her attention away from the face that suddenly seemed twice as handsome as it had the day before, she latched onto the sight of the framed artwork leaning against the dresser and moved toward it.

Sidling around him, she gestured to the two pieces. "Some last-minute additions to the room?"

Before she could lay a finger on the taller of the two, Barnabas zipped around and blocked her path.

Phoebe immediately stepped back, retracting her outstretched hand. "I'm sorry. I shouldn't have presumed—"

"No reason to be sorry. I just . . ." He blew out a breath. "Only one of them is for the room. The other is more . . . personal."

Seeing the unflappable businessman . . . well, flapping, Phoebe grinned and took pity on him.

"Tell you what," she said. "I'll close my eyes while you hide the one you don't want me to see. Then, when it's safely hidden away, you can show me the other."

Barnabas visibly relaxed. "Excellent suggestion." His confidence flooding back in, he raised a brow of challenge at her. "Why don't we make it interesting and see if you can guess what is in the frame?"

"All right." Getting into the spirit of the game, Phoebe closed her eyes, then cupped her hands over her spectacle lenses. "Is it a picture of a tree? That does seem to be the prevailing theme of the room."

"You picked up on that, did you?" His voice sounded warm, as if a chuckle were just beneath the surface. "Yes, the artwork features part of a tree."

"Is there a couple sitting beneath the branches?" Such a tableau was probably more romantic than anything he'd actually choose, but it would make for a lovely addition to the room. This space was cozy and intimate, but there was nothing distinctly *romantic* about it. Perhaps adding such a painting would give it that missing touch.

"There are no people in the picture," Barnabas said from somewhere behind her. The wardrobe hinge creaked. "But couples are represented in more abstract fashion."

Abstract? "Like a pair of lovebirds sitting on a branch with their beaks touching?" That would be sweet.

"No. Much simpler." The wardrobe door clicked shut, and his shoes scuffed softly against the floorboards as he made his way back to the bureau. "In fact, I'm regretting asking you to guess. You're bound to be disappointed when you see the actual piece. It can't compare to that vivid imagination of yours. It's only a sketch. No color."

"I'm sure it's wonderful," she assured him.

"We'll see. Just lower your expectations before you open your eyes, all right?"

She shook her head. “Not on your life. I’m raising my expectations. You’ve given me no reason for disappointment yet.”

“Yes, well, you’ve never seen one of my sketches before.”

One of *his* sketches? Phoebe yanked her hands away from her eyes and peered at the framed sketch he held in front of him.

She inhaled a shaky breath. Her fingers trembled as she reached out toward the immediately recognizable rendering. “*You* drew this?”

He shifted his weight. “It’s not real art, I know, but I thought it might lend a sentimental touch to the room.”

“Not real art? Barnabas, this is . . .”—she struggled to find the right word—“amazing.”

He’d captured the trunk of the Kissing Tree in dark charcoal on ivory paper. The weathered bark. The carvings. *All* the carvings. He’d drawn them all. Exactly as they appeared on the tree. Every nuance. Every imperfection. Every ragged slip of the knife. It must have taken hours of study to perfect each detail. Yet Barnabas never did anything halfway. Somehow he’d captured the very essence of her beloved Kissing Tree.

And with it, she very much feared he’d captured her heart.

He might have intended the sketch as nothing more than a clever business strategy, tying the room to the romance of the tree, but she felt the touch of it travel all the way to the depths of her soul.

Tears misted her eyes as she stroked the edge of the frame. “It’s perfect.”

Six

As Phoebe blinked moisture from her eyes, an alarming mushiness afflicted Barnabas's chest. He'd done a few quick sketches for clients before, to help them visualize his plans for a particular property, but never had he tried to create an actual piece of art. It had taken him a week of sneaking away to the tree when she wasn't watching to get the scale and shading just right. He'd burned his first few attempts when they'd failed to capture the essence of the tree's heart, but seeing her reaction now, satisfaction swelled within him.

"I'm glad you like it." And by *glad*, he meant euphoric. If the pleasure pounding through his veins didn't regulate soon, he might start listing sideways and spouting horrendous poetry due to excessive inebriation. Not exactly the behavior of a professional business consultant.

Barnabas turned with the artwork and forced his attention away from Phoebe's lovely face and onto the nail protruding from the wall instead. The softness in her expression was wreaking havoc on his pulse. Not to mention fuzzing his brain.

"Who taught you to draw like that?" she asked.

He closed his eyes briefly to defend himself against the admiration in her tone. A man could forget he was merely a hired hand with that tone slithering over him like fine silk.

"My mother," he finally managed to get out as he hooked the frame over the nail. Taking longer than necessary to level the corners—since what he was really leveling was his head—he steadied his hands and his breath before pivoting to face the woman whose approval grew dangerously more important to him each day.

She's the boss's daughter, genius. Off limits.

He'd come to Oak Springs to preserve his job, not exterminate it. Fraternizing with Hollis Woodward's daughter was guaranteed to kill his career faster than munching on a cyanide sandwich.

Barnabas cleared his throat. What were they talking about? Oh yes. His mother. "She's a master at turning ordinary items into works of art," he bragged. "My father left us when I was just a boy. Mother kept a roof over our heads and shoes on our feet by turning people's castoffs into desirable items she could sell at a profit. Beads from an unwanted purse dressed up an ordinary bodice and transformed it from a day dress to formal attire. A torn piece of lace became trim for a lady's handkerchief or sleeve. Strategically placed embroidered patches brought new life to thinning upholstery." He gestured to the picture he'd just hung. "Pressed leaves and charcoal sketches become fine art for nothing more costly than time and framing materials."

Phoebe smiled. "So the magician learned his tricks from a master sorceress."

Barnabas dipped his head. "Indeed."

"She undoubtedly also influenced your sense of style." Her smile twisted into a wry expression. "Something I'm beginning to suspect I lack."

He opened his mouth to argue, but the look she shot him told him not to bother. She wouldn't welcome polite half-truths.

She held up a hand. "Oh, I'm not saying I'm ready to concede our contest just because a few people mentioned that they find the inn's new green exterior more flattering than the pink. Nor will I completely forfeit flowers and cupids just because the man who cautions against them happens to wear dapper suits and sports disgustingly perfect hair and charmingly chiseled features. I still believe my romantic sensibilities will carry the day."

Wait. Had she just called him dapper and . . . *charmingly chiseled*? Barnabas's pulse leapt to a gallop like a thoroughbred reacting to the drop of the starting flag. He'd overheard ladies describe him as staid, steady, or even stodgy, but never stylish. And certainly not charmingly chiseled. Was that really how Phoebe saw him?

"Come on." She grabbed his hand and dragged him out of his stupor.

Only then did he realize she'd been talking to him while he'd been stuck on chisels. Of course, the moment her hand clasped his, all ability to focus on anything other than the feel of her skin against his palm abandoned him as well. Her next words barely registered.

"It's only fair that you get to see mine since I saw yours."

Thankfully, her meaning didn't take long to decipher when she pushed open the door to the room she'd been decorating and led him inside.

The moment he crossed the threshold, it occurred to Barnabas that a man really shouldn't join a lady in a bedchamber while under the influence of ego-enhancing compliments and feminine hand-holding. Despite the fact that the door was wide open and workmen could interrupt at any time, Barnabas started backing out of the room.

"I shouldn't be in here," he said, heat rising up his nape.

"Don't be silly." Phoebe yanked him deeper into the room. He stumbled a bit as she conquered his feeble resistance. "It's only fair. I examined your room. You can examine mine." She looked at him expectantly, and the fog around his brain cleared enough for him to recognize the vulnerability in her brown eyes. "I'd like to hear what you think."

Get your mind off your own ego for a minute and pay attention to hers. She's nervous.

A crowd of people was about to descend upon the inn and cast judgment upon the design she'd been working on for weeks. It was only natural for her to feel anxiety. Especially since he'd been pointing out her failings since the day he arrived. Yet despite that, she peered at him with a shy desire to please. Nibbling on the corner of her lip, she turned to gaze at the room she'd put together and gently squeezed his hand before releasing it.

She respected his opinion. Perhaps even hoped to impress him. And like a dunce, all he'd been able to think about were improprieties that only existed in his mind.

Barnabas straightened his shoulders. Time to think about *her* for a change. Well, he *had* been thinking about her, but he'd do so in a strictly businesslike manner from this point on. He was here as a consultant. He might as well consult.

Giving each of his coat sleeves a sharp tug, he stepped into the center of the room. "Very well. Let's see what we have." He paced in a slow half circle, surveying her handiwork.

Careful to keep his expression neutral as he made his examination, Barnabas fought to remain objective. The rococo-style wallpaper was far frillier than he would prefer, with its curling feathers, draping flowers, fluttering ribbons, and golden scrollwork, yet it was so completely Phoebe that he found it more quirky than annoying. And truth be told, he could see restraint in the pattern she'd selected.

The colors were muted—golds, greens, and dark pinks—so the overall effect did not overwhelm the senses. And the artistic scene within the scrollwork that repeated in a checkerboard pattern every twelve inches or so couldn't have been a better fit for the Inn of Wooing Woodery. A young country lass leaning against a fence with a playful pup pawing at her skirts. A besotted swain on the opposite side, elbow propped on the top rail, eyes gazing longingly into the face of the fair maiden. And a tree standing in the background, sheltering the courting couple. Phoebe being Phoebe, it would have been impossible for her *not* to have chosen this design.

What really surprised him was her choice of bedding. With all the pinks and reds in the wallpaper, he would have expected her to select one of those feminine hues, but she'd opted for a light green covering. The color was perfect for the room, but it was covered in a fancy cutwork ivory lace that, while sure to be attractive to those of the female persuasion, would leave a man feeling like he couldn't relax for fear of snagging the fine lace on a trouser button or boot buckle. The impractical coverlet would fray and tear easily with guest use, leaving it looking ratty instead of romantic after only a handful of visitors, but she was on the right track.

A matching dresser scarf further feminized the room, but she'd kept the knickknacks to a minimum. Though he nearly cracked a smile when he spotted the small cupid on the soap dish on the washstand. Somehow he knew that was a deliberate jab at him. He rather liked the idea of her thinking of him as she decorated. Even if it was only in a teasing capacity.

She'd brought in a chaise longue in a dark wine-colored fabric that looked sturdy even with its tooled legs. Best of all, there were no crazy designs in the fabric. The pattern was so subtle that it looked more like a textured solid than a pattern. Of course, she did have a rather flamboyant floral pillow tossed atop it, but a man could *accidentally* kick that piece of hideousness under the bed if it proved too disturbing.

"I'm impressed," he finally said, and surprisingly enough,

he meant it. "You managed to stay true to your aesthetic while toning things down to appeal to a broader clientele." He turned his gaze on her. "Nice job, Phoebe."

A delighted smile blossomed slowly across her face before bursting into full bloom. An answering unfurling stretched inside his chest.

Good grief. What was happening to him? Even his analogies were becoming botanical. The flowers in the room must be addling his mind.

No, he thought, fighting the urge to caress the side of Phoebe's face as she gazed up at him with pleasure. The addling was all *her* doing.

Forcing his gaze away from hers, he caught sight of a hat rack standing in the corner on the far side of the wardrobe. The large clothes cabinet hid all but the top of a black hat, but when he shifted sideways for a closer look, he knew immediately that this couldn't stay.

He strode forward, clasped the hat rack by the neck, and dragged it away from the slender nook between the wardrobe and the wall.

"Hey!" Phoebe lunged after him. "You can't move things around before the judging. That's sabotage!"

Barnabas would not be dissuaded, even when she grabbed hold of his arm. "The bigger crime would be leaving this tucked away in the corner where it could be missed. This is the best piece in the room, Phoebe. It needs a place of honor."

Her cheeks turned a lovely shade of pink as her hand slid off his coat sleeve, no longer intent on stopping him. "You like it?"

"It's the perfect blend of sentimentality and practicality."

Why did it suddenly feel as if the hat stand wasn't the only occupant of the room for which that description fit?

Phoebe fingered the lace of the wedding veil, the wreath of silk flowers that formed its crown looped over the top hook. A man's black top hat hung from the opposite hook, leaving the lower hooks free for guests to utilize.

"I needed something tall and thin to fill the space on the other side of the wardrobe and got the idea to use my daddy's wedding hat and my mama's veil. If our pretend clients like it when they come through this afternoon, I'll get replicas made before opening for business. Although I suppose I could leave these on display. It's not like they were doing anyone any good locked away in a trunk."

Barnabas frowned. "Do you not wish to wear your mother's veil at your own wedding someday?" He couldn't imagine a woman with such intense romantic sensibilities not wanting to keep a token of the mother she adored close to her on such an important day.

"Oh, I won't be marrying." Phoebe flung the statement past him as if it were a foregone conclusion.

"Why not?" How could a woman in love with love not dream about her own romantic future?

"You're a clever fellow. One who understands the law of supply and demand. It should be obvious." Her tone grew tight. "Plain, bespectacled women over a certain age are not precisely a prime commodity in the marriage market. Especially when they tend to be a tad eccentric, spending all their time with books and trees." She shrugged to minimize the statement, but her eyes told the real story. Showed her hurt. She turned her back and paced toward the window. "A few gentlemen have made offers over the years," she said, pushing back the lace curtain so she could gaze across the yard to the tree he was beginning to suspect had never seen her kissed beneath its branches, "but I knew they didn't really want *me*. They wanted the connection to my father."

She dropped the curtain and pivoted to face him, the fire in her expression taking him by surprise. "Practical marriages may work for some. Political alliances. Societal connections. Security. Children." She stumbled a bit over that last one. "But I have no need of such arrangements. I am free to marry whomever I choose, and I refuse to settle for anything other than soul-stirring, fully reciprocated love. Spinsterhood over settling, that's my motto."

Phoebe grinned as if it were all some kind of joke, but he found nothing humorous in anything she'd just revealed.

Barnabas searched for something to say, something to let her know how much he respected her for not compromising her standards. How he saw so much more in her than the paltry statistics she used to describe herself. But before he could find the right words, she brushed at her eyes with the back of her hand and all but ran past him.

"Excuse me. I need to speak to the workmen."

Barnabas made no move to stop her. He did, however, pace over to the wardrobe and shove it into the corner so that the wedding hat stand could be displayed in a prominent, impossible-to-miss place.

Just like where Phoebe should have been all this time. How could the men of Oak Springs not see the treasure they had right under their noses?

Plain? Old? Odd? Was that really how she saw herself? How others saw her? She was bright, imaginative, full of life and dreams. How could they not see that in her?

Or did they not see her at all?

Barnabas stared at the empty doorway. *He* hadn't seen her. Not really. All those company dinners. Those quiet hours reading together in her father's study. He'd failed to truly see her.

Now he could see little else. Think of little else.

He exited Phoebe's room and reentered his own. He walked over to the wardrobe, pulled open the door, and collected the second drawing he'd made. The one he'd drawn for her. Not for the inn. Not to help him keep his job. Just to please her.

Would she see his heart on the page when she saw it? Or would he be as invisible to her as she had been to him all these years?

Seven

Phoebe watched the ballot completion from a wingback chair in the corner of the parlor. She tapped a finger against one of the bare shelves on the bookcase beside her, the one she planned to stock with a selection of novels, poetry, and biographies of famous couples. If Barnabas had his way, there'd be a few business journals, almanacs, and historical treatises included as well. Perhaps on the bottom shelf. Fashion not requiring a corset made low-shelf retrieval a much simpler matter for men, after all. And that way, should a male guest really want one of those stuffy business journals, at least his wife would have the pleasure of seeing him get down on one knee.

Peering into the dining room through the open doorway that joined it to the parlor, she tried to gauge the progress of their judging panel. She couldn't see all the couples who'd just completed their upstairs tour, but she could see the Fishers and the Bresdens at the table, their heads bent over questionnaires like students in a classroom.

Her stomach twisted as pencils scraped against paper. The parlor-decorating plans she'd been using to distract herself faded into the background of her mind as new, louder thoughts took precedence.

What were they writing? Did they like her room? Hate it? Did they think the inn itself completely ridiculous? Barnabas had, at least initially. He hadn't said it in so many words, but she'd sensed his true opinion. He seemed more supportive of late, however. Invested even, as if he truly wanted her inn to succeed, and not just to please her father and the Woodward Land Development Company.

She cast a glance toward where he stood by the mantel, near the corner where she planned to install a phonograph with a selection of recordings fit for sweethearts. The center of the room would intentionally be left open to provide space for dancing, while the furnishings arranged around the outer edges would remain grouped in pairs, each twosome centered around a different activity. Music, reading, a game table for backgammon or checkers, and a writing desk for correspondence, particularly love letters. Phoebe intended to place her favorite poetry volumes there, along with a not-so-subtle hint of letters tied in a bow for inspiration. Any husband taking care of last-minute business concerns would be reminded of his purpose for staying at the inn.

Barnabas had suggested the desk as a concession to practicality. Phoebe was resolved to transform it into another mechanism for romance. Even the most pragmatic item could become something chivalrous with a little imagination.

Could the same be true of a *person*?

Phoebe's pulse gave a little hiccup as she examined Barnabas in his stiff collar, well-pressed suit, and clean-shaven face. Her father's associate was the epitome of rationality and common sense. Yet he'd created a piece of art that had moved her nearly to tears. What might he reveal himself to be if she applied a little creativity while interpreting his actions?

Barnabas glanced over at her, and their gazes locked. He crossed the room. The strains of a waltz began playing in her mind. She imagined him stopping before her, extending his arm, and saying . . .

"It'll be over soon."

Not that.

Phoebe blinked, and her brow scrunched.

"The waiting," he explained, as if a normal person wouldn't have understood his meaning at once.

Of course, a normal person would not have been dreaming up imaginary balls and invitations to dance.

Barnabas slid into the chair beside her and took her hand in his. His fingers gently clasped hers, and she immediately forgave him for not asking her to dance to music only she could hear. He offered camaraderie. Reassurance. Friendship. Tangible treasures that would go much further in the real world than mere wisps of whimsy.

Finally, their visitors began to stir in the other room. Barnabas gave her hand a squeeze, then released it. Strange how she felt the loss of his touch so keenly when it had lasted such a short time. He stood, then offered her his assistance in rising. Fitting her hand into his, she absorbed the sensation of his fingers wrapping around hers once again before slipping free of his grasp as propriety demanded.

"Before I hand these over," Bella Fisher said as she entered the parlor, holding the stack of folded papers in front of her, "I have something to say to Mr. Ackerly."

Barnabas nodded politely. "Of course, Mrs. Fisher. I'm at your service."

"Collecting data is all well and good, but there are intangible influences that should not be overlooked in this process."

"Such as?"

Phoebe met her friend's gaze. What was she up to?

Bella's small smile failed to reassure as she turned on Barnabas like a mother hen preparing to peck an encroaching rooster. "I have read every one of Phoebe's tales, and there is a reason *Lippincott's* keeps asking for more. Her stories touch the heart. Not only mine, but hundreds of others. She's too modest to tell you this, but I know for a fact that she has an entire hatbox filled with letters from readers who have been captivated not only by her stories, but also by her depictions of our Kissing Tree."

"Bella!" Phoebe croaked, heat rushing to her face.

"She's already cultivated the market for this inn all on her own, Mr. Ackerly. And while I concede that there is wisdom to be gained from seeking multiple opinions on décor and other superficialities, I would caution against using the results of this feedback to stifle the spirit that brought this inn to life in the first place."

Bella's passionate defense left Phoebe torn between the desire to hug her friend and strangle her. Before she could decide which would prove most satisfying, however, Barnabas stepped forward and gave a small bow.

"Well said, madam. I couldn't agree more." He turned to look at Phoebe, his expression softening, effectively dissolving all lingering strangulation urges. "Without Miss Woodward's imagination and romantic sensibilities, the Kissing Tree Inn would be just another lodging. It is her spirit and heart that make it unique. Those must be preserved at all cost."

It must have been a trick of the light, the sun glinting off one of Barnabas's buttons, but for just a moment, Phoebe could have sworn his fine wool suit had transformed into one made of shining armor.

"Excellent!" Bella's voice restored reality, as well as a healthy dose of embarrassment. "Then I gladly hand these results over for your consideration." She extended the papers toward

Phoebe, the smile on her face a little brighter than the occasion warranted. Bella glanced to Barnabas and then back to Phoebe, her eyes dancing. "I shuffled the ballots so you won't know whose are whose."

Phoebe accepted the forms from her friend, barely resisting the impulse to swat her with them. "Thanks."

As Barnabas moved forward to shake Adam Fisher's hand and mingle with the other men, Phoebe found herself herded out into the hall and surrounded by five women.

"That Mr. Ackerly seems taken with you." Mabel Cassidy, who was pushing sixty-five, winked at Phoebe as if she were a girl in short skirts. "Better not let him get away."

"Such a gentleman. So polite and well-mannered. Comes to church every Sunday. A girl could do much worse." Hester Washington, the preacher's wife, actually waggled her eyebrows.

Good heavens. Phoebe needed to nip this matchmaking in the bud before things got out of hand. "Mr. Ackerly is here in a professional capacity, ladies. Nothing more. Once the inn is finished, he'll be returning to Huntsville."

A rather depressing thought, now that she considered it. She'd grown accustomed to having him around the last couple of weeks. Their rousing debates and this room-decorating competition had fired her blood and drawn her out of her quiet, internalized existence. Would she revert to her introspective, spinsterish self when he left? Was that who she still wanted to be?

"I saw him holding your hand." Freda Bresden grinned. "A man doesn't do that in a *professional* capacity. That's a *personal* gesture."

Phoebe's heart thudded against her ribs. Could it be true? Could Barnabas truly be interested in *her*, not just her inn? She shoved the question aside, too afraid of what the answer might mean to ponder it more deeply. Besides, this wasn't the time for a discussion of this nature. Nor the place. Heavens, Barnabas could walk through the parlor door at any moment and overhear.

"All right. Enough teasing, ladies." Bella Fisher wrapped an arm around Phoebe's shoulders. "Our Phoebe has a business to run and an inn to finish." She caught Phoebe's gaze. "An inn that is shaping up into an incredibly charming retreat. One I'm looking forward to trying out myself after it's up and running."

"Me too!" Freda said. "When I heard you were giving away a free stay in exchange for opinions, I insisted Max join me. He grumbled the whole way here about not caring two figs about feminine doodads and fancy furnishings until Mr. Ackerly explained that you wanted the male perspective as well as the female. Max got into the spirit after that. He said if he had to stay here at some future date, he might as well do what he could to protect himself from overzealous flowers and excessive figurines."

"Men." Mabel Cassidy shook her head. "If it were up to them, we'd be living in plain wooden boxes void of anything sentimental or interesting. Rather like a coffin."

A startled laugh burst from Phoebe to join the titters of the other ladies.

"Mabel?" A scratchy male voice fell into the laughter like a scoop of gravel and dispersed the merriment into small ripples. "Time to go."

Mrs. Cassidy smiled toward the parlor doorway, where her husband of forty-seven years leaned a shoulder against the doorframe, waiting for her. "Yes, dear." She turned back to the group and lowered her voice. "Cater to them a little, Phoebe. Be thoughtful about their preferences. Adjust your designs to accommodate their comfort. But stay true to who you are too." She patted Phoebe's hand as she edged away from the gathering. "That's how you'll find harmony. In your rooms *and* your relationships."

Mabel smiled at her husband, fit her fingers to his arm, then let him lead her toward the front door. Alvin Cassidy seemed to stand taller with Mabel on his arm, his bent frame straightening, his eyes coming to life as if he were not only happier but stronger with her by his side.

The other men filtered out of the parlor to claim their wives, as well, and Phoebe couldn't stop her gaze from seeking Barnabas. When he came to stand beside her as they wished their guest judges good-bye, it seemed the most natural thing in the world for him to be there. She nearly reached for his arm in mindless mimic of the others.

After the last couple exited the inn's foyer, Barnabas closed the door behind them. When he turned, he looked to the folded papers in her left hand, then clapped his palms together. "Ready to read the results?"

Phoebe's brows arched. "Awfully eager, aren't you? That confident your room will win?"

He grinned. "I'm confident the *inn* will win."

She rolled her eyes. "Always so diplomatic. It makes me wonder if I'll ever know what you really think about anything."

His smile flattened, and something fierce ignited in his blue-gray eyes. "You want to know what I think?"

Her breath caught in her throat. Somehow she managed to give a tiny nod even though she was pretty sure his question had been rhetorical. He didn't seem to need a response, as he was already striding forward, his gaze locked on hers.

"I think you are an amazing woman who knows exactly what she wishes to create yet has the humility to seek advice and use it to inform her choices. Do you know how rare that is?"

Her heart throbbed. He looked so . . . *passionate*. She'd never seen him this way. He visibly vibrated with energy. Any minute, his starched collar was sure to pop open from the effort of containing his zeal.

"Most of the clients I work with either cannot see the value in what I propose until I've created it for them, or they are so set on their own vision that they refuse to listen to anyone else. Neither circumstance brings about the best results. But you . . ." His words faltered.

Embarrassed by his praise, Phoebe fiddled with her glasses and shrugged, her gaze falling to the tiny bit of floor space that separated the toes of their shoes. "Daddy always says a good businessman has to know who to listen to and who to ignore." She lifted her eyes to meet his once again. "It didn't take me long to decide that your advice was worth heeding."

"Phoebe, I . . ." He reached out, and for a breath-stealing moment, she thought he would take her hand, but his fingers closed into a fist and dropped slowly back down to his side. Then his hand relaxed, and he favored her with a sheepish grin. "I admit that when your father first told me about your inn, I thought it was a terrible idea. But he demanded I look past my first impression, and I'm glad I did. Once I started spending time with you, I came to see the heart of the inn. Your heart. The logistical difficulties ceased to matter."

He reached for her again, and this time he didn't stop himself. His warm hand settled over her upper arm, then slid down to cup her elbow. Delightful tingles danced over her skin. "I believe in this place, Phoebe." He grinned. "In fact, I'd invest in it myself if you were looking for a partner."

Good heavens. What was she to say to *that*? Especially since the only partnership that came to mind was of the matrimonial variety, and he surely hadn't intended such an intimation.

Or had he?

Afraid to probe into meanings that might or might not actually reside in his statement, Phoebe opted for a safer path.

She returned Barnabas's smile and waved the ballots in the air between them. "Well, *partner*, shall we get down to business and examine these? We still have a winner to crown, you know."

He followed her lead, releasing her elbow to extend his own. "May I escort you to the dining room, my lady?"

Phoebe bobbed a small curtsy. "'Twould be an honor, kind sir." She slid her fingers into the crook of his arm, irrationally thankful to have an excuse to continue touching him.

He led her to the chair at the head of the table, then placed himself in the seat to her right.

It didn't take long for them to discover the truth she'd suspected from the beginning. There was no winner. Five voted for Maiden Faire, the room she'd decorated and dubbed—each room needed its own identity, after all—while the other five had voted for Oakhaven. The divide obviously fell along gender lines. However, what became evident as she and Barnabas combed through the comments was that neither room was perfect. Both could benefit from the strengths of the other. Maiden Faire could use more practicality and a simplification of design in order to appeal to men. Oakhaven could use a few feminine touches to make a woman feel immediately at home.

As Barnabas spread the pages on the table and started organizing them based on similarity of comments, Phoebe watched him from behind lowered lashes. This inn needed his influence. No, *she* needed his influence. His grounded nature. His pragmatism.

And maybe . . . just maybe . . . he needed her influence as well.

Someone needed to ruffle that perfect hair of his and remind him he was more than just a persona. He was a man. A man who just might benefit from a woman of whimsy messing up his perfection.

Eight

Barnabas pulled the pair of draft horses to a halt, set the brake, then did something so ungentlemanly that his mother would have taken a switch to his backside had she borne witness. Thankfully, she was half a state away. The female reaction he most cared about belonged to a woman much closer. One inside the green building in front of him.

As if he were Jesus calling forth the entombed Lazarus, Barnabas cupped his hands around his mouth and bellowed with absolutely no chivalry whatsoever. "Phoebe Woodward! Come out!"

He didn't have long to wait. Less than a minute later, the door flew open, and an adorably bespectacled woman rushed out onto the porch. Her light blue skirt whipped wildly about her ankles until she reached the stairs. She grabbed hold of the railing with one hand and yanked herself to a halt.

"What on earth?" Her eyes widened. Her gaze drank in the conveyance he sat perched upon—the yellow wheels, dark red body, *three* black leather seats, surrey top with rolled canvas curtains, and hefty rear luggage rack—then finally meandered up to his face. "Barnabas? Is that a . . . a . . ."

"A Studebaker Mountain Passenger Wagon? Yes, it is." He grinned. Smugly.

He'd been looking forward to this moment for weeks. He'd stumbled across this beauty in a carriage shop in Huntsville when he'd gone to find pieces for the room-decorating contest. The vehicle had been a mess. A wheel missing. Paint worn clear away. Leather trim disintegrated from weather and heavy use. The owner had parted with it for less than $200. Barnabas had snatched it up without hesitation and delivered it to the carpenter who handled most of his restoration projects. A new wheel, fresh paint, reupholstered seats, a few repairs to the undercarriage, and he had the perfect coach for a budding hostler.

Phoebe crept down the stairs as if she were afraid the carriage would turn into a pumpkin if she approached too quickly. Barnabas disembarked and hurried around the team of draft horses he'd rented, eager to show off his acquisition.

"Father told me he wasn't ready to invest in a carriage yet," Phoebe said, her voice soft, her brow furrowed. She tentatively approached the carriage and ran her fingers along the red-painted wood that formed the body.

Barnabas clapped a hand over the edge of the frame, a mere inch from where her fingers traced the wood grain. "I convinced him to reconsider when I found this lady for such a bargain. Barely one-third the cost of a new one, even after all the repairs."

Man, he wanted to hold her. To sweep her into his arms and celebrate their victory with gusto. To feel her wonder-filled smile against his mouth.

The workmen might be gone after the month they'd spent painting, papering, and installing, but he and Phoebe weren't alone. Even now, Mrs. Roberts, the widow they'd hired as the inn's cook—and unofficial chaperone for Phoebe once she decided to take up residence in the innkeeper's personal chambers downstairs—was walking out onto the front porch.

"Land sakes, Miss Phoebe. What's all the commotion?" The middle-aged woman wiped her hands on her apron.

Phoebe clapped her hands beneath her chin as she spun around. "Isn't it the most beautiful thing you've ever seen?" The disbelief that had initially kept her in check disappeared completely beneath a burgeoning joy that took Barnabas's breath away. A smile beamed across her face, and laughter bubbled from inside her. "Our guests will ride in style, thanks to Mr. Ackerly." She turned to regard him, the admiration in her eyes making his heart squeeze. "You truly are a magician, Barnabas."

Perhaps, but *she* was an enchantress. Sometime over the last month, he had fallen completely under her spell. So far, in fact, that she had him thinking all kinds of crazy thoughts. Like giving up his career as a property developer to become an innkeeper's assistant.

The impoverished kid in hand-me-down clothes—the one who'd driven himself to excel in order to escape the limitations of poverty and establish a name respected by others—that same security-starved kid was actually considering gambling away all he'd achieved to stay with the woman he loved.

"Would you ladies care to go for a drive?" he asked. Having Phoebe all to himself would be preferred, but he couldn't exclude Mrs. Roberts from the invitation without being rude.

"I'd love to!" Phoebe immediately gathered her skirt and reached for the nearest handhold.

Barnabas took her elbow to support her climb, smiling at her blatant enthusiasm. After she settled on the front bench, he turned back toward the inn. "Mrs. Roberts?"

The cook waved him off. "You two young'uns go ahead. I've got cookies in the oven." The wink she sent him made him doubt the veracity of that statement, but he wasn't about to question her.

Feeling exceptionally good about the choice they'd made in their cook—staff at the Kissing Tree Inn would need to be skilled in facilitating romantic moments for the clientele, after all—Barnabas tipped his hat to the older woman before taking his place in the driver's seat.

He collected the reins, released the brake, then turned his full attention to the woman at his side. "Where would you like to go?"

"Wherever you'd like to take me." Her lashes lowered a little, and a touch of pink kissed her cheeks, sending his pulse into an erratic pattern of elatedness.

"Perhaps we could scout out some picnic locations? To recommend to guests." He added the last phrase as an afterthought. His main concern was securing a bit of privacy.

"The spring that gave the town its name is north of the gristmill. It's surrounded by three oaks and has a nice stream running from it. There's even a tiny waterfall. We'd have to hike a bit from the road, but it's a pretty spot."

Barnabas grinned. "Sounds perfect." Especially since they didn't have company.

He wished now that he'd brought her gift. He'd been waiting for the right moment to give her the second sketch he'd made of the Kissing Tree carvings ever since the day of the judging, but the moment had never felt right.

Tonight. It had to be tonight. Her father was coming to town tomorrow to inspect the inn. To check on his daughter. To take care of his usual Oak Springs business. Barnabas had no guarantee that after her father learned of his desire to switch careers that he'd be allowed anywhere near Phoebe. The gift would have to be given tonight.

"I've been working on that ad copy you asked me to write," Phoebe said, interrupting his plotting.

Barnabas steered the horses away from town and toward the

gristmill. "Great! I scribbled down a few ideas too, but they'll need to be dressed up with your professional author skills." He grinned at her and shifted the reins to his left hand so he could dig a piece of paper from his coat pocket. He held it out to her. "Here. Let me know what you think."

Paper crinkled as she unfolded the sheet. She read the contents aloud. "'Want your wife to brag about you to all her friends? Be the first of your peers to celebrate an anniversary at the Inn of Pecking Pulp Providers—'" A laugh burst from her belly. "What?"

Heat radiated up Barnabas's neck. He'd forgotten about using that latest alias in his rough draft. He grabbed for the paper, but she twisted to the side, and his fingers bounced off her elbow. Impressive reflexes for someone laughing so hard.

She wiped at her eyes with the back of her hand and fought to catch her breath between lingering giggles. "The Inn of Pecking Pulp Providers? Really?"

Well, at least she wasn't insulted. He supposed it could be worse.

Recognizing the humor in the situation, he chuckled along with her. Feeling a bit sheepish, he shrugged and admitted the truth. "I started coining alternative names for the inn from the day your father gave me this assignment. At first, they were a way to deal with the frustration of being tasked with a project I didn't want, but after the first day of working with you, they evolved into teasing nicknames. The kind of thing friends or family members do out of fondness. I meant no offense, I promise."

Phoebe grinned. "None taken. Although it's a shame you didn't share this with me before we had the sign installed. The Inn of Pecking Pulp Providers has quite an alliterative ring to it."

"I thought you wanted people to actually come to your inn."

She laughed again, the sound buoying instead of worrying

him this time. Her amusement was unrestrained and beautiful. Her face tipped back toward the sky. Tiny lines danced at the corners of her eyes, above cheeks flushed pink with delight. It made a man hunger to repeat the experience. Often.

Spotting the mill up ahead, Barnabas slowed the team, wanting to prolong their moment together.

Phoebe's laughter drifted away on the breeze, but she quickly filled the quiet by resuming her recitation of his less than admirable advertisement copy.

"Let's try this again, shall we?" She aimed a grin at him that made his insides feel as if a family of tail-chasing squirrels had just taken up residence. "'Want your wife to brag about you to all her friends? Be the first of your peers to celebrate an anniversary at the'—*ahem*—'Kissing Tree Inn. *Don't worry. There's stuff for you here too*.'" She raised a teasing brow at him. "Well, *that's* a ringing endorsement."

Barnabas chuckled. "I figured you would flesh it out. I mainly wanted to construct phrasing that would appeal to male readers. I knew you would write something romantic and enticing to engage the hearts of female readers. Those could be placed in ladies' magazines and your literary magazine. But I thought we should place a few ads in business journals and newspapers that cater to men of means. Those types are most susceptible to ploys that stroke their ego."

Phoebe leaned close as he steered the team to the side of the road and reined them to a halt. She folded his atrocious ad copy and slipped it into the pocket of his coat, her fingers inadvertently nudging his side. His breathing shallowed.

"So if I were to compliment your intelligence, tell you how much I admire your business instincts, and gush my amazement over the way you transform unwanted objects into treasured essentials, I'd increase my chances of adding a chandelier made of bronze cherubs to the inn's foyer?"

Her eyes held him captive as her fingers came to rest atop his forearm. He swallowed. Reminded himself to breathe. And completely lost track of what she'd been saying. Something about cherubs?

He expected her to tease him for his lack of response, but she seemed equally distracted. She made no attempt to retrieve his dropped conversational thread. In fact, she stared up at him as if he were the most interesting man in the world.

One of the horses shook its head, rattling the traces and reminding Barnabas that they were on a public road in full view of anyone who happened to pass by. Not the right place for a first kiss, even if his mind could think of little else at the moment.

Forcing his gaze away from Phoebe, he set the brake and clambered down. He hurried around to her side and helped her alight. Then, tucking her hand into the crook of his arm, he started to climb the small hill that led to a trio of oaks at the top of a knoll. He assumed that was where they'd find the picturesque spring she'd mentioned. To be honest, he didn't care what they found as long as her arm remained twined with his.

About halfway to the trees, they met up with the stream that ran downhill to power the mill. The gentle sound of water tripping over stones and roots accompanied them the rest of their journey, putting Barnabas at ease. Before they reached the trees, Phoebe slowed and pointed out the miniature waterfall that stood all of eighteen inches high.

"This has always been my favorite spot," she said. "If the sun is too bright, guests can enjoy the shade of the trees farther up, but I imagine many will choose to stop here. I know I would."

"Then let's stop." Barnabas took a step away from her and shrugged out of his coat. Snapping it against the breeze, he laid it on the grass near the bank of the stream.

"Barnabas! Your coat," she protested. "It's going to get terribly wrinkled."

"I'm not afraid of a few wrinkles. Are you?"

Her eyes sparked at the challenge, and she immediately lowered herself to sit upon the coat, tucking her legs behind her. He joined her, taking off his hat and dropping it over one knee. Her attention shifted to his hair, and an odd look came into her eye.

"Barnabas?" She shifted until her knees came under her, then rose slightly so her face was even with his. "If I asked to take liberties with your person, would you grant me permission?"

His throat went dry. "What, uh, kind of liberties?"

"Nothing indecent." She smiled, and he knew he'd give her permission to do whatever she wanted. "I just wish to assuage my curiosity on a particular matter."

His heart pounded like a steel forger's hammer. "All right, then. Assuage away."

"Close your eyes."

He complied, but every other sense remained heightened as he focused completely on her. The rustle of her skirt as she adjusted her position. The smell of her hair as her face inched closer to his. The tingle of her touch as her fingers brushed against his forehead.

Sitting still was the hardest thing he'd ever done. His arms screamed to reach for her. His lips begged to press against hers. But he held his ground and remained outwardly calm even as gunpowder fuses sizzled with fire inside him.

Even with his eyes closed, he could sense her nearness. Feel her warmth. Then her fingers moved, burying themselves in his hair. Shivers danced over his scalp and down his nape. It felt marvelous. Invigorating and relaxing all at once. Until her fingers left his scalp to tousle his hair with all the vigor of a wet dog shaking dry.

One eye popped open. Directly in front of it was her chin and her full, pink lips. It was too bad her curiosity had centered more on his hair than his mouth, but the way her upper teeth caught her lower lip soothed his disappointment.

His other eye opened. “You were curious about my hair?”

“Mm-hmm.” She gave it one more good ruffle, then sat back on her heels to survey her handiwork.

Barnabas itched to smooth it back into some semblance of order, knowing how wild his wavy hair could get when not properly tamed, but the look on her face kept his hands at his sides.

“You’re always so perfectly turned out,” she said. “Never a wrinkle or hair out of place. It can be difficult for someone who’s always been an odd duck to feel comfortable next to such a majestic swan. So I brought you down to my level. Just for a moment.” Her lashes lowered. “I hope you don’t mind too much.”

“Mind?” Barnabas shook his head and chuckled softly. “I feel freer in this moment than I have in a long time. I’ve had to fight for every opportunity that came my way. Had to be smarter, more skilled, more professional than my competition. I couldn’t afford to be anything less than perfect if I wanted to escape my past. My appearance became my first line of defense. If I looked like a professional, it was easier for others to believe in my capabilities. Easier for *me* to believe.” He captured her hand with his. “I don’t want to wear armor with you, Phoebe. Yet until this moment, I was afraid to let you see inside, afraid you might not like the man beneath the veneer.”

“Oh, I like him.” Her voice came out whisper-soft and brushed against his heart like fine wool. “I like him very much.”

Nine

Phoebe cupped Barnabas's square jaw. His skin was smooth from a morning shave and warm from the afternoon sunshine. His lips beckoned. His chin tilted. His neck stretched. Anticipation swirled like a whirlwind of fall leaves in Phoebe's belly. Heavens, how she wanted him to kiss her. To see what love tasted like.

She leaned forward.

"Phoebe Woodward! Is that you?"

Jerking backward, Phoebe dropped her hand from Barnabas's face. She thought she might have heard Barnabas groan, but she couldn't be sure. Not when her ears were full of the strident tones of Esmerelda Clovis.

"It *is* you. I knew I recognized those spectacles."

Esmerelda must have eyes like a hawk to recognize a pair of spectacles from thirty yards away. Biting back a sigh of severe disappointment, Phoebe stood to greet the huffing woman as she ascended the hill with surprising agility for a mother of three. Although Phoebe really shouldn't find Melda's energy surprising. Clovis females thrived on gossip, and if taking an uphill hike meant getting the scoop on the town spinster and the handsome land developer before her mother-in-law did, no climb would be too steep to keep Melda in her little black buggy.

"What can I do for you, Melda?" Phoebe asked, making an effort to keep her tone from sounding too perturbed. Not that she had much success, but her conscience insisted she at least try.

Esmerelda Clovis pressed her palm to her chest as she fought to catch her breath. Then, of course, she ignored Phoebe's question and addressed the issue most of interest to her. "Mr. Ackerly! What a surprise to find you out here with our dear Phoebe." She looked down at the coat lying on the grass before aiming a sly glance at the man bending down to retrieve it.

Thankfully, Barnabas had managed to smooth his hair into some semblance of his normal tidiness. Phoebe hated to think what conclusions Melda might have drawn had she seen the tousled mess Phoebe had so imprudently made of his hair moments ago.

Acting as if nothing were out of the ordinary, Barnabas fit his hat to his head, then retrieved his suit coat and shook the grass from its underside. He smoothed the fabric with a long swipe of his hand, draped the garment over his arm, then finally turned his attention to their nosy intruder. "I don't know why you'd be surprised to find me in Miss Woodward's company, ma'am. It's well known that I have been employed to assist her in the development of her inn. We are often in each other's company."

Barnabas's innocent deflection was impressive, but Melda was no novice to be put off so easily. She and the rest of the Clovis Busybody Society ran the Oak Springs grapevine with the efficiency of a mechanized mining operation. She wouldn't be deterred until she uncovered the juiciest tidbit.

"Of course," she said as she gave Barnabas's shoulder a decidedly patronizing pat. "But finding the two of you together *away* from the inn, and looking so cozy, is certainly of interest."

She smiled as if privy to a secret already shared. "An experienced woman such as myself knows courtship when she sees it."

"Excellent!" Barnabas's cheery enthusiasm caught Phoebe off guard. "That is precisely the effect we were hoping to achieve. Thank you, Mrs. Clovis, for confirming our hypothesis. Miss Woodward and I were on the hunt for romantic rendezvous locations to recommend to the inn's future clientele. You've just ensured that this spot will be added to the list. Although . . ." He lowered his voice and leaned close to Melda, darting his eyes about as if fearing someone might overhear what he was about to say.

Melda tilted her head toward him, unwilling to miss a single syllable.

"We might need your help putting it about town that should one come across a couple sharing an intimate picnic or other private moment in a picturesque setting, one should practice discretion and leave the couple to enjoy their solitude. We wouldn't want the inn's guests to be made to feel uncomfortable in any way. Not when they are bringing so much business to the local area."

Phoebe had to stifle a laugh. He had Melda eating out of his hand. Even while scolding her for interrupting them, Barnabas cleverly invited her into his confidence and soon had her pledging to do her part in protecting the privacy of future guests.

While they spoke, Barnabas escorted Mrs. Clovis down the slope, leaving Phoebe to follow in their wake. Not that she minded. Avoiding the scrutiny of a female Clovis was always a blessing.

Barnabas handed Melda into her buggy, continuing to work his management magic. As she took hold of the reins, however, her attention suddenly lurched away from Barnabas and jumped onto Phoebe.

"I nearly forgot! There's a photographer headed to your inn.

He stopped by the livery to ask for directions while I was fetching my buggy. I overheard him say that Mr. Ackerly had hired him to take some publicity photos. I didn't think much of it until I ran into the two of you out here, but you better hurry back. He's probably waiting on you. The, ah, rendezvous hunt will have to wait." The long, slow wink that accompanied that pronouncement was anything but subtle.

Apparently the Oak Springs grapevine would be buzzing with news of Phoebe's little outing with Barnabas after all. She'd probably be the talk of the town before the photographer even finished setting up his camera.

She stifled a groan and forced her cheeks to crease in an expression she hoped passed for a smile. "Thanks for the warning, Melda. We'll head back right away."

Phoebe didn't wait for Barnabas to help her into the carriage. While Melda waved and aimed her horse toward town, Phoebe climbed into the front seat of the inn's new carriage, keeping to the edge so she wouldn't be seen sitting too close to the driver. A spinster had to take care with her reputation. Especially one who wanted to run a respectable establishment for married couples.

Barnabas tried to offer reassurances, but he didn't know Oak Springs the way she did. He'd leave in a few days, and she'd be left to face the pitying glances and wagging heads. Instead of Phoebe Woodward, innkeeper and entrepreneur, she'd now be Phoebe Woodward, abandoned spinster who'd lost the one man who'd ever shown an interest in her.

She stole a glance at the man by her side. He'd given up forcing conversation on her and now stared straight ahead, contemplating the road before them.

What if he *didn't* leave her? What if he stayed? With her. Her father managed to conduct business both in Oak Springs and Huntsville. Surely Barnabas could too. If he wanted to.

Would he want to?

Phoebe bit her lip. How did one handle this kind of situation? Should she ask him to stay? Offer to give up the inn and move to Huntsville? But they'd worked so hard on the inn. She didn't want to give it up. It had become *their* project.

The thought momentarily stunned her. Their project. Not hers. *Theirs.* Barnabas's style and influence were visible in every corner of every room. Even her private chambers, the one room for which he'd offered zero advice. She'd been tempted to cover it in wall-to-wall flowers and cupids just because she could, but in the end she'd selected a simple damask pattern of white and silver flowers on a deep blue-gray background. A color reminiscent of Barnabas's eyes. A happenstance she hadn't recognized until this very moment.

Oh dear. It was too late to save herself. She'd gone and fallen completely, irrevocably in love with him.

"You all right?" Barnabas arched a brow at her as he turned the carriage down Kissing Tree Lane.

Phoebe faked a smile and nodded. "Yes. Just working through a few things in my mind."

"Well, if you want to talk them out, I'm here."

For how long?

But she didn't voice that thought. They had a photographer waiting on them. Now wasn't the time to bare souls.

So she pasted on another insipid grin and said, "Thanks."

She turned away from his too-perceptive gaze, knowing he'd see right through her. His inspection lingered, but he didn't press her. Probably because they'd reached the inn.

"Keep the horses back," a man called from where he was adjusting a camera on top of a tripod at the far edge of the road. "I want a clear shot of the inn."

Barnabas reined in the team and set the brake. "Edward Cooksey, I presume?"

The photographer finished adjusting his equipment, then turned, a smile stretching his bushy mustache across his upper lip. "Yes, sir." He strode toward the carriage. "And you must be Mr. Ackerly. A pleasure." He gave Barnabas's hand a firm shake. "I hope you don't mind me setting up early. The cloud cover that recently rolled in makes the lighting ideal. No glare off the windows or undesirable shadows. I wanted to start taking photographs before the conditions changed. One never knows what the weather will do in Texas."

"True enough." Barnabas twisted on the seat and gestured to Phoebe. "This is Miss Woodward, owner of the Kissing Tree Inn."

Mr. Cooksey tipped his hat. "Honor to meet you, ma'am."

Phoebe dipped her chin. "We appreciate you taking time out of your schedule to make these photographs for us, Mr. Cooksey."

Had she just said *we*? And *us*?

Don't panic. You and Barnabas have been working together on this project. We *isn't too big a slip.* Even if the *we* she'd accidentally implied had expanded their current temporary partnership into a more permanent *personal* version. At least in her mind.

"That's one of the things I like best about the photography business, ma'am. The chance to get out of the studio and see new places." He turned back to the inn and waved his hand toward it. "I'll take a photograph of the front of the inn where the sign is visible, as you requested, but I also think an image should be made with that magnificent tree at the heart. The inn will be partially out of frame, but the result will make for a more compelling shot. People have seen quaint inns before. What they haven't seen is a tree like that."

Phoebe smiled. "I see why you came so highly recommended, Mr. Cooksey. You have the eye of an artist and the mind of a merchant."

"You're too kind, miss." He gave a small bow, then met her

gaze, his eyes glowing with respect as he turned his full attention to her as the owner instead of defaulting to Barnabas as the nearest man. "My business relies on the satisfaction of my clients. It is my job to find the best possible image and capture it for your use. Before the day is out, I'll present you with at least four high-quality photographs to choose from. If none of them are to your liking, you are under no obligation to purchase."

"I have a feeling that finding a suitable photograph will not be a problem. Selecting only one will present the true challenge."

Mr. Cooksey tipped his hat again. "I will endeavor to perform up to your high expectations, Miss Woodward. Now, if you'll excuse me, I'll get to work. If you and Mr. Ackerly would be so kind as to remain out of frame over here until I signal?"

"Of course." She smiled at the photographer as he hurried back to his camera, only then catching a strange look in Barnabas's eye. One that looked decidedly grumpy. Perhaps even . . . jealous?

Because she'd been exchanging professional courtesies with the photographer they'd hired?

Or because she'd been smiling and complimenting a man—someone an ill-informed suitor might consider a rival? An artistic type who surely understood romance and emotional renderings better than a stodgy man of practicality?

Phoebe turned her smile on Barnabas, then scooted closer to him on the bench. She'd developed a definite fondness for stodgy practicality of late, and no artistic fellow, or gossipy busybody, would change her mind—or heart—on the matter.

"You did it again, Barnabas."

A furrow creased his brow. "Did what?"

"Brought the inn exactly what it needed. I hate to think what the Kissing Tree Inn would be without your influence." *What*

I would be without you in my life. "I needed you more than I ever imagined." *And not just for the inn.*

Embarrassed to have said more than she intended, she pulled away from him and set about disembarking from the carriage. Barnabas hurried around to assist her, reaching her just in time to fit his hands to her waist as she set her shoe on the step. He lifted her down, his hands strong and secure about her, his gaze searching. Her feet touched the ground, but she paid the earth little mind. How could she, when her heart was taking flight?

"All right!" Mr. Cooksey called from behind his camera. "Nobody breathe!"

An easy order to obey, seeing as how Barnabas had stolen all the air from her lungs.

The photographer's voice broke the spell, however. Barnabas dropped his hands from her waist and took a step back, creating a proper distance between them. A distance she no longer wanted, even if it was necessary.

The photographer removed the cap from the lens, waited several heartbeats, then replaced it. "Done!"

For the next twenty minutes, Phoebe and Barnabas watched the photographer position and reposition his camera in search of the perfect angle. No words passed between them. Sidelong looks were another matter, however. By the time Mr. Cooksey finally moved to the Kissing Tree, Phoebe was fairly certain her heart rhythm had been permanently disrupted by all the erratic dips and surges thrust upon it from the silent, charged atmosphere encircling her and Barnabas.

Mr. Cooksey carried on, completely oblivious to the undercurrents afflicting his clients. He made his first photograph of the tree but grew agitated over something as he searched for the perfect final shot.

He came out from under the canvas flap at the back of the camera and waved his hands about in frustration. "No, no, no. This just isn't right. It doesn't say *Kissing Tree.*" He paced around the yard, mumbling to himself, before glancing up and spying Phoebe and Barnabas looking on. All at once his face cleared. "Yes. That's it. Come." He gestured toward them, his movement growing more frantic and urgent by the second. "Come! Hurry! Before the lighting changes."

Phoebe looked at Barnabas, who did little more than shrug before responding to the call. Mr. Cooksey met them before they'd made it halfway across the yard and circled around behind them, pushing on their backs like they were children who were late for dinner.

"What are you . . . ?" she sputtered.

"This is a romantic retreat, is it not?" the photographer asked while continuing to usher them forward.

"Yes, but—"

"Then we need a romantic image to capture its essence. Without kissing, this is just a tree."

"What?" This from Barnabas, who finally decided to balk.

Mr. Cooksey waved their concerns away with an impatient hand. "Don't worry. You'll be in silhouette. No one will recognize your faces. Think of it as treading the theatrical boards. Just a bit of playacting. That's all."

Without pause, he placed Barnabas and Phoebe precisely where he wanted them, arranging her hand on Barnabas's shoulder, his hand at her waist, scooting them closer together until almost nothing separated them. With a frown, the photographer snatched the spectacles from her face, leaving Phoebe blinking and blushing.

Barnabas's hand squeezed her waist. "For the inn," he whispered.

Her eyes met his. Her nerves quieted a bit at his calm demeanor. If he could endure this embarrassment with dignity, so could she. "For the inn."

Mr. Cooksey stomped off to his camera and ducked beneath the flap. An instant later he popped back out. "You're too stiff," he called, thankfully without marching forward to try to fix the problem himself. "Pretend you actually care for each other. Look into her eyes, Ackerly. Hold her as if she's the one true love of your life."

"She is." Barnabas's murmured words nearly buckled her knees.

Phoebe's eyes found his, thankful he was close enough to be in perfect focus. "Barnabas?"

"I love you, Phoebe." His hand slid up from her waist to her back, pressing her even closer to his chest. His other hand settled at her cheek, his fingers delving into the hair at her nape. "So much."

He tilted her face up toward his. Her gaze fell to his mouth.

"Yes, that's it. Hold it right there!"

But she didn't want to hold it right there. She wanted to kiss him. To pledge her love in return. To hold him and never let him go.

She did none of that, however. Not until Mr. Cooksey gave the all-clear signal. As soon as he did, she lifted up on her toes, intent on claiming the kiss she craved, but Barnabas's hand fell away from her face, and he set her away from him.

Disappointment stabbed her heart, dimmed only slightly by the regret she saw in his eyes.

"Did you get what you needed?" Barnabas called, striding away from her.

"Yes, indeed. I'll just require some time in a dark room to get the images developed. Your cook mentioned a large pantry that might prove suitable."

"I'll show you the way," Barnabas said.

He never looked back. Just focused on the photographer and left her standing beneath the tree. Alone.

Phoebe pressed a hand to her stomach, surprised at how much it suddenly ached.

For the inn. That was what he'd said. For the inn.

He needed the inn to be successful for his career. He'd admitted as much to her. He said her father had given him no choice about taking on her project. Was that why he'd said what he had? To seduce her into creating a romantic image suitable for promotion? Had it just been playacting? Nothing more?

Stumbling deeper beneath the branches of her beloved tree in a less-than-graceful manner—Mr. Cooksey still had her glasses—she made her way to the branch where her parents' initials were carved. Uncaring what it looked like for a grown woman to scramble across limbs like a hoyden, she hiked up her skirts and straddled the branch where it dipped close to the ground, then scooted her way to where her father's carving lay. Wrapping her arms around the branch, she lay flat against the bark as she had as a young girl and let the tears fall.

Her head insisted that Barnabas was too honorable to say love words without meaning them, that he could have teased her into relaxing, had that been his true purpose. His apparent coldness after the fact was simply a measure to protect her reputation. With Esmerelda Clovis priming the pump, townsfolk would be all too eager to believe a traveling photographer's tales of how a pretend kissing pose had turned all too real.

Yet even with that solid logic to lean on, her heart wavered. Other potential suitors had viewed her as a rung on their career ladders. Maybe Barnabas did too. After all, she was no catch. A spinster past her prime, possessing an odd temperament and an atrocious sense of style. Peculiar. That was what the school children had called her in their taunting singsong voices. And it had been true. She *was* peculiar. Always had been. Always would be.

She closed her eyes and squeezed the limb tighter. "Mama. I wish you were here."

To hold her. To comb her hair with her fingers and assure her that everything would be all right. To impart words of wisdom that would help Phoebe determine truth from fiction.

But Mama wasn't here. To comfort. To advise. To hold her while she cried.

Phoebe's eyes cracked open. But there was another. One who offered all she sought and more. She released her grip on the branch and slowly pushed up into a sitting position, her gaze lifting to peer past the canopy of leaves into the cloudy sky above.

I need your help, her spirit whispered to the God who could see into the hearts of men—into her heart, into Barnabas's heart. The God who could fathom all mysteries. *Show me what is true. Please. I don't know where to go from here.*

Ten

He should have kissed her. Barnabas's gut clenched as he silently backed away from the tree after searching Phoebe out when she didn't return to the inn. He'd hurt her. The way she clung to her parents' branch like a child seeking comfort shouted that truth so loudly that it deafened him to everything but self-recrimination.

He should have kissed her. Heaven knew he'd wanted to. He *still* wanted to. He wanted to walk up to that tree branch, take her into his arms, and kiss her until she forgave him for being the least romantic man on the planet.

Only an emotionally stunted man would tell a woman he loved her and then immediately give her reason to doubt his declaration by acting as if he couldn't get away from her embrace fast enough. Yes, he'd been thinking of her reputation, but he should have handled that better. Much better.

Afraid to make things worse by interrupting Phoebe when she obviously wished to be alone, Barnabas crept back to the inn.

Some magician he was. Instead of inducing Phoebe to fall under his spell, he'd made her disappear.

Barnabas kicked at the gravel in the newly installed path that led from the tree to the inn's back porch. He had to make this right. To convince her of the truth of his affection. Perhaps some kind of grand gesture. Something he couldn't mess up with ill-timed words.

The drawing!

His chin lifted at the thought. Yes. The drawing. He'd intended to give it to her tonight anyway. He'd just retrieve it earlier than planned. Perhaps he could even make it back before she returned from the tree.

"Mrs. Roberts?"

He burst through the back door with such force, the cook gasped and spun away from the stove with a wooden spoon poised in sword-like readiness.

Upon recognizing him, she lowered her weapon and pressed a hand to her chest. "Land sakes, but you gave me a fright."

"Sorry." He didn't have time for a longer apology. "I just wanted to let you know that I'm running back to town. I need to grab something from my room, but I'll be back to help Phoebe with the photographs."

Mrs. Roberts eyed him suspiciously. "Don't take too long. That camera fellow has them pictures hangin' up like clean laundry on a line in my pantry. He said they'd be dry soon." She stepped closer and lowered her voice. "Did you find Miss Phoebe? Is she all right? It ain't like her to run off for no reason."

Unfortunately, she *had* a reason. Him. A situation he aimed to rectify as soon as possible. "She's spending some time at the tree," he said as he straightened his hat. "If she returns before I do, let her know I'll be back shortly."

Before the cook could do more than nod, he was off. He commandeered the carriage and dropped it off at the wagonyard where he'd contracted storage space for it, then hustled the few blocks to the Woodward home and the small guesthouse at the back where he'd been staying.

Barnabas retrieved the framed drawing from under his bed, glad he'd had the forethought to wrap it in brown paper a week ago. He blew away the thin layer of dust that had accumulated on top of the package, then stripped out of his wrinkled coat. A man should look his best when trying to convince a woman of the sincerity of his love.

He eyed himself in the dresser mirror, picked up his comb, then halted, arm in midair. Frowning at his reflection, he dropped the comb and ruffled his hair with a vengeance. No more veneer. His desire to preserve appearances was what got him into this mess. Baring one's soul demanded vulnerability. So he'd leave his armor behind. No suit coat, no combed hair. He wouldn't even take his hat.

Feeling exceptionally daring in his bare head and shirtsleeves, Barnabas tucked Phoebe's gift under his arm and marched out the guesthouse door.

And nearly plowed into his boss.

Hollis Woodward had come home early.

Hollis raised a brow as his gaze raked his employee from head to toe. Barnabas's fingers itched to straighten his hair, but he resisted the impulse and simply lifted his chin.

"Mr. Woodward."

"Ackerly. You look . . . changed."

"I am changed, sir. Thanks to your daughter." Heart pounding, Barnabas faced his mentor with respect and a touch of defiance. "Phoebe's a remarkable woman."

Hollis crossed his arms and widened his stance like a warrior ensuring his footing before battle. "That she is." His frown darkened. "It's about time you noticed."

Barnabas faltered. *What?*

Hollis stalked forward one step. Then another. Until his face loomed mere inches in front of Barnabas. "The question now is . . . what are you going to do about it?"

Was he implying what Barnabas thought he was implying?

"I, ah, planned to speak with you tomorrow about that, sir."

"I'm sure you did." Hollis grinned. Not a comforting sort of grin. More the type reserved for cats playing with trapped mice. "But since we're both here, why don't you speak with me about it now?"

It wasn't a question.

Barnabas swallowed. He'd hoped to have time to compose his thoughts. Create a list of the benefits he could offer as Phoebe's husband. Figure out whether or not he should try to keep his job with Woodward Land Development or offer his resignation. Which would be more compelling to a man of Hollis Woodward's stature? Barnabas needed a way to provide for a wife, after all. And he didn't want his future father-in-law to think he was trying to take advantage of Phoebe by assuming he'd step in as inn manager. Phoebe was more than capable of handling that on her own. So what should he—

"Quit thinkin' it to death, son. Just speak from your heart."

That comment severed Barnabas's thoughts with the skill of a master swordsman. Nothing remained but raw truth.

"I'm in love with her, sir." Barnabas met his mentor's gaze, unsure of what he'd find there. "I haven't quite figured out what that means for my job with Woodward Land Development, but I know I don't want to live the rest of my life without her by my side. There are men with better pedigrees than mine. With more to offer when it comes to wealth and security. But I assure you, there is no man alive who loves her the way I do, who will work his fingers to the bone to provide for her should hardship arise, who will put her needs above his own, work by her side, respect her, honor her, and cherish her above all other women. If you see fit to give your blessing, I intend to ask Phoebe to become my wife."

A grin split Hollis's face before he tipped his head up toward the sky. "You hear that, Laurel? The boy's finally come to his senses." He slapped Barnabas on the back. "I'd nearly given up on you, Ackerly. I've known for ages that you and Phoebe were perfect for each other. You've always gravitated toward each other at social events despite being complete opposites in temperament. My Laurel and I were the same way. From two different worlds, yet made for each other."

The older man smiled, and Barnabas immediately saw the love he carried for his departed wife.

"Phoebe's my dreamer," Hollis continued. "She needs a man who can appreciate her dreams while grounding her in reality. And you, my dear boy, are the most capable, down-to-earth man I know. When Phoebe came to me with this inn idea, it was as if Laurel had whispered into God's ear and the Almighty saw fit to send me the perfect solution: force the two of you to work together, let you get in each other's way and get to know each other. If nothing sparked . . ." He shrugged. "Well, I knew you'd see that her inn was a success, so there'd be no harm done. But if something *did* spark . . . well, then. We'd be having a whole different conversation. One rather like this one, right now."

A weight lifted from Barnabas's shoulders, leaving him nearly giddy with relief and excitement. "So I have your blessing?"

Hollis planted his large palm on Barnabas's shoulder and squeezed. "You've been like a son to me for years. I'd be honored to make it official." His gaze honed to a sharp edge, and his grip tightened. "*If* Phoebe welcomes your suit."

"I think she will," Barnabas said, "if she'll forgive me for blundering earlier today." He pulled the paper-wrapped frame out from under his arm. "I came back to get this as a way to make amends." He turned his head in the direction of the inn. "I've already been gone longer than I intended."

Hollis released his grip on Barnabas's shoulder and gave his back a firm pat, the kind that would have sent a less-prepared man sprawling. Thankfully, Barnabas was well accustomed to Hollis Woodward's thumps and had braced for the impact.

"Don't let me stop you," the big man boomed.

Barnabas nodded his thanks and strode forward, only to be stopped a few steps later when his future father-in-law called out to him.

"Hey, Ackerly!"

Barnabas turned. "Yes?"

"You'll need this." Hollis tossed him a small object.

Barnabas snatched it out of the air, his pulse stuttering when he realized what it was. A pocketknife. An old one. One that had probably carved the very initials featured in the artwork he held in his hands.

He looked back. Hollis nodded. Approval. Acceptance. Even a wish of good luck.

Barnabas returned the nod. Time to carry on the family tradition.

At the sound of the back door opening, Phoebe glanced over her shoulder. Her heart gave a painful throb in her breast at the sight of Barnabas striding through the doorway, but she'd been mentally preparing herself for this moment and was determined to act as if nothing were amiss.

"Oh good. You're back." She returned to her inspection of the photographs laid out across the kitchen table. "Mr. Cooksey has produced some marvelous shots." She smiled politely at the preening photographer standing on the other side of the table. "I'm leaning toward the inn view for the advertising we do in the newspapers and men's periodicals, but I think we should use the tree view for the ladies' magazines as well as in *Lippincott's*. It would be the perfect companion to my column, don't you think?"

Her heart ached every time she looked at the photograph of her and Barnabas embracing beneath the branches of the Kissing Tree, but she recognized the marketability of the image. Mr. Cooksey had utterly captured the romantic magic of the Kissing Tree. She'd be a fool not to use it, no matter what painful emotions it stirred.

When Barnabas made no comment, Phoebe finally turned to face him. A tiny gasp escaped her. He was completely disheveled. Hair wild, no coat, no hat, his gaze filled with worry and regret. All thoughts of photography fled her mind.

She took a step toward him, her hand outstretched. "Barnabas? Are you all right?"

"No. I'm not. I need to speak with you." He glanced to the photographer, then to the cook, who had just reached for the kettle and the cup Barnabas preferred. "Alone."

Phoebe didn't hesitate. Whatever was bothering him, it was serious. She'd never seen him like this. "Of course. We can talk outside."

He gave a sharp nod, then pivoted and marched out the back door. She muttered a quick apology to Mr. Cooksey, then hurried after Barnabas, expecting him to be waiting for her at the base of the porch steps. He wasn't. He was striding down the path to the Kissing Tree.

Not there. She shook her head. Her heart was still too raw. Too confused. But she didn't have a choice. He needed her. She'd just have to ignore the tree. She'd listen to what he had to say and help him if she could. That was what friends did for each other. And she was determined to preserve their friendship. It might be all she had left.

By the time she caught up to him, he was ducking under the branch that held her parents' initials. Ignoring the pang in her chest at the sight of the place where she had wept out her hopes and dreams less than an hour ago, she focused her gaze, instead, on the marble bench that seemed to be Barnabas's destination.

He paced in front of the bench, some kind of package in his hands. Finally, as if coming to a decision, he halted, set the package down, then turned to face her. Before she knew what he was about, he captured both her hands in his and peered into her eyes with an intensity that made her warm and cold all at once.

"I hurt you today, Phoebe, and I'm sorry." He squeezed her hands. "So sorry."

She dropped her gaze, embarrassed. Shaking her head, she tried to reassure him despite the fact that she couldn't manage to meet his gaze. "You have nothing to be sorry about. You know how I am. Overly sentimental and foolish." She shrugged. "I got caught up in the moment, is all." In the words. She could still hear his declaration of love cooing in her ears. Thank heaven he couldn't see her eyes. There was a definite sheen collecting there. She did her best to blink it away.

"You're *not* foolish. I am. Look at me, Phoebe. Please."

Compelled by his plea, her chin came up. Her eyes met his.

"I meant what I said earlier today. I *do* love you. So much that it terrifies me to think I might have destroyed any chance of you returning my feelings because I chose practicality over romance in the moment that mattered most."

Phoebe couldn't move, could barely breathe as the hope she'd thought unraveled now knitted itself back together with miraculous speed.

All at once, Barnabas dropped down on one knee. "Phoebe, I'll never be a romantic hero who sweeps you off your feet with grand gestures."

"I don't know," she murmured. "This gesture is pretty grand."

He faltered a bit at her interruption, but then a light came into his blue-gray eyes that brought a smile to her face.

"Can you forgive me for being a clod who did more to protect appearances than your feelings?"

His face tilted up to hers, so earnest, so full of longing. A longing her heart recognized, for it matched her own.

She squeezed his hands. "Of course I forgive you."

He bounded back to his feet and drew her over to the bench. Picking up the package, he urged her to sit, then lowered himself beside her. "Here. This is for you."

Feeling the shape, she guessed the contents before she had it fully unwrapped. The frame he'd tried to hide from her the day of the room judging. It had been for her?

She pulled the last of the paper away, and tears immediately filled her eyes. He'd sketched her parents' initials just as they appeared on the tree, the details vivid and lifelike. Not only that, but he'd woven a laurel of grasses to encircle the drawing beneath the glass. A laurel—to represent her mother. And he said he wasn't romantic.

"It's beautiful." Her fingers traced the letters through the glass before she turned to the thoughtful man at her side. "I love it."

"I was thinking I might have to redo it," he said.

"Absolutely not!" She clutched the frame to her chest and scowled at him. "It's perfect just the way it is."

"Well, I was thinking I might need to add another set of initials. *BA* and *PW*. To the sketch . . ." He paused and pulled a knife from his pocket, a knife she recognized. "And to the tree."

"Barnabas?" Her heart beat so hard and fast, his name barely made it past her lips.

His hand cupped her face, the sweetness of his touch turning her insides to mush.

"Will you marry me, Phoebe? And spend the rest of your days teaching me how to be the romantic man of your dreams?"

Setting the frame aside, she covered his hand with hers and

peered into his face. "Oh, Barnabas. You're already the man of my dreams."

A clink of metal on stone told her he'd dropped the pocketknife a heartbeat before his left hand caressed her other cheek. He drew her face toward him and met her halfway with a passionate eagerness that dissolved the last of her doubts.

His kiss was tender yet urgent. Full of passion. Adoration. Never had she dreamed that a simple kiss could make her feel so cherished, so wanted. So . . . *not* peculiar. She clung to his shoulders, letting him anchor her in a swirl of sensations that left her deliciously dizzy.

If her parents' love story had taught her one thing, it was never to take a single moment for granted. As her future husband's kiss gentled and he tucked her face into the hollow of his shoulder, where she could hear the beating of his heart, she vowed to love him to the best of her ability every single day.

After a blessedly long moment, Barnabas straightened and touched his lips to her forehead. Then he smiled and reached for the pocketknife that had bounced off the bench to land in the dirt beneath.

"I guess I better get carving."

Phoebe removed her glasses and used the edge of her skirt to clean away the smudges left behind from their enthusiastic embrace. "While you do that, I'll make mental notes."

He smiled over his shoulder as he walked over to the branch. "For your column?"

Phoebe shook her head. "No. This Kissing Tree tale will be strictly for our children."

Epilogue

I'm telling you, Oliver. It's *them*."

Phoebe hid her grin over the not-quite-whispered comment made by their most recently arrived guests. Mr. and Mrs. Edmondson stood in front of the parlor fireplace, admiring the room's showpiece, a large framed photograph of a silhouetted couple embracing beneath the branches of the Kissing Tree.

"Don't be ridiculous, Matilda. The Ackerlys are far too sensible to pose for such a photograph. They probably hired actors to portray the scene. It's just another accoutrement designed to heighten the romantic atmosphere. It's not real."

"I assure you, it's very real," Barnabas said as he crossed the room and extended a hand to his wife, where she was pretending to read in the corner. "Isn't that so, dear?"

"Absolutely." Phoebe placed her hand in his, her pulse fluttering in anticipation.

Barnabas helped her to her feet, then with a flourish, pulled her into his arms and pressed her close. Her head fell back just as it had during their photography session, and she gazed up into his adoring face as love bloomed anew in her heart.

"I'm a stickler for authenticity, you see," Barnabas said, just as he did every time one of the inn's guests got mired in too much stodginess. He caressed the side of Phoebe's face, then stepped out of their embrace, being sure to keep an arm about her waist. He never left her alone after one of their affectionate displays. "Everything you see in the Kissing Tree Inn was designed while my wife and I were falling in love. The courtship was real, and it's reflected in the very walls around you."

At least in the wallpaper, Phoebe thought as she grinned at her husband. She loved it when his inner romantic came out. Almost as much as she loved the practical mind that had made their inn a spectacular success. They'd been open for only two months and were already booked for the next three.

They'd waited to accept guests until after their wedding, a small outdoor affair beneath the arms of the tree that inspired so much love in the Oak Springs community. Barnabas claimed the delay was a sound business decision, explaining how the inn would fare better with a newly wedded couple as innkeepers instead of a single woman in the midst of a courtship. They couldn't have the innkeeper so distracted by her own love story that she neglected the stories around her. In private, however, Barnabas admitted that he'd really just wanted an excuse to move up the wedding date. And having Phoebe all to himself for those six weeks had been well worth the money they'd lost in postponing the grand opening of the Kissing Tree Inn.

"Bravo!" The couple in the game corner set down their cards and applauded. "Good show, Ackerly," Mr. Winchester said. "You remind me of myself when Beatrice and I were first married." He winked at his wife, the two of them in their early forties. "The question is, if we come back in twenty years, will you still be singing the same tune?"

Barnabas turned to look at Phoebe, his blue-gray eyes softening with promise. "After twenty years of practice, sir, I imagine our song will be even sweeter."

From Roots to Sky

AMANDA DYKES

To all whose homes are havens of
hope, life, and refuge.

God places the lonely in families;
he sets the prisoners free and gives them joy.

Psalm 68:6

Prologue

DECEMBER 24, 1944
BATTLE OF THE BULGE

"Dear Hannah." Luke's hands shook as he spoke the words and tried to form the letters on a torn paper sack. His breath puffed into the dark night, then dissipated into stars above, the sound of shells and shots ringing in the distance.

"Concentrate." The word escaped raggedly. If that was what he sounded like, he must look worse than the piles of rubble peppering this landscape. Having your plane shot down in battle and falling from the sky into waves of snowy drifts would do that to a guy, he guessed.

He glanced around, confirming yet again that he was alone. Had been alone in the plane, as its lone pilot. So much was a blur—but yes, that part was clear.

Lights danced into his wobbly consciousness. A tiny Belgian village on Christmas Eve. Home fires burning, soft carols filling homes and chapels, and here he sat, half buried in snow with at least one broken leg and a smattering of other splintered maladies inside, leaning up against his impossibly cold plane. Or what was left of it. The remains of an old stone barn sat a stone's throw away, its bent weathervane sprouting crookedly from the ground, creaking its own Christmas melody into the night. Its off-key groan, pitiful as it was, seemed to speak hope to him.

"Concentrate." Again, through gritted teeth. He gripped the pencil and willed it to move. He may not be able to drag himself to safety. He might well die this night. But he would fight for his life with the weapons he had: pencil, paper, and a pen pal he'd never met, halfway across the world in Texas.

Where it was warm.

He fisted the pencil and forced his hand to form shaky letters. If he did not move, he would close his eyes. If he closed his eyes, he would sleep. If he slept, he would die.

D-E-A-R

H-A-N-N-A-H

The cold burned colder in the blur in his mind. He dug through the mire of his thoughts to the nearest clear memory. Danny Garland, tossing that ridiculous half grin at him before he'd left for duty six months back. Throwing him his notebook. *"Hey,"* he'd said. *"You write to my sister while I'm out. Keep sending her those drawings—just till I get back."*

He had never come back. So Luke Hampstead, whose own last letter received had been of the "Dear John" variety, took up writing to a stranger in Texas . . . and kept it up when her brother no longer could, his life claimed by the war.

And now she would get him through this cold. *Please, God . . .*

He had never written her much in the chatty way. Only technical notes explaining his sketches, to keep her brother's promise. But now . . .

"H-h-h-how are you?" He breathed the words, small talk freezing into ice and dropping to the ground. It figured. He never was good at small talk. He wrote the words anyway to the tune of shellfire and distant caroling.

It went on this way for hours, on into the silence. Fighting back the creeping fingers of cold with the warm promise of golden Texas light. When dawn crept over the jagged-tree horizon of the Ardennes Forest, Luke Hampstead beheld three impossible things . . . and laughed the prayer of a man so grateful his words had long, long run out.

The first impossible thing: his letter. Which he had labored over with more dedication and concentration than he could ever remember pouring into a single effort in his entire life . . . was a meager few sentences long, looked like a kid had written it, and bore the ramblings of a man convinced of his own demise. This pitiful excuse for a letter was what he'd exhausted his entire being to write?

The second impossible thing: his breath. Coming in shorter, quicker beats now—but coming still, its puffs illuminated by a sun he'd thought he'd never see again. He was *alive.*

And the third impossible, beautiful thing: a man and woman in humble farmhouse garb, running up the hill toward him with what looked to be a homemade stretcher. Gesturing back at a chimney, smoke curling out, with cinnamon on the air. The woman uttering something in Dutch to the man. "*Leven. Leven.*" Muttering urgent and low, like a prayer, then leaning in to hear his breath. Declaring, "*Leven—Life*! Amen. You are *alive*!"

If this wasn't heaven, it sure felt like it. And if this wasn't heaven . . . he sure had a lot of life left to live. And a letter to deliver . . . and a promise yet to keep.

One

May 1945
Oak Springs, Texas

The farm truck that had picked him up somewhere on the road from College Station, Texas, groaned a metallic farewell. A cloud of dust and wayward bits of straw engulfed Luke. They billowed and settled, revealing a main street approximately twenty strides long with a looming gray water tower standing at the end. Oak Springs Welcomes You, it read in large painted letters, and looked for all the world like an overgrown tin man standing guard over the yellow brick road. Only instead of yellow bricks, it was sidewalk-lined asphalt with a lone blue model A pickup truck parked in perfect parallel with the curb.

"No place on earth like Oak Springs," Danny had said.

"Really, Danny? Looks like you landed me in Oz." Luke wished he could sock his friend on the shoulder right about now.

Unfolding his map, he looked from this spot—so small it wasn't even named in writing—to the place he was headed for: New York. People's hopes were high that the war would end soon, and the world of air travel was on the brink of big changes . . . changes he would be a part of. An honorable discharge followed by a long and confining rehabilitation, in which he nearly went mad, had set him ready to be back in the sky in a matter of months. This time, blazing the postwar trail in commercial flights, bringing war-weary Americans to places over the sea once more. *Please, God.*

Traveling to New York via Colorado with a detour to Oak Springs, Texas, may not have been the most expedient choice. And his wallet was nearly caving in on itself with emptiness because of it. But he had a delivery to make, and it was one that he'd agreed in his soul had to be made in person. Hannah Garland had saved his life, though she didn't know it, and this one small thing was the least he could do to close this chapter of his life. Judging by the size of this town, it shouldn't be too hard to find one woman. He had her address, of course, but no knowledge of where in this town or its reaches it might be.

He approached the first in a row of brick storefronts—Tom's Diner. His stomach growled at the thought of a plate of steaming breakfast, though it was well past dinner, as proved by the locked door handle. *Be back at sunup*, the note on the door said.

Across the way, a tall brick theater with light-studded letters dubbing it the Orpheum Cinema touted in rounded black letters upon its marquis that *Meet Me in St. Louis* would open there this evening.

He passed a few other storefronts—Nettie's Notions, its window display featuring fabric bolts lined up like so many books. The Chili Parlor, the air lingering with spices of cayenne and onion making its Closed sign a special brand of cruel. And the Ice Cream Emporium, where a lone busboy swept up the gleaming wooden floor inside.

Faint whistling sounded, and a man whittling in a rocking

chair a few doors down gave a wave. His denim jeans were dusty and his plaid shirt had seen some trials in its day, but they suited the man and his entire come-sit-awhile demeanor just fine. "Howdy, soldier," he said, chewing on a long piece of straw. "Not from around here, are ya?"

Luke slung his kit bag over his shoulder and approached, taking the man's proffered hand.

"No, sir, I'm not." He wasn't exactly a soldier, either, but didn't want to correct a perfect stranger. His uniform made him conspicuous out here, he'd realized on the journey. But that empty wallet—it didn't have any hidden stores for purchasing extra clothes. He had a few civvies, but they were worn and dusty from travel, and this delivery deserved every ounce of respect he could muster in his meager possessions.

The man squinted at him past bushy dark brows, inviting more of an answer.

"I'm looking for someone, actually. A Miss Hannah Garland. You wouldn't happen to know where I could find her?"

"Hannah Garland." The man repeated the name as if it were the most perplexing thing on this green earth. "Now, what'll you be wanting with Hannah Garland?"

Luke removed his hat, holding it to his stomach. "I knew her brother, Danny," he said. "I just came to . . . to . . ." To what? Offer condolences? Which he'd already done by mail, when they'd first started writing. Deliver a letter on a paper-sack scrap that looked like a tot had written it? Which he could've done just as easily by mail.

He didn't know quite how to explain to a stranger what he was doing here. Which was ironic, since Hannah Garland herself was essentially a stranger to him, too.

"Never you mind," the man said, and the tangle of words fell away from Luke, as they always did when he got tongue-tied. "You might check inside," he said. "They're still open and might know Hannah's whereabouts. Hard to keep track of that one." He chuckled, shaking his head.

Luke studied the man, trying to grasp his meaning. The way Danny had talked about his older sister, she was a steady sort of presence who kept to home, holding down the fort there on the farm and keeping things running. He'd gathered from her letters that she was highly intelligent, and the sketches she had shared proved to be the careful work of someone extremely level-headed. The work of a mature soul, in both mind and body. Danny had always spoken of her with great respect.

"Yes, sir," Luke said at last, and turned to go in the door indicated. Bresden's Feed and Dime, the sign said, and a cardboard cutout of a man grinning over his tray of green-tinted 7Up bottles welcomed him inside. A bell jingled, and the warm scents of beeswax and sorghum-sweetened horse grain filled the place.

"Come on in," a voice said, its source darting behind the storeroom door. "Got your snaffle bits up here, Jerry."

But "up here" seemed to have four different directions, for the way the figure darted out of the storeroom, stuck a paper bag up in the air near the front of the store, ducked behind the counter to retrieve something, bumped her kerchief-covered head on the way back up, and was gone again in a flash.

He made his way to the front counter, which bore scratches and dings in its dark stain from decades upon decades of grain sacks and coin payments.

Reaching it, and with no sign of the proprietress, he cleared his throat. No response.

"Hello?" he said.

"Hey, Jerry, just take 'em. I'll add 'em to your tab."

"I, um . . ."

The kerchiefed figure emerged, bright cornflower-blue eyes glued to a paper she carried as she snapped a measuring tape absently in her other hand. Young—perhaps midtwenties—she wore denim overalls over a blue-and-white checked shirt like a modern-day Dorothy. She looked about as befuddled as if she'd just landed in Oz, too. *That makes two of us,* he thought.

She nearly bumped into the post between them, her hair gold as the wheat fields, a loose curl brushing her delicate chin.

"Watch out for the—" he started to say, but she dodged it without looking up.

"But that won't work," she mumbled to herself, tapping the paper with her thumb. "Assuming the width is twenty-six feet, then scaling it down to a quarter of the size would be . . ."

"Six and a half feet," Luke said, at the same time as she.

"Right." She slapped the paper on the counter. "Which won't work with the current dimensions of the—" She snapped her attention up, as if realizing for the first time that she wasn't alone.

"You're not Jerry," she said.

"No, ma'am."

"Jerry doesn't do numbers," she said.

"Yes, ma'am," he said. He didn't know Jerry, but he wasn't about to argue with the narrowed eyes that seemed to be doing ten thousand calculations a minute as she looked him over, uniform and all, as the color suddenly went from her face. She gulped.

"Closed," she said, in nearly a whisper.

"I'm sorry?"

"We're—we're closed." She scratched her head, flustered. Looked at the clock. Stacked her paper on top of ten others like it, each one worn but kept with care. She gathered them up, crossing her arms over her heart with them held close.

"Great gumdrops, I lost track of the time. Pete'll have my hide for closin' late again."

Grabbing the paper bag containing the snaffle bits, she lifted the hinged portion of the counter, ducking beneath to come out and show the way to the door. When she reached it, she paused with her hand on the knob and turned to face him full-on. He paused, too, hat in hand. "If you could just tell me where to find—"

She backed up a smidge, eyes on his uniform again, and nearly toppled a display of Murphy's Oil Soap bottles behind her. He dove to catch the wire rack before it hit the ground, realizing he'd braced her elbow, too, steadying her. He froze, and so did she. Silence ticked between them. As he took a step back and withdrew his hand to regain a gentlemanly distance, she rolled her shoulders forward as if to settle something within herself. At their feet lay her beloved papers, and Luke stooped to gather them.

Hastily she joined him, scurrying with lightning speed and pressing the papers close to herself once more, this time with corners pointed every which way and the crinkle of paper filling the space between them. She stuck out the paper bag to him and opened the door, practically pushing him out.

"But these aren't my—"

She pulled the last remaining paper from his grip, with a quick smile said, "Thank you, sir," and shut the door. But not before he glimpsed the stick-straight etching on the paper. His thoughts slammed as worlds collided.

That—that was his drawing.

One—or one of the many, rather—that he'd sent to Hannah Garland.

If the ridiculously straight lines and too-sharp angles didn't give it away, his trademark signature in the bottom right corner did: *Keep well, Hannah*.

He never signed it *sincerely*. Too many people signed letters that way and didn't mean it. He should know.

Echoes of the jangling bell laughed at him right along with the man in the rocking chair.

"Find what you were looking for?" the man said.

He glanced through the glass door at the whirlwind of a woman flitting about, turning off lights. She looked away at rapid-fire speed the one time she glanced over her shoulder at him. If this was Oz . . . was she Dorothy or the tornado?

"Y-yes," he said slowly. "I believe I have." And she was not at all what he'd expected. "But I'll have to try again tomorrow, I think."

"You *think*," the man said, and laughed deeply. "Tell you a secret, son. There's a time for thinkin', and a time for actin', and many a fool get the two mixed up."

"That may well be, sir, but I'm afraid today is not my day for acting. Is there an inn or a boardinghouse here?"

A fresh wave of laughter from the man was less than comforting. "Sure is," he said. "Down the road a piece. Take a right at the windmill. Keep going toward the big tree. You'll see it. Can't miss it."

"Thanks," he said, the paper bag crinkling in his arms and reminding him of its presence. With the store dark as night behind them now, he had no chance of returning the snaffle bits to tornado girl. "Do you know a Jerry?"

"Sure do," the man said, standing stiffly, so that the echoes of the creaking rocking chair seemed to reverberate in the man's bones. He stuck out his hand. "Pleased to meet ya."

"Jerry." Luke shook the man's hand.

"Last I knew, that's me. Sat down a spell to rest my rusty old joints before goin' in for my snaffle bits. Looks like you saved me the trip, and I thank you for it. And you are?"

Lost, he thought. "Luke," he said. "Luke Hampstead."

"Well, Luke Hampstead, stick with me. I'll show ya where you can stay, and you can try again tomorrow with Ms. Hannah."

Two

S*omeday, I'll keep going. Just up and up and up, and I'll see the world."*

Hannah lay on the grass beneath the great old oak as purple-gray dusk slipped through the branches above. She could almost hear her childhood self saying it, hair flying wild behind her as she swung from the swing that hung from the big branch.

And even more, she could hear her brother's laugh. *"I know you will, Hannah,"* Danny had said when they were kids. *"And I'll build a house and put down roots right here, and you can come home whenever you need a place to rest those wings."*

She remembered how he'd stood so proudly, looking out on their grandparents' farmland to the east. The tree didn't belong to them, but the innkeeper who owned it on the next parcel over never minded their playing beneath it, so long as they steered clear of the weddings and such.

It had been a magical childhood, growing up there, with the inn's lights glowing into the evenings, its player piano piping ragtime that tumbled down the hill to her and Danny. She used to spin herself around, fancying she knew all the loveliest dance steps, while Danny rolled his eyes and kept to his books.

And then the inn had fallen silent and empty, those months after Black Sunday. She remembered that day in vivid detail—the tinny voice on the radio was somber with news of the great wind that picked up the earth itself from all that farmland, up in Oklahoma, spun it up in the air, and blew it clean away. So far that it blackened their skies down here in Oak Springs, its doomsday effects killing the land and sucking the life right out of towns like theirs, with farmers picking up and heading west before they lost everything.

Couples seeking a romantic getaway stopped coming to the Kissing Tree Inn, and the old Victorian had been boarded shut for a decade now.

But the tree lived on, bearing story upon story in its carved trunk.

"Just not mine," she said, breathing out. She had never launched from that swing, kept on flying to see the world. And, ironically, Danny had been the one to be plucked from the land, until the war had claimed him for good. So here she was, planted in the grass he'd loved, fresh off from making a fool of herself to that nice airman today.

"What's the matter with you, anyway, Hannah Garland?" She hopped to her feet, ready to give herself a proper scolding. "A man serves his country in this awful war, comes back, finds himself in the Feed and Dime, and all you can do is hush up like a silent old grave and push him out? Great gumdrops, you fool. You should've rolled out the red carpet! Pulled out a trumpet! Baked him a cake!"

The tirade against herself was off to a good start, but it hadn't tapped into the tempest inside of her. Approaching the trunk, she leaned her forehead against it and let out a wail. A fake wail, but she'd long given up thinking she'd ever cry again. When news of her brother's demise reached her, she hadn't shed a tear. The pain went too far down, way past the place of words, and stopped up her tears forever, it seemed. The guilt over that seared her something fierce.

The truth was, that same force—whatever had stopped up her tears—had resurfaced again today. When that airman stood looking at her with solemn hope in his gray eyes, she'd wanted to hug him for whatever he'd been through, and she wanted to slug him for not being Danny, and she felt eternal remorse for the latter. The whole crisscrossed mess inside of her just stopped up her words and turned her into a bumbling fool. Well, even more of a bumbling fool than usual.

"Make it right, Hannah." She closed her eyes as she felt the bark of the tree press into her forehead. Lifting her head, she rubbed the spot and took a shaky breath. "Get to work."

Pulling the papers from her satchel, she spread them fan-like in her hand. Danny had sent some, and his friend Luke had carried the torch when Danny no longer could. The two men's drawings were as different as night and day. Her brother's were haphazard in scale and captivating to behold. When he'd been drafted into this war and she'd been the one to put down roots to hold down the family farm, he'd promised to send her the world, one picture at a time. And he had. Sketches of London from the air, of a tiny chapel in the Alps, of a cathedral in Italy. The focus of his sketches had kept narrowing, from castles down to homes, until that was almost exclusively what he'd sent. *Homes,* he'd written. *To give us hope for when I return and you can take flight, Hannah.*

It was then she'd determined that they'd be kept more than on paper. She'd bring them to life, in a house right here. Danny's house, and it'd be waiting for him when he got back. A place to hold the broken things he'd seen and taken such care to remember . . . and a place to hold him, too.

Luke's sketches, when he'd taken over, had been a scalding oil and healing balm all at once. The unfamiliar hand—the absence of Danny's trademark scribbles—broke her heart. And yet Sergeant Pilot Luke Hampstead's attention to detail, to scale and measurement, was a boon. His sketches came with a few lines of correspondence and no more. He was a man of few words, it seemed, but the places he chose to sketch proved he had great heart. *These places have been destroyed by war,* he'd written. *But at least they might keep in these humble sketches. Keep well, Hannah.* He always signed it that way, and it always struck her. Simple and yet—so different. She felt an ache in the words. As if he meant that though the world before him crumbled, if he could just know the people back home kept well, then he might keep on.

He drew images side by side—what a building looked like after it had been reduced to rubble, and what it had looked like before its demise. He captured so much life in these that she had asked him, once, how he knew what they had looked like before their destruction. He'd written back: *You can tell a lot if you watch and listen, and study a thing closely. Its surroundings, the buildings nearby, the person who built it, the people who knew it well.*

His words surprised her. They made her feel that she knew these buildings well, too. And somehow, in the process, she was known a bit more. She felt those drawings etch right into her being. The quirky centered doorknob of a rowhouse in Rotterdam. A carved welcome in the wall of a French farmhouse—*Bienvenue.* A turret-like gable from a Scottish castle in Clydebank, vanished after two nights of blitzkrieg.

It lit her imagination on fire, and sent her back to her and Danny's construction site, with the rest of the town's hearts breaking right alongside hers, and their hands and arms swinging right alongside hers, too. It had given them something to set their hands to in their grief—some way to fight for hope, one nail and one plank at a time. They'd nearly finished Danny's house over the past few months in stolen moments between plantings and harvestings. If not for him, then for her.

And now here she was. So close to being done, but with planting season in full swing, she was hard-pressed for time. She'd taken on the job at the Feed and Dime to earn some money to fund the project, but truth was, she had enough on her hands helping her grandmother on their own farm, too.

So the nights were hers. Her only time to fight the dark, to make sure this house was finished, once and for all, even if it was just her pounding nails late into the night. With a fortifying breath and a nod at her papers, she marched off into the growing dark for the job that filled her nights and fueled her days. There, at the edge of her grandparents' land, stood the silhouette of a building. A small one, but when she thought of what it did—or would one day do, if she could ever finish the thing—it seemed the grandest building in all the world.

Picking up a hammer from her brother's old toolbox, she got to work.

Three

"Here y'are," Jerry said, planting his feet in the Texas soil and looking proudly up a gentle hill. "The inn."

Luke could feel Jerry's study of him and was thankful for his well-practiced deadpan face from his missions. He couldn't let on that the place before him was—well—how could he say it nicely? . . . It looked more like some of the war-ravaged farmhouses back in Belgium than a Texas inn extending the state's famed hospitality.

"It's . . ." Luke cleared his throat. "I could help with that," he said, pointing at the crooked sign, which had come loose from one of its chains. Stepping closer, he read the words aloud: "The Kissing Tree Inn." The sign swung in the light breeze, a weary welcome.

Jerry stroked his stubbled chin and work-weathered skin, lending the moment all the gravitas as if Luke had just read aloud a treatise.

"What's that mean?" Luke asked. "The Kissing Tree." He could feel his face burn as he repeated the words.

"That, over yonder," Jerry said, gesturing down a hill to the left and beyond the inn, where a lone tree stood, "is the Kissing Tree. Or the Big Oak. Old Oak. Oak of Shame, depending on who you ask. Folks've been carving initials in its wood for decades now, and still it stands."

"Can't say as much for the inn, eh?" Luke said, beholding the place that was clearly once a prized property. But the windows were boarded up, the pale green paint peeling back to reveal—was that pink? Belay that. *Bright* pink—and what once was a gravel path was now a scattered vestige of a former byway.

"Fell on hard times, like most of this part of the country, the past ten, fifteen years," Jerry said. "But it's got itself a new owner, and that owner's got hisself a new caretaker, and that's yours truly." Jerry stuck his thumbs under his suspenders, snapping them proudly. "Which means, you can stay here, far as I'm concerned, so long as you don't mind it ain't up to snuff, being that I just started working on the place."

"I don't want to trouble you," Luke said.

"No trouble. You won't find any other inns around here, so unless you want to set up camp outside somewhere, you'd best come with me."

Luke followed. It'd only be for one night, after all, and after years of barked orders, droning plane engines, and Luftwaffe attacks, well, the man's rambling ways were a welcome change.

Inside, Jerry set to work laying a fire in the parlor, where an old photograph hung of a silhouetted couple beneath a tree, keeping watch over the empty tables and chairs.

Something cracked inside him, along with the log that had just caught fire. This hollow place, in the face of what it—according to the photo—once represented. It felt . . . too real. Too close. He thought of his own story, one that was once supposed to have ended in marriage. That, too, had gone hollow and empty.

"You can pick any room you want," Jerry said. "I've got the downstairs one, keepin' it for me and my grandson, Arnie. He's coming out here to live with me, if I can get the place fit for a kid.

He's stayin' with an aunt right now who's none too keen to have him, so by George, I'm making a place for him here. A kid needs room to roam, you know? Fresh air and sunshine and a place for life to get back inside him, after all he's lost." Jerry didn't elaborate, but the way his stubbled chin trembled and he shook himself out of that thought, Luke hoped his grandson would find his way here very soon. It seemed the two needed each other. "Anyhow, grab any other room you like. Have a look."

Luke did, mounting the creaking stairs. He passed the first room—Maiden Faire, the brass plate on the door declared it—and felt he'd be an imposter in there. The next room's plaque called it Oakhaven, and Luke ducked inside, where muted tones of hunter green hushed the world around him.

He deposited his kit bag on the bed, ignoring the cloud of dust that rose in response, and took himself to the window. May as well earn his keep. Finding a shoehorn in the dresser drawer, he used it to pry off the wood that boarded the window and discovered that the view overlooked the sprawling old oak. He could see why it had taken on such a life, so much lore and legend to it. It seemed to lay its branches upon the ground like unfolding fingers, inviting one to climb up inside and stay awhile.

He unzipped his bag, unfazed by the scant number of belongings inside. He'd learned to travel light, and he'd needed to leave room for the rather awkward, spindly yet bulky bundle he'd hauled all this way to deliver to one Hannah Garland.

Still, for all the places he'd been, there was one possession he always took with him. He pulled it out now, unwrapping the bundle from a scrap of old canvas.

Letters. For a man who'd gone so long in the war with no word from home but that fateful "Dear John" letter, he hadn't known where to begin when he'd taken up writing to Hannah Garland. So his letters had always been short. When her first letter had arrived, he'd not opened it for three days, not knowing what to make of it. He had no family. No home or history, other than the Chatham home for boys back in New Jersey. He had thought he would have all of that one day, but that hope had been crushed to bits. And so for Danny's sister to write him out of the blue, he felt like a big fake—undeserving of her words. But he'd opened that envelope and found a simple thank-you. Short, but kind, written from a broken heart. *Thank you for the drawings*, it said. *They mean the world.*

So he'd kept them coming, and she'd kept her letters coming. Always short, sometimes newsy about plantings and harvests, and always a hearty thank-you.

And at the bottom of the stack . . . was the other letter. Caroline's. Like always, he shoved it back into the dark of his bag, closing the door on that part of his life.

Opening the window and leaning out to fill his lungs with the sweet air of farm country, he inclined his ear. What was that he heard, reverberating so sharply? It stopped, and after a beat an owl hooted somewhere in the tree. Then it started again. A thwack and an echo, a thwack and an echo, again and again. Someone was building now, with so little light? Surely that wasn't good for the eyes.

A cry of pain sounded, confirming his fears but bowling him over in surprise. It was the voice of a woman. And not just any woman. There was no mistaking the voice when it piped up again with all the frustration in the world: "Jumpin' gumdrops!"

He was out the door with a quick "I'll be back" to Jerry before he could think better of it. Long strides carried him swiftly up the old gravel path, beneath the tree whose branches created a tunnel of sorts, and out the other side to the pasture beyond. With the moon rising now, he paused to catch his breath and take in the sight before him.

A small two-story white house—or most of one, anyway. A

ladder leaning against it, and perched at the very top, the same kerchiefed, overalled Hannah Garland he'd seen earlier. This time sporting a headlamp and a hammer in the dusky pink sky. She paused hammering to lean in and examine something, muttered a few words, and clambered down the ladder at a speed that made even him nervous—he, who was used to soaring thousands of miles above the earth.

She disappeared up a hill beyond. In her absence, he closed the distance between himself and the house. When he drew close enough to touch it, he stopped in his tracks, jaw dropping.

This was—what? Words pounded in succession for trial, none of them quite enough. Incredible. Creative. Singular. Heartbreaking. Healing. It was—it was—

"Impossible," he said out loud. He stepped closer, the structure drawing him. It was, at first glance, no different from many a country farmhouse. But the gable on the left corner of the house was no gable at all, but rather a turret in miniature. Plucked right out of the castle he'd seen in Clydebank before the Luftwaffe descended upon Scotland.

And the doorknob in the middle of the door was distinctly un-Texas-farmhouse-like, and very distinctly European. He had drawn one such from a sketch he'd sent from the Netherlands, after Rotterdam had been blitzed and that bright blue fallen door had reached out from the rubble, with its plucky tarnished brass knob in the middle.

Though Hannah's pounding hammer had silenced, it seemed to take up residence now inside his chest. He stepped up the makeshift porch steps—placeholders, he assumed, for something more permanent to come, and reached a hand out to feel for himself what his eyes could not believe: etched letters, deep in the wood, as they had been in their original stone back in France. *Bienvenue.*

Welcome.

A home, welcoming him, when he had no home to speak of.

"Hey!" said a voice, in a less-than-welcoming tone.

He turned, his hand lingering on the carved word. "I-I'm sorry, Miss Garland. I didn't mean to intrude. I just came because—"

"It's you," she said, her voice softening. "From the Feed and Dime. Listen, I owe you an apology. I was all addlepated today—you just took me by surprise is all. Standing there in uniform, fresh out of the air from heaven-knows-where, and I was late in closing, and I'm all thumbs and two left feet as you saw, and it flustered me something awful and I—there I go again, railroading you with my words. Gran says I get to ramblin' more than a tumbleweed when my words go. Like a full-force faucet, she says."

If she was a full-force faucet, he was a stone wall, all the words caught somewhere deep and silent inside. "I, uh—"

She picked up a hammer from the steps, disappearing around the side of the house. Grabbing the tin can of nails, he followed.

"So if you'll forgive me for my *abysmal* behavior, mister, I'll let you be on your way. Where you heading to, anyway?" She held a hand out for a nail.

"New York," he said, handing her three. She stuck two in her mouth and climbed halfway up the ladder, pounding a nail into a piece of trim with remarkably swift accuracy.

"Roo Rork," she said around the nails, eyebrows raised. She removed the nails. "What're you doing way up there?"

"Flying." Why was his vocabulary suddenly limited to one-word answers?

And yet that one-word answer halted her as if he'd just delivered astounding news. She clambered back down the ladder and pointed at him.

"You're a pilot," she said. "What's it like up there?" There was a thirst in her words. "I always imagined it'd be like one great big reverse-falling into the most beautiful place in the world. Like swimming in the sky, or breaking into some sort of other world up there."

He thought of the war-torn skies, rent with blitzes and falling planes. Of sitting near-freezing on Christmas Eve alone in a field in Belgium.

He thought of the toy biplane he'd soared as a kid, skipping it over the rock walls surrounding the tiny yard of the boys' home, and how his very soul took flight at the thought of piloting a plane one day.

There was a disconnect there . . . and this girl's vibrant blue eyes, so eager for a hope-filled answer, seemed to bridge it. To remind him of the promise of the skies.

"It's . . . remarkable," he said. And meant it.

"I knew it. Danny said so, too. My brother," she said.

He nodded slow, about to speak. To tell her he knew exactly who Danny was, how he'd pulled Luke up out of the mire when his future looked so dark he couldn't see his way forward. To relish speaking to another soul who thought of him—well, in her case, who truly knew him—as a brother.

"Well, mister, I don't mean to keep you here, and you must be needin' to get someplace. I'll say good-bye, then." She stuck her hand out to shake it.

He, tongue-tied yet again, cleared his throat and took her hand, holding it as he locked eyes with her, inviting her to hear him. Hear his heart.

"I'll see you tomorrow. Keep well, Hannah."

As he retreated, his footfalls in the tall grass were the only sound. This time, she was the one rendered speechless.

Four

I'm a fool," Hannah said, flipping a fried egg with more force than she intended. Its yolk splatted in the skillet with just as much gusto and failure as she had shown, prattling away last night.

"There I was, Gran, just prattling away like Harry Granger's old Ford, and blowing as much smoke from my head, too. Foolish talk about swimming in the sky and I don't even know what. And all the time—it was *him*."

Gran stopped her quick whisking of her cinnamon muffin batter and tilted her silver-braided head. "Who, darlin'?"

The woman had the patience of a saint. "*Him*. Luke Hampstead, of the 311th Photographic Wing. How is it that I can recite his address like it's my own last name, but I can't recognize him when he's standing two feet from my own face?"

"Well, it was dark, certainly, right?"

"Yes, and truth is I've never seen a picture of him, but shouldn't I have known, somehow? Shouldn't I have—I don't know, sensed those were the hands that had drawn those sketches? Made the cottage possible? And there I was, talking on about Danny, never thinking—"

Gran's hand was on hers, stilling the flailing spatula. Hannah spoke with her hands, and Gran swore one of these days it'd end with putting someone's eye out.

"Today is a new day," Gran said.

Hannah breathed in her words. "A new day," she said and pointed her spatula at Gran with conviction. "Right."

Gran gently pried the spatula from Hannah, removing a smoking egg from the skillet and depositing it in the pail for the pigs.

"Right," she reiterated. "It's a new day, so go and seize it."

She did. Hannah seized it while slopping the pigs, addressing them as if they were Luke Hampstead and she were a girl who actually kept her head about her.

"Why, hello, kind sir," she said. Porky, the biggest of the lot, grunted back at her. "I see by your uniform that you have served our country with great honor and distinction. Distinguishment? Distinctionment. And I thank you, truly." She swirled her hand in a bow. Ranger, Danny's horse, who was as old as Methuselah and just as wise, hung his head over the fence. If Hannah didn't know better, she'd have sworn he just gave a solemn and approving nod, which she returned gravely. "Thank you, Methuselah," she said, using Danny's old nickname for the horse. "Now *that* is how a hero should be greeted, and don't you forget it." She sloshed the remains of the buckets with abandon.

"Forget what?"

Hannah spun to face the voice. It was him.

"Distinquilment," she muttered.

"Pardon?"

"I mean—hello," she said, setting the bucket down, brushing her palms against her apron, and tugging at the sprigged green calico as if primping her barnyard dress might somehow undo all her foibles. "You're Luke. Luke Hampstead." She stuck her hand out to shake his.

Something akin to mirth sparked in his gray eyes, and he

appeared to be trying to keep back a smile. It dimpled his jaw somethin' handsome. Somethin' awful, she meant.

"And you're Hannah." He took her hand and gently shook it. "Hannah Garland."

They beheld each other, shaking hands right there by the pigpen after introducing each other to themselves, until she laughed first. His laugh followed, deep and pleasant.

"Well, Luke Hampstead, you'd better come and see the cottage properly," she said. "Since it's all your fault. And I mean that in a good way."

"I'd be honored. I don't want to keep you from your work, but if I can help—"

"*Help*," she said. "Sir, you already have. Come see."

She led the way down the farm's dirt driveway, through a pasture of growing cotton, and to the pasture's edge where the cottage perched with the big oak rising beyond. He studied the house, and she studied him. The way his dark hair was so different from Danny's blond. The way his demeanor was steady, serious, but with some current of buried laughter flowing somewhere deep within. She could see why the two had been fast friends. Danny would've been well-balanced by a friend like this.

"You did all this," he said, shaking his head in what seemed to be wonder.

"Well, me and a whole army," she said, leading him up the steps and into the structure. "Bill Clois built that stairway while I manned his livery. Elmer Longstreet put the windows in, in exchange for a couple pots of chili."

"Must be some chili," Luke said.

Hannah laughed. "Must be some nice people, more like," she said. "Gran says my chili's hardly fit for the chickens. I don't have much of a head for the kitchen."

"But you have a great mind for figures and numbers, it seems."

She shrugged. "They make sense. Most of the world doesn't. So when Danny started to send those sketches of places around the world, I decided I'd surprise him. Put 'em all into one house, the one he'd be building himself if he were here today."

She felt the familiar sadness descend. She'd resigned herself that his absence would never stop feeling like a great gaping hole. A cruel presence in itself. So she'd resolved to fight that by pouring herself into this house. Honoring who he was.

Luke ran his hand up the banister as he climbed the narrow stair to a loft above. "And who did you barter with for this?" He clapped his hand onto the banister. It was singular. With the curves and juts of a branch, but all the soft smoothness of the finest lumber.

"I, um—well, truth be told, I snatched that up from the ground. From the old oak after a storm. Sanded it down and fixed it to the wall there, and there it'll stay, I hope." She put her hand on it, too, running her fingers along its surface. "Helps me think, sanding away knots and bumps. Irons out the knots and bumps in life, too, somehow."

Luke nodded. "I know what you mean," he said. "It felt the same whenever I put pen to paper to send you a sketch. Like taking hold of something that had disappeared from the world, capturing it one last time on paper—it made the destruction feel a little . . . less."

She stared, wide-eyed, and let out a low whistle. "You said that a whole lot better than I could've." Then, after thinking a moment, she tipped her head up. "Go on up," she said. "You might like it up there."

He obliged, leading the way up the rest of the narrow stair to the loft, which opened by railing to the two rooms below. One wall was lined with shelves following the slope of the ceiling all the way to the floor, a circular window at the center of it all.

"For Danny's books," Luke said. "Right?"

"How did you—"

"We figured out quick which books we both grew up on," Luke said. "*Swallows and Amazons*, *The Story of Ferdinand*, the Hardy Boys books."

Hannah rolled her eyes. "Those Hardy boys. If I could count the number of times they fell off cliffs and got all tied up by bad guys." She whistled a descending whistle. "Danny would lie under that tree and read them aloud."

"And what were you doing while he read?"

She could feel her cheeks grow warm. "I, um—I climbed."

"I'm sorry?" Luke leaned in, apparently trying to decipher her mumbled words.

She threw up her hands. "I climbed. Up and up and up until Danny told me I'd get myself stuck in the clouds." She laughed. "I told him someday I would. That I'd just keep on going on that upswing, fly far away to see all the world." She grew serious. "But—some dreams fade away when you grow up, and I s'pose that's all well and good. We trade them in for other dreams." She looked at the cottage. "Worthier dreams. I know I belong here, now, just like Danny always knew he did. I couldn't leave Gran or the farm." She inhaled deeply. "Besides, there's a whole world of adventure right here in Oak Springs, you know." She said it firmly, trying to convince herself.

In his eyes, she saw a depth of understanding she could not account for, in a soul she'd only just met. And with it, a longing. Like the man wanted to wrap up her words and keep them safe.

"That had to be some tree," he said.

"See for yourself." Hannah gestured toward a doorway, which had yet to be closed off with a door. "This'll be one of those Dutch doors someday," she said. "The kind where the top opens separate from the bottom. From one of Danny's sketches," she added.

"I remember that one. He was proud of that sketch. Borrowed a village girl's pencils to give it color, if I remember correctly."

"That's right," Hannah said, leading the way through the imagined Dutch door. Outside, a balcony spread wide, covering the full length of the cottage. A sturdy railing secured the edge, and Luke rested an arm on it. Hannah watched his eyes roam over the stretching green of the fields and settle close on the tree.

"You almost feel like you're in the branches," he said, shielding his eyes against the morning sun. "It makes you feel closer to the tree than we actually are."

"Exactly," Hannah said. "Danny told me I'd be stuck in the clouds, and all he wanted to do was put down roots like that great-grandfather tree over there. So I planted his house in the branches. Or at least as close as I could without making it a bother to the inn, if they ever get running again."

"They're planning on it," Luke said.

"That's what Jerry says. He's got high hopes of settling in there once and for all with his grandson, Arnie, being caretaker and all. I sure hope for his sake that it works out, though I don't know what a young boy'll do in a place so fine," she said.

"It sounds like Jerry intends to give him all the time outdoors that he can," Luke said.

Silence settled between them.

"Mr. Hampstead," Hannah said, unsure what to make of the man's presence here. It felt right, somehow, but she could not for the life of her account for the reason behind it. "Can I ask what brought you here?"

He seemed torn. The look in his eyes as they met hers was that of a man with a story, but he seemed reluctant, somehow.

"Miss Garland," he said slowly. "I . . . have a little time, before I need to be in New York."

"Well, thank goodness for that. It's a good bit down the road from here. Or so I hear."

He smiled. He had the sort of smile that took its time finding its way to the surface, so that by the time it reached its destination, it was as real and hard-won as a thing could be. "I have even more time than that," he said, brows furrowing as he studied the perfectly parallel boards at his feet. It was a strangely fulfilling sensation, having a man who flew the skies of the world stand now supported only by boards she'd laid with her own two hands.

"Might I . . . that is, if I won't be too much in the way . . ."

"Out with it, Mr. Hampstead." Hannah laughed. "Promise I won't pounce on you."

"Well—could you use a hand? With the house, I mean."

Hannah studied the man before her. The hands stuffed in his pockets. Hands that had sent her the world.

"Mr. Hampstead, I would be honored to have your help finishing this little old cottage."

Five

Luke could picture Oak Springs as it would look from the air. With its shops lined up all down Main Street like so many storybooks upon a shelf, bookended by the timeless water tower on one end and the white-steepled country church on the other.

It was the latter he sat in now, in the very back pew on a Sunday morning in Texas. The organist played "A Mighty Fortress Is Our God" as people trickled out after the service and paused to shake the preacher's hand.

Luke went last, hoping to escape unnoticed. He didn't want to disrespect anyone, and one look around showed him that this town, humble though the people's means were, took their Sundays seriously. Joyfully, but seriously, as evidenced by the number of ribbons and flowered straw hats, bright-patterned dresses and men in suits and ties. He'd learned they were farmers, most of them—and yet it was he who looked the part of a man just come in from the field, with his travel-worn clothes, dull from one too many washings in sinks along the way. He'd planned to buy new clothes once he landed in New York, and he meant to travel light until then.

Well, the kind folks of Oak Springs were likely well on their way home to Sunday dinners just now, and none would be the wiser that a man resembling a vagabond had been in their midst.

After shaking the preacher's hand to the organist's last measures, he stepped into the sun and loosened his collar at the shocking heat of midmorning Texas. What was wrong with him? He'd endured extremes worse than this. On the cold end of the spectrum, but still. He swiped his arm over his forehead, letting his eyes adjust.

"What's wrong with you?" he asked himself aloud—and opened his eyes to see twenty faces, all answering with welcome grins.

Luke gulped.

It seemed the residents of Oak Springs were *not* well on their way home to Sunday dinner. They were scattered in groups and pairs, chatting across the emerald-green lawn to the chorus of cicadas droning in the trees beyond.

"What's wrong with *us*?" Jerry piped up. "What's wrong with you, more like! You look like you just crawled out from under a rock, blinking like a baby," he said.

Hannah's grandmother—*Gran*, he'd heard her call her—strode over and thwapped Jerry in the shoulder with her red purse.

"You look just fine, darlin'," she said. "Now, come on home with me and Hannah. We have a roast in the oven and we'll need someone to carve it for us."

Hannah slipped in next to Gran and looked askance at the notion that they needed help with such a task, but then her grandmother gave her a look that silenced her. He had a hunch these two women knew their way around carving a roast better than most army air force pilots, but he recognized a lifeline when he saw one. She was throwing him a rope.

"Luke Hampstead," Gran said, sweeping her arm toward him in one grand introduction to the town, "this is everyone. You'll get their names in time. Everyone, this is Luke. Helpin' out on the farm for a little while." Her proclamation was met with furrowed brows and puzzled glances, as if "for a little while" wasn't a saying they heard much around here. "He's just back from the war, for goodness' sake. Is that how you greet a war hero?"

At this, they came alive in an outburst of jovial exclamations, and before he knew it, Luke was enveloped in a cloud of handshakes and hearty claps on the back and several dinner and supper invitations. Gran intervened again, though, reminding them with a wink that they needed him to carve that roast.

That roast—together with the plate full of skillet potatoes, gravy, and hot butterhorn rolls—showed him for the first time he could recall what a true home-cooked meal was. The memory of the smells filling the farmhouse stayed with him all that day and night, as he thought back on the kindly women who had welcomed him in.

If Hannah was a human tornado, Gran was the gentle, warm wind that blew in with the sun. He didn't know what he had to offer them but prayed his time here might bring some of that kindness back upon them, too.

That week, his hope got off to a rough start. While Hannah was away working at the Feed and Dime, he spent the days familiarizing himself with the status of the cottage. Finishing off projects where he could—a bit of trim here, a shelf or two there—but found he needed Hannah's insight with most of the bigger projects. Not knowing just what she envisioned, he didn't want to presume.

On his third day, he'd secured the branch railing in a few loose spots, touched up some paint, and sanded some rough patches on the stairs. Sitting on the floor in the loft, the sun pouring through the open door, he recalled Hannah's plans for a Dutch door there someday.

"Today," he said aloud. "Someday is today." He recalled

Danny's sketch of the door. Could even picture his friend bent over the drawing as if it were an invasion plan to end the war.

He set to sorting through the lumber in the back, listing hardware to purchase on a scrap of paper, making measurements, sawing marked lines. Perhaps it was the noise of his back-and-forth sawing, or the way the project had swallowed him up, mind and body, but he was entirely consumed with the work when a tap on his shoulder made him jerk in surprise.

"Hey!" he said, a little too loudly. He could still hear the grating cry of the saw ringing in his hears, though he'd stopped work. Hannah stepped back, hands in the air in surrender.

"Hey," Luke said again, calming his voice. "I mean, hello. Hello, Hannah."

She tilted her head quizzically. "Hi, Luke." Her voice mimicked his serious and schooled tone. "What are you working on?"

"A door," he said, the words coming out too hurried and sounding more like *adore*. Hannah's pretty mouth turned up at the corners, mischief in her eyes. "A door," he repeated, with a painstaking pause in between the two words.

"So you said," Hannah replied. "Well, it looks mighty fine, Mr. Hampstead," she said, nodding an official approval. "It looks a sight better than the one I tried to make," she said, laughing.

"You made one?" Luke kicked himself. He knew he should've waited and asked before blazing forward like this.

"See for yourself," Hannah said, leading the way to a scrap pile around the corner and gesturing at a piece of wood no longer than his own legs. It was a door, true enough—and an impressive one, at that. Just . . . small. "Ladies and gentlemen, the revolutionary miniature door! Only one of its kind in existence, and sure to go fast, so don't hold your wallets too close, now."

Luke chuckled, scratching his head. "How . . . I mean, I saw you with your measurements. You're very accurate. How did this . . ."

"Happen? Glad you asked, my good man." She carried on in her salesman impression. "This here is what occurs when a perfectionist starts with *the* perfect size of wood, but then also wants *the* perfect cut, *the* perfect sanding, *the* perfect ornamentation, and keeps slicing off little corners and cuts to slice off mistakes and make it appear just so. What you get is, indeed" —Hannah held up a finger for emphasis—"the perfect door. In miniature. The *just-so* door, if you will." She rested her hands on her hips proudly, though the blush on her face told him she was, under all that show, embarrassed by her endeavor.

He'd known his fair share of embarrassments in his time and felt a sudden camaraderie with this girl. *Woman*, he corrected himself. There was no mistaking that; her loveliness was only emphasized by her girlish enthusiasm.

He studied her, then crouched, running his finger over the door. It was truly a work of art. She'd carved vines into the upper arch of it, sanded it to velvety smoothness, and it pained him to see it lying here in a pile of scraps. It seemed to go against the very nature of the cottage that salvaged broken things and gave them a place to live forever.

"This doesn't belong here," he said simply, rather enjoying the confounded look she gave him.

She held a palm upward toward it as he stood. "What do you mean? It's clearly—well, too small. Too big for a doll's house. I can't give it to one of the neighbors for that. Too small for the cottage . . ." She let her thoughts trail off, eyes big as she stared at him.

He pursed his mouth. "Leave it to me," he said thoughtfully, seriously. He had an idea brewing.

"Alright, Mr. Hampstead. You do whatever you like with that."

"Are you sure?" He needed her permission for what he had planned but didn't want to give too much away.

"Entirely. It was bound for the big bonfire we have come harvest time, so you can make a suit out of it for all I care." She brightened. "Say, that's not a bad idea. Mrs. Hollis came into the shop today and was saying how you were in need of a suit. She told me to tell you to stop by the fabric store this week and she'll get you all shipshape."

Now it was his turn to feel the keen heat of embarrassment. "I can't argue that," he said.

Later that week, when Luke arrived around the time he'd noticed Hannah usually came, his stride carried him under the arching branches of the reaching oak to reveal a sight that set him running: his Dutch door, swinging in midair over the balcony railing. Hannah was stationed up on the balcony, her face beet red, holding her breath as she leaned backward, leveraging the rope and pulling with all her might to get that door upstairs. But the door barely budged, the rope snagged on something on the railing. She was barely hanging on, keeping it from crashing into a window or the ground below, and then they'd have two doors bound for the bonfire.

In a matter of seconds, Luke had bounded up the stairs, freed the rope from its snag, and taken hold of the coil to help Hannah hoist it over the rest of the way. They worked in tandem, pulling in perfect time until the door appeared at the railing. He was thrown back to the singular and satisfying feeling of striving together with someone toward a common goal and finding in it a brotherhood. The last person he'd worked so in stride with had been Danny.

With a quick nod from Hannah silently affirming his plan, he left her side and eased the door over the railing. Their eyes met, shared victory brimming in both of them. He felt he should salute her, offer a handshake, or show some gesture of that shared brotherhood. Only . . . looking at this fount of words and energy, the way she looked fit to burst with joy, he had the sudden urge to gather her up in an embrace instead.

That was different from a brotherhood. Very different.

He cleared his throat, shoving back the ridiculous notion. Of course it was different. She wasn't a brother. If anything, she should be like a sister to him, seeing as how Danny was like a brother. That was logical.

The ache in his arms without her in them was not logical.

"Good work, pilot," she said, her smile dimpling rosy cheeks.

"Same to you," he said. "That was a good idea, the pulley you rigged up to get that upstairs."

She shrugged. "Maybe in theory. But if you hadn't come along when you had—I'm afraid my pulley would've been the death of your beautiful door, there. Speaking of which . . ." She dashed inside to the loft area and snatched up a carefully folded paper bag. "I come bearing gifts."

He opened the bag and saw everything he'd listed on his scrap of paper earlier that week. Hinges, screws, all of it. "How did you know?"

Again with her nonchalant shrug. "A girl knows things. What can I say?"

He was impressed.

"Plus, I snatched up your list when you weren't looking." She winked and, without missing a beat, sidled up to the door again. "Now, let's get this door up, shall we?"

By the time they'd released the Dutch door from its rope binding, rigged up a way to hang it, secured all the hardware, and tested it out, it was clear that Hannah Garland was a force to be reckoned with. Brilliant and bright, intense and jovial, all wrapped together.

He pulled the door closed with her on the other side for one last test, and listened as she unlatched the top half of the door, pulling it open on her side. She rested her elbow on the ledge, leaning her head into her fist as she studied him.

"I don't know about you, Mr. Hampstead."

"Luke," he said, the word coming out too quick. "You can call me Luke."

"Alright, Mr. Luke. I don't know about you."

"What don't you know?"

"Well, you're a mystery, is all. You come over and spend the whole evening listening to me blabber away, and by the time we part ways, I feel like I know you. But that doesn't add up. How you could speak three to ten words, and I could speak a hundred—"

He stifled a laugh.

"Okay, ten thousand."

He nodded, raising his eyebrows with a suppressed smile. That was a better estimate.

"And then I wake up the next morning and can't wait to see you again? It doesn't make sense at all. I mean—" She stopped. Her hand flew to cover her mouth, eyes round as saucers. "I didn't mean that. I mean, I did, but I didn't mean anything by it or—well, I just mean—"

This was where he should jump in and say something nice, something smooth and gentlemanly to get her out of her bind. Goodness knew he understood what it felt like to be trapped by one's own words. *Think, Luke. Think . . .*

"I don't blame you," he said. There. That would show her he understood. That he felt the same about her and looked forward to their time together. Right? Why was she looking at him like her whole being was laughing and she was barely holding it in?

"Really, now," she said. "Well, thank you for deigning to grace me with your presence." She laughed.

And then it hit him. What he'd said, how it had sounded.

"No—no, I meant I enjoy my time with you, too," he said, rubbing his temple with his fingers and wincing. "I should be going." He tried to open the door to move past her, disappear down the stairs as fast as he could, maybe find a way to disappear entirely.

But she held that door latch tight.

"Never you mind, Mr. Hampstead."

"Luke," he mumbled. He lifted his eyes. He could do better.

"I knew what you meant, Luke. And I'm the one that got all tongue-tied. But what I'm getting at is, who *are* you? How is it that you can spend all this time *here* when the great city of New York is waiting for you?"

His shoulders eased. This, he could answer. "Pan-Am is just making preparations right now. Anticipating the end of the war, but no one knows when that might be. So I wait to hear from them. I've sent them my address at the inn, and they'll let me know once they're ready."

Hannah tilted her head, waiting. She was a good listener, it turned out.

But he didn't know how to put this next part into words. It felt too . . . torn. "I know a lot of guys who'd switch places with me in a heartbeat," he said. "Guys still up there flying, fighting." He nodded up at the sky. "To get to come home, to have a job waiting when the time is right—and when this war ends, there are going to be more pilots freshly trained and home from the war than this nation has ever seen at once . . . but fewer jobs. I'll have to jump on that job right away when word comes, or there'll be a hundred guys waiting on the sidewalk to take my place."

He paused, breathed deep.

"But . . . ?" Hannah opened the door, letting him in from the balcony. She settled into a sun patch on the wooden planked floor, and he followed suit across from her. The loft was so small, their feet nearly touched.

"I know I have a lot to be thankful for. I'm lucky to be alive," he said. This, she grew serious at. But that was a tale for another day. "I'm here, alive, healed, and with a job waiting. I'd just—there's part of me that would give anything to still be in the fight," he said.

Especially looking at those blue eyes of hers, the earnest sincerity and openness of them. As long as there were people like Hannah Garland in the world, it was worth fighting to protect them.

She drew in a long breath and let out a whistle. "I guess it's true what they say," she said, studying him.

"What's that?"

"Still waters run deep. You've got a lot going on inside of you."

He dropped his gaze. How had she done that? Pulled so much up out of him?

"Well, you'd better keep that coming. Don't let me talk so much." She pointed an accusing finger at him. "Say more. I like it. And by the way, I'm glad you're here. I'm sorry for what you went through, and what you had to leave behind. And I mean that. But at the same time—maybe you were born for such a time as this."

He leaned forward, hoping for more.

She obliged. "Seems to me whenever a body finds themselves in a place they never thought life would take them, there's purpose there. They were born for that moment, even though it might be hard. And you, Mr. Luke . . . you are full of purpose, sure as the day is long."

She rose to go, looking at the sky. "It's late—Gran'll be comin' after me soon if I don't get home."

"I'll walk you," he said, standing.

"Mighty chivalrous of you, but don't you worry. I know the path home like the back of my hand. And I've got your words to keep me company. Besides, you'd best head on home, too. Jerry'll chew my head off if I hog you. He likes having help around."

Luke stuffed his hands in his pockets. "I have one or two things to wrap up here, and then I'll head back," he said.

She narrowed her eyes. "One or two things," she said. "That sounds mysterious."

"You'll see."

And she would. He made sure of that. In the alcove beneath the narrow stair, he worked late into the night removing a piece of the wall to make a small storage closet and inserting a smallish door carved to perfection. *Just-so door*, he wrote on a note, and left it wedged there for her to find.

He thought of her words as he swung the door closed with a quiet *click*. "For such a time as this," he said. "May it be so."

Six

June 1945

Four weeks. Twenty-eight days. Six hundred seventy-two hours spent here in Oak Springs, and at least three boxes of nails expended on siding, trim, windowsills, shingles, and shelves on a tiny cottage in the shadows of a sprawling oak.

At night, Luke dreamt of the frigid dark on the outskirts of the Ardennes, fingers so stiff he could barely form a single word.

During the days, he soaked in the warmth of the Texas sun, and the warmth that was the girl who'd gotten him through that frigid night in what felt like another lifetime. Never had he imagined he'd still be here—and still had not given her that letter, nor the package he came here to deliver.

He didn't know why. At first it felt presumptuous. Embarrassing, even, to relate that tale to a near stranger. But each day, he realized more and more that she was no stranger at all. Strange, perhaps, in a most wonderful way, and he laughed thinking of her near misses walking into posts and beams when her eyes were glued to sketches. But she was no stranger.

And then the prospect of giving her the parcel became fear. It was so very rustic compared to what she deserved. She'd lit up like a Christmas tree at the sight of the just-so door when she'd discovered it. He'd do anything to see that same thrill upon her face. Or rather—saturating her being. For nothing with Hannah Garland was confined to the surface. Whatever she felt, she felt it straight through. Whatever she did, she did with everything in her.

He was beginning to feel less a stranger here, too. Hannah's Gran made sure of that, demanding he sit down for a full breakfast each day, and sneaking him a plate of hot sausage links when the toast served him by Hannah crunched like steel. But he finished every bite of that toast, too, his smile sincere. How had he ended up here? At a warm kitchen in a family home, when he had never known such before. The sky had been his home, and he'd been fine with that.

But now . . . when he thought of New York, of taking to the skies once more, a strange ache cracked open inside of him. All through the war, he'd had no home to be homesick for. And now . . . he was pining for a home that was never his, and he wasn't even gone from it yet.

"Pull yourself together," Luke muttered to himself.

"What're you mutterin' about now?" Jerry piped up between bites of his sandwich. They were sneaking a quick bite in between repairing part of the inn's paneling. Luke was dead tired after working all afternoon at the cottage with Hannah, but he was earning his keep here at the inn by helping Jerry into the evening.

"Nothing," Luke said. "Just thinking."

"Thinkin'," Jerry said, sounding like the idea was as absurd as swallowing a frog.

"Yeah."

"That'll get you into trouble. How much should I wager that you're thinkin' on that pretty, young Hannah Garland?"

Luke had to stifle a laugh at the man's description. Hannah

was pretty, yes. Prettier than he had words for. And true, she was a young woman. But when he thought of Hannah, a thousand other words burst into thought, too. She was bright. Brilliant, really. Ambitious. Undaunted. Spunky and quirky and plucky, and yet just when she risked fooling everyone into thinking she was clumsy and scatterbrained, she stopped the world with some stroke of genius.

More than all that, though . . . she was kind. The sort of kindness that made a man not know what to do with himself, when she looked at him with those clearer-than-the-sky blue eyes and saw right down to his soul, stopped what she was doing, and listened. Understood.

"Well?" Jerry's voice grated into his thoughts.

"I might've been thinking about her," Luke admitted, quick to pick up a two-by-four and measure it. Hopefully Jerry would let it be.

"Well, what're you gonna do about it, son?"

Luke propped the wood against the wall. "What can I do? I'm leaving in a few weeks. Maybe a few months."

"See? Look at you. You're already solving it. Stretch those weeks on into months, those months on into years, and before you know it, you'll be as much a part of this place as old Jerry here, and then there's no leavin', no matter what."

"I don't think I *can* stay," Luke said, thinking about the scarcity of that pilot job. A man needed to earn a living, especially if he had hopes of providing a home for someone someday. The very idea of having a someone was miraculous. His heart's door had been firmly shut after everything with Caroline, and yet the thought kept knocking on it. And the irony of him needing to leave town to make that possible urged him to pound a bucket of nails more into that place inside, nail it firmly shut forever. Luke narrowed his eyes. "But even if I did, that doesn't mean she'd want me to. I just showed up out of the blue one day and inserted myself into her life. A girl like that . . . she doesn't need me getting in her way."

"True, you are in the way more often than not," Jerry said, chewing on his straw.

"Thanks."

"Just sayin'. But who's to say she doesn't want you in the way? Many a fella's tried to court Hannah Garland. Just none of 'em can keep up with her, is all. She's got twelve schemes and ideas in her head if she's got one, and never has there been any room there for a fella, too."

"You sure know how to give a guy hope, Jerry."

"Pipe down, I wasn't finished. I was gonna say . . ." He leaned in, a conspiratorial twinkle igniting in his eyes above his stubble. "*Until now.*"

"Until now?"

"Shoot, do I have to spell it out for you, son? The girl thinks somethin' of you, so quit your thinkin' and go talk to her, for Pete's sake. And I mean that. Pete Bresden's gonna be in a world of hurt at his Feed and Dime if his countergirl can't concentrate."

Luke resumed his work, the thought enveloping him again. Maybe the man had a point. Maybe he needed to get his head out of the clouds and go talk—really talk—to Hannah. They'd conversed for hours every day, except for the times when their work in tandem slipped into easy comfortable silence. But never had either of them mentioned this growing . . . *presence* between them. Whatever it was.

He became aware of someone deeply impatient watching him. Looking up, he saw Jerry drop his jaw in frustration, gesturing with his hand.

"What. Now?" Luke said, straightening.

"Now! What're you waitin' for, lightning to strike?"

And with that, he was out the door, the deadbolt locked

behind him by an emphatic Jerry. He looked at his watch—7:00 p.m. A bit late for visiting when farmers around here retired plenty early, but he knew Hannah kept odd hours. Stuffing his hands in his pockets, he took the path beneath the tree, past the cottage, and through the cotton field. He was three-quarters of the way there before he realized he should've brought something. A man shouldn't come empty-handed to see a lady, that much he knew. And though all he had to offer her every day were empty hands—and she filled them, gladly, with hammers and nails—he felt the pull tonight to bring her *something*.

A quick detour to a patch of purple wildflowers found him stumbling into a mucky bog where the field drained. With a dubious glance at the brown mud caking his shoes, he narrowed his eyes at the patch of wildflowers that had gotten him into this mess and determined that nothing would stop him. Not mud, or the deceptively strong stems that did not want to snap at his demand, or the way his palms burned after wrestling them into a haphazard bouquet. Hannah would have fresh flowers, by golly, and now it was personal.

When she answered the door to his knock with the sky dusking quickly, she took a look at the state of him, and a look at the flowers, and appeared speechless.

"These are for you," Luke said, refusing to let this maddening heat overtake his face. He offered the flowers to her and she took them slowly.

"Thistles," she said, her voice low.

Great. He had made himself into a swamp creature in order to bring the girl he—admired—*thistles*? He was sending the wrong message, on all fronts.

She swiped a tear. Oh no. This was not good.

Then she looked at her fingers, freshly wet from that tear, and gaped at him. "You made me cry," she said, mouth open in astonishment.

"I'm so sorry," he blurted. "I just wanted to bring you something nice, and—well, I didn't know they were thistles. You have to believe me."

"Thistles," she murmured again, running her palm gently over their tops and . . . smiling?

A great rush of relief flooded him. Perhaps he hadn't blundered as badly as he'd thought.

"Would you like to walk with me?" he asked, trying to salvage the evening.

For the first time, she turned her wide, tear-flooded eyes to his, and held them. "I would be honored, Luke Hampstead," she said. "And I'll just bring these right along, if it's all the same to you. I should perhaps explain myself." She lifted her chin with gathered resolve, her smile dimpling.

He offered an arm, and they strolled deep into the cotton field. It was like a sea of white-capped waves in the moonlight, tossing in the breeze, making an island of the two of them.

"I'm sorry the flowers weren't something more," he said, breaking the silence.

She stopped and faced him. "The flowers are everything, and don't you think for a minute otherwise. I assumed Danny must've told you."

He tilted his head, questioning. "No, I don't think he did. They just—they looked nice, and they made me think of you," he said. Why wasn't he better with words? They stumbled out of him and flopped miserably in their attempt to show something of what he wished to offer, from the depths of himself.

"Well, let me fill you in, then, Mr. Hampstead." She resumed walking in a roundabout way toward the tree, skirting a pond where frogs sang into the night. "When I was sixteen, I was supposed to go to the watermelon festival with Burl Taggart. Only he never came. I showed up at the town hall that night with Danny for the dance, and do you know who was there?"

"Don't say Burl."

"*Burl.*"

"The fiend."

"Yes! Fiend! With Marybeth Hendricks on his arm. They're married now and have four children and I love all six of those Taggarts dearly, but let me tell you, I did *not* love them dearly that night. I ran home and climbed up in this old oak." She gestured to where it stood as they drew closer to it. "Danny rode his old horse Methuselah up—galloped him up that hill like a brotherly knight in shining armor, only he wore a plaid shirt and his cowboy hat. He came knocking at the trunk like it was a door, telling me to come down, that he'd found my corsage, and we'd better get to the dance before I missed my favorite part."

"Which was . . . ?"

"Watermelon seed spitting after the dance. What else? Anyway, I climbed down, ready to just turn in like the spinster I was meant to be, and Danny was standing there with his hand behind his back. He pulled out a bundle of purple flowers tied up with baling twine from the hay barn, secured it around my wrist, and escorted me to that dance like I was one of the English princesses! Margaret or Elizabeth, I can never keep them straight. Anyway, Danny danced the night away with Sarah Brighton, and I'm glad of that, but I'll never forget that he picked me up from my wallowing pit and helped me look Burl Taggart and Marybeth Hendricks in the eye with my corsage of thistles. I don't blame Burl for choosing Marybeth. I'm an odd duck and I know it, and truth was, we'd have been a terrible fit all around. But Danny told me something that night that I'll never forget. He said, '*You're not like anyone else, Hannah, and you're not supposed to be. God knew just what He was doing when He made you, and one of these days you're going to take flight, I just know it.*'"

“That sounds like Danny,” he said. “He would pull those one-liners out of nowhere, and they’d just sink right into us. He was the morale of our entire division. I saw him one time, kneeling in the chapel on base, before we were shipped out. I didn’t mean to intrude, and I turned to leave, but he told me to stay. We just sat there a long time, him praying and me wondering, until finally he said it was okay to ask questions. That God was big enough for questions, and how would I ever know Him if I didn’t ask? So I did. I started asking questions. To Danny, and then reading that Bible he gave me, and something strange happened. The more I asked, the more I felt—at home. I had never known a home, not really. But I found a home in the Psalms and in the stories of a man who gave of himself beyond reason.”

“I believe it,” Hannah said. “Danny lived and breathed that sort of love.”

She took a shaky breath and looked to the sky as crickets began their evening song. “Methuselah misses him.” She glanced back toward the old barn. “Just hasn’t been the same since he went away.” She sighed and spoke more quietly. “Nothing has. I miss him.” She swiped another tear. “And that!” She held out her freshly tear-kissed fingertips to him accusingly. “That’s all thanks to you.”

“I’m so sorry . . .”

“No, it’s a good thing. Something’s been wrong with me since we lost Danny. The loss—it was so deep, I couldn’t even cry, somehow. The tears were there, I could feel ’em welling way down in there, with no way out. And then you and your—your thistles.” She waved the bouquet in between them for emphasis. “It’s a gift, is all. And I thank you.”

He beheld her. Tried to find the right words in his ever-failing vocabulary. *I’m sorry. I wish he was here with you. I hope time heals your wound*. None of it sounded . . . enough. “I miss him, too,” he said at last.

She sniffed and nodded, giving silence to the thought. Then she reached a hand to touch the etched bark of the oak. "I come here sometimes to look at these letters," she said. In the moonlight, the initials scattered among the leaves and branches took on a lofty and magical feel, as if touching any one of them would cause the couple's story to play out in the light of the fireflies darting among the leaves.

"What are you looking for in them?" Luke touched one, too, wondering what it would be like to be carved here, with someone, for all time.

"It's silly," Hannah said. "You'll laugh."

"Try me." He smiled.

She watched him suspiciously a moment, then nodded. "A name. Something for the cottage. I want it to be called something that'll honor what you've done, sending me these pictures of places that are lost in their original homes, but will always be remembered in this house's very bones."

Luke stared, feeling as if someone had just seen straight into him. "Not silly at all," he said, his voice strangely thick. "Have you struck on any names?"

She smiled. "Well, there's Hal," she said, pointing at a place where Hal had proclaimed his love for Sally once upon a time. "But that doesn't seem the right fit somehow."

Their laughter mingled, the tree's leaves trembling in a night breeze as if joining in.

She shook her head, growing more serious. "I've tried spelling out names from initials scattered all over this tree. But nothing is quite right. I keep thinking something like . . . the keeping place. Or the gathering. Or—I don't know, something that speaks of safety, and holding. New life."

"Maybe that's it," Luke said. "Your name."

She blinked, summoned from deep thought. "But my name's Hannah," she said.

He grinned. "The name of your house, I mean."

She laughed, showing she'd known just what he'd been getting at.

He continued. "Life house, or . . ." he looked to the side, thinking.

"I keep thinking something like—maybe *haven.*" Her voice grew quiet.

The word struck something in his memory, summoning it across the frozen fields of Belgium and over a raging ocean into this very moment. *Leven*, the woman had said in Dutch, the pronunciation rhyming exactly with haven. *Life.*

"Did I say something wrong?" Hannah's face was concerned. "You look like you've seen a ghost."

He shook his head. "No. That word—*haven.* It sounds so much like another I heard, once." He told her the whole story of that long cold night. Of the bent weathervane singing its melody in the morning, of the couple come to rescue him. He told all but the part about the letter.

Hannah stood up straight from where she'd been leaning against the trunk, soaking in his every word. "Luke." She shook her head. "You went through all that—and here you are, standing right in front of me, all the while keeping a story like this? What other tales are you holding in that big quiet of yours?" She said it like a badge of honor—*big quiet.* He'd always thought of his reticent ways as a shortcoming. But here she was looking at him like he was a treasure trove of cherished things.

"*Leven.*" She tried the word out, and he loved it in her voice, on her lips. "*Leven. Lay-ven.* Lay-ven. Haven."

Their eyes met, and they burst into laughter at the way the rhyme rather undid the tender meaning of it all.

"Alright, so maybe not Leven Haven. But that word." She shook her head in wonder. "You've hit on something, Luke Hampstead. Let's hang on to that."

Hannah stroked the soft tops of the thistles with her fingertips, then ever so softly slipped her hand into his. And without a thought, for it was the most natural thing in the world, he closed his hand around hers, wishing he could hold her close and safe always. They began the walk home to her farmhouse, crickets singing and fireflies dancing in the dark.

"This watermelon festival," he said at length. "They have it every year?"

"Yes, sir," she said. "Coming up next month, as a matter of fact."

"You . . . uh . . ." No, that was all wrong. Burl Taggart had jilted her at this festival. She did not deserve a bumbling *You, uh,* tongue-tied invitation. The girl before him—the one smiling at the dance of fireflies skimming over cotton—she deserved on-purpose, all-heart words.

He cleared his throat. "Hannah. Would you do me the honor of accompanying me to the Oak Springs Watermelon Festival?"

She whirled to face him, and he worried she'd given herself whiplash. Her eyes were wide as saucers. "Me? With you. Me?"

"I know where I can procure an authentic purple thistle corsage," he said. "If that puts a shine on the invitation at all."

She smiled, and his muscles eased at the sight. "Well, I'd be honored, Mr. Hampstead."

Seven

July 1945

The twenty-first annual Watermelon Festival of Oak Springs was a sight to behold for anyone. But Hannah was especially enjoying seeing it through Luke's eyes, which were huge as dinner plates at the moment.

It was a bit of a spectacle, she realized. With Main Street bedecked in bunting that remained up for the whole month of July, the road blocked off with barrels, and people milling about in their Sunday best, it seemed to make Luke stand a bit straighter.

"Penny for your thoughts?" she said, tilting her head.

Luke shrugged a shoulder. "It's nothing," he said.

"Well, *nothing* sure looks like a whole lot of *something* on you, pilot. Tell you what, I'll make it a slice of pie for your thoughts, and you can pick any kind you want from the pie jubilee."

He coughed. "Did you say pie *jubilee*?"

"Oak Springs does nothing halfway, sir. See for yourself." She led him beneath the covered walkway to a long table spread with blue-and-white gingham, where plump pies of every kind awaited in varying states of having been devoured. Blueberry, pecan, peach, sour cream apple, and the ongoing joke of the town: Mr. Jones's mincemeat pie, which was rumored to be the same returning relic, year after year, always going untouched.

Luke's stomach growled, and Hannah was swift to take note of which pie had captured his attention. "Ah, I pegged you for a pecan pie man. I see I was . . . correct?"

He gave a sheepish nod. "But please," he said, "let me. What'll it be?" He was becoming easier in her presence, and she couldn't quite put her finger on the feeling, but she felt . . . honored, somehow, by that. That this man with the treasure trove inside him would choose her to be comfortable around.

She opted for her favorite, sour cream apple pie. He paid discreetly, though she couldn't help but notice it was twice what he owed. The pie was served up on the diner's mixed china, and they strolled a bit while eating. Their wanderings took them past the Chili Parlor and its robust, tantalizing aromas, through a clutch of children gathered around a box of free kittens, around a crowd gathered to measure competing watermelons, and to a booth serving up ice cold glasses of watermelon sweet tea, of which they heartily partook.

"So . . . watermelon festival," Luke said. "Don't most towns just have a county fair?"

"Yes, sir. But Oak Springs isn't most towns. Or rather—our fair *was* like most towns, until the great storm of '24." She told of the tornado that had torn through the town that year, destroying all crops but the watermelons. "No one had any warning, you see."

Luke's face showed sheer befuddlement, as well it should. "You don't have warning sirens?"

"No, sir. Most places around here still use church bells to warn, and that's if they are allowed to."

"Allowed?"

She leaned in and lowered her voice as if to impart a great scandalous secret. "We couldn't even *say* the word *tornado* around here till 1938, when the last real bad one ripped through here. Mayor thought it caused too much panic. And certainly no warning bells. But that's all changed now. Church bells ring for three reasons: the watermelon festival kickoff, Sunday services, and tornado warning."

"So now you have both warning bells *and* a watermelon festival, all because of those storms," Luke said.

Hannah nodded. "The town had two choices after that: shrivel up on the vine and be defeated, or turn lemons into lemonade."

"Or watermelon sweet tea." Luke raised his glass. She clinked his cheerfully, and they meandered away from the crowd to a grove of trees, where a creek babbled happily on by, swallowing up great green islands in its gentle currents.

"Are those more watermelons?"

"Indeed they are," she said. "And it'll be just about time for the tastin', too. Folks stick them in the creek to chill, and then everyone has a bite of everyone else's ripest melon. Of course there's a blue ribbon to be awarded, too. Tell you what, I'll take our dishes back if you get started hauling these up. We all help out. Be back quicker than lightning."

And she meant to, except that Marybeth Taggart intercepted her, her brood of four children gawking at the kittens.

"Hannah Garland," Marybeth said. "Who is this handsome airman of yours that everyone's been talking about?"

Hannah nearly dropped her dishes, sputtering. She set them in the appropriate collection basket before she had a chance to shatter them, and in time to shatter this rumor that had apparently sprung up like so much buckwheat.

"He's not," she said quickly.

Marybeth tipped her head quizzically.

"I mean—not to the handsome part. To the *mine* part. He's not mine."

"So he is handsome."

"I didn't say that."

"But you just said—"

Marybeth was direct. It was one of her best qualities, and once Hannah had gotten over Burl Taggart being swept away in her presence enough to forget his date with Hannah, she'd once again counted Marybeth as one of her dearest friends. But right now, she was nothing short of maddening.

Or maybe it was Hannah herself who was maddening.

"He's—he was a friend of Danny's," she said, and Marybeth's entire stance softened immediately. "He's just staying a few weeks to help Gran and me put the last touches on the cottage. Then he's off again to take to the skies. So no, he's not mine."

"But he is handsome." Marybeth's smile dimpled, and Hannah swatted her on the shoulder.

"Maybe."

"And full of grit, that one is." Gran's voice popped in as she sidled up from her walk down the boards. "Judging by the way that man saws through your biscuits each morning, he's got teeth of steel, and courage even stronger."

"Gran!"

"Hannah, I love you, darlin', but you know it's true. And that's a good thing. The man is brave." And just like that, Gran popped back out of the conversation, leaving a gobsmacked wake for Marybeth to revel in.

Which she did, entirely. "So he came to finish the cottage?"

"Well, no, not as such, but once he saw it, he offered to stay."

"So—why did he come?"

Marybeth's question was simple. So simple it irked Hannah something awful that it hadn't struck her in all this time. Irked her so much she spun in a blur of frustrated thought and made a beeline for the creek to get to the bottom of it, posthaste.

But Luke was nowhere to be seen, and neither were the chilled watermelons. By the time she tracked him down, slicing melons with the Watkins twins, who had taken to him like a third brother, he was swallowed up whole by the town. It seemed they'd all noticed him in his weeks on their outskirts and had decided to make the festival one giant welcome to a serviceman, channeling all their patriotism and gratitude and the missing of their own sons and husbands into a great and mighty welcome.

He served up melon. Was ushered up to be the honorary awarder of blue ribbons. Acquiesced to the crowd's prodding for him to kick off the apple bobbing, and all without a single complaint. Hannah knew enough of Luke Hampstead to know that being in the spotlight was not his cup of sweet tea, but he took it with true grit and kindness. And before she knew it, the sun had set, the torches were lit, and the town was funneling into the town hall for the evening's culminating activity—the dance.

Somewhere in the hubbub, Luke was swept into the current of incoming dancers, and though he kept looking back, his eyes earnest and searching, his gaze never quite landed on Hannah. An old dread crept up in her. She had been here before, here at the doors of this dance, all alone. And while then it got her ire up, this time something worse began to grow. The opposite of a feeling. Cold, hollow resignation. This was getting to be a pattern in her life—being left behind. Unseen, overlooked. And she didn't mind, not most of the time. There was so much to be busy *doing* that, honestly, who cared if anyone was thinking of little old Hannah Garland? She had enough humility to know the world did not always need to be thinking of her.

Still, this hollowness—it dug deep tonight, for some reason. This feeling of being forgotten.

A quick scan around the room saw Luke had been cornered by the three Drexler sisters—Peony, Rose, and Freesia, each of them fanning her fan and batting her eyelashes and putting on all the feminine charm that Hannah knew nothing of. Watching, she narrowed her eyes in an attempt to mimic them. How *did* they do that with their eyelashes? Winking one eye closed, then another, then rolling her eyes up at the ceiling, she determined that no amount of eyeball acrobatics could turn her into an eyelash batter, and perhaps that sealed her fate as a spinster. Well, so be it. She could swing a hammer, and there was work to do, and that would be enough for her.

Burl and Marybeth Taggart danced on by, a vision from the past. Marybeth caught her eye, giving a not-so-subtle jerk of her pretty head over toward Luke. "Go," she mouthed.

But Marybeth did not know that Hannah could not compete with the eyelash batters. So Hannah did the only sensible thing and headed for the punch table, over near the string quartet.

Armed with a cut glass cup of pink liquid that at least provided some small buffer between her and this whirling room, she filled her lungs and smoothed out the pale blue taffeta dress that made her feel like she was walking on a cloud. She rolled back her shoulders, lifted her chin, turned to face the world—and nearly collided with Luke Hampstead.

"Great gumdrops, you scared me," she said. Flustered, she held out the cup. "Here," she said.

"For me?" He was pulling up that grin, the one that seemed mined from the very depths of the man.

"Why, sure," she said, as if she'd meant to do that all along. When she had no earthly idea why she'd gone and shoved a cup of pink punch in the man's hands.

He took a sip politely and nodded in approval, then set the cup down. "Mighty kind of you, Miss Garland, but I confess I was hoping for something a little different when I came this way."

She scanned the far side of the room, spotting the Drexler girls fanning their fans and looking none too pleased toward them. He had—left them? To seek her out? She ran her hand along the table behind her, nonchalantly. As if it wasn't keeping her from falling over like a featherbrained idiot. She was not sixteen anymore. So why was she acting like it? "O-oh?"

He held out his hand. Looked pointedly at Burl Taggart, who, along with the rest of the room, was completely oblivious to the crisis going on inside of her. "Miss Garland, would you do me the honor of granting me this dance?"

Hannah's eyes grew wide. She swallowed. Gripped the table harder. This was entirely out of her element—and yet she could not refuse the earnest and open gaze of the man before her. The way he stood, hand outstretched, in his dark uniform.

"If you can swing a hammer, you can dance around a room for four minutes," she muttered to herself, not believing a word of it. Then clapped a hand over her mouth. She hadn't meant to say that out loud.

Luke leaned forward ever so slightly. "True, Hannah. You can. You can do anything."

And with that, she unlocked her grip from the table, rested her hand in his, and let herself be swept onto the dance floor for the first time since the Burl Taggart incident, when Danny had come to her rescue.

Couples around them bobbed gently to the plucky tune of the band. Hannah couldn't imagine how they were keeping time, with her heartbeat pounding out its own rogue tempo so loud it was likely to trip them all.

Her feet took a bit to slip into the rhythm, but Luke's gentle strength at her back eased her into it, until it felt oddly natural.

"I like the music," he offered, and she breathed easy at the silence between them being broken.

"Do you?" Pride swelled up in Hannah at her town's band.

"Oak Springs is lucky to boast our very own string quartet," she said. "Not many small towns can say that."

"String quartet?" Luke said, surprise in his voice.

"See for yourself." Hannah led him to the low stage, where Ralph Gleason fingerpicked his fiddle, Sam Granger strummed his guitar, and Jake Eden plucked a long string tied to a stick at one end and an overturned washbasin at the other—a contraption he called the "gut-bucket."

"Sarsaparilla's Orchestra, they call themselves."

"After the soft drink?"

"No, after the lone donkey who resides in the barn where they practice. Though now they've taken to calling themselves *Uncle* Sarsaparilla's Orchestra. Our own USO. They feel very patriotic about it."

Luke laughed, and Hannah felt it resonate right into her.

"Where's the fourth member of the quartet?"

Hannah sobered slightly. "Off at war," she said. "We all hope he'll be back safe and sound, maybe sometime soon. In the meantime, these three carry the torch and do a mighty fine job keeping Oak Springs in Bing Crosby."

As if on cue, the trio wound down their rather tinny rendition of "Don't Fence Me In," their concluding chord a little off-key.

Which was exactly how Hannah felt. What now? Was she supposed to stay? Were they done dancing? She'd just found her land feet, so to speak, out here on the dance floor, and they'd hardly had a chance to talk.

"Stay?" Luke said, as if reading her thoughts. The deep green of his uniform jacket and the gold of its buttons called to her. She closed her eyes, seeing the deep green leaves of her oak and the golden light slipping in through its branches. Mingling with the greens and golds of his uniform until she didn't know where one stopped and the other began, and she felt just as home in the arms of this man as she did in the limbs of that tree. They dipped and moved to the plodding, plucky tune, she hardly noticing a note of it.

She opened her eyes again as the band began to play "Stardust," and saw Luke Hampstead as he was: the embodiment of something faithful and true, strong and adventurous, steady and kind. Like her tree—but—real. Or human, rather.

And like her tree, he seemed carved, in his very soul, with stories. Stories she wished to know.

His single-word question from minutes before marched through her mind. *Stay?*

And her answer was, resoundingly, *yes*. For the first time in the history of Oak Springs, Hannah Garland dreamed not of flying, or leaving, or taking flight . . . but of staying.

Eight

August 1945

For the next few weeks, Luke replayed that dance in his mind more times than he cared to admit. It wasn't until Jerry called him a "human jukebox" for whistling "Stardust" one too many times that he realized he had, perhaps, lost a grip on reality.

"Hey, Jukebox," Jerry said one day as the August heat drove them to work on inside projects.

"Yeah?" Luke said with some difficulty from his place holding up the mantel—the extremely heavy mantel—as Jerry mounted new braces for it.

"You still planning on leaving?" Jerry asked, in uncharacteristic simplicity. So direct the question scalded him.

"I . . . don't know," Luke said. "Don't know where else I'd go if not New York, with the job waiting. They're holding it since they can't start commercial international flights up again just yet, but it's only a matter of time."

Jerry reached out a hand and flicked Luke hard on the forehead.

Luke exhaled in pain. Convenient that Jerry had waited until he couldn't defend himself to mount his attack.

"What'd you do that for?" he asked

"'Cause you're dumber than an ox with his head in the mud," Jerry said. "Nobody around here has seen Hannah so—so alive—since her brother passed." Jerry turned his attention slowly back to hammering a nail in place.

"That's good," Luke said. "I'm glad to hear she's doing well."

Jerry tossed his hands up in the air in frustration, letting his hammer fall to the ground. "I'm glad to hear she's doing well," Jerry said in a nasal tone. "You hear yourself? You sound like a heartless old catfish."

Luke braced his shoulder beneath the weight of the mantel, flushing in heat from the strain of it, and from frustration at his own self. Why was he so bad at saying what he meant? He propped the mantel up with the ladder and crossed his hands over his chest, facing Jerry.

"I just mean that if anyone deserves joy, it's Hannah."

"Good," Jerry said. "'Cause you know if you up and leave to New Jersey or New Connecticut or wherever—"

"New York," Luke muttered. Not that it mattered.

"New Timbuktu, for all I care! If you leave, you leave that girl in a world of hurt. So you'd better change one or the other of those things. Either don't you leave, or you better tell her now that you're not fixin' to stay."

The words settled heavy in him. The truth was, he'd give anything to stay. But who was he to presume a place here, with a girl like Hannah Garland, who could have any fellow in the world? She deserved the very best.

"Or take her with you," Jerry said. "She ain't married to this land, you know."

That didn't mesh with what she'd told him when he'd first arrived. It was clear Oak Springs and Hannah Garland were a part of each other. How had she put it? *"Some dreams fade away. . . ."*

Still, the truth of Jerry's words resonated with something that had been tumbling around inside of him for weeks now. So, he took himself to his room that afternoon and did what he did best: reconnaissance. It had been his mission in the war. He'd been so proud to be a part of the army air force, had studied hard and pushed himself to be one of the few who would be assigned not to bombers but to reconnaissance planes. To observe. Map. Photograph. Chart. In essence, to use reality to plot a navigable course for others whose lives depended upon it.

From the bottom drawer of the old bureau, he pulled his few possessions of significance from the shadows and laid them out in the light.

Letters.

Three rows and four columns of them, evenly spaced, until he could see the familiar handwriting stamped upon each envelope again and again and again. Just as the writer of those letters was stamped upon his very soul now.

And then there was this last letter. Not from Hannah . . . but from Caroline. Spilling her self-proclaimed broken heart onto paper, about how it was killing her, not knowing whether he was safe, not knowing when or if she'd see him again. How she had to "set him free," that he could fight better, unshackled by thoughts of a girl back home. She had signed it with the word he would never use to close a letter again: *Sincerely, Caroline.*

That letter had not unshackled him but untethered him. Snapped his last link to any semblance of home or family, and sent him floundering in a sea of unbelonging. He had written back, taking painstaking care not to fumble his words as he always did, to assure her she never had shackled him. It had taken everything in him to write that letter—and his only answer had been silence. That is, until a cousin of hers had seen fit to mail him her wedding announcement from the *Herald*, claiming he deserved to know. He could still feel the hollow sickness of the months that followed.

Until Danny had happened along, clapping him on the back and calling him "brother." Bidding him to write to his sister, who—Luke laughed dryly recalling this—he had imagined to be a spinster. He hated himself for having categorized someone so, regardless of age or circumstance, without ever having met them. Truth was, even if Hannah had been much older than she was . . . and even if, at that age, she had never wed, *spinster* was the farthest term from that woman's soul. He wished to banish the word from the English language, for all the single-dimensioned presumptions it made about a person.

The letter in his hands felt hollow, somehow. In the end, it was true that Caroline had been kind. A bit dramatic, perhaps, but a nice person, even if she'd reduced him to a *Dear John*. And just as she'd set him free of herself, this letter . . . it had no place in his present. No place in his future. When he looked at the field of riches that lay before him in Hannah's grid of perfectly spaced letters—he knew exactly what he had to do.

Standing, he strode to the fireplace. Pulled a dusty jar of matches from the mantel, struck one—and watched as flame took to the paper that had once charred him. He held it a moment, watching the paper disappear before his eyes—and moved to discard it in the fireplace.

"Luke?" The voice came floating up the stairs, followed by soft but eager footfalls. Hannah.

He froze. Caught between everything right—the letting go of this letter, the approach of Hannah Garland—but feeling everything wrong about it. She would see. Her letters laid out so meticulously. Him with Caroline's letter, one he should have left behind long, long ago.

His thoughts slowed into a maddening muddle and then—she was there.

"Luke?" She stood in the open doorway, hand poised to knock, and face full of eager joy.

"H-Hannah," he breathed, her name coming out like the truest thing he'd ever spoken.

The next second seemed to slow. He watched her take in the scene before her. Watched her face register her own letters, and the one in his hand. Watched as that smile, which could warm straight through ice, melted into crestfallen hurt.

And that was when he remembered he was holding fire. Or, rather, the fire reminded him, reaching his fingers and causing him to drop what was left of Caroline's letter, the pain of it paling in the wake of that look on Hannah's face. It was written there clear as day: She believed he'd burned one of her own letters.

"I—I'm sorry," she said. "I should go."

"Wait," he said, urgency telling his feet to fly him to her, but the smoldering embers of the fire requiring him to stay, to stomp them out where they had fallen on the floor.

By the time he caught up with her, she was outside and halfway to the safety of her white-as-snow fields of cotton. She heard him, glanced backwards, and just as quickly fixed her gaze on the path before her, which carried her into the low-hanging branches of the oak.

"Hannah, please," he said. He saw confirmed upon her being what she had perceived—that the letter in his hand had been one of her own. That he was destroying her words, committing them to flame. And judging by the look on her face, it may as well have been her heart.

He laid a hand on her shoulder, and she stopped, shoulders heaving.

"I shouldn't have come up there," she said. "It's none of my business what you do with your things. They're just papers." Her words were winding up, gathering speed. Her arms regaining some of her usual animation as she raised a palm to her forehead. "I mean, I hardly knew you when I wrote those. I didn't know you at all. Why should you keep them? I thought we were friends—and maybe we are—but—come on, Hannah. *Keep well, Hannah*, your letters always said, and it just sort of got inside me, you know, and made itself a part of me until you showed up and said them in *person*, of all things—*Keep well, Hannah*—and I guess seeing the hands that wrote those words burning one of my letters . . ." She paused, taking a deep breath. "Stop it, Hannah. Compose yourself."

She had stopped talking to him at some point and slipped into lecturing herself, rendering him suddenly an eavesdropper. And a gentleman should always make his presence known when in danger of becoming an accidental eavesdropper.

Even if it was on a conversation between a woman so maddeningly wonderful he got tongue-tied in her presence . . . and her own self.

He cleared his throat.

She was pacing now, and glanced up at him as if he were some distant apparition. "I'm positively mortified at myself, Mr. Hampstead," she said. "I don't know why I reacted like a skittish old deer. I just—I saw those letters and I saw the one in your hand and the—the *fire*—" She stopped and brightened, as if a lightbulb had just gone on in the ether above her hair that circled her head in a braided ring like a slightly off-kilter halo. "Say, did a candle fall on it? Is that why it was burning? Maybe you were saving it." She scrunched up her nose and shook her head. "Don't answer that. It's none of my business. Only . . . did it?"

Her eyes were so vibrant blue, so full of hope, and his words were stopping up all stumbly again. So his feet did what his words failed to. They closed the distance between them, until his hand reached up to trace her face.

"Hannah," he said.

She swallowed, waiting. A breeze rolled through the oak's reaching branches, setting its green leaves to trembling in a dance of light and shadow.

And those words, they stacked up in the unspoken place. *There's no one like you on God's green earth.*

He let his thumb linger, brushing her soft cheek in its rosy glow. This woman . . .

"The candle didn't fall on the letter," he said, unwilling to leave her anguished question a second longer. "But—it wasn't yours," he said.

"It wasn't?" She bit her lip, and it was all he could do to keep from gathering her up entirely. That all of this should have meant so much to her . . . it was more than he'd dared to hope.

He shook his head. "I could never do that to your letters."

"You—you couldn't?"

Oh, if she only knew. How her letters had been his lifeline. His warmth. But for that . . . she deserved more than words.

"Can you meet me this evening? There's something you should know," he said, finally withdrawing his hand from its place cradling her face. Her hand flew up, her fingers touching the place he just had.

"This evening," she said. He didn't know if he ever had or ever would see Hannah Garland so at a loss for words.

"At the cottage," he said.

"Well, I normally help Gran with her pies on Monday nights, but she's off for a visit to her sister over in College Station for the week, and I guess I—" She looked up, apparently seeing the same anguished waiting on his face that he'd seen on hers just moments before. "I'd be honored," she said.

Those words surrounded him with the rush of the wind as it drove him home to the inn. It was time, at last, to do what he had come to do.

Nine

Hannah was jitterier than a jitterbug, and it was rubbing off on the animals as she made her rounds. The hens dashed around their pen like spooked things.

"I know how you feel, girls," she said. "What's it mean, anyway? *'There's something you should know.'* What is it? Is he leaving?" The black-and-white barred Rock cocked her little hen head, staring an inquisitive red eye at her before ducking away with the others behind a bush. "Smart," she said, pointing. "Take cover. Maybe I should take a cue from you."

The pigs were no better, with Porky grunting to beat the band, and Porky's little ones squealing something awful.

Still, it wasn't until she reached Methuselah's trough in the grazing pasture that it struck her—something else was going on. Methuselah paced the fence, bobbing his roan head, the wild whites of his eyes scanning the horizon.

Hannah reached an arm under and around his head, stroking his muzzle. "Hey, boy," she said, following his gaze to the field path Danny had always walked home on, whistling up a storm.

The only thing that whistled now was a rogue gust of wind, setting the cotton to bobbing eerily in the darkening sky.

"He's not coming, boy." Hannah felt the burn in her throat

as she spoke the words, resting her forehead against the horse's soft neck.

Methuselah trembled, and when a second gust of wind kicked up, he reared back.

That was when a cannonball sank right down into her stomach. She'd seen this behavior before. Back in '38—the year of the last big tornado.

Don't say that word. The old warnings of the townspeople whispered among the whistling cotton, sending a shiver up her spine.

Surely it wasn't a coming tornado. Surely not now. Still, that cannonball in her stomach seemed to grow weightier by the second. A scan of the horizon a few miles yonder showed the thick gray of a cloud aloft dripping its middle into a sickening funnel and telling her one thing: *run.*

She did. She ran from pen to pen, opening the gates, setting the animals to running. They knew what to do, and one girl alone wouldn't have time to get them all to shelter if she tried. She'd do them more harm than good. Being set free gave them their best chance of finding cover, with the tornado so close at hand.

But when she got back round to Methuselah's pasture and opened it, he slowed his stamping foot and hung his head. Still as a statue, but for the way his mane rippled and whipped in the growing gusts.

"Get on, boy," she said. "Go."

But he wouldn't budge. He looked again to Danny's ridge, still maddeningly empty. The church bells rang out from town with wild abandon, pealing the storm warning as far as they could possibly fling such news. Time was short.

"He'd want you to go," she said, her voice growing thick. "*Go,*" she said. But when he didn't respond to her prodding, her clicks, her signals to gallop and "git on," she knew it was time. She had to get to safety, too, and her only prayer was that if she left this gate open, he'd change his mind and flee.

But at the last second, just as she was about to go, she spotted his halter and lead. The same one Danny had used every day with him. Maybe if she tried that . . .

Quick as the lightning flashing over the Fishers' field yonder, she buckled the halter around him and led.

He did not come.

Rain from a purpling sky began to pelt her, driven in the growing wind.

"Please," she said, her voice cracking the embodiment of anguish she felt. How often had she prayed that word? Asked as a girl to take flight from this place. Begged for God to let Danny come home. Pleaded, then, for her brother's death to be untrue. And finally, after time had stemmed the flow of her wild grief, asked, as in the eye of a storm, for the honor of building Danny's cottage in his stead.

And now the plea flew from her again, embodying all of those desperate cries. "Please," she groaned, falling to her knees as her shoulders shook and her tears mingled with the pelting rain.

"Please," she whispered. To the horse—but more so, to heaven. For help. Direction. Salvation from this mire she knelt in, and the mire of her confusion in this life.

In the distance, she heard a voice fighting through the wind. "Hannah!"

She scrambled to her feet. Methuselah, too, stood at attention, his ears angled forward. A posture she hadn't seen on the gentle beast in years. And there, there on the horizon he'd watched with wild eyes, came the figure of a soldier.

Not Danny. But one with the same courage, the same strength of heart, the same compassion.

"Luke!" she cried, hope shooting through her whole being, straight down to her fingertips. She jumped, waving. "Luke!"

And he was there. Running full force, wrapping his hand around hers, around the lead, and bending straight into the force of the coming storm, horse plodding faithfully behind.

It was a blur then. The battle with the barn door as they pulled it open together, despite the angry protest of the fighting wind, and set the faithful old beast free inside. It was the best shelter for him, and he'd weathered tornadoes here before. But when she and Luke latched themselves inside, too, it was to see the view through the old knothole that the tornado was headed straight for them. Growing larger than life, its force tearing through everything in its path.

"We have to go," she said. "There's a storm cellar at the cottage. It's closer than Gran's house. If we go through the other door—"

Luke looked at her, his face a meeting of strength and desperation as his eyes drank her in. "Yes," he said. "*Go.*"

He made for the horse, and Hannah loved him for it. But she knew there wasn't time. "Come on," she hollered, the roar of the storm growing louder. "He'll know what to do!" It wasn't ideal—it would have been best if Methuselah could have stayed in the barn—but letting him run free was his last hope.

That phrase—*last hope*—pummeled her with as much force as the whipping wind. With a mighty burst out through the far end of the barn, the three of them flew. Methuselah dashed over the hill beyond the old oak. Luke yelled Hannah's name with more intensity than she'd ever heard from the man, his eyes wild as he pulled her to himself. A screaming force passing behind her pressed her into him, and she looked to see a rogue, shredded piece of a tin roof spin past the very spot she had just stood.

Their eyes met for an instant, both of their shoulders heaving. He took her hand, and they ran with everything they had for the cottage. Branches flew and wooden shingles catapulted and the air pressure around them dropped like a vacuum ready to devour them as they ducked and dodged and pressed on to outrun the impossible monster at their backs, the storm's out-cry so loud they could not speak, could not hear each other, until they'd reached Leven House, standing with its little turret and centered knob. Her heart hurt, thinking of it facing this, all of its carefully kept elements in dire danger.

It took them both pulling with every ounce of strength in them and more to open the storm cellar door. Luke held it, propping himself between it and the ground as Hannah dashed down the stairs and looked up in time to watch him leap. The door slammed shut with sickening force—and darkness swal-lowed them whole.

Ten

Luke knew this place. He had been here before. In the cold . . . in the dark . . . the thought of a soul named Hannah keeping him conscious.

Only—was he conscious? His head pounded something fierce, and an odd memory of something slamming in the darkness assaulted him. Had it been the plane? He'd been shot down, in the snow. The tree line of the Ardennes in the distance, silhouetted against the stars.

He opened his eyes and strained to see it, but saw only oppressive pitch black. Some great hollow howl sounded, a ravenous predator on the prowl.

He knew he was in the snow. But when he pictured it, it was a field of sun-kissed white fluff, not the diamond-dusted drifts of a barren Belgian winter.

Past and present wrestled as his mind waded through visions of war and visions of watermelon festivals. Of plotting out reconnaissance and plotting out footfalls of a dance with a girl in his arms.

"Hannah," he said into the darkness.

"I'm here." The voice was so sweet it rolled right into that tangle of consciousness like a beam of light.

It was the voice of the girl. The real, live, breathing and blue-eyed Hannah. Not the faceless pen pal he'd regarded . . . but the woman he loved.

"Keep well, Luke," she said. His words, on her lips. The ones he'd penned with his last ounce of energy on the brink of death—calling him back to life now. "You'll be just fine." And then, in a whisper, "Please, Lord."

He hoisted himself up to a sitting position and heard the strike of a match. It flickered into life, casting bouncing shadows around him. It was a small space—an unfinished cellar, by the looks of it. Hard-packed dirt on all sides, the spice of the damp earth bringing clarity to his muddled thoughts. Tendrils and gnarls of tree roots protruded from the corner nearest them. He ran his hand over them, trying to orient himself.

"We're under the cottage," he said, feeling the pinch of his forehead, the ache behind it. "Is—is that right?"

"Yes," Hannah spoke.

"These are from the old oak, then," he said.

"The Kissing Tree itself," Hannah said, doing something with the candle she'd just lit. Securing it to something. "I didn't realize its roots reached so far. Part of the reason for how small the storm cellar is. When we hit the roots, we stopped digging. Didn't want to harm the old tree, though I doubt anything in this world could do that creature in. It's a tree for the ages."

"It is, at that." It had ushered him beneath its branches, like some portal between the inn and the cottage, depositing him right in the middle of Hannah Garland's life.

He nodded, then raised a hand to his pounding head. "The tornado," he said. "Has it gone?"

Hannah turned, a single candlestick wobbling in its tarnished holder in her hand. She steadied it, inclining her ear toward the storm cellar door at the top of the steep wooden stairs.

"I'm afraid not," she said. "Sounds like it's still near. It won't be long, though, unless it changes course again." She paused a moment, grave concern etching her delicate features. "You took a fall, Luke. When the wind slammed the door on you. You were gone only a minute or two, but it was so loud." She neared, smelling of honeysuckle and sunshine and wind, kneeling beside him. Reaching up and running a thumb over his brow. "Are you alright? It must hurt somethin' awful."

Right now all he could register was pounding in his head, and pounding in his chest at her nearness. He would be alright, once he spoke what he had to say.

What he had to say. His hand flew to his shirt pocket, a sudden vision of the papers he'd carted like a fool from across the world being shredded to pieces by a Texas tornado.

His pocket crinkled in reply, and he dropped his shoulders in relief. Lifting his hand, he took hers from where it rested, still, on his face.

"Hannah," he said. "I—I know I'm not much for words."

She dropped her gaze, a smile spreading. That smile . . .

"We're a fine pair, then, aren't we? My mouth runnin' a mile a minute all the time. Gran says I should let you get a word in edgewise once in a while, and I know she's right."

Luke laughed. "I'd be glad if you never stopped talking, Hannah. But . . . there is something I should say."

She pursed her lips, nodding earnestly, her eyes wide as saucers. He wished he could take her in his arms and kiss those lips that liked to run a mile a minute with words. But first, his turn for words.

"I have a confession," Luke said. "When Danny used to talk about you—about the sister who stayed back home, kept the farm running, and was the lifeblood of this place—I never pictured you right."

"You pictured me? Well, do tell, Mr. Hampstead, what did you picture?"

"Someone . . . steady. Reserved. And . . ." He felt embarrassed for this, fearing it would embarrass her. "Someone much older than Danny."

"Ha! I don't know which of those is most preposterous. Although according to Oak Springs standards, twenty-four is well and solid in the spinster realm, so maybe you weren't so far off."

"That night I told you about in Belgium," he said, and shuddered at the thought of that biting, numbing cold. "Christmas Eve, when my plane was shot down. I nearly froze to death that night." He shook his head. No, it was more than that. "I *should* have frozen that night. By all counts. The doctors couldn't figure out, later, how I'd survived. All I know is, with the night so bright and the snow so cold and the village lights flickering like they were, I could only think of one person I wished to talk to." He drew in a breath, shuddering around the ache. The longing. "You."

"But—you hardly knew me."

He reached inside his pocket, pulling out that scrap of paper, scrawled with his frozen-fingered scratch. Placing it in her hands, he tapped it.

"I knew if I fell asleep—if I surrendered to the cold, that would be it. So I did the only thing I could think of to stay awake. I wrote to you."

Hannah held the paper, slipping both hands around it as if she'd just been handed a treasure of glass, and she meant not to shatter it.

"It's not much. I could hardly think—and could hardly move my fingers." He laughed dryly. "It took me all night to write those few lines. But it—that is, *you*—kept me awake. And that kept me alive."

She looked at him then, eyes welling with tears. "Can I . . . ?" She lifted the paper ever so slightly.

Luke nodded, the throbbing in his head beginning to quiet.

She opened the paper. Traced the words with tender touch. "'Dear Hannah,'" she said.

Luke straightened, alarmed. "You don't have to read it aloud."

Hannah shot him a look. "If you think that a man can carve a letter out of his very own frozen being and carry it by hand half a world away, and then build a *house* just so he can deliver it—and not have that letter be read out loud—then you are sorely mistaken."

He held up his hands in surrender, warmed by her proclamation.

She cleared her throat. "'Dear Hannah,'" she began again. "'How are you?'" She peeked above the top edge of the letter. "If I were writing to this man in return," she said, "I would tell him I'm just fine, thank you, thanks to the rescue work of a friendly neighbor man who saved me from a gargantuan tornado. Now, carrying on . . . 'I want to thank you. For so many things. For sharing your brother with us—the best friend I ever knew. For giving me a place to send the broken things of this world, for safekeeping. I don't know what you're doing with the sketches, but from all that Danny told me of you, I know they'll be safe. Honored, just by being cherished. Not a lot of people take the time to do that, you know. To witness broken places, and to take the time to simply see them. Remember them. It's a very hope-filled thing, you know. It matters, and I bet it seeps into every bit of your life, too. I don't know if I'll make it any farther in this life than tonight—'"

She broke off, her voice cracking. Her chin dimpled as she pursed her lips around unreleased tears. "Wish you'd tell this man not to talk like that," she said, sniffling around a manufactured laugh.

Luke shook his head. "He should've died that night, and he knows it. But he's thankful he didn't . . . and he has a lot more to say to the woman he was writing to."

She tilted her head, her golden hair a beautiful mess where it'd been pulled from her braided halo by tornado-force wind. What was it he'd labeled her in his head, when first he'd encountered her at the Feed and Dime? "Tornado girl," he muttered.

"Pardon?"

"That's what I called you when I met you, before I knew your name. You were blustering all over that store, handing me Jerry's snaffle bits and who knows what else, and I thought—*she's a tornado*."

She nodded. "Destructive, upending, chaotic, and leaving a wake of debris. Sounds about right."

"No. Not that. I just mean—you have a way of tearing through a man's life and ripping the gray sky away so the sun can break through. Since I came here, Hannah—knowing you, spending days with you, building something good and life-honoring with you—it's done something to me. When I left the Ardennes and the snow, I was frozen straight through. Stayed that way long after I'd rehabilitated, been transferred to different hospitals, been discharged and shipped back to a homeland where I had no home. I wandered into your town and you collided with me and it just cracked that ice clean away. You've been light, and warmth. You've been everything real. Honest and true. You have dreams bigger than the entire state of Texas, and I wouldn't be surprised if you were hiding wings in there somewhere, and might just break them out and fly off to bring that warmth to the rest of the world one of these days. But—"

He stopped, wincing at the pain in his head, the ache in his heart. He had laid out everything in him. For better or for worse, he had to finish that. "Could you finish the letter?"

Hannah watched him as if she meant never to tear her gaze from him, but nodded at last. Outside, pelting rain—or perhaps hail?—pounded upon the door, punctuating the sheer agony of unspoken truth. The storm door trembled.

"'I don't know if I'll make it any farther in this life than tonight, but if I do, I hope to thank you in person one day. Sincerely, Luke Ham—'"

Hannah swiped tears, which spilled freely down her cheeks. "I don't know any Luke Ham," she said, again trying to make light of her tears.

"That was when the townspeople came," he said. "When dawn broke. No time to write the rest of my name." He eased forward, taking her hands in his, catching her tears. "I should go back and fix that," he said. "I should go back and add a few important details, too."

Hannah sniffed, offering a half smile. "Oh?"

"I should write—*I hope to thank you in person one day. And every day, Hannah. I'm not much for words, but these words are very much a part of me, if you will permit me to speak them.*" He lifted a hand, breaking away from the imagined text of the letter and speaking the rest right here, right now, right between them. An offering of himself, just as she had given so much of herself into his life. "I love you, Hannah."

The hail stopped. The door lay still, all quiet but the beat of two hearts melding into one.

Hannah looked at him, stunned. Then shook her head, gesturing with the letter clutched tight in her hand. "But—I'm just me. And you're Luke Hampstead."

He smiled. "So you told me. And you're Hannah Garland."

"But you—I mean, I'm just—I mean, I just live here and burn biscuits and swing a hammer and make a general mess of things, and you—you—you fly those skies and dance to 'Stardust' and help Gran and basically save the world, quite literally, surviving snowstorms in Belgium and gathering up broken places for safekeeping, and I just—I don't see how—"

He watched those lips run a mile a minute. Felt the angst of her heart and cherished every bit of it—and in one motion, dearly hoped that in quieting one, he might quiet the other for her. He lifted a hand, smoothing those storm-swept hairs of hers, soaking in the feeling of holding this brilliant mind and tender soul—and he kissed her. Right in the middle of her stream of words, he kissed her and drank in her warmth and assured her, without a word, that in all the world, Hannah was his dream.

His hand cradled the back of her head as their foreheads met, their own silence joining that of the dissipating storm above.

Her fingers came up around his, lacing themselves into his in a weaving that would never be undone. "I love you, too, Luke."

He pulled back to behold her, candlelight dancing around her as if it had been drawn from the sky by the roots surrounding them and scattered in dust to light this moment.

Against all reason, Luke wished to stay here. Right in this moment, in the dark, holding Hannah Garland's heart close to his. For when they emerged . . . *please, God*. He didn't know what to pray. If the cottage was damaged—it would destroy her. He couldn't bear to think of it. Hannah, who had lost so much already.

And yet if it had withstood the storm, what reason could he give, now, for staying? The work was done. His job was waiting in New York. And without it, he had nothing to offer the girl who deserved the whole world.

Eleven

Hannah paused at the top of the cellar stairs. With one mighty push, she would have that door open, and there was no turning back from whatever awaited them. A quick look back at Luke showed the same trepidation on his face, though when he saw her looking, he gave a reassuring smile.

God bless that man. Bolstered, she took the plunge into the twilight above. As she turned in a slow near circle, her hand pressed to her heart, the ache of what she saw before her digging deep, so deep. Snapped branches strewn about like pick-up sticks. An eerie stillness lingered, air laced with the smell of thunderstorm mixed with fresh-cut grass, spiced soil, fresh lumber. All such comforting things, on their own . . . but in the wake of a tornado louder than a train and with a thousand times more force—they brought heaviness to the atmosphere.

The field that had glowed white in moonlight just twenty hours before—it was snapped. Ravaged. Cotton flung every which way, the only spinning it would ever know was that of a tornado.

The little victory garden Hannah had planted to the east of the cottage—plowed straight through, the picturesque white picket fence a sickening pile of splintered shards. Cornstalks and strawberries long, long gone.

In the middle of an empty clearing stood, eerily, the steps that once had led to the cottage. Leading, now, to nowhere. A sound escaped her, a breaking inside. Half groan, half cry.

She took a step, and her feet stepped on something hard. She bent to pick it up, smoothing dark soil from its white surface and straining to see in the dimming light.

"Leven House." She whispered the words etched before her, hands trembling.

Luke braced her hands with his, brushing the remaining soil away, plucking a rogue leaf from its surface.

They had pounded this sign to the house so securely, weeks before. She had penciled the name in careful script upon a plank; he had carved and burned the letters to stand the test of time. Their two sets of hands, set on this task that had somehow wrapped their hearts together, changed the course of everything. If that cyclone had managed to pry it loose from the cottage—then what had become of the cottage itself?

"I can't look," Hannah said. She heard the words come out of her mouth and detested the defeat in them. "But I will look," she said, squaring her shoulders, closing her eyes, turning to orient herself toward the cottage. Waiting a second to gather her courage. And just—just a second more. And maybe one more. Or two.

She groaned, hating herself for this weakness. "But I can't," she said.

And then a low, steady voice beside her, a squeeze around her hand that clutched the wayward sign. "But you must," it said. Was that—hope? Notes of hope, carrying that invitation to her heart. "Look," Luke said.

Slowly, Hannah opened her eyes.

There was the sky, coral purpling into post-storm gray in

that show of utter peace and unspeakable color that only follows upheaval. As if all the turmoil and chaos had lifted into the sky, its intensities wrapped in vivid light.

There was the top of the oak, peeking up beyond the cottage like fingers offering a timid, hopeful wave.

And there was the cottage. Standing. Its small turret and quirky centered doorknob and its welcome in a language she did not speak—waiting there, storm weary with shingles plucked from its roof and a window blown out. But looking right back at her, all the same, as if it and the land beneath them heaved a great sigh of relief that the storm had gone, and life remained.

On the ground beneath the turret, a plucky, endearingly off-key melody sounded, and she went to examine its source. A weathervane. Its arms a little bent, its song a little beaten, but spinning, slowly, with hope.

She picked it up, fingering a tag that had been tied on with a piece of twine and written in an oh-so-familiar hand. *To: Hannah. From: Luke. Given to me by a couple in Belgium from the remains of their stone barn . . . for your collection of keeping things.*

Tears welled and laughter sprang, a tempest of all her fears and joys together.

"Where did this come from?" she asked, sniffling.

Luke lifted a shoulder, his quietness returning. "Like it says," he said. "Belgium."

She socked him on the arm. "I mean right now," Hannah said.

"This was what I invited you to the cottage to show you tonight," Luke said. "But when I saw the tornado headed your way—I guess I dropped it when I took off running for you. Can't believe it's still here." Luke's arm came around her shoulder, pulling her close as they took in the miracle before them. "This is why I came to Oak Springs—to deliver this—and that letter."

Hannah turned to face him, tipping her gaze up to meet his and drink in all the unspoken words this quiet man was saying with this, the gift of his heart. His life.

"Thank you, Luke," she said, and sank into his arms, savoring the heart of a man who saw so much.

Twelve

September 1945

That hope-filled embrace stayed with Hannah in the days that followed as they and the rest of Oak Springs set homes and barns to rights. As they rallied to raise a new wall to replace the Fisher barn that had splintered away in the storm. As they cleared debris from the spring and waterfall, righted the waterwheel at the old gristmill, and righted wayward railings on the water tower. Methuselah often led the pack with his harness, pulling with all his age-old might. The old horse seemed to have been hit with a new wave of life after facing the storm. Hannah would never know what exactly had happened to him out there, but he'd returned two days later with a new vigor inside of him.

The list of reconstruction tasks was long, and full of items big and small. In quiet moments when they returned to the farm bone weary, she mourned the snapped ropes of the old swing beneath the oak. But with homes and structures and businesses needing attention, that was one task that would have to wait, and rightfully so.

It was hard work, the rebuilding. Soul-rending work, good

work, heart-healing work, this putting together of things lost. It seemed fitting that it had come just as the newspapers and radios both crackled with news of the war's final end. Great hope on the horizon, and great chasms and wounds across the landscape of humanity. There was work to be done.

It was the same goodness of work that the building of the cottage had been. And Hannah couldn't help thinking that it had kept Luke here a little longer, when he was set to leave Oak Springs for his big New York job. All the while, as she watched that man slip into Oak Springs life like one of the locals—holding up beams with the men, digging in the earth like he was a part of it, wiping his mud-streaked brow, and pausing to smile at her, a smile so deep it felt like he was offering her his very heart—an ache began to grow inside of her.

He was leaving. He had to. As much as he seemed a part of this place, there was a part of him that would never be at home with two feet planted firmly on the earth. She knew it as much as she knew herself, for wasn't she the same? The call of the sky, the way the clouds beckoned until she felt homesick—she could see it on him. But she could see a growing unrest in him, too. A sadness and silence whenever the topic of his leaving came up. The way he stopped to look at the For Sale sign in front of the old Whitlock homestead, the way he glanced back at her, and back at the sign, and up at the sky.

It broke her heart right in two. So when she returned to work at the Feed and Dime and picked up the post for Gran and Jerry on her way home one September night, she thumbed through the three envelopes. A smudged envelope marked in childish handwriting for "Grampa Jerry at the big hotel" tugged at Hannah's heartstrings, and she sent up a prayer that little Arnie could come soon to be with this man who gave every last ounce of energy in his wiry, wind-weathered body to bring him to a good life. She flipped past an issue of

Woman's Home Companion for Gran and stopped cold at the last envelope.

Addressed to Mr. Luke Hampstead, care of the Kissing Tree Inn. She had to smile at the incongruity of those two names together, for he was everything reserved and steady, the sort she was sure would save anything to do with *kissing* for an audience of just one. She recalled that kiss in the cellar, and what it felt like to be that one singled-out soul. There was something about Luke Hampstead that told her a kiss like that—a man like this—came but once in a lifetime . . . and when he gave himself, he gave every last bit of that deep-running man.

Then she saw the return address: *Pan American Airways.*

She froze in her tracks, right there in the middle of the dirt-packed road home.

"This is it," she said. "This'll be good-bye."

So when he met her coming up the road with an eagerness of a little boy, wrapped up in the form of a man, she smiled. She took his offered hand, relished the strength of it for what might be the very last time. Tried to muster happiness—and managed a smile as she asked him, before they parted ways at the drive, to meet her in an hour beneath the oak.

She would give him his letter. She would give him her heart, in the very most complete way she could: She would let him go.

Every step up the slow rise to the oak felt impossible and good, an hour later. She drank in the golden air, filling her courage coffers with visions of Luke soaring in the clouds. She could be a part of making that happen.

"You're going to fly, Mr. Hampstead." She practiced her line, which she'd planned carefully on her way through the tornado-snapped cotton field, trying *not* to think of the visual irony of it all. Wading through broken things with a broken heart to offer her broken hopes in order to give the man she loved flight. Life. *Leven.*

Her voice was all wrong. It sounded like a limp wet rag. She needed it to convey the fullness of heart she felt when she thought of him soaring. "You're going to *fly*, Mr. Hampstead," she said again, infusing strength into the words. But it still wasn't right. "Fly," she tried, on a quieter tone. "Fly!" she shouted, fisting the air with a small leap. None of it seemed quite right.

She reached the top of the hill and saw his silhouette there, bent like one of the branches, hovering over something. As natural as if he were a part of the tree itself.

"You're going to fly, Luke," she said, and this time, the smile on her lips was as sincere as it could be. He belonged up there as much as Danny had belonged to this land. Where she fit in all of it, she did not know.

The silhouette straightened and approached her. As he emerged from the shadows of the Kissing Tree, his smile washed over her with the answer: *with him. You belong with him.*

"I'm going to fly?" he asked.

"Oh!" Her eyelids flew open wide. "You heard that?" She gripped the letter behind her back, slipped it quietly into her skirt pocket. Not ready to let go just yet. Or ever.

"I have a question for you," he said in answer. "How would *you* feel about flying?"

"Me?" she said, her voice curving down around the word that made no sense.

"You. How did you put it? '*Up and up and up . . . to see all the world.*'" He led her into the gentle cover of the tree's canopy. It was another world, in there. A cathedral of light and green, shifting shadows and glancing sunrays, birdsong falling like rain. There, in the middle of it all, was the swing. Ropes repaired, plank securely tied. The place her dreams had once lived.

"You fixed it," she breathed, a smile overtaking her whole being.

He gestured to the seat as a gentleman might to a fine lady in a refined restaurant. "Care to fly?"

Hannah bit her lip. She shouldn't. She should do what she came here to do. Give him his final summons to the great far-off north, for surely that was what lay in the envelope. The war was over, thanks be to God. And those flights would be up and running as soon as the airline could manage, eager to beat their competition back into the air.

But he was behind her then, pulling the ropes back. Pausing for half a second as her breath caught—and releasing her into the sunlit air.

She gripped the ropes, face to the sky, soaking in the warmth and allowing herself to remember, just for a moment, that bygone dream of flight. Back and forth she swung, the billows of her skirts like ruffling wings as she gained height. And just as she'd done when she was young, she waited until that breathless moment hanging in the balance between upswing and down, right in that space where anything seemed possible, to open her eyes.

As she did, time slowed. The branch just out of reach was stark in the richness of its bark against the blue sky, but for one place where freshly carved lines revealed new, light wood. An etching of wings, and in the glorious space between, two sets of initials:

HG

+

LH

"But that's us," Hannah breathed. "That's—that's me."

And then, as if her words had severed a cord between her and the upward ascent, the hovering swing succumbed to gravity and swung down, down, down . . . where the sight awaiting her caused her to dig her heels in and stand, hand to her mouth.

Luke knelt before her on one knee, his expression one of utter openness and heartrending hope.

"Hannah," he said, voice husky. "My heart is yours. It's not what you deserve, not even close to being enough. But if you'll have me, if you can put up with the life of a pilot, if you maybe wouldn't mind even coming with me sometimes—because truth be told, Hannah, I can't tear myself away from you. Can't imagine tearing myself away from you to fly those skies, and if anyone belongs up there, soaring, it's you. If you could do with a life like that—"

"*Do* with a life like that?" Hannah's hand transferred to her heart. "Do you not know?"

Luke furrowed his brow, and she wished to kiss every doubt away from the contours of his handsome face.

"Luke, I would give anything for a life with you. But more than that—I'd give anything for you to have the life you were meant for. I came here today to give you this." She reached into the pocket of her skirt, pulled out the flight-wrinkled envelope. "They're ready for you. I know it."

He took the offered letter. Beheld it for a moment and shook his head. "That might be," he said. "But I'm not ready for a life without you. Hannah Garland . . ." He opened his palm, where a tiny glint of light danced up at her from a simple ring of gold. "Will you marry me?"

"Yes!" she said, then clapped her hand over her mouth at the embarrassing force and speed at which that word had come out. "I mean—I'm just me and you're you and I don't know if you've really thought this through, Luke, but if you think you can do with me at your side, then I—"

He was up then. Kissing her in a way that told her she'd been wrong all along . . . that his home wasn't in the lofty skies above these branches. It was, miracle of miracles, with her.

Epilogue

Christmas Eve 1945

"Dear Hannah."

Dear, dear Hannah.

Luke spoke the words, felt them engrave into the deepest parts of him, and halted. He remembered so vividly another night, one year ago, when he penned those words and held fast to the thought of this woman. She had saved his life then. God had filled his life with the gift of her since then.

And now, he had traded that star-studded, frozen sky for a shower of sunlight slipping through oak leaves that clung to their green, even in December. They stood together, hand in hand, heart in heart, beneath the great oak, before God and all these witnesses. Here, he would give everything he had, and ever would have, to her. In the two months that had passed since he'd gone to New York, their letters had flown across states at a dizzying speed, and engulfing length. Sketches from time to time, for old times' sake—but the quiet man had a deep-running well of things to say, it turned out, and Hannah happily continued to be a fount of words and joy. The time had simultaneously crawled excruciatingly by and flown at alarming speed, bringing him at last back down from the skies and to this singular tree and this moment in time.

It was all he could do to keep from reaching out right then and lifting the veil that happily did a very poor job of concealing the bright blue of her eyes, the breathless smile on her face. All he could do to keep from running his hand along that cheek of hers. He was fit to burst with gratitude, and the only way for it now was out. In words.

He repeated after the preacher, with solemn honor and deepest hope. "With this ring, I thee wed, and all my worldly goods I thee endow. In sickness and in health, in poverty or in wealth, till death do us part."

He nearly gathered her up in his arms on the spot when she began by uttering beneath her breath, "Great gumdrops . . ." and then letting the rest of the vows march out in her sweet voice, with all the conviction in the world.

Hannah and Luke Hampstead's hearts beat as one, there upon the ground where their story was embedded and held deep in the roots, and high in the branches above. Looking on through its wide-eyed round windows was Leven House, sunlight glancing on the windowpanes like a wink as the weathervane above the turret sang out a clear, bright song.

This was the house that had given their hearts a home . . . and now, with greatest hope and hardest good-byes, it was time to take flight. But they wouldn't leave without first doing for the house what it had done for them: giving the home . . . a heart.

Amid a whirlwind of dancing beneath and around the tree, Uncle Sarsaparilla's Orchestra—all four members—played "Stardust" with every bit of soul they could muster, and the couple pulled Jerry into the shadow of the cottage and handed him an envelope.

Onlookers—and being that Oak Springs residents loved one another's business as much as they loved one another, there were plenty of onlookers—would later tell how Jerry stuck a thumb under that envelope's flap, pulled out a paper, read it, and looked at them in confusion. How you could've tipped him over with a feather, he seemed that shocked. How his chin trembled somethin' awful until he took the newlyweds in his arms and squeezed them in a hug but good, and how he then demanded two things. That if he did this thing—if he indeed took up residence in Leven House, made it a home for his Arnie, a new life for them both, then they owed him two things: a good long visit every time they came across these parts or anywhere near . . . and a bag of snaffle bits, which an awestruck young airman had failed to deliver to him when he first came to town.

Luke happily did both. In the years that followed, every time they came to Oak Springs and stayed at the farmhouse, there were great pots of chili and bouquets of thistles on the old plank table; the occasional batch of burnt buttermilk biscuits, which Hannah plated up with her winking and squinting rendition of eyelash batting; Luke's ladling of his hearty gravy, concocted over the years as a companion to those biscuits to the cheer of every mouth; and a merry band of souls gathered in the kitchen of the cottage or farmhouse.

And as the "grown-ups" among them talked long into fireside tales of travel and home, Luke would watch his own young daughter slip away into the long grasses, chasing Jerry's grandson, who always held a sparkle in his eye and a fire in his heart for their girl. He watched from afar as their feet flew beneath those branches, fireflies dancing to light the way, and the boy would set the girl to swinging high in that sky.

His heart, and Hannah's, were full. Light dancing from above, roots plunging life through dark, and warmth all around.

Heartwood

NICOLE DEESE

To all those who have lost someone precious
and are brave enough to love again.
This story is for you.

The Lord is close to the brokenhearted;
he rescues those whose spirits are crushed.

Psalm 34:18

One

A tittering laugh sailed under the arch of the rose trellis and ribboned through twenty rows of alpine-white wedding chairs to where Abby Brookshire crouched in the west garden, tidying up from her meticulous pruning before guests arrived. With her hands full of trimmings, she glanced over her shoulder just in time to see today's groom sweep his blushing bride into his arms and plant a flirtatious kiss on her mouth. It was a display she'd seen countless times over the years, and yet it never failed to press against an emotional bruise that refused to heal, no matter how much time had passed.

As the photographer rotated around the blissful couple like paparazzi, capturing every angle of their magazine-worthy poses, Abby focused once again on the azaleas she'd been tending to. She had no doubt that all the pictures taken today at the Kissing Tree Inn would be stunning. After all, she'd been told most of her life that this particular wedding destination had once been voted eighth on the coveted Top Ten Most Romantic Venues in Texas.

But Abby knew a secret even the most intuitive bridal magazine editor did not. The magic found in Oak Springs had less to do with a romantic inn and everything to do with the nature surrounding it.

She brushed the dirt off her knees and stretched the stiffness from her back. Having been raised on the inn's twenty-six acres, her familiarity with each patch of grass and flowering plant was equal to that of the cozy two-bedroom groundskeeper's cottage she'd grown up in with her father. Even now, as she gazed over the expanse of manicured lawns and groomed walking paths, her recollection of the hide-and-seek games played in the bushes after school, and creek frogs captured on scorching summer days with the Malone boys, and applesauce jars stuffed with seedlings and planting soil were as vivid as they were visceral. And it was those memories, those past heartbeats of happiness and stability, that would keep her here forever. No matter how tempting the offer. Or how tempting the man who had dared to make such an offer.

Gingerly, she bent to pluck a twig from between a row of yellow tulips and tossed it into her wheelbarrow. She traipsed along the stepping-stones her father had laid nearly two decades prior, her trusty rubber half boots leading the way. Unlike most females in their midtwenties, Abby's shoe selection wouldn't fit the majority of social occasions attended by her peers. No, her fashion choices followed one simple motto: If she couldn't wear it in a garden, it didn't belong in her closet.

Mindful of the pre-ceremony photography session taking place on the south side of the property, she worked her way east, past the river rock water feature, a row of juniper trees, and the flowering golden dewdrops dotting the path to the creek—all locations that ticked like clockwork in Abby's mind: eight, nine, and ten. Her father had trained her to visualize the land like the numbers of an incongruent clock face: "*If you follow the sequence of the clock, no flower, bush, or plant will ever be neglected.*"

As she rounded the greenhouse and approached twelve o'clock on the property, her grip on the wheelbarrow handles tightened, as if by that action alone, she might prevent the one memory she wished she could forget more than all. But the ruggedly handsome face who appeared in her mind each and every time she reached the massive live oak near the front of the inn would be as impossible to erase as this century-old landmark would be to uproot.

The instant she stepped beneath the oak's sprawling branches, she jerked the wheelbarrow to a stop, her eyes straining to make sense of the scene before her. Neon yellow caution tape wrapped the circumference of the oak's thick trunk. A swaying branch overhead caused her attention to shift to the shadowy figure climbing high into the tree's crown.

What in the world? Abandoning the wheelbarrow, Abby jogged toward the man standing on the opposite side of the oak, the one dressed in a sleek business suit and taking pictures of the area with his fancy new iPhone. Bradley, the eldest son of the Malone family line—and the inn's newest owner—had become a daily test of patience for Abby.

"Bradley, what's going on?" She didn't bother with the formality he preferred while in earshot of their guests. He may be her direct boss now, but their childhood history made that easy to forget, especially when said history included him stranding her in this very tree without a ladder during the summer of her sixth-grade year. If not for Bradley's slightly older, slightly more attractive cousin tackling him to the ground until he apologized and retrieved the ladder, she might never have found the boldness to stand up to him. But Griffin had always been the Malone to push her to be more. Because Griffin had always believed she could be more. "What's with all this caution tape? And who's that up in our tree?"

He released a weighty sigh, as if the very thought of having to interact with his head groundskeeper exhausted him. "As I've already told Annette, incident reports are time-sensitive. Insurance adjusters don't wait on wedding ceremonies."

Ah, Annette. So that's why his mouth looked as if he'd been sucking on a sour candy for hours. Not only was Annette the best wedding coordinator in their town, she was also Bradley's ex-wife, an unfortunate combination for everybody employed at the Kissing Tree Inn.

"Wait, does that incident report have anything to do with the teen who fell and broke his arm last weekend? Because that was clearly his fault; he was the one who ignored the No Climbing sign and—"

"Doesn't matter," Bradley said, as if he were chiseling the words out of granite. "The inn is still liable for his fall. At least, that's what the stack of medical bills on my desk tells me." With a frustration that seemed ever present these days, he glanced up at the climber, who was tying off on a higher branch.

Abby breathed through her nose and tried to tap into the diplomatic tone her father had mastered in tension-filled moments. "Okay, well, while I can understand your frustration over the unexpected medical bills, you still have a responsibility to follow protocol." A conversation she'd had with him multiple times regarding the oak. "The county's Live Oak Protection Act is very particular about requesting proper clearance for climbers, and it's even more particular about hiring certified arborists only."

"I'm aware of the protocol, Abby," he said dryly.

"So then you're also aware that the fines for noncompliance can be upwards of ten thousand dollars?"

Since Bradley's parents had retired from the inn last year, there had been plenty of tighten-the-purse-straps budget meetings, especially when it came to anything he considered expendable or extraneous. Often, her groundskeeping budget fell into this category. She'd already had to switch to a lesser fertilizer, and her small staff had been reduced, not to mention her ignored requests for new gardening tools. So if he was upset about the costs of a broken arm, then a fine from the state wouldn't bode well for any of them.

"I won't get fined."

The arrogance in his voice heated her blood. "Being a Malone won't keep you from a citation. The rules are in place for a reason—to protect one of our town's most precious historical landmarks." The Malone family might be one of the most reputable families in Oak Springs, but not even they could outpower a more than one-hundred-fifty-year-old oak tree.

"He's certified," he continued.

"What?"

"My climber." Bradley flicked his hand north.

She squinted through the setting sun's glare. She didn't recognize the man's gear or his profile. "What company is he with? Because I've never seen that logo before." And Abby was fairly certain she knew every certified arborist within a ninety-mile radius of Oak Springs. *Not to mention the one arborist who moved far outside that ninety-mile radius two years ago*. But most importantly, Winston Hawks, the older gentleman who had serviced their tree since she was a young girl, was still back east, visiting his ailing mother. "And what exactly is this guy supposed to be doing up there, anyway? Our next pruning isn't scheduled until June."

Bradley closed his eyes and massaged his right temple. And something about that gesture reminded her of when they were kids, back before braces had fixed the gap between his two front teeth and before LASIK had fixed his nearsightedness. "Do you realize what could have happened if that kid's parents had decided to sue us?"

"Yes, but even if they'd tried, there were too many witnesses to—"

He continued as if she hadn't spoken. "And do you have any idea how much the average pruning invoice runs us on the oak these days? Or any of the extra costs associated with the specialty irrigation plans and climbing equipment for its unusual height and width?"

As he spoke, a branch snapped from somewhere near the top of the crown and pinballed its way to the ground, shattering upon impact.

"Well, no, but I—"

"We can't afford it. Not ten years ago, and certainly not now." His pause caused her to hold her breath. "The very preservation act you seem so fond of places one hundred percent of the financial burden on the property owner. And yet I have next to zero rights when it comes to making decisions about the property I own surrounding this tree, or regarding the tree itself. Not without facing a severe penalty."

Cold dread crept up her spine. "So what are you saying?"

"I'm petitioning the council for a removal."

"You're *what*?" Her voice was little more than a squeak, as if with that one pronouncement, he'd yanked all the fight right out of her. "A removal? But you can't . . . you can't do that." She wracked her brain for an argument, anything that might appeal to a stuffy businessman like Bradley Malone. "The inn is called *the Kissing Tree Inn*. It's integral to every part of your branding and one of the key reasons we're booked to capacity every wedding season. Every bride wants their picture taken right here."

"A name change is the least of my worries, and we have plenty of beautiful scenery to be photographed beyond this tree." He slipped his phone from his pocket and tapped furiously on the screen. "The wedding season is only three months out of the year—four at most. It's not what will sustain us." He leveled his gaze on her once again. "Guests will book with or without that tree looming in the background of their photos. The inn has over a hundred years of history in this town."

"As does *this tree*!" Fear like Abby hadn't known since the day her daddy told her of his prognosis flooded her heart. Though Bradley had complained about the high costs associated with tending the tree before, he'd never threatened to repeal the protection order, and he certainly hadn't threatened a removal. *A removal*. Just the thought of it made her sway on her feet. "*Please, please* don't do this." Her voice flexed with hidden emotion. "There has to be a way to keep the inn from financial hardship *and* keep the tree. We just need some time to brainstorm, to plan."

For a moment, the hard exterior Bradley had worn since his divorce last January seemed to peel back a layer, exposing a fleeting glimpse of the man she believed he could still become. But then he shook his head and shattered her hope. "It's too late. The repeal process has already started. I've hired an arborist I trust to provide the committee with a full health assessment report for the council meeting at the end of the month. If you have questions, you can direct them to him."

She swung her focus back to the small-boned man rappelling off the trunk. Why would Bradley trust a stranger with something so important? Had he paid this guy off somehow? She scrutinized the climber's shiny, unfamiliar gear—all of which spoke of a recent hire. It was that revelation alone that soothed the growing anxiety within her. This age-old tree wouldn't be taken down by someone so inexperienced. It wouldn't be written off by someone who lacked the respect for such a historic piece of nature. The town's committee wouldn't stand for it. And neither would she . . . no matter what it might cost her in the end.

From the youthful look of this guy, he couldn't have had his arborist certification for more than what? A month or two?

Absurd. She'd spent the better part of her twenty-eight years elbow deep in this soil, planting and pruning and experiencing the world through the gentle guidance of a master gardener who'd spent his life teaching her to respect God's creation. And while she might not be allowed to climb the protected oak herself, some out-of-town kid wouldn't tell her anything she didn't already know.

Because she *knew* this tree. The same way she knew every square foot of these twenty-six acres. This land, much like this old oak, was a part of Abby, an extension of her broken heart. And if she lost it, there would be nothing left inside her to keep on beating.

From somewhere not far behind her a throat cleared, and the familiar rumble of it sent tiny goose bumps racing down her neck and spine. She didn't need to turn around to identify the man who now stood at her back. Because he was the same man who showed up uninvited in her dreams. The same man who had kissed her in the greenhouse during a hailstorm on her nineteenth birthday. The same man who'd held her for hours the night her father had breathed his last breath.

And he was the same man she'd vowed never to give her heart to again.

Griffin Malone.

Two

Griffin had spent the better part of his four-hour drive from San Antonio to Oak Springs readying himself for this exact moment. Heck, who was he kidding? He'd spent the better part of the last two years readying himself for this moment. And while he knew that dropping in unannounced for a round of Ghost from Girlfriend's Past would smart a bit, it wouldn't come close to the permanent fracture Abby's rejection had caused when she'd shut him out of her life.

As if overnight, Abby had become an impenetrable fortress, hiding herself away from the world—from *him*—despite his best attempts to reach her. No matter what he'd said, she'd refused to hear the truth: He loved her too much to watch her waste her talent on the inn . . . and so had her father.

And while he knew showing up on her turf today with job orders from his cousin wouldn't be a surprise Abby would appreciate, it was quite possibly his only chance at closure. And closure, he realized, seemed to be the one thing he couldn't manufacture on his own. Building a successful arborist business? Done. Hiring reliable employees? No problem. But letting Abby go while the promises he'd made to her dying father remained unfulfilled?

Impossible.

On the long drive over, he'd prepared himself for the sight of Abby's sleek, sunbathed skin and her dark walnut eyes. He'd forced himself to remember the lone spattering of freckles that arched the bridge of her nose and highlighted the tempting peak of her top lip. But he'd failed to prepare for what the sound of her voice would do to him. Because she wasn't just speaking, she was pleading. For the life of this tree, much the way she'd pled for the life of her father the day he'd decided to stop treatments.

Griffin cleared his throat and shook the difficult memory away. He shoved his hands into the pockets of his work pants and stepped toward her, fighting against the invisible power of muscle memory that ached to pull her into his arms.

"Hey, Abby."

She turned around slowly, blinking him in as if she, too, was struggling to sort the past from the present. "Griffin."

He'd thought of a dozen opening lines, a dozen different ways to stay indifferent and unaffected—all of which evaporated the instant she spoke his name. It was the first contact they'd had since she'd told him off in this very spot. Nearly two years ago.

A distant part of him was aware of his cousin's impatient mutterings about "not having much daylight left" and something else about "finishing the report before Annette flies over on her broomstick and curses them all," but Griffin ignored him, too transfixed by the face he'd convinced himself couldn't possibly affect him after all this time. But he was about as good at self-deception as he was at giving relationship advice.

There was only so much Bradley and Annette drama he could handle in a single afternoon. A quota that had been filled in the first ten minutes of his arrival at the inn. Granted, he knew it couldn't be easy for his cousin to work in such close proximity to his ex-wife, but even still, Griffin had zero counsel to offer on how to get a stubborn inn owner and an eccentric wedding planner to see eye to eye on, well, anything. He had his own relationship woes to sort out with Abby, which was exactly what he intended to do with the time he'd been given here.

He smiled as he took in the beautiful woman in the green garden boots. "I see you still have Kermit."

Abby lifted the toe of her short rubber boot and gave a noncommittal shrug, even though the evidence of his handiwork—a humorous frog drawn in permanent black marker under her ankle—was still in place for the world to see. "They've still got a few years left in them."

He chuckled at that. Always the practical thinker, his Abby. Well, not *his* Abby anymore.

Bradley made another one of his aggravated huffs, and Griffin finally shifted his eyes from Abby to his apprentice, who'd just scaled down from the oak. Abby twisted to face the tree as well, her intoxicatingly familiar scent shifting downwind to meet him head on. *Torture. Pure torture.* He moved to stand even with her. *Better,* he thought. *But also, worse*—since now he could feel the heat radiating off her tanned arms.

He concentrated on the task in front of him like a doctor assessing an injury. It didn't take a certified arborist to determine that the tree had seen better days. Much, much better days. Days he remembered fondly. With Abby.

"So, you're the one he hired to write the repeal report?" Her voice shook ever so slightly as she spoke to him.

"The assessment report, yes."

She wouldn't look him in the eye now, her gaze fixed only on the tree. "I've scheduled all the services for the tree for the past two years and kept all the records. You can see the file. It's all there."

"I'm sure you have it all in order." After all, she was Arnie's daughter.

She dropped her voice to half volume, as if speaking to herself. "There's no sound reason the council will grant a repeal, not when we can prove it's healthy and strong."

He didn't miss the side-eye she shot him at her accidental slip of *we*. But yes, he had indeed caught it. Just like he'd caught her restless fingers playing an invisible piano solo on her hip. A nervous tic he used to tease her about in their teen years.

He removed his hat and ran a hand through his cropped hair. Maybe the action would reattach his brain to his skull. Because he hadn't come here to reminisce. He'd come for closure.

Exhaling, he plodded to the left side of the wide trunk, following the buckled root system that extended toward the foundation of the inn's screened-in porch. He frowned.

"It's all a tangled mess, boss," his apprentice, Jason, pointed out unhelpfully. "And the crown's not much better. Think I saw some blight on a few of the leaves near the top, too."

Griffin nodded stiffly, hoping the kid would take his silence as a cue to shut his trap. If only Jason's mouth had come with a mute option when he'd first hired him.

"Blight?" Abby's attention was on them both now. "No, that's impossible. I'm always checking for signs of sickness. And this tree isn't sick."

Griffin saw the instant Jason registered the beautiful woman speaking to him.

"Ah, so you must be Abby, then? It's a pleasure. I'm Jason." Jason's introductory handshake-and-grin routine was one Griffin had watched him use on many a female. But little did Jason know that Abby Brookshire would never be won by charm alone. "Well, ma'am, no offense, but the diseased leaves I spotted were up pretty high. So, unless you want me to give you a boost, there's no way you could spot it from down here." He looped his thumbs through the belt loops of his climbing harness and leaned back on his boot heels.

Idiot.

If Griffin could have thrown a tranquilizing dart right then, he'd have aimed it straight for Jason's neck.

"Jason, is it?" Abby asked in a tone that could have frozen the extra-hot drip coffee Griffin brewed for himself every morning. "How long have you worked as an arborist?"

"Uh . . . about five months."

"And how many century-old oak trees have you assessed in that time?"

Griffin muttered a choice word under his breath and shook his head. This wasn't going to be good. Abby rarely got worked up enough to speak her mind fully, but when she did, a man should be given a warning to take cover.

"This is my first, ma'am."

"Right. Well, that big, burly tree right there once weathered a tornado that nearly obliterated our entire town. It's stood tall through blazing August heat and frigid December ice storms. It's been abused and neglected and greatly undervalued throughout the years"—she shot a fierce look at Bradley—"but this tree has proven one thing over and over again: It's stronger than anything nature or man can throw at it. So don't think for a single minute that some little patch of blight you may or may not have seen up there will be what takes it down. Because it won't. It will heal, and then it will outlive you and your great-grandchildren."

Jason's gulp was likely audible to the early wedding guests arriving in the parking area behind Griffin's work truck.

"We're not making any official diagnoses yet," Griffin said pointedly at Jason. "We're simply taking in information. Lots of information." He held his palms out to her. "Nobody here wants to put a healthy tree in an early grave, Abby."

The instant it was out of his mouth he wished he could take the words back. *Stupid. So, so stupid.*

The tension crease between her eyebrows went slack, and there was little wonder where his careless statement had taken her thoughts, down a road paved with grief and regret. Griffin reached out his hand to—

Everybody jolted as a fiery comet with burnt-red hair, dressed in spiked heels and a tailored black pantsuit, broke into their group. Annette, Bradley's high school sweetheart and recent ex-wife, jabbed a finger in the direction of the wedding setup.

"I told you this had to be cleaned up by five. It's now ten after. There's a wedding starting in just over an hour, and strangely enough, the bride's family did not pay for this yellow murder-scene tape to be in the background of all their ceremony photos."

"Sorry, Annette," Griffin offered cautiously, giving his cousin a moment to collect himself—though he likely didn't deserve one. "The delay is my fault, but I promise we'll have the whole area cleaned up shortly."

Immediately, the fierce redhead switched her southern charm to ON and grinned up at Griffin. "Which is exactly why you continue to remain my favorite ex in-law." Her shrewd eyes flicked to Bradley and back. "If only chivalry was passed through bloodline." She reached up to pat Griffin's cheek, which was quite the reach considering she barely hit the five-foot mark. "Success looks good on you, Griff. I always knew you'd make it."

He dipped his head in thanks, noting the flicker of interest that crossed Abby's face. "Thanks."

Annette's gaze drifted to the only woman Griff had ever loved. "Oh, and, Abby, before I forget, that keepsake you created for the bride's late mother? It. Was. Stunning. Everyone in the bridal suite had to get their eye makeup redone before we could start pictures."

"I'm glad she liked it." Abby's humble nod was indication enough that whatever she'd created was obviously something meaningful.

How long had it been since he'd seen Abby's full talents on display? Far too long.

Annette's charm dimmed to gray as she turned back to address Bradley with all the warmth of a striking cobra. "No more tacky caution tape while there's a paying wedding party on the premises. Get it taken care of."

Bradley's face reddened. "It's a liability to have the tree exposed to the public, Annette. We've already discussed that."

"And as we have also discussed, I will make a formal announcement during the reception. I've got it covered. Remove the tape."

The air crackled between them as they all waited for Bradley's response. He waved a hand at Griffin and spoke in a sharp staccato. "Fine, get this stuff cleaned up. We'll start fresh in the morning."

Without another word to each other, Bradley and Annette stormed off in opposite directions. Fitting.

"Aye, aye, Captain," Griffin mumbled as he searched for his employee to put him to work. Not shockingly, Griffin spotted Jason several yards away, speaking to a giggling young woman in a bridesmaid dress. Also fitting.

"I hope your little Romeo over there is better with the ladies than he is at tree work." Abby's words dripped with sarcasm.

"Listen." Griffin faced her. "Jason may not be the most socially aware at times, but he's a good kid. Dependable and honest. One of the best recruits I've had thus far."

She gazed up at him with a curiosity that made his blood thicken. "And how many is that?"

"Employees? I have five that are full-time now. Most are back near San Antonio, finishing up some storm work."

She glanced at some point he couldn't identify in the property beyond them. "I heard that was a big one out there."

"It was." And so was the paycheck his company had collected. But it wasn't trees or storms or even his growing business that he wanted to discuss with Abby. This wasn't the conversation he'd been rehashing in his head since the night they'd spread her father's ashes. "How 'bout I buy your pizza tonight so the two of us can . . . talk."

"My pizza?"

"Yeah," he answered confidently. This was an Abby Challenge he could win easily. "Your favorite Veggie Delight on thin crust with added salami and double pineapple. The same pizza you order every Saturday night during wedding season."

A reluctant smile sneaked onto her mouth as she crossed her arms over her chest. "Who says I haven't changed my order?"

"Fifty bucks says it's still your standing order and that it's set to arrive at six thirty sharp."

Something like defeat crimped her brow before she dropped her attention to her grass-covered boots. "You really should have called first. I hate surprises."

"I know you do." He lowered his voice. "But I can't say that I've been the biggest fan of your voicemail, either." And they both knew that's exactly where she would have sent his call.

She bit the corner of her lip, guilt clouding her features.

There were a lot of things he owed her an apology for, but showing up today wasn't one of them. "All I'm asking for is a slice of pizza. Possibly two." He didn't take a step toward her; he simply remained where he was, willing her to accept his offer. "What do you say, Bee?"

For the longest time, she said nothing at all. He could only guess at the battle happening inside her head right now, the weighing and analyzing of all her options.

When she finally lifted her twinkling eyes to his, his breath stilled. "I'll tell Freddie to add an order of cheesy bread for you. Don't be late." And then she turned and started for the stone-paved path he'd laid with her father the first summer he'd worked at the inn.

He studied the way she strolled over each smoothed stone, her hips swaying side to side in a cadence he'd memorized long ago, the same way he'd memorized the flutter of her short hair against the nape of her neck in the breeze. A familiarity that sparked something inside him to question his original motive for coming today.

Because maybe he hadn't only hoped for closure with Abby. Maybe, he still hoped for a second chance. To keep his promise to her father.

And maybe, just maybe, to win her back.

He stuffed two fingers in his mouth and whistled for Jason. They needed to get this area cleaned up. And then he needed to duck into the back of the cab of his truck and change into a clean flannel. If he only had one evening to spend with Abby Brookshire, he wouldn't waste a single moment of it.

Three

The instant the front door of her cottage latched behind her, she collapsed against it, her legs shaky and unwilling to support her for another minute.

He was here. Griffin. *Her Griffin.* In Oak Springs. And in less than an hour's time, he'd be at her door and then inside her home and then sharing in her veggie, salami, and pineapple pizza . . . which he'd remembered perfectly.

Her breath came out in short, uneven pants, her chest rising and falling at an unsustainable rate. She squeezed her eyes closed. How had she forgotten the intensity of his gaze? His face? His . . . well, his everything. Her memory should be fired. Its one and only job was to recall such details accurately. And today it had failed at an epic degree. For nearly two years, she'd been dreaming of Griffin through a hazy lens. But staring into those fern-green eyes tonight while he said her name . . . it was all too much.

Too much.

Gahhh. "Stop it, Abby! Pull yourself together." She glanced at the clock on her microwave. She had forty-five minutes. She looked down at her work clothes and gave a self-deprecating laugh. Who was she kidding? All she had in her closet was more of the same. Tired cotton T-shirts and faded work jeans.

She trudged to her bedroom, cursing herself for never taking Annette up on a single one of her shopping invitations, and slipped out of her gardening attire. She reached into her closet and selected a clean shirt—blue it was—and then tugged on a fresh, but certainly not new, pair of light denim pants.

Abby doubted Griff had any expectation that she would have transformed into some kind of fashion diva since their breakup, but the thought sparked a wandering trail in her mind . . . starting back at his fancy new work truck. And then to his shiny climbing gear and Asolo boots. And then to his confident demeanor as a boss of five employees. He'd done exactly what he'd said he would do when he left Oak Springs, and Abby, well, Abby had also done exactly what he said she would do, too . . . she'd stayed exactly the same. She shoved the condemning thought out of her mind the way she often did, and made a quick call to Galaxy Pizza to update her order.

After running a brush through her short hair and swiping some unflavored lip balm across her lips, she added a few strokes of who-knows-how-old mascara to her eyelashes. Somehow, even after all that, she still had fifteen minutes to spare.

She glanced around the front room for something to tidy, but there wasn't much to clean in this little cottage for company's sake. Living alone had turned her into even more of a minimalist. She ate on the same plate—to avoid having to wash multiple dishes—used the same silverware, coffee mug, and the occasional wineglass. The only knickknacks in the cottage lived on the mantel above the fireplace: trinkets her father had crafted out of fallen branches around the property when she was in middle school.

But she had loved this old cottage—rich with history from her father's ancestors, the cottage had been passed down to her dad, Arnie Jr., as a wedding gift, which had been enjoyed by her parents until just two years after Abby's birth, when her mother had fallen asleep at the wheel after working the night shift as an on-call nurse. Her mother had died in that car accident, a tragedy so unexpected it had formed an unbreakable bond between her and her father, one she never thought could be broken . . . until death had come again.

Her father had wanted to keep everything in the cottage the same as it had been before her mother passed away—the welcome sign on the outside of the house carved in French that only the sharpest eyes could detect as reading *Bienvenue*, the strange middle-of-the-door doorknobs all throughout each bedroom and closet, and the miniature turret on the left side of the cottage that her father teased was built for royalty. And much like the exterior, the interior of the home hadn't changed much either.

She glanced to the petite staircase leading to the loft. Just beyond the small Dutch door was her favorite place to think and reminisce: the wraparound balcony. From up there, she could view nearly the entire property.

The knock at her door released the anxious butterflies she'd been holding back for two years.

She exhaled and pulled open the door to her past.

Griffin's eyes softened on her immediately. "Blue's always been my favorite color on you."

Before she had a chance to contemplate if she'd chosen the blue shirt for him consciously, he extended a single fuchsia saucer hibiscus from behind his back. She recognized the picture-perfect flower immediately, from the shrub near the inn's front porch.

"It's a good thing you didn't let the gardener see you pick that—I hear she can be fairly particular about her hibiscus shrubs."

The right side of his mouth ticked north as he stepped inside her home. "I was hoping she might take pity on me since I couldn't show up at a pretty lady's door empty-handed."

"I thought you were just here for my good taste in pizza."

"I am."

Oh, he so was not. She didn't know what all Griffin had done to himself in the hour they'd been apart, but it was entirely unfair that a simple flannel change could dial up his appearance by a factor of ten. And why did he smell so . . . so . . .

"Are you wearing cologne?" Her question was far too abrupt to be considered casual. *But when had he started doing that?*

"Oh, uh . . . yeah." He shrugged as if he'd been caught doing something wrong. "One of my temp guys left it in my truck before he moved back to Oklahoma. You don't like it?"

"I didn't say that, it's just . . . I don't know. You'll always smell like trees no matter what you squirt on your shirt. Nature's in your DNA."

A cheeky grin snaked onto his face as he stepped into her little house and crossed into the living area. "Hate to break it to you, Bee, but it's in yours, too."

She worked to ignore the warm rush of familiarity his nickname caused her and gestured for him to choose a seat in the living area. The choices were limited—a small sofa and an armchair with more history than a library could contain.

Griffin stood for a minute, saying nothing as he faced her father's old leather recliner. "Wow." He cleared his throat. "I'd forgotten about Arnie's chair."

She didn't move, unsure if his statement meant he wished to sit in it or avoid it altogether. That was the strange thing about grief: Sometimes you wanted to wrap yourself in it like a thick winter quilt, and other times you wanted to throw the blanket to the ground and pretend you wouldn't be cold without it.

He started toward the chair and then hesitated. "Do you mind if I . . . ?"

"Not at all. You loved him, too." The words came out so freely, so naturally, as if that particular truth had been waiting to leap off her tongue since the moment she'd seen Griff out by the oak tree. The rest of the truth was that her father had loved him, too. Deeply. Like a son.

With a reverence that caused the tip of her nose to tingle from oncoming tears, Griff lowered himself into her father's chair and rubbed his hands along the worn cracks running the length of both arms—those threadbare places her father used to rest his elbows after a long day of working the land. She could still see him there, balancing a book on his lap with his head resting on his open palm. And then, without fail, his breathing would deepen and his heavy eyelids would surrender to sleep. His elbow would dig into the leather, slipping inch by inch until he woke to re-situate himself every few minutes, refusing Abby's suggestions to go take a nap on his bed.

Griffin remained quiet, pensive, and she wished she could tap into his mind and peek inside his memories. What she wouldn't give to capture a piece of her father through someone else's lens. "I think about him often," he said.

She sank into the sofa cushion, the bones in her legs suddenly more liquid than solid mass. Discussing her father with Griffin danced dangerously close to the topic of their last conversation, one she hoped not to revisit any time soon.

Their gazes collided. "I think about you, too, Bee. All the time."

And there it was. He'd been inside her home for less than five minutes, and this was where they were again. Right back to where they'd started—trapped inside a revolving door without an exit strategy.

"Griff." She shook her head as a familiar sadness crept up her throat. "*Please*." But there was no request that followed her plea. Her excuses for shutting him out had dried up long ago, as had her anger toward him. And perhaps the emptiness she was left with now was worse than either.

He pushed to the edge of the chair, his focus honed on her face. "Do you have any idea how many times I talked myself out of showing up here after I left? I guarantee it was a lot more than the forty-eight unanswered texts I sent you. Or the thirty-two times you sent me to voicemail." He exhaled and raked a hand down his face, no doubt replaying the awful things she'd said to him the last time they'd spoken. She replayed them, too, often. And yet, nothing about their situation had changed. Not really. Griffin had coped with his grief by living out his dreams far away from Oak Springs, while she'd chosen to stay in the only place that would ever feel like home.

He continued. "Losing Arnie and then losing you only a few months later was . . ." He shook his head and let out a short, self-deprecating laugh. "I'm fairly certain my tree work was the only thing that kept me sane."

The admittance was as shockingly raw as it was exposing. Their breakup had been complicated, a tangled mess surrounding the most devastating loss of her life. Yet she'd loved this man once—more than she could ever imagine loving someone else in the same way.

I'm sorry. I'm sorry. I'm sorry.

The phrase repeated over and over in her mind as Griffin continued speaking as if her living room was a confessional, as if he needed to say the words more than he needed her to hear them. "Despite everything that's happened between the two of us, when Bradley called and asked me to assess the oak . . . I couldn't say no." He paused, then released a breath. "And I want to believe I made the right decision."

Bantering with Griffin was much easier than where this conversation was headed—far more detached from all the tender places he was pressing on now. But this was the role he'd always played in their relationship, the strange sort of magic he possessed. No matter how hard she fought to hide behind locked doors, he never failed to break through the deadbolts of her heart in record time.

She didn't know how to answer him, or if there even was a question to be answered in what he'd just revealed. But as soon as she felt brave enough to open her mouth and utter a response, Freddie the pizza man was at her door.

"Abby? You in there? Pizza's here," Freddie hollered from her front porch in his usual unfriendly tone.

On legs that didn't feel quite walk-ready, she stood and started for the door, but Griff beat her to it. "I've got it."

Looking as bored as ever, the late-twenties college dropout wore his usual hunter-orange ball cap and a faded black T-shirt with a giant pepperoni pizza smack-dab in the center of the Milky Way. He presented the box to Griffin without hesitation, as if Griffin opening her front door was as routine as her Saturday-night order. "That will be eighteen eighty-two."

"I have cash ready right here," Abby said, swiping the money she'd left on her counter for just such a delivery. But once again, Griffin had already reached into his wallet, pulling out several crisp bills and handing them to Freddie.

"Uh . . . thanks," the chronically bed-headed employee uttered, glancing at the cash in his hands.

"You're welcome. Have a good night, Freddie," Griffin said as he shut the front door, armed with the pizza and cheesy bread.

"You really didn't need to do that," Abby said, trying to soften the edge in her tone. She might not have much to show for these last two years, but she could certainly afford to pay for their pizza. Truth be told, her savings account told her she could afford a lot more than that, but like usual, her inheritance was as untouched as her most secret of dreams. "I'd planned on paying."

"That makes two of us, then." He readjusted the boxes in his arms and winked. "Now, where we headed with these? You still use your balcony like a viewing platform?" The twinkle in his eye deflated the tension building in her chest.

"Who needs reality TV when you can watch it live from your own backyard every weekend?" She'd witnessed many a town drama from her cottage balcony—groomsmen fights, secret rendezvous, and a few shady business deals.

"Lead the way."

She gathered the plates and utensils and napkins, as well as some soft drinks, and together they climbed the steps to the loft. Griffin ducked under the A-frame roofline the way he'd done since they were teens, and Abby pushed open the Dutch door to the balcony with a perfect view of the inn's reception area.

Abby set the plates and other items on the small oval patio table and made room for Griffin to add the steaming boxes. She opened the top lid, comforted by the sight of a pizza she'd been ordering for more years than she could recall. In her mind, there was no better combination—plenty of the veggies she loved with her favorite choice of meat topping, and the pineapple added the perfect balance of sweet to the mix of savory.

Griffin trailed to the edge of the landing and craned his neck to the left to glimpse the ceremony site. "Looks like they just finished taking communion. The party should be kicking off soon." He moseyed back to the table and pulled out a chair for her.

"Thank you," she said, handing him a soft drink before they sat down across from each other.

"So, what's the inside scoop on tonight's bride and groom?"

"Um, well, they're a couple from Georgia. They booked over a year ago through the website after they fell in love with the setting."

"Kudos to you," Griffin said with a smile.

"Hardly. I just maintain what's here." What her father had dreamed and created at the inn decades ago. "Go ahead, you're probably starving." She gestured to the pizza box, but Griffin shook his head.

"Ladies first, always."

She lifted out a slice, focusing intently on the stringy mozzarella instead of the rush of heat to her cheeks at his chivalry. As Griffin helped himself to pizza, she continued on. "That's been happening more and more actually—the inn bringing in out-of-staters. Bradley's thrilled of course, says his new marketing manager in Dallas is a genius." She picked at an olive, her stomach souring at the thought of all the changes Bradley had made since her father's passing.

"Sounds like the inn could use all the business it can get." He took a greedy bite of his pizza and groaned approvingly. "Mmm. Just like I remembered it."

Her polite smile fell flat. "I'm not so sure about that. The way Bradley talks about expansion plans for the future, I think the inn's doing better than he's letting on." She wiped her fingers on her napkin, her mind immediately circling back to the tree. "What do you really think about it, Griff? The live oak."

He took another bite, likely a strategic delay to give him a few extra seconds. But he always told it to her straight—sometimes too straight. "I'll need to climb it myself to get a better read on what's going on up at the crown." He paused. "But I do have some concerns. Not only about a possible blight . . . but about the irrigation system, too." Though Griffin's words were said softly enough, the impact of them was anything but.

She leaned back in her chair, wracking her brain for how she could have missed that—had the tree's irrigation been in distress for long? She walked by that tree at least four times a day. How could she possibly have—

"Stop," he said. "None of this is your fault."

Her eyes shot up to meet his. "But I should have seen if there were changes to—"

He shook his head. "You aren't responsible to see every little thing that happens on these twenty-six acres."

"But anything you find is a point for Bradley to plead his case to the council."

Ever the diplomat, Griffin's face held steady. "I won't smudge the truth to make it sound better than it is, Bee. Nor will I smudge it to make it sound worse."

A fact she knew better than most. She locked her jaw in place, refusing to be the first one to break eye contact.

A loud cheer cut through their stare-down, followed by the accompaniment of a live band and a pronouncement that Mr. and Mrs. Collins had now joined the club of Happily Ever After. Over a crackling speaker, the guests were invited to celebrate at the reception site while the bridal party continued their wedding pictures. Several people made their way to the dance floor set up just a few hundred feet away. Among them, Griffin's protégé.

"Wait, isn't that . . ." Abby started, squinting to focus her eyes on a man who had just dropped into a full breakdance routine.

"Yep. That would be Jason. He dances more than any human has a right to." The humor in Griffin's voice warmed the chill between them. Obviously, his care for the kid stretched beyond the standard employee-employer relationship.

The DJ mixed a pop song with an aggressive beat that had guests gathering around the floor, clapping and cheering for the wedding crasher spinning against gravity on the toe of his dress shoe. Jason had the build of Toby Maguire and the confidence of a shirtless Matthew McConaughey. Abby couldn't help but giggle at his comedic antics and the way he involved the onlookers. Several guests joined in on the fun, and Abby felt her own face break into a smile when she noticed the groom laughing as he snuck glances at the party going on across the way.

Soon enough, the crowd broke and the music changed once again to something swoony and sweet as the DJ announced the grand entrance of the bride and groom. It only took three-point-five seconds for everyone to scurry toward the buffet lines, including Breakdance Jason.

With a fresh quip about wedding buffet manners on her tongue, Abby refocused her attention on Griffin, only his gaze was already resting on her face. "It's good to see you smile again."

And just like that, she didn't feel like smiling anymore. She felt like crying—all those tears she'd refused to shed since the night she'd told Griffin to take his offer and his plans and leave without her.

Four

Much the way Griffin knew Abby could identify the exact location of the hibiscus he'd picked from the front shrub, Griffin could identify the meaning behind every one of her smiles. Not so long ago, he'd been the leading consumer of them. But the sweet, spontaneous smile that had graced her mouth a mere moment ago as she'd swayed to the DJ's beat had since returned to the sorrowful curve he could trace in his sleep.

"How've you been, Bee?"

Those big brown eyes darted back to his, and once more, he fought the urge to touch her. To draw her close. To erase the last two years of rejection and regret and work to embrace the reality they'd been left with: a life without Arnie Brookshire, the only man he'd ever considered a true father.

He clamped his hands together under the table and waited for her to answer.

"I've been . . . okay." She pursed her lips together, as if that was the only adjective she could drum up. "But I know what you must be thinking." Doubtful, considering she was often oblivious to what he thought about her. Or how much.

He leaned back in his chair and crossed his leg over his knee. "Yeah? And what's that?"

"That everything here is just the same as when you left—but it's not."

He could sense a list coming his way. Abby was an excellent list maker.

"Once the wedding party leaves tomorrow, you should take a walk around the place. We reworked the landscaping near the walking bridge at the creek, and last fall we expanded the pond to almost double its size. Oh, and did you see the new perennial garden I planted near the west lawn?"

"I haven't, but I'll be sure to take a tour."

She nodded once and then absently pressed her fingertips to the glass tabletop in a way that would have made every church organist in Oak Springs proud. "How about you? Has the storm chasing been everything you hoped it would be?"

How could he possibly answer that? Nothing was as he hoped it would be without Abby by his side. But he knew not to say that out loud. Pushing her too hard, too fast was a lesson he'd learned the hard way. "All things considered, the storm business has gone better than expected. Arnie's generosity played a big part in that."

She glanced up at him. "He'd be proud of you."

A sentiment that meant more to him than he could ever express. "I sure hope so."

Abby pulled her knees up on the chair and wrapped her arms around them as if to warm herself, though it had to be at least seventy-five out. She was a Texan through and through. "What's next for you, then? More employees and expansions to new cities?"

"I'm not sure, actually." Only, yesterday, he'd been quite sure. The adventure of chasing storms had always thrilled him. New places, new people, new challenges of how to fix the damage done by raging rain and wind. Yet somehow, sitting here, with a woman who felt as familiar to him as the trees he'd been groomed to climb since boyhood, brought more into question than he was prepared to ask himself.

A glint of silver caught his eye at the corner of the balcony, and without hesitation, he pushed out his chair and moved toward it to get a better view.

Abby was up on her feet in an instant. "Oh, that's not . . . it's nothing. Just something I play around with from time to time."

He cocked his head to the left and then to the right as his fingers grazed the beautifully sculpted miniature garden scene before him, complete with succulents, moss, river rock, and reflective glass in the shape of a tiny pond. Several figurines in fairy form gazed into the still water. "You made this?"

"It's not finished yet."

He smiled at her evasion. "That's not what I asked."

He could almost feel the heat spreading down the thin column of her neck. "It's a hobby more than anything."

Which meant this wasn't her first creation. Not by a long shot. He studied the intricate details of the miniature garden and then remembered something Annette had said earlier that afternoon. "Is this what Annette meant about you creating something for the bride's mother? Some kind of keepsake?"

Again, Abby squirmed under his gaze. "It wasn't exactly like this one, but a similar idea, yes. Minus the fairies." She took a second before continuing on. "A few weeks ago I heard that today's bride had recently lost her mom to cancer, and I wanted to create something special for her—a memory garden that would resemble the inn's venue on her wedding day. I added a rock with her mother's name and dates, along with a little note that she was here in spirit even though she couldn't be here in body."

Griffin's chest tugged at her words. "You make . . ." He searched his mind for a description. "Memorial gardens?"

She nodded. "I guess you could call them that, only not everyone I give them to has recently lost a loved one. Sometimes I just make them to brighten someone's day. This one is for a teen girl who broke her leg during her first soccer game of the season." She paused and picked up one of the fairies to reposition it closer to the miniature pond. "It's become a therapy of sorts for me—when my work is finished on the grounds and my hands are still in need of something to do, I make these."

Just one of the many differences between them. Griffin spent his time tearing out the old, dying, and dead, while Abby spent her time planting seeds with the hope of sprouting new life. "So, you just . . . give them away after you make them?"

"People have offered me money for them, but I don't feel right about taking it. I don't look at these like a business for me or anything."

"Yet it could easily be one if you wanted it to be." This wasn't some kid's arts and crafts project. This was original art. And it was as fascinatingly unique as Abby herself.

"Nature has always provided me a peaceful escape on my hardest days, and I wanted to give that gift to others, even those who've never handled potting soil a day in their lives. These gardens are easy to care for and tend to, and they can be kept indoors." She shrugged and began to shake her head in that stop-making-such-a-fuss way of hers. "Again, this isn't a big deal, they're just—"

"Beautiful," he finished. "I want to see more." He glanced around the balcony, searching behind the stack of chairs in the corner. "Where are you hiding them?"

She laughed, and the sound was sweeter to his ears than the acoustic medley coming from the reception tent below them. "I don't have any more. Not here, at least."

He raised an eyebrow. "So just how many more handcrafted

masterpieces has one Abby Brookshire made for the residents of Oak Springs?"

A humble shrug that led to an even more humble estimation. "Somewhere around fifteen or so, maybe."

"Then I'll be on the lookout."

With their gazes still locked, they fell quiet once more as a song pulled him into a memory he knew neither of them could pretend to have forgotten. "*Dream a Little Dream of Me*" crooned in the background like a moonlit serenade of their past, back to a time when all seemed right with the world. When Griffin had pulled Abby close and danced with her in the grass under the sprawling branches of a tree they loved. He'd kissed her for the first time that night, promising himself it wouldn't be the last.

Abby was the first to look away.

"I can't save that tree on my own, Bee." He stepped closer to her, mesmerized by the light of a waning moon on her left cheek. "After that boy broke his arm last weekend, Bradley's case for a repeal based on financial hardship has become pretty convincing."

"But his motivation is bigger than that, Griff. I know it is. Something's off. I think he just wants to use that land to expand the inn and fill his pockets."

"That land has been in his family for generations."

"Yes, but it belonged to our oak first, and it should be able to stay that way for as long as it's alive."

Griff dipped his head and released a long exhale. "I don't disagree with you, but I do think you need to prepare yourself for either outcome."

As if she could snap on determination like armor, Abby narrowed her eyes at him and spoke with a conviction that caused her voice to waver. "I'll do whatever I need to in order to save that tree, Griff. I just need you to promise me that you'll do the same."

Five

Abby listened intently for the whir of Griffin's chainsaw to halt, knowing his warning shout would soon echo through the inn's property. Sure enough, it came only a moment later as a freshly cut branch pinballed its way to the ground and broke into four large chunks upon impact.

Jason, who'd shown up at the tree this morning looking like he'd been dragged behind a semitruck for the better part of a week, was not nearly as energetic as he'd been on the dance floor last night. If the dark circles under his eyes were any indication, the kid had been out much, much later than his boss, who'd said good-bye at her door without so much as a pat on the arm. But what had she expected from Griffin? A lingering hug? A good-night kiss? *Ridiculous.* That type of shared affection was ancient history between them now, had been for going on two years. Griffin wasn't here for a second-chance romance; he was here for a job, and she had no right to get in his way, no matter what kind of regret had surfaced in her since his arrival. He deserved to move on from her, to live and love and find happiness outside of this small town . . . and her even smaller dreams.

Jason gripped the largest of the splintered branches and dragged it over to the chipper, where Abby waited. "All clear!"

He leaned the branch on the back end of the machine and gave her a huge smile paired with a thumbs-up, indicating he was ready to load. Together, they slipped their ear protection on once again and worked to feed the growing pile of pruned branches into the open mouth of the chipper.

So far, things had been going as planned. Griffin had spent over an hour in the canopy of the tree, identifying unhealthy branches and pruning accordingly. Due to the vast expanse of the tree's crown, Abby estimated he'd still have at least a few days of work ahead of him in order to write a thorough report for the preservation committee. And though Bradley's patience was thin to begin with, Griffin wouldn't be rushed. He might be brutally honest, but he was rarely hasty.

She watched Griff climb to a new height, up several more branches, tying himself off and inspecting something too far away for her to make out. She'd forgotten how intriguing it was to watch him work in his element. So much of an arborist's job was instinctual. Of course, there were books, classes, and tests involved during the certification process, but as her father pointed out on many occasions, intuition couldn't be taught in a classroom. It had to be felt, fed most by time and experience.

Her father had seen that special intuition in Griffin early on. Even from that first summer when he'd shown up at the inn to live with Bradley's family permanently at age fifteen. Abby hadn't known then what all had gone wrong in his childhood home, or with his parents, but she'd heard enough rumors whispered of substance abuse and child endangerment to know it was bad. He confirmed these ugly details to her as their friendship progressed over time. Just a year later, his parents' rights had been severed and his visitations with them had stopped completely.

But Abby's father hadn't let him disappear into himself; instead, he capitalized on Griff's intrinsic affection for the great outdoors. Her father had recognized it as more than just a passing fascination of a city boy who'd been set loose on acreage, but rather as a love that seemed to grow and mature with age. Much the way her own admiration for all things nature had grown over time. To an outsider, Abby and Griffin's roles might seem opposing—him hauling away the dead and her nurturing the new—but ultimately, their goal was the same: to steward God's creation the best way they knew how.

As Jason fed more dead oak into the chipper, adding to the mound of fresh mulch and filling the air with one of her favorite aromas, her gaze settled back to the heavy foliage where Griffin worked. Something in her stomach grabbed as she watched him scale down, climb back into the boom of his truck, and lower himself to the ground. Tucked into his belt were several shoots sprouting a dozen or so leaves. The second he hopped off the platform, he unclipped his safety harness and headed straight toward her.

"What is it?" she asked, trying to decipher the expression on his face. *Not oak wilt*, she prayed silently. *Please, God, don't let it be the wilt*. Even the sturdiest of oak trees could be taken down by the aggressive fungus, and rarely did the costly treatments work in time. Her father had told her multiple stories of mature trees taken out by such a blight in as little as thirty days.

Griffin plucked a branch from his belt and held it out for her to inspect. "It wasn't easy to find, but Jason wasn't wrong when he said he spotted a blight. This is a rare variety, and one that typically only appears after a season of heavy rains, but I'm fairly positive it's *Cryptocline cinerescens*."

"Translation please." Flowers and shrubs she knew—along with most species of grass, plants, trees, and herbs—but textbook terms for agricultural fungi . . . that wasn't in her area of expertise.

"It's essentially an oak twig blight—not to be confused with an oak wilt."

"We can thank God for that," she said under her breath. "Is there a treatment plan? How bad is this? I've never even heard of a twig blight before."

"It's not too common, but can you see the anthracnose on these leaves? The dark spots here and here? That's the fungi. It attacks the new growth shoots first and then spreads to the leaves, eventually contaminating the crown."

She took the blanched twig in her hands. "So new, and already dead."

He took off his hard hat and swiped at the sweat beading on his forehead. The temperatures hovered in the low eighties today, and cloud cover had been scarce all morning. Texas in springtime was fickle: one minute scorching sun, the next a storm warning. April was a constant guessing game. "Luckily, I think we caught it early enough. I'll need to make cuts in the healthy tissues under the infected branches as I prune, and I have a systemic fungicide I can apply a week or so after I finish pruning. The crown will likely be thinner next year, but with proper irrigation and fertilizers I think it can be strong again."

"Really?" Relief and possibly another unidentified emotion swarmed her insides—partly because Griffin's report to the committee would reflect this new hope, and partly because his treatment plan guaranteed he'd be sticking around in Oak Springs for at least another week, unless . . . "Will you be the one to do the treatments? Or will you need to head back to your storm crew?"

He shaded his eyes against the sun's intensity. "I'm not planning to leave until the job is done."

Why did she get the distinct impression that the job he referenced was bigger than the fate of this live oak? And furthermore, why did she hope it was?

"Hey, boss?" Jason hollered at them over the grinding motor of the chipper. "Do you know that lady?"

Both Abby and Griffin followed his pointer finger to the minivan with more political stickers than passenger seats, and then on to the string-bean woman with the overly made-up face now streaking her way across the grass with some kind of device clutched in her hand. A name surfaced in Abby's mind just as the fuzzy end of a microphone jabbed in her direction. Was this *Gladys Applebottom*, Oak Springs's unofficial tell-all radio station host? If so, she certainly wasn't who Abby had pictured when she listened to the show in the mornings with the cook over her toast and coffee. Abby had imagined someone with a bit more . . . substance, whereas this woman looked a sneeze away from breaking in two.

But Abby couldn't be happier to see her here.

"Are you Abby Brookshire—the groundskeeper for the Kissing Tree Inn and an employee of Bradley Malone?"

Griffin clamped his hands on Abby's shoulders protectively and tugged her back a step, as if to shield her from another potential microphone attack.

"Ma'am, I think it's best you start by telling us who *you* are, and why you're storming onto private property." Griffin spoke with a confident calm that made Abby's heart march to a silent parade inside her chest.

Gladys's frost-blue lined eyes, circa 1986, took Griffin's measure without batting a lash. "Ah, so you're the one who's been hired to destroy our beloved oak tree? Well, not if the residents of Oak Springs have something to say about it, you're not. If you so much as pluck one more leaf off this historical landmark, I'll see to it that you'll be sued for everything you're worth. This tree is protected by the state of Texas—and by its citizens."

Griffin stood his ground, though his hold on Abby tightened ever so slightly. "Sorry, but I'm still waiting to see some form of identification."

Before Gladys had a chance to respond, Abby found her voice. "This is Gladys Applebottom." She tipped her chin up and twisted to face Griffin, who looked utterly confused at how she knew this Aqua Net lover's name. "She hosts a local radio program about current events and happenings within our town. Our cook, Mrs. Madden, listens to her show every morning." She turned back to Gladys. "It's an honor to meet you. A report you aired on missing pets actually helped her find her missing black Lab last winter."

Something in Gladys's severely bronzed cheekbones softened, and her apricot-brushed cheeks lifted into a grin. "Yes, that's right, I'm Gladys Applebottom. I've been a news professional since the early eighties—a former lead anchor for KEVI in New Mexico, followed at the *Desert Sand Gazette* as an investigative crime reporter."

She paused as if to leave room for Abby and Griffin's affirmation of her accolades. Apparently neither Griffin nor Abby responded quickly enough, because she slashed a hand through the air and continued. "I found my true calling in radio nearly three years ago, right here in this charming town I now call home. It's not all crime I cover, of course, but I feel it's my duty to inform the locals of all the happenings—the good and the bad." Her eyes narrowed on Griffin once more. "And losing the namesake of this town due to some chainsaw-happy millennial would be *very, very bad*."

Abby saw the twitch in Griffin's right cheek as he made eye contact with Jason, who now stood just a few steps behind Gladys. The kid had been pointing at his chest with a pick-me-please expression on his face since the moment Abby had outed the radio host in their midst. *Oh good gravy*, he'd just upped his pleading eyes to add animated praying hands. If Abby didn't take charge of this situation soon, Jason might derail the reason Abby had secretly left a voicemail for one Mrs. Gladys Applebottom early this morning.

Abby stepped away from the two men, working to block Jason from her peripheral vision. "Uh, Mrs. Applebottom, can I ask who told you that Griffin was being paid to remove the oak?" Because she certainly hadn't indicated that in her message, had she?

"I can't reveal my sources."

She really should have seen that one coming. "Right, well, then I'd like to set the record straight. Griffin was actually hired to give an accurate report on the tree's health, not to cut it down. The appeal to remove the protection act from this live oak is now in the second stage with our town council and the protection committee. Griffin will present the report next week, and then we'll wait on their recommendation and decision." She took a breath, and hoped she could persuade Gladys in a new direction. "Perhaps your radio show might help spread the word about what's going on. I would think there would be many residents in Oak Springs who would have an opinion on this tree's future fate."

Gladys didn't blink as she studied Abby with the intensity of a bounty hunter searching for a lost target. But it was Griffin's scrutiny that Abby felt the strongest. She refused eye contact with him.

"Everything Abby said is true, Mrs. Applebottom," Jason said, as if unable to hold himself back from the microphone a second more. "And I'm willing to go on record with that."

Griffin groaned as Gladys swung around to find Jason standing in wait. "And who are you?"

"I work for Malone Storm Services—Griffin's company." Jason offered his hand with much too big a grin. "I'm Jason Reddit—apprenticing arborist at your service. And I've been told by numerous women that I have a face for radio."

Abby stifled a laugh, but much to her surprise, Gladys shook his hand and then held out the recording device for him. "Based on your expertise, Mr. Reddit, and the evidence being transcribed in the arborist's report, what is your opinion on the fate of this oak?"

Abby held her breath.

"I'm not a doctor, but I'll level with you, Gladys. This tree's in critical condition. We have a treatment plan in place for the old girl, but we can't do it alone. We need to get the word out, to band together in the solidarity of one clear goal—to save this big, beautiful oak and watch her prosper for generations to come." He pounded his fist to his chest twice, and Abby fought the urge to hug him.

Though she had no idea why the kid had chosen tree work over starring in a daytime soap opera, that plea was a thousand times better than she could do any day of the week.

Obviously moved by Jason's speech, Gladys nodded and then spoke directly into the recording device. "You heard it here first, folks. The fate of our town's most cherished historical landmark is in jeopardy. If you care about this tree, won't you take a moment to make yourself known? Share your story with us so that we can band together and fight this appeal as one voice. No act of support is considered too small. We'll be back with more from the Kissing Tree Inn in the days to come. This is Gladys Applebottom from *Your Good Neighbor* 93.8, keeping our town clear of crime, one rotten apple at a time."

Griffin winked at Abby, and she couldn't help but smile back.

Whatever had just been transmitted into the airwaves of

Oak Springs, Abby knew one thing for certain: Where one person's cry could be easily ignored, an entire town would be much harder to silence. In only a matter of minutes, Gladys Applebottom had given wings to her weary heart and voice to her vision.

Six

Abby headed out her cottage door for the second time since finishing up her rounds in the gardens a smidgen after sunrise, switching out her windbreaker for a hooded sweatshirt. The morning had been noticeably cooler than yesterday. A crisp breeze wrestled through the bushes and trees, and heavy clouds pregnant with precipitation formed overhead. She glanced up at the sky and then back to the shadowed cobblestones her feet had walked countless times since her youth.

Absently, she wondered just how many more times she'd travel this path from her cabin to the grand oak. A hundred? A thousand? A hundred thousand?

To her surprise, Griffin wasn't at the tree when she arrived at the trunk. There was no chainsaw or climbing equipment on the ground, no chipper waiting to be fed a fresh round of pruned branches, and no fame-seeking Jason anywhere in sight. Where was everybody? Abby had finished her maintenance rounds by seven thirty, expecting Griffin to be ready for the day's work by eight like he had the day before. Perhaps he was still inside the inn talking with Bradley?

As she strolled past the trunk of the oak to get a better view of the parking lot and check for Griffin's work truck, a stark shade of white caught her eye. There, amid the bumpy ridges of bark and hundreds of initials and heart carvings, was an envelope pinned to the trunk of the oak. *What is that?* Gingerly, Abby pulled out the pin and opened the envelope that was simply addressed, *To whom it may concern.*

She slipped the contents out and unfolded the handwritten letter.

To whom it may concern:

After hearing the broadcast on Your Good Neighbor *yesterday, I was moved to take a moment and write down a memory about the oak tree next to the inn. I don't enjoy large crowds of people, and I'm not the type to speak up at a town council meeting, but I can share a story with anybody willing to listen.*

Like my parents and grandparents, I grew up in Oak Springs. I've watched the town grow from two stoplights and one elementary school to a miniature city with chain restaurants and coffee stands on multiple corners. I'm not complaining about the growth—the extra revenue has helped a lot of hardworking families stay afloat during lean times . . . mine included. I've worked as a waitress for thirty of my sixty-two years, and my daily commute takes me by the old oak on Acorn Lane. I've seen a lot of life happen under that tree—weddings, picnics, parties, and even a proposal once. I've also watched teenagers carve their initials into the trunk, just like I did once with my high school boyfriend after our senior prom. We'd made plans to elope after graduation (our parents thought we were too young to be so serious). But we were in love and I knew he was the only one for me.

When the day came to meet at the tree and leave town

together, my boyfriend never showed up. I was heartbroken and devastated. Weeks later, I received a letter from him, explaining how he'd joined the army with his older brother. He said he was too young to become a husband, and that he needed more life experience before he settled down to start a family with me. He asked if I would write to him during the war so that he'd have a connection to home, and to me.

But I refused to write back. I was too hurt, too angry, too justified in how wrong he'd been for standing me up without being courteous enough to tell me in person. As the years went on, bitterness grew in my heart like a vine, causing me to become untrusting and cynical of men—even the man I was married to for nearly twenty-two years. After his death, I was certain I would end up alone. It's what I deserved. I'd become a victim of my own making.

Last fall, during a rather routine shift at the diner, I served breakfast to a man I barely gave notice to, other than the fact that he was in a wheelchair, one leg amputated at the knee. When I picked up his check, there was a note written on the back side of the receipt. It said: I earned a Purple Heart in battle, and yet I'm little more than a coward when it comes to you. I never should have left without saying good-bye. I loved you. I think I always will. Please forgive me.

My heart cracked in two as I fled the diner in search of him. I drove all through town, scared I'd missed him, scared I'd never have the chance to free the pain I'd harbored for so long. But then, on my way back to the diner, I saw him. He'd parked his chair in front of that old live oak—contemplating life, love, and all the regrets sandwiched in between. That was the day I spoke the words I should have said decades earlier: I forgive you. Will you please forgive me, too?

This month marks ten years of a second chance I never should have been given. We were married under this tree eight years ago, and we pray each night that the good Lord will use our story to free others from the same prison of guilt and unforgiveness.

Much love,
Priscilla Burns

Abby's throat constricted, her chest tightening with a mounting pressure she'd come to know all too well over the last two years. Though she'd been able to hide from Griffin, ignore his texts, and decline his phone calls, she hadn't been able to avoid the guilt for the way she'd ended their relationship. At times, that pressing guilt had been more consuming than her grief.

As had her resentment.

Fresh conviction knocked on her heart as hot tears gathered on her lower lashes. She dashed them away with the back of her hand, only to see Griffin coming toward her in the distance, trudging his way through the damp grass.

"Unbelievable," he muttered on the tail end of a chuckle. "You'd think we were celebrities in hiding by the amount of phone calls I've had to field after Gladys aired another show this morning. My voicemail is full for the second time today, and that's after I spent an hour dealing with the first round. Some guy actually called to ask if he could bring his bongos to the tree and beat on them while I pruned—said there was new scientific evidence that a good reggae beat brings healing to distressed nature. Please tell me you haven't heard of such a thing, because it was all I could do not to burst out laughing and—"

"I'm sorry, Griff." The words tumbled out of her without hesitation. She didn't want to live another day, or even another second, without offering him a proper apology for her actions.

He stopped just shy of her, blinked, and then closed his mouth, as if whatever he was planning to say next no longer mattered.

Spurred on by the letter still clutched in her hand, she willed herself to continue this difficult conversation that should have happened long ago. "I shouldn't have waited two years to say this, but I was wrong to cut you out of my life, as if you hadn't meant anything to me . . . or to my father. Because you did mean something." *You still do,* her heart pleaded. "I know now you were only trying to help me believe things could be different . . . that *I* could be different. But I was too hurt to see that in the moment." She took in a shuddering breath and then exhaled. "I'm so sorry. I hope you can forgive me."

She'd watched movies where time appeared to slow when people spoke significant things to one another—a confession, a proposal, a buried truth resurrected. And as the background music quieted, the viewer of such pivotal moments in time could almost hear the pounding of heartbeats and the frosty puffs of breath. Abby couldn't be sure how much time ticked by in the space between her words and his, but she was certain she felt every millisecond in between.

"Thank you," he finally said. "I do forgive you, Abby, and you're not alone in your regrets. There were lots of things said and done that night that I wish we could go back and change."

"I know; me too. But we can't," she amended softly. "Part of me wonders if . . ." Only she couldn't finish that thought. Not yet. Not with him. Apologizing and asking Griffin for forgiveness was one thing, but exposing such a deep vulnerability? That was a level of intimacy she couldn't share, especially in light of all Griffin's shiny accomplishments and successes. "I just hope you don't have regrets about leaving Oak Springs. You did the right thing in going; I hope you believe that."

He shortened the distance between them and reached for her, his hands wrapping her upper arms as if to ground her here in this present moment. "Hey . . ." he said, concern lacing his voice. "What's brought all this on this morning? Did something happen?" He paused a beat and then let out an exasperated sigh. "Wait—have you been getting crazy calls from the radio show, too?"

She shook her head, this time her chest loosening on a laugh. "No, no calls, but I did find this." She held out the piece of paper, and confusion crimped his brow.

"A letter?"

"More like an inspiring story involving our faithful tree here. It was pinned to the trunk for someone to find."

A mix of curiosity and understanding softened his features. His eyes drifted from the letter back to her face once more. "My only regret in leaving Oak Springs was that I couldn't convince you to come with me."

"My home is here, Griff." A statement she'd made countless times, and yet this time the words seemed less convincing while standing in the shadow of a man whose presence warmed her like the summer sun.

He pulled her to his chest and pressed a kiss to the top of her head, the way he'd done years before their *just friends* label morphed into the *something more* category. "I know it is."

They stood that way for several minutes, locked in an embrace under the sprawling limbs of the same old oak where their relationship had both begun and ended.

She heard an unmistakable rumble coming from Griffin's abdomen and pulled away slightly.

He chuckled. "Sorry, I missed breakfast. Bongo Guy was pretty long-winded."

"I hope you told him he could come out and play; I have a few rose bushes that could use some reggae encouragement."

"You're out of luck there." He gave her a wink. "But I'm thinking I'll call an early lunch break today. How do pancakes sound?"

"Lunch break? But it's still morning, and you haven't even started work yet today."

"That's the glory of being the boss." His smile made something expand in her chest. "Jason should be rolling in any minute. I had him go to the supply store to pick up a few things. He can finish the pruning today, and then we can start on the next part of the treatment phase this afternoon. I have to turn in the arborist report to the council by the end of next week."

Abby stepped out of his embrace and returned the letter back inside the envelope. "Sounds like a good plan."

His face twisted in confusion. "What part?"

"The part where we leave Jason to work and go out for pancakes." And with that, she started for his truck, leaving him to jog after her.

Seven

After a hearty breakfast sponsored by applewood bacon and maple syrup, Griffin decided to take the long way back to the inn. Partly because he wanted to see the changes Abby had described to him over a shared buttery tower of flapjacks, but mostly because he wanted more time alone with her.

Just a few streets into downtown, he could clearly see that Abby's assessment of the town's growth had been spot-on. Oak Springs had expanded from the small town he'd known since he was a teen into a miniature city of booming potential. New businesses, restaurants, schools, subdivisions, and even rumors of a superstore coming their way early next year. And yet unlike so many of the smaller towns he'd visited, the residents of Oak Springs didn't seem to adopt the antigrowth mindset. Even the table of retirees who sat in the booth next to theirs at breakfast—a group of men he remembered as Piggy Pancakes regulars from years ago—seemed optimistic about the changes in town. Griffin's ears had perked up as their conversation shifted from last week's church sermon to the increase in job opportunities in the area. *"I say, whatever it takes to keep our kids and grandkids local, then it's fine by me. Community is a mindset, not a population size."* The other men concurred.

For the first time since he arrived, he could understand his cousin's desire to offload the financial burden of the massive oak and do something different with the land he'd inherited. Griffin had seen the sketches for a more distinguished common area and park, and for a few vacation cabins that would help bring in more revenue during the peak seasons. And though he disagreed in principle with removing a live tree before its natural death, he believed the heart behind Bradley's ideas wasn't all bad. As the preservation act stood now, Bradley couldn't add anything to that part of the property while the tree was still standing. Every move he made was scrutinized by the committee.

He also knew his cousin was still mourning the loss of a marriage he never anticipated would end.

"You seem to have forgotten your way," Abby said, her tone light and engaging as she looked from the road to him.

He stopped by the water tower at a sparkling new intersection that was once just a four-way stop. "Just enjoying the scenic route is all." Truth was, though, Griffin had forgotten many things over the last two years, not the least of which was how good Abby felt wrapped in his arms. Her presence, much like this town, always had a way of grounding him, of reminding him that even as a grown man, he couldn't escape his longing for home.

Running from city to city, chasing storms, adrenaline highs, and a growing bottom line had certainly taken the edge off, but it hadn't cured him of what he wanted most. And it wasn't the thrill of packing up at the dead of night to follow the wind radar for limb cleanup.

As he followed the curve of the road, his attention continued to gravitate to Abby—the way the sun haloed around her chestnut hair kept drawing him back. She'd kept her hair the same length for as long as he'd known her, a few inches or so below her chin. It was just one of the many ways Abby proved her steadfastness.

"My home is here, Griff."

Her earlier words took another stab at his conscience. Abby had apologized for blocking him out of her life, and yet he'd failed to reciprocate in kind. Not because he didn't have things to apologize for—there were many things he wished he could go back and do differently in those final grief-ridden days and hours. And yet, he'd never once considered his request of Abby to have been anything less than a white-stallion rescue, a chance to spread her wings and try on a different kind of life, one her father had urged her to experience. A life of adventure outside the one he'd passed down to her at the inn.

Fueled by a dying man's wish, Griffin had felt justified in his position to push her to leave with him. His promise to Arnie—to take care of his beloved Abby, to protect and love her until his own last breath—was one he imagined would be as easy to keep as it was to make. But there had been nothing easy about holding on to a woman who had needed a place to call home more than she had needed him.

Abby shifted in her seat, sitting up straighter as he pulled onto the road where Arnie had taught him to drive with his learner's permit. Smithe Farm Road.

"You almost gave my dad a heart attack on this road."

Griffin smiled. "I remember."

"I'm pretty sure that was the closest I'd ever seen him come to swearing."

He chuckled at the memory that flooded his mind. "Oh, he came more than close, Bee."

"*What?*" Abby rotated as much as her restraint would allow. "No way, you're joking. I'm not sure my father knew a single curse word, much less how to use one in a sentence."

At that, Griffin let loose a real laugh, full and deep. Her father had been the truest of gentlemen, a reputable deacon at Tenth Avenue Chapel, and the kind of man who was more comfortable pruning a rose bush than holding a rifle. But the afternoon Griffin nearly drove them into the ditch that ran alongside the Smithe property line was . . . *wait*.

He slammed on his brakes, and Abby yelped.

"Griff! What are you—?"

But he was already turning in to the driveway, curious about the dusty *For Sale* sign staked to the side of the entrance.

"Wow . . . when did this place go up for sale?" he muttered aloud, surveying the property through his road-trip splattered windshield. The last time he'd been here was on a raspberry picking excursion with Abby some four or five years back, before the farm had turned into this overgrown jungle of weeds.

"About a year ago—officially, anyway. It was held up awhile before that in an estate feud between family members."

He popped his door open and scrutinized the old rancher building in front of them. The house, at least, didn't look as bad off as the grounds. It was dated, to be certain, but it still appeared to be structurally sound.

Abby hopped out of the passenger's seat and closed the truck door behind her. "You want to see something?" Without waiting for his answer, she beckoned him to follow her around the house, and like a smitten puppy, he willingly obliged.

Truth was, Griffin didn't want to be anywhere that Abby wasn't.

They trampled over weeds and stumps and a giant overgrown blackberry bush until they reached the back of the old yellow house.

And then she stopped.

"It's beautiful, isn't it?" A hint of reverence lit up her voice in a way that had him wondering if they were seeing the same thing.

He continued to scan the wasteland in front of them. Barren fruit trees, a dried-up pond little more than a hole in the ground, and several dedicated garden areas so full of debris they were almost unrecognizable.

Griffin suddenly wished for the ability to see this land through her eyes, because whatever Abby saw in this place had transformed her entire countenance. She radiated a hope he hadn't seen on her face since . . . since before her father became ill.

As if in a daze, she moved toward a nearly shriveled rose bush and knelt in front of it. She touched the lone bud on the vine with her fingertips. "I stop here sometimes and just . . . I don't know. I guess I imagine what this land could be if it was tended to properly." She stood tall and again surveyed the acreage. "The potential feels limitless here."

A stark contrast to the grounds at the inn, where everything had been polished and pristine for decades. Maintaining was not the same as designing.

"Like a canvas waiting for the right painter," Griffin said as understanding dawned.

"Yes, exactly."

Griffin strolled on ahead of her, making a mental checklist of issues needing attention. "How many acres is this?"

"Nine-point-two."

He spun slowly, eyebrows hiked. "So, you've called on it, then?"

Her shrug didn't fool him one bit. "Only out of curiosity."

"Have you walked through the house, too?"

"Both of them, yes. They could use some updating, but they're actually in pretty good shape."

"There's two dwellings?"

She nodded. "There's a two-bedroom cabin on the opposite side of the property. It actually has a separate driveway I didn't know was there until Sheryl, the agent, pointed it out."

The wistful note in her voice made his heart stretch wide. She reached down between her garden boots to pluck two dandelion weeds out of the dried soil. "It'd make for a perfect rental . . . ya know, if somebody needed income while they were fixing up the property and the main house."

"Huh. Sure would," he said, eyeing her as she tucked her hands in her pockets and released a weighty sigh.

He stepped even with her and nudged her shoulder. "So, why can't you be that somebody, Bee?"

"Me?" She laughed, dismissing the idea instantly. "No. I could never."

"Why not?"

"I have the cottage and the grounds to tend to."

He proceeded with caution, careful to avoid talk of the promise he'd made to her father about helping her move on from the inn, of not letting her talents go to waste on the same grounds Arnie had tended to for decades. "But the inn has no real outlet for your creativity. Even if Bradley doesn't get the expansion he's pushing for now, it will happen eventually. And that will leave you even less land to tend." He paused, silently asking God to give him the right words. "When I look out at this"—he waved a hand over the acreage—"I see a mess ready for the burn pile . . . but you see hope for the future. That's a gift, Abby." One he'd been the recipient of on numerous occasions.

She shook her head slowly, as if arguing more with herself than with Griffin. "It's too much money."

"And yet something tells me you could afford it if you wanted it badly enough. I'd bet my work truck that you haven't touched a penny of the inheritance Arnie left you."

She studied her Kermit garden boots. "I haven't, no, but even still, all the renovations it would need wouldn't be cheap. Or easy."

"So, you get a steady renter and you start selling those awesome succulent gardens you create on the side and you make it work. *You. Could. Do. This.*"

She lifted her chin to meet his gaze, but the high color in her cheeks had already begun to fade, along with the sparkle in her eyes. "Yeah, I don't know, maybe."

He flexed his hands into fists, debating how far to push this conversation. He knew exactly why she wouldn't allow this dream to become a reality. "Bee—"

The phone in his front pocket trilled, alerting him to a text message. And then to a second one immediately after. And then to a third.

"You should probably check that," she said quickly, though he had little doubt that she was as grateful for the escape as he was annoyed by it. "It's probably Jason. We've been gone for a while."

She was already three steps to the truck when he slipped the phone out of his pocket and read Jason's messages.

Hit a snag. You might want to head back.

Soon.

Before Griffin could reply, a picture came through.

He pinched the screen to zoom in, struggling to comprehend what he was seeing. "*What on earth?*"

Abby twisted around, her hand reaching for the truck's handle behind her. "Something wrong?"

He sprinted to his driver's side door and then hopped into the cab with Abby. "Has everybody in this town lost their minds?"

"Careful now," she said in mock defense. "I live here, too, ya know."

He flipped the screen around for her to see the crisp image of a young boy and girl holding hands while chained to the tree, a padlock between them.

"Oh my . . ." Abby gasped. "Seriously? Is this for real?"

"Unless Jason has figured out how to use Photoshop between pruning and irrigating, then yes. I'd say it's very, very real."

Abby barreled out of the truck before Griffin had even thrown the gearshift into park, but she was far from the only adult on the scene. A news truck from their neighboring city was parked catawampus in the grass, as was Gladys's radio van. Both vehicles were surrounded by a sea of fresh-faced picketers who couldn't be much older than sixteen.

Abby jogged toward a girl who held a sign that read *Trees have feelings too! Leaf them alone!*

"Hey there, um, can I ask where y'all are from?"

"Oak Springs High School. We're in Mr. Brower's junior and senior speech classes. We're exercising our right to protest."

Abby scanned the crowd to find Mr. Brower, the same speech teacher she'd had nearly eleven years prior, seated in a canvas camping chair at the far edge of the parking lot. As she caught his attention, he flashed her a peace sign similar to the one on his tie-dyed tank top.

"O-okay. Well, yes, I suppose it is your right to protest, but this isn't really the time or—"

Before she could finish, Griffin stormed past her toward the oak, more specifically, toward the two teen boys climbing on his new wood chipper.

"Uh, hold that thought," Abby called over her shoulder as she rushed after him.

"Griff, wait—"

"This is *insane*."

"True, but you can't just—"

He halted a foot in front of the equipment. "If you aren't off my machine in three, two, one—"

With fear-rounded eyes, both boys leapt to the ground, their hands raised high. One stayed to apologize while the other ran like he was about to be smashed by a rolling boulder. A small part of Abby wanted to laugh at the circus of it all, but there was simply too much chaos to focus on any one thing. A cameraman set up his tripod about twenty feet out from the live oak, no doubt capturing the teen boy and girl shackled to its robust trunk—only upon closer inspection, the apparatus holding them hostage to the tree looked as if it could double for a ten-dollar bike chain and combination lock.

The ash blonde with the highest ponytail Abby had ever seen bobbed her head as she spoke to the reporter. "It's our year to carve our initials on the trunk. We've waited for this since we were freshmen. It's tradition. No one should be able to take away our rights without a fight."

"Yeah, and we're prepared to stay here for days if necessary. To make our point," the boyfriend said, his navy beanie so low he appeared to have lost his eyebrows in the wide knit.

"Days?" Jack Johnston, the reporter from Channel 9 News repeated. "So, then, you must have a plan for food and water? But what about when you need to use the restroom?" Obviously, he was finding as much amusement in this ridiculous scenario as Abby was.

"I've gone two full days with nothing more than an apple during summer cheer camp," the girl announced proudly. "We're hard-core."

Beanie Boy appeared far more doubtful of his girlfriend's apple-a-day diet plan, but he managed to add, "And I once drove all the way to Colorado Springs with my folks without having to make a single pit stop. We can hold it."

The reporter turned back to the camera, a smirk pinching his right cheek. "There you have it, folks. Teens in love and committed to saving the life of a legendary tree. In a world where our next generation gets a lot of pushback, may we all rest a bit better tonight knowing that the youth of Oak Springs have die-hard spirits and ironclad bladders. This is Jack Johnston for Channel 9 News. Back to you, Kelly and Adam."

The reporter and cameraman packed up a few minutes later, after taking several selfies with the picketers and getting a token interview with Mr. Brower in his Grateful Dead lawn chair.

Gladys Applebottom made her way over to Abby. "This old tree continues to make quite the ruckus, doesn't it?"

"I'd say so. Between this and all the phone calls Griffin's been getting and the letter I found this morning on the tree . . . it's been a full day."

"You got a letter?" Gladys asked. "Good! I was hoping people might take that approach. I mentioned it on the show yesterday."

Abby nodded, remembering the convicting words of Priscilla Burns. "If more letters come in, I'll be sure to turn them over to the council before the big committee meeting."

"Perfect. I have a feeling you'll be hearing from a lot more people before this thing is said and done."

Abby looked from the teens chained to the tree, to the picketers in the street, and then finally to the argument happening between Bradley and Griffin on the front-porch steps of the inn, where Jason sat undisturbed eating a sub sandwich. But even in the chaos of it all, she couldn't ignore the warmth spreading through her entire being at Gladys's optimism: Nobody in their town was gonna let this tree be taken down without a fight.

Eight

The next five days passed without much protest, at least, not in the way of teenagers chaining themselves to the base of a legendary oak tree—a fact Griffin was grateful for, even though it meant he'd lost his bet with Abby. While Griffin predicted the Tenacious Tree-Loving Teens, as the local news had deemed them, would make it at least six hours before tapping out, they'd only made it to three, which was exactly what Abby had guessed. He should have known they would call it quits early when Lover Boy started complaining that his body was "shutting down" on account of starvation just after hour two. Abby's big win had involved another delicious round of veggie and salami pizza with a hefty side of gloating.

But Griffin would lose a bet to Abby any day of the week as long as it involved spending more time alone with her . . . which had grown increasingly more difficult to do as the live oak had grown in celebrity status. Gladys Applebottom informed him that the Kissing Tree of Oak Springs now had its own Facebook following and Twitter account. He didn't doubt it. The way residents had flocked to his job site unannounced, bearing gifts like free sandwiches and cupcakes as well as handwritten letters detailing their reflections on the tree, had kept him in a continual state of wonderment.

Griffin's favorite visitors of the week had been the preschoolers. Fascinated by chainsaws and chipper trucks, they'd come with colorful drawings and smiles that could warm even the hardest of lumberjacks. He wasn't sure when his occupation had become field trip worthy, but such was life in Oak Springs—a life he'd missed more than he realized.

Today's guest, though, was one he'd invited—Winston Hawks of Hawks Tree Services.

As the most reputable arborist in town, and one of Arnie Brookshire's oldest friends, it didn't seem right to seal up this arborist report without a sign-off from Winston. Thankfully, he'd just rolled back into town last night after visiting his aging mother on the East Coast—Connecticut, if Griffin remembered correctly. Winston had spent the better part of the morning giving Griffin his two professional cents on the old tree, signing off in agreement with Griffin's assessment and treatment plan, as well as his recommendation for the tree to remain where it stood.

Griffin stepped forward to shake the man's hand. "Thanks for your time, Winston. I appreciate you coming out, especially when the weather's about to turn and you have a crew to manage."

"Ah, you know how it is. A little rain is good for the soul." Winston tipped his wide-brimmed hat and glanced up at the graying sky. "Although my gut says this rain might be brewing into something bigger. You best get your fancy new equipment under cover."

Griff's focus hadn't been on the weather as much as it usually was, but even still, he knew Winston was right. He felt it in his gut, too. The gathering clouds had a violent look about them.

"Will do, sir." He'd forgotten how much he enjoyed conversing with Winston. Arnie had set Griffin up with an apprenticeship with Hawks Trees right after he graduated from high school, and he learned some invaluable lessons that summer, along with some good inside jokes.

"And you tell me if those boys and girls on the preservation committee give you any trouble. They're a good bunch overall, and I trust they'll make the right decision, but I do feel for Bradley." He shook his head and glanced at the inn. "The caregiving bill for a tree this age and size will just keep growing as time goes on, no matter how many discounts he's given." He gestured to the tree. "But the fact remains: This tree may be geriatric, complaining of its aches and pains, but it ain't dead yet."

"Well said. See ya around, Winston." Griffin laughed and started back to where Jason was busy spreading fungicide near the roots.

"Hey, Malone!"

Griffin turned to find Winston inspecting his work truck appreciatively. "If you ever tire of the fast pace of storm life and need a place to settle down, come talk to me, will ya? I might have something of interest to you."

"Oh yeah?" Griffin wiped his hands on his work pants and took a few steps closer, intrigued. "What might that be?"

Winston's grin widened as the wind began to pick up. "I'm pushing retirement age, son." He hitched a thumb back at the tree. "But like our oak friend here, I'm not done living yet—just done climbing. I've built a steady business over the last three decades, consistent work up and down I-45. But my own boy just partnered with a law firm in Dallas. He doesn't have interest in tree work."

"You're selling Hawks Trees?" The question was cradled in surprise.

"Not today, and not necessarily tomorrow either, but the

time for change is coming soon." He shrugged as if he hadn't just offered Griffin the opportunity to acquire a reputable business in Oak Springs. "Just something for you to ponder while you're here." Again, he tipped his hat. "Have a good day, son."

"Yeah . . . you, too. Thanks." Griffin's words were lost on a powerful gust of wind that had Jason whooping in delight as he fought to balance the heavy spray pack on his back.

Before Griff's thoughts had a chance to take root and allow him to contemplate the offer he'd just been given, the sky's grumbling mood demanded his attention. "Hey, Jason, it's time to pack up the equipment. We're about to get soaked."

"Got it," Jason answered, shrugging out of his pack and dropping the sprayer to the ground.

Thoughts of Abby in the gardens around back caused Griffin to quicken his steps, gathering his supplies and tossing them all into the back of his unhitched trailer while Jason turned on the weather radar in the cab of Griff's truck. He flipped the tracking device around, the red zone hard to miss. "It's gonna be a biggie, boss."

It was an announcement that usually came with a rush of adrenaline and a surefire excuse to hit the road without a care in the world. But not this time. This time Griffin had no intention of leaving town. Because this time, the person he cared most about in the entire world was right here.

And suddenly, *right here* was the only place he wanted to be.

Abby regretted not grabbing her parka when she had the chance, but it was too late to run back to her cottage now. By the looks of the temperamental sky, she would have only minutes to prepare her gardens for the coming rain. Her body was sturdy enough to handle a spontaneous downpour from the heavens, but her most delicate of flowers and vegetation would not be.

She sprinted to the toolshed in search of the cloches and heavy stakes that would act as a protective shelter for her most fragile of plant life just as an aggressive onslaught of wind caused her to stumble into the shed door. *Where did all this wind come from?* The weather alerts on her phone had indicated precipitation was in the forecast, but the too-close rumble of thunder sent a jolt of fear down her spine.

She dragged thick plastic coverings from the shed to the gardens, working in vain to straighten them out as they slapped against her chest and face so many times that her frustration matched the angry rain that soaked her hair and pale gray T-shirt. Without a second pair of hands to help secure the stakes into the ground, this job would be nearly impossible. But there was no one she could call for help. Griffin and Jason were likely in a similar predicament over at the tree, sheltering the high-dollar machinery and gear.

She'd just have to power through the way she'd always done.

Despite her rain-slicked hair that caught in her eyelashes, she drew back the heavy mallet and drove it into the stake, pinning the corner of a tarp to the pooling soil. It took seven strikes for the ground to yield to her strength, as if refusing to wave the white flag no matter how badly her muscles ached to call it quits. The sky bellowed again, the sound crackling in her ears and rattling her teeth. She willed herself to work faster, tugging again on the plastic tarp until it was taut over her favorite spotted bee balm, begonias, and irises. Her garden boots slipped on the wet earth as she found her footing at the opposite corner of the raised bed.

She had gripped the mallet to strike at a new stake when warmth wrapped around her wrist and stilled her swing.

"I got you!" Griffin hollered over the raging storm, piercing her with a confident gaze. "I'll hammer; you straighten the tarps. We need to be quick."

Grateful beyond words, she nodded and reached for the opposite end. This was a rhythm they both knew well, a partnership based on an efficiency that complemented their strengths and covered their weaknesses.

With no further communication needed, the remaining three corners of the garden bed were sheltered in a matter of seconds. Fighting against horizontal sheets of rain, they raced back to the shed, tossing the tools inside and latching the door closed. The first rod of lightning lit up the ground around them an instant before they reached the front steps of her cottage.

They barreled inside her living room, both a storm-soaked mess of dripping hair, clothes, and work boots.

Griffin swiped an arm across his eyes and then peered down at her drenched shirt. "Where's your jacket?"

It was such a ridiculous question, in light of the widening puddles at their feet and the flash flood happening on the other side of the cottage walls, that she couldn't help but laugh. She pressed a palm to the chest of his saturated black cotton tee, lifting it away just enough to see a perfect indentation of all five of her fingers. "Looks like I could ask you the very same question."

He caught her hand in his, the warmth of his skin a welcome contrast to the chill creeping through her body. "I'm sorry I couldn't get to you sooner. One of the gears in the chipper jammed, and we had to push it to the clearing."

At the sincerity of his voice, her throat tightened. "Your timing was perfect. I don't think I could have finished it in time without your help."

His thumb slid over the pulse point in her wrist and she shivered. "We make a good team."

And something about the present tense of that statement, the here and now of it, caused her mind to fog with possibility. "We do."

The splatter of water pooling around their boots cut her attention away from the earnestness of his gaze. "I'll get us some towels and see about finding you some dry clothes of my dad's. You can have the bathroom first."

She twisted toward the linen closet, but he caught her arm once again and drew her back to his chest. "Wait."

Though he said nothing more with his mouth, his eyes were alight with a desire that waged war against the last of her willpower. Because keeping Griffin out of the very space he'd occupied inside her heart for so many years was as futile as demanding that the wind stop blowing.

"Yes?" she asked a bit too breathlessly.

"I just wanted to look at you a little bit longer."

Self-consciously, she touched her soggy ponytail stub. "I'm sure I look like I fell out of a tornado cyclone."

"No, you don't." He stepped toward her. "You look beautiful."

She didn't flinch when he dropped his hands to her waist or his gaze to her mouth. Instead, despite all her resolve to lock him out of her life, she reached for him, too, skimming his cheek with the same inquisitive touch she used to greet a budding flower petal. She relished the familiar feel of his lips parting hers for the first time in much, much too long. And just like that, she allowed the bleak realities of her world, the concrete walls she'd lived inside, to break away. She explored each forbidden sensation she'd fought to block since Griffin arrived—the woodsy scent of his skin, the secure hold of his embrace, the low rumble in the back of his throat as his fingers skimmed her rain-slicked hair.

Neither of them reacted to the flicker of lights overhead or the wailing shrills of wind outside her door. Because for those few precious minutes, the only thing Abby could focus on was a feeling she hadn't allowed herself in the two years since her father's death: hope.

Nine

Griffin's skin hummed with an awareness he couldn't disregard. He'd kissed her. Or maybe, she'd kissed him. Whatever the case, the end result was the same. And he couldn't—wouldn't—go back to pretending he wanted any kind of life apart from Abby. That particular facade had vanished in full the instant her lips had brushed his.

As he heard the shower water turn on in the bathroom at the end of the hallway, he searched for a much-needed distraction. Something to do with his hands, somewhere to take his thoughts, someplace to redirect this unharnessed energy pumping through his every cell. He braced the back of his neck with both hands and exhaled slowly. He'd spent years falling in love with Abby the first time around. A patient friendship birthed from long summers tending to the same land, and yet this time, his feelings for her had rushed back without preamble or apology.

He flipped on the tap at Abby's kitchen sink and chugged a cold glass of water, but as he tipped his head back for the last drop, a pile of letters on the dining table caught his attention. He wandered over to them, recognizing a few of the envelopes immediately, given he'd been the one to hand them to Abby for safekeeping. Several still had pushpins poking out through the corners.

He riffled through the mix, skimming over the familiar names and scanning the memories with a smile, even chuckling a time or two at the way the residents recounted their favorite events with the Kissing Tree. As he stepped away from the table, he noticed a blank envelope on the floor, wedged next to the foot of a wooden chair leg. It had likely blown off the pile when the wind wailed through the cottage as they'd come inside. He swept the unaddressed letter off the floor and made to add it to the collection with the others, only before he released it, he flipped the envelope over and slipped the folded paper into his palm.

He recognized the loose script immediately—the swooping tails that rounded each letter and the slashes that dotted the i's and crossed the t's. But even if the writing hadn't looked so familiar, he wouldn't have needed to read any further than the first two words to identify the author.

Dear Daddy,

I thought sitting down to write you a letter would get easier with time, but I don't think that's true. The words rolling around in my heart feel just as difficult to think as they do to write. But once again, I'm forced into a timeline I didn't choose and can't control.

The fate of the oak tree is in question, and the sentimentalities of our town have come out in force. Most of the memories shared are of events—first kisses, promposals, marriage proposals, special moments enjoyed with siblings and children. But for us, that tree was a part of our daily life together.

It was a shady spot to work on my homework while you pulled weeds nearby. A place to eat leftover pizza and read novels and work out funky dance moves during the livelier reception parties happening on the north lawn. But those memories feel harder for me to recall now. Because no matter how hard I try to go back to those happier moments, I can't seem to move past that night. The night you told me about your prognosis, and ultimately, about your decision not to pursue treatments.

The truth is, part of me is still there, Daddy. Stuck at the base of that tree, where I hoped I could escape the reality you'd already come to terms with. I felt as frozen as the world around me, and yet I would have given anything to have frozen what little time I had left with you.

I wish you were here to nudge me forward, give me your famous dad look with those untamed eyebrows of yours. I wish you could tell me that it's okay to want something else . . . something different than the life you made for us here all those years ago. Because the truth is, I'm not sure how to reach for something new when I'm trying so hard not to let go of everything we shared.

I know you warned me not to be like the servant in Matthew 25, the one who buried his master's talent in the ground and then went back to his life as if nothing had changed . . . but I also know I won't survive losing you twice. So how can I honor your life by walking away from the one place I feel you the closest?

Yours forever,
Bee

"What are you doing?"

He hadn't heard the shower turn off or the quiet sound of her footsteps padding down the hallway. He'd been totally engrossed, totally consumed by the vulnerability inside her letter—one he had no right to read and yet couldn't tear himself away from.

Griffin turned to face her, his eyes glassy and his breath far more shallow than his lungs demanded. "I found this on the floor. Thought it belonged in the stack for the town council."

Her gaze steadied on the letter in his hands, a frown tugging at the corners of her mouth. "It doesn't."

"I'm sorry, Bee." For more than he could ever name. The loss. The pain. The grief he tried and failed to rescue her from. But he knew better now.

Abby hadn't been wrong to stay. He'd been wrong to ask her to leave. Grief was a process, a path that had to be traveled. He'd tried to be her getaway car, an escape from the hardest steps of her journey, and yet each new step was dependent on the last. He could see that now. Abby hadn't given up; she'd been stumbling forward the best way she knew how.

Desperate to pull her close again, he fought his instincts and remained where he stood, silent and waiting for her to put a voice to all the thoughts swirling in her head. Because this was her turn to speak, not his. He may have started this conversation with her two years ago, but his timing had been way off. And so had his desire to remove her from pain. Griffin wasn't about to get his part wrong on this second time around.

"Some days I don't know what I fear more—staying stuck, or moving on."

Her honesty caused him to consider her words with a question he hoped she would be able to answer.

"And what if fear wasn't part of the equation?"

She tilted her head, as if waiting for him to expound. But Abby wasn't a dimly lit bulb in a corner closet. On the contrary, she was one of the brightest minds he knew. Much like her father, she lived scenarios out in her head first, processing things to the fullest before she ever spoke a word.

"If fear wasn't part of the equation . . ." she repeated, releasing a long exhale. "Then I'd invest my father's inheritance in the Smithe Farm and work that land the way he once worked the inn's property."

The pronouncement had come with a boldness he hadn't anticipated. Though he'd recognized her joy at the property that day, he wasn't sure she'd been able to. Apparently today was full of surprises.

She fingered the strings on her gray hooded sweatshirt. "Maybe I could do it, start a new dream, one that was my own and not . . ." She let the sentence hang there as if she couldn't quite bring herself to finalize it.

"Your father's?"

Her nod beckoned him to still the fidgety movement of her hand with his.

"I think that's exactly what he'd want you to do. Not just with the money, but with all your other giftings, too."

"But what about all he's done here? All the time and effort he put into every square inch of this land? How could I ever walk away from that?"

He squeezed her hand, rubbing his thumb along the ridges of her knuckles. "Your loyalty is one of the things I've admired about you most. But you aren't rooted to this place forever."

"My heart is."

A truth-tipped arrow that plunged straight through his chest. Despite her post-shower clothes and drying hair, he moved in close and wrapped his arms around her. "I know it must feel that way to you now, but—"

A sharp crack of splintering wood muted his next words. He spun her away from the large picture window and sheltered her body with his own, unsure if a wind-borne branch would be crashing in on them next. Another giant break was followed by a blinding flash of fire, the last light they saw before the room went black.

Ten

Abby opened her kitchen cabinet and handed Griffin her emergency flashlight, her hand still shaking from the sudden surge of adrenaline.

"Thanks," he said. "I'm gonna take a look around upstairs in the loft, check out the balcony to make sure nothing's fallen on the roof."

"Be careful." She felt compelled to say it, though she trusted Griffin's skilled eye and experience. The man had weathered many storms—tracked them, followed them, ridden them out. But that had been the closest lightning bolt Abby had ever witnessed, and she couldn't shake the unease growing in her abdomen. She tried to see out the windows again, but the constant rain kept her vision limited to the cobblestone steps that curved around her little cottage.

"I will." Griffin touched her cheek. "With the power out, we won't be able to see much until morning, but it's not safe to go poking around outside with only a flashlight. Don't worry, okay? Whatever mess is waiting for us tomorrow, we'll fix it together. The worst has already passed."

"Okay." A word she spoke but didn't mean. Not in the slightest.

Though she couldn't see what kind of damage lurked beyond

her darkened windows, she was certain whatever was to come was far from over.

Before the first hope of daylight winked over the horizon, a chainsaw whirred outside her window, revealing Griffin was already up and at work. He'd offered to take the old futon upstairs in the loft while she hunkered down for a night of tossing and turning in the bedroom. Apparently insomnia was contagious.

She pulled on a fresh pair of jeans and a lightweight sweatshirt before bustling into the kitchen. If Griffin was committed to starting out this early, then the least she could do was find a couple of thermoses for their much-needed caffeine intake. She searched for her father's old Coleman thermos, the one he sipped from on chilly mornings while he worked the land. Rummaging past the pots and pans, she found it hiding behind a colander and hugged it to her chest.

She'd let Griffin use this one today.

Only, as she crossed the kitchen toward the front door, two steaming thermoses in hand, Griffin came inside, wearing an expression that made the static in her chest return.

"Hey," he said. "I didn't know if you'd be up yet."

"How come you didn't wake me before you went out?"

"I thought you could use the sleep." His gaze fell to her father's thermos as she handed it to him with a smile. "Thanks." But instead of bringing it to his lips, he set it on her table and pulled out a chair, as if there wasn't a night's worth of storm cleanup waiting for them beyond her dining room walls.

"Uh . . . what are you doing?" she asked as he sat and placed his elbows on the worn table's surface. "This coffee is designed to be portable, Griff. Let's go get to work. I'm ready."

"Abby." Griffin sighed and let his head fall heavy into his hands. "I need you to sit down for a minute."

"But why? Is it worse than you thought out there?"

"Please." He gestured at the chair across from him.

Robotically, she did as he asked, keeping her eyes locked on his drawn features.

"Whatever it is, Griff—just say it. What?" Anticipation of any kind wasn't her friend.

After a forceful scrub down the sides of his face, he leveled his gaze on hers once more. "The oak didn't make it."

The oak didn't . . . But no matter how she repeated it in her head, she couldn't make sense of his words. "What?"

"The sharp crack we heard last night, that splintering of wood, it was a lightning strike. A bolt shot clean through one of the branches at the crown and then straight into the trunk. We're fortunate it didn't catch fire."

She shook her head. "But trees get hit by lightning all the time. That doesn't mean it's—"

"It reached the heartwood, Abby." Words that clenched around her lungs and squeezed every last ounce of oxygen from her chest. "The internal blisters have already started. It's not the kind of wound a tree can heal from—not even one as resilient as ours. Not this time. I'm sorry."

She tried to stand up, to push out her chair, to go and see for herself just how wrong his assessment had to be. Because their tree had survived over a hundred years' worth of storms and blight and disease—even fire! This couldn't be how it ended, not after all they'd done to save it. Not after their entire town had been rooting for it to stay put and outlive their children and grandchildren.

"There has to be something more we can do for it, Griff. We just need to think. Research all our options. It's too soon to make that kind of call."

He reached for her wrist as a familiar warning chimed in his voice. "Abby."

"No." She shook her head again. "I won't accept that. I can't. I need to see it for myself."

"I figured you'd want to, which is exactly why I told you first—before I call Winston or my contact on the committee. I knew you'd need a few minutes."

"A few minutes?" A humorless laugh bubbled up her throat. "To do what, exactly? To be fine with just letting the tree die when there could still be options to save it? No. I won't let you give up on it, not without a fight. Not this time."

The stricken look on his face told her exactly where the statement had led him, because it was the same place her mind had traveled. Back to that stuffy living room in late August when her father had announced he wouldn't be receiving treatment.

"Don't go there, Bee. This isn't the same as what happened with your dad." His words may have been quiet, yet his meaning was a volcanic eruption of stuffed emotions. "Your father had a choice. And he chose to live out his days the best way he could. *With you.*"

She ripped her wrist away. "And yet never once did you try and change his mind." Angry tears rushed behind her eyes, but she refused them release.

"Is that really what you believe?" Hurt flashed across his features. "That it didn't crush me when your father told me he wasn't going to accept medical intervention? Because that's a lie. It *did* crush me, and not only because of the loss *I* would feel, but for you, too, Bee. I knew what his death would mean for you. What it would cost you." His voice hitched, broke. "And I loved you too much not to beg him to research every possibility out there before he made up his mind."

Tears slipped down her cheeks and dripped off her chin.

Griffin gentled his voice, his face softening with a compassion that only increased her pain. "The risks were too high; the odds too low. He refused treatment because he didn't want you to watch him suffer."

Her throat ached as she remembered her father's words to her that night. *"I want you to remember my joy, not my suffering."*

She swiped at her cheeks and studied the floor beneath their feet, allowing an eternity of silence to fill the space between their unspoken thoughts.

"If there were something more I could do for that tree, I'd do it. But wishing things were different doesn't make the truth any less true." He exhaled a weary breath. "It will have to come down—*soon*. Many of the crown's branches are in rough shape from the storm. One already punctured the roof of the solarium."

"Then just cut the bad branches down."

"Abby, you know I can't prune a dead tree for the sake of nostalgia."

She squeezed her eyes closed. "So what then? You just chop it down and haul it away and rid our town of a namesake? A legacy?" She shook her head, wanting nothing more than to cover her ears and make his prognosis disappear. To make this entire conversation disappear.

She started for the door, thermos forgotten on the table, along with her foolish dreams for the future.

Griffin swiped the pile of letters off the counter and held them high in the air. "The heart of this town has little to do with the dying heartwood inside that old oak. It's in here. In these letters. In the memories that have spanned more than a century and through multiple generations." His voice grew husky, tender. "I know what that tree represents to you, but saying good-bye to it doesn't have to change this new path you're on. It doesn't have to mean—"

"I'm not on a new path, Griffin." She pushed past him. "This land is where I belong, where I'll always belong. I was a fool to think I could ever be somewhere else."

"You're not a fool for believing there's a life outside this place. Look at me." He blocked the door before she had a chance to yank it open. "Your father isn't on these grounds or at this inn or even a part of that great beautiful namesake of a tree outside. *He's inside you.* He's a part of your creative eye and your compassionate spirit." He paused to release a breath. "He was patient and dependable and had a knack for loving people who didn't believe they could ever deserve a second chance—and yet he proved them wrong." Griffin's voice strained on the last word. "And all of that helped to shape the person you are today—that's the real legacy of Arnie Brookshire. Not the land he worked, but the daughter he raised. *You* are his living legacy, Bee. And only you get to decide how you're going to live it out."

Without another word, he twisted the knob and pulled the door open wide for her, allowing her an escape to find solace in the land she'd grown up on, the land her father had taught her to memorize like a clock face. Only, this time, when she stepped onto the same cobblestone path she'd walked thousands of times before, she'd never felt more lost.

Eleven

Abby had been up before daybreak thousands of times in her life. Much like the plant life she tended, she was used to the sun warming her back and the crisp spring breeze riffling her hair. She knew how it felt to touch dew-kissed petals and cultivate soil for fresh seed to be sown. But rarely, if ever, had she been outdoors at this time of day without a task to manage on the grounds.

She rubbed at the thin fabric covering her arms and forged a trail through the wet grass to a tree she'd been keeping her distance from for the past hour. Griffin was right: She couldn't avoid the truth forever.

The charred scars of the Y branch that split off from the main trunk, along with the giant slabs of bark scattered across the ground, had been visible even from the other side of the property. But now, up close . . . she reached her hand out, brushing her fingertips along the bubbling, black blisters. A sign that all the gasses inside the sapwood and the heartwood had turned to liquid.

That lightning bolt had been a death strike.

Just like Griffin had told her.

Griffin. He hadn't come after her. Hadn't asked her more

questions or debated her reasons for wanting to stay at the grounds. He'd simply opened the door and allowed her to walk away. Alone.

He'd driven off in the direction of town soon after, without a good-bye or an explanation of when he might return. He didn't owe her one. Truth was, he didn't owe her anything at all.

Another stiff breeze lifted her hair off her neck and across her cheek. She pinned it behind her ear and glanced over her shoulder at the memorial bench several yards out from the oak. She moved toward it as if it were the only answer she could locate for a problem far bigger than she could solve on her own. She tucked her legs under the cold stone seat meant to be a place of reflection, a spot to observe the beauty of the gardens and, of course, the Kissing Tree. But what purpose would this bench serve once this century-old tree disappeared from its sacred home forever?

Abby couldn't even imagine the scarred ground that would be left in its absence. She hugged her arms around her chest, forming words in her mind she couldn't yet speak out loud, when another voice interrupted her thoughts.

"Mind if I join you?" A question almost as surprising as the mouth who spoke it: Bradley Malone.

She shrugged and slid to the farthest side of the bench, watching him out of the corner of her eye as the toes of his polished dress shoes pointed at the massive ten-foot scar in the oak's trunk.

For several minutes, neither of them spoke, yet she couldn't help but wonder what he must be feeling in a moment like this. After all, he'd been the one pushing for the tree to go, pushing for financial relief at the cost of a premature death. Well, he'd won.

Only nothing about Bradley's demeanor resembled that of a victor. Oddly enough, he looked deflated, maybe even a bit defeated.

"I know you must think I'm the enemy." He bent forward, elbows to knees, and clasped his hands together. "And I suppose I haven't given you much reason to believe otherwise . . . but this is not how I hoped things would end."

Leery, she gave him another side glance, refusing to appease whatever guilt he was feeling now with platitudes she didn't mean.

"My hope in starting the repeal process was to eventually settle on a compromise with the council—to transition at least half of the maintenance fees over to the Parks and Recreation Department and to share in the liability the oak's location represents to the inn. I researched several counties up north of landowners caught in similar predicaments and was impressed by the agreements they reached."

Startled by his unexpected proclamation, she broke her silence. "But you were the one petitioning for it to be removed so that you could expand and build on to the property—"

"I asked for it to be removed, yes, but only so they would hear my case in person. If I came only asking for money to help with the costs, without any leverage, my request would have been denied immediately. My father tried that approach years ago, back when the financials were half the cost of what they are now. I would like to expand our lodging options one day, but those plans were never the driver behind the repeal, nor were they dependent on the removal of this oak. The north lawn only represents a small fraction of our buildable acreage."

Her expression was likely equal parts confused and curious. "So why didn't you say something to us sooner? Why not tell us your real motive for the committee meeting?"

"I couldn't risk it leaking out. We live in a very small town when it comes to the speed of information travel. Besides, the town's involvement in wanting to keep it only helped my cause. It's also why I hired Griff. I knew his bent would be to do everything in his power to keep it healthy." And then his gaze drifted to a place beyond the charred remains and the fallen branches. To an unknown location she couldn't see. "I have a lot of good memories in this spot. A few from when I was a boy, goofing off with you and Griff. But others, too." He pinched his lips closed, breathing through his nose for several seconds. "And a few that are more painful than they are pleasant now."

Abby thought back to when she'd attended his wedding, six or seven years ago. It had been right here, of course, at the inn. A beautiful catered affair with twinkle lights ribboning throughout the branches of this very tree. A ceremony that matched every perfected detail for two polished professionals. Only, their fairy tale had come crashing down without a happily ever after ending.

He shifted in his seat, straightening out the curve in his spine. "I don't understand a lot of things about life, but I have learned a few lessons over the last year or so." He rotated the shiny silver watch on his wrist and fingered the clasp. Abby recognized it as a gift Annette had given him on their first anniversary. "When things feel completely out of my control, my options become very simple: I can either tighten my grip and hang on no matter how much that hold might hurt myself or others, or I can open my fist and trust in a process much bigger than myself . . . and let go." He unclasped the watch, studied it for several seconds, and then slipped it into his coat pocket, leaving the ghost of an outline on his wrist.

It had been years since she and Bradley had engaged in any kind of interaction beyond the boundaries of an employer-employee relationship, and even in those years, their conversations had often revolved around their differing life goals regarding future plans. But the Bradley sharing with her now was neither an arrogant teenager nor an aloof boss. He was simply a man who had been broken by pain and scarred by loss.

Two things her own heart could relate to well. Two things that bonded even the most opposite of personality types.

"I'm sorry, Bradley. For everything you've gone through this last year with Annette." It was the first time she'd spoken those words to him since his divorce had finalized, though she realized now, she should have said them much sooner. Hurt didn't discriminate in heartbreak. It just . . . hurt.

He glanced at the toe of his shoe and gave a stiff nod in reply. "I'm sorry, too. About the storm. And the tree." He pointed at the dying oak. "I'm sure this brings up some difficult memories for you. It makes me wonder what Arnie would have done."

Bradley and his family had known her father for decades—he'd been a man loved by a small circle of friends, and the Malone clan had filled many places in that circle.

She lifted her eyes to the tree once again, letting his thoughtful statement wrap around her heart until it provided a response. "He would say a blessing, for all the years this tree has served our town and for all the years to come without it, and then he would say good-bye in that calm yet heartfelt way of his . . . and then he'd let it go." Her bottom lip quivered as she thought of her father's commitment to honor the nature God had created for His children to enjoy.

In her father's time on this earth, he had planted many seeds. He'd nurtured, tended, and pruned many maturing plants and trees. And he'd reaped a harvest hundreds of times over from the land he'd dedicated his life to. He never questioned the rhythm or cycle of the seasons, nor did he doubt the master plan behind it all. He'd simply accepted life and death as they came—in their due season and in their due time. The very thing she'd struggled to accept for the past two years. A thought struck her then, one that burrowed deep inside her. "I think my dad would want everyone who loved this tree to have the chance to do the same—to say good-bye and look ahead to a new beginning."

Bradley looked at her, seeming to turn her words over in his own head. "Then I think I should probably make a few phone calls."

Tears shimmered in her eyes as his meaning became clear. "I'd be happy to make some, too."

He gave her a single squeeze on the shoulder before he stood and faced the path back to the inn.

"Bradley?"

He twisted back, waited.

"Thank you," she said. "For this . . . but also for all the decades your family invested in my father's vision for these grounds."

"You're welcome." He scrutinized her face for a moment more. "Why do I get the sense there might be something more you need to say?"

"Because there is." On her next exhale, she spoke the words she never thought she'd find the courage to believe. "I think it's time for me to let go, too. I need to find a vision of my own."

Twelve

Will you meet me at the creek? texted Bee.

Even after several days of living a stone's throw away from the woman he loved, reading her name light up his phone screen caused his gut to seize. Just like it had when he'd watched her walk out her front door this morning. But if Griffin had learned anything since coming back to Oak Springs, it was that he couldn't manufacture closure. He couldn't will it into existence just because it would be easier not to feel the pain.

True *closure*, it seemed, was a daily walk, the same one Abby had taken for the last twenty-three months, two weeks, and four days.

He watched her now, her elbows pressed against the railing of the ten-foot cedar bridge, while she peered into the water below . . . the same place they'd released her father's ashes only a month after his funeral. Griffin was close enough to see her lips moving, yet too far to hear the prayer she whispered. A bucket of rocks and debris was propped beside her right boot, evidence of the time she must have spent combing the bank before he'd arrived.

Careful not to startle her, he slipped out of the grouping of juniper trees he'd been stationed near for longer than he realized, and started toward her.

Though he knew Abby tracked him out of the corner of her eye, it wasn't until he reached her on the bridge that she acknowledged him fully, sliding her open palm toward him on the railing. Both a peace offering and a gift. He wouldn't take either for granted.

The soundtrack of spring played in the background as his hand enveloped hers. "Abby, I'm sor—"

"No." She shook her head. "I'm sorry, Griff. For everything I said—for everything I chose to believe about my dad's treatment decisions. I wasn't brave enough to ask the harder questions back then, because I was too afraid to hear the answers. I wanted something else—*someone else*—to blame for my pain." She interlocked their fingers. "But that's the risk in loving people. The depth of heartache often matches the depth of the love."

A profound statement, and yet one he'd done everything in his power to avoid since Arnie's death. He leaned on the railing beside her, her hand tucked firmly in his. "I convinced myself there were better opportunities for you and me outside of this town. That I'd have a better return on Arnie's investment in my business while helping you explore your talents in a bigger city . . . but the truth is, I wasn't strong enough to stay. I wasn't strong enough to face the grief of a life here without your dad. He was the best man I've ever known, Bee. And I'm a better man for having loved him." *And for having been loved by him.*

Emotion crept up his throat and stung at his eyes. He hadn't allowed himself to feel this—these tears, this absence, this overwhelming ache. But this was a part of the journey. He'd wanted to believe that if he wasn't here, he could outrun it, outlive it somehow. "I was wrong to give you an ultimatum."

A tear slipped down her cheek, followed by another one. "But I can understand why you did."

"And I can understand why you stayed."

She twisted to face him, to touch her palm to his damp cheek. "Thank you for coming back, Griff. I needed you to come back."

"I needed it, too." More than he could even say. He lifted their joined hands to kiss her knuckles before moving in to press a kiss to her mouth, when he stubbed the toe of his work boot on the mysterious bucket of rocks at her feet. "Mind if I move these?"

"*Oh*—I forgot those were there." She bent to reach for the handle, but he beat her to it, waiting on her next instruction.

"Where would you like them? Are these for a new project you're working on?" He peered into the random collection of rocks, sticks, moss, and sand, and when she didn't answer him immediately, he glanced up to see her transformed by an emotion he wasn't sure he could name.

"What . . . what's that look about?"

"I did it." She bit her lip as if trying to conceal a smile much too uncontainable to be controlled. "I called the agent and put in an offer on the Smithe Farm." Her elation was contagious. "I'm ready, Griff. I'm ready to chase a new dream. You helped me see that."

"You . . . you made an offer? Wow. When? This afternoon?" He could hardly believe it. Abby was many things, but spontaneous wasn't usually one of them. Then again, she'd obviously been dreaming of that property for quite a while.

The laugh that escaped her made something in his chest pinch. "Yes. A cash offer, pending inspection, of course. Sheryl said if everything goes according to plan, it could close within thirty days." She pointed to the rocks still suspended in his grip. "And those will be a housewarming gift to myself—I have plans to create a memorial garden with key pieces I find around the grounds where my dad worked." She touched his arm and pressed a kiss to his cheek. "Bradley gave me his blessing to take anything I wanted from the land, as long as I promised to come back and check in on the gardens from time to time."

Another surprise Griffin hadn't seen coming. She'd talked to Bradley? Just how many hours had he been away this afternoon? Although, he supposed he had a few things to update her about as well, starting with his offer from Winston. If all went well at his meeting tomorrow afternoon, he hoped it would end with a plan to transition back to Oak Springs permanently by summer.

"I'm so incredibly proud of you," he said. "And I know Arnie would be, too."

"Thank you." She placed a hand to his shirtfront and seemed to consider her next words. "I know there's a lot of work ahead with removing the old oak, Griff, and I'm prepared to help you in whatever way you need me to, but . . ."

His need to kiss her was growing by the millisecond. "Yeah?"

"I had an idea I'm hoping you might be willing to help me with first. It will likely delay your timeline by a week or so, but I think it's important for our town to be given the chance to say good-bye to such a significant part of its history."

The cramp in his bicep might have been reason enough to put the bucket down, but it was the ache to hold the woman he loved in his arms that convinced him to let it go. He drew her close and pressed a kiss to her mouth. "Your timeline is my timeline."

Thirteen

The weather couldn't have been more ideal for an outdoor event—*"a perfect day to shed happy tears,"* Gladys had said to Abby when she'd rolled up in her van bearing donuts and to-go coffee for their busy crew. They didn't have much time to set up between the back-to-back weddings hosted at the inn between Friday night and then again on Saturday afternoon, but Bradley and Annette had each agreed—which might have been a mini miracle in and of itself—that this event was too important to their town to decline.

Griff and Jason had worked tirelessly, carrying chairs, tables, speakers, and even creating a platform angled to fit the base of a tree she'd drawn dozens of times as a child from memory. And though today marked the ending of one era, perhaps it also marked the beginning of a new one. A chance for new history to be made, new memories to be penciled, colored, and stuck to refrigerator doors.

"You ready, Bee? The chairs are filling up quickly." Griff's voice at her bedroom door bolstered her courage and calmed her nerves. Though her part in the tree's memorial service was minimal in comparison to Griffin's, she'd never been a fan of public speaking.

She cracked her door open slowly, stepping out in a turquoise sundress she'd borrowed from Annette's bountiful closet. It had taken nearly twenty minutes for the bobby pins she'd used to create something that looked less like a work-ready ponytail and more like something semi-elegant she'd done on purpose.

"Wow," Griffin said, his winsome smile warming her cheeks. "You look gorgeous."

"I figured a dress would be more appropriate for today than my faded jeans and gardening boots."

As if that was the only invitation he needed to touch her, Griffin wrapped his flannel-clad arms around her and said, "I fell in love with the girl in the faded jeans and garden boots, so no matter what kind of fancy clothes she puts on for a day, I'll always be partial to the former."

She raised her chin to search his eyes, his declaration moving her in a way she hadn't prepared for. It had been a long time since they'd used the word *love* in regard to their relationship, and while hearing it now had caused her heart to double in size, she had so many more thoughts than time to articulate them fully.

With misty eyes, she attempted the impossible. "Griffin, there's so much I want to . . ."

But he didn't wait—he simply lowered his face to hers and kissed her in a way that could have made even the harshest skeptic a believer in second chances.

"To be continued," he whispered against her mouth before taking hold of her hand and leading her out of her cottage and into a crowd of people who needed the same encouragement Griffin had just offered her.

Gladys, Bradley, and Jason stood at the corner of the stage, giving Abby a nod that assured her all was in place and ready to begin. Their guests were seated, the podium and microphone in place, and the abundant basket filled with tiny tokens of hope was all set to be shared at the completion of the service.

Abby took her place next to Bradley, the first speaker of the day, and she couldn't help but smile as Jason greeted Griffin with a smack on the back and a too-loud whisper of *"Looking forward to hearing you preach, boss."*

If not for the crowd of several hundred people staring up at the stage, she was certain Griffin would have pinned Jason into a headlock in under five seconds flat. But instead, the five of them sobered quickly, ultra-aware of the unique atmosphere surrounding them. Abby scanned the faces of the crowd, overcome by the multitude of townsfolk. Many of the residents in attendance worked weekend retail and service jobs at their local shops and restaurants, sacrificing their time and paychecks to be here this morning. Others were reputable business owners she knew by name, sharing this moment with staff and customers alike. And dozens more were grouped by families—grandparents, parents, and children old and young. But no matter their differing life stages and seasons, all had come for the same cause: to honor the life of a legendary oak tree.

A quiet reverence hovered over the crowd as Bradley opened the service by sharing a brief history of the families who'd homesteaded their town over a century ago, recalling the documented events and records of the live oak throughout the decades. And then, with a pounding heart, it was Abby's turn to share with her fellow townspeople. Griffin squeezed her hand twice, and she squeezed back before stepping up to the podium.

It took her a minute to catch her breath and find her voice, but then the words were there, waiting and ready for her to share. "Today we say good-bye to a tree that's become more than just a landmark in our town, but a friend. My father, Arnie Brookshire, used to say, '*You can never outtalk the listening ear of a tree.'"* A gentle laugh rolled through the gathered crowd. "And certainly, that's been true of our town's namesake." She paused, forcing a shaky smile onto her face. "So, as we honor the life of a friend who's been a listening ear for many of us here today, let's take some time to reflect on the legacy we're passing down to our future generations."

She could feel Griffin's presence at her back the entire time she spoke, a reassuring support. And when it was time to pass off the microphone to him, he was there, as ready to take the lead as he was to follow.

Abby had always respected Griffin's unwavering confidence, his ability to direct a crew and communicate a solution as problems arose, but in this moment, it was his willingness to meet a need that she admired most.

"When I first started working with trees," he began, "I didn't know much about the components that made up a tree, other than the obvious trunk, branches, and leaves I've been drawing since my toddler days." The crowd chuckled and Griffin smiled good-naturedly. "But the more time I spent with trees, and the people who loved them, I've learned a bit more."

He pulled back from the microphone momentarily to point at the massive oak trunk behind him. "The wood you see behind me has several different functions—all of them layered and complex, all of them formed to meet the needs of a living tree. One layer carries water from roots to leaves. Another transports nutrients. And another, at the very core, offers support and stability. The heartwood's strength allows the tree to stand through the harshest elements any season and circumstance can bring. It also serves to preserve and protect the tree. Without the heartwood, there would be no tree in any town that could outlive a single generation, much less multiple."

Griffin reached for Abby's hand, and she gave it to him willingly, her own heart bursting with pride at the passion in his words. "Our town can learn a lot from the heartwood inside this beautiful old oak. Because its legacy is here—in this town, and in each other. It has lived a life we can be proud of, one of strength and purpose, one that continues, even now, to bring friends and families together." His gaze moved over the crowd. "It's our turn to do the same. To be the type of community that supports and strengthens each other. That protects our future by preserving the memories and stories from our past. And above all, to carry on as a living heartbeat, even after our tree is gone."

Not a single whispered word buzzed through the crowd as he stepped away from the mic stand. A single clap broke through the silence, multiplying into a deafening applause by hundreds of inspired people. Tears shimmered on the cheeks of many, including Abby's. Oh, how she loved this man—his strength, his heart, his ability to connect God's creation to His people. He was so much like her father, and yet so different, too.

"In light of what Griffin just shared," Gladys began, leading them in the last part of the service, the benediction, "this basket of acorns is a gift from our beautiful tree—to you and your families. They are for planting in your yards, your businesses, and in the common areas we walk beside every day. Griffin's absolutely right—the legacy we've been gifted by this tree doesn't have to end today. It's our privilege and honor to spread it and share it with others. To enjoy its shade on hot days, its beauty throughout the seasons, and its steadfast, listening ear. May your homes be blessed with love and laughter, and may your hearts be open to receive the gift of God's beautiful creation. Let's bow our heads."

Griffin's arm snaked around Abby's shoulders as Gladys spoke a prayer to close out one of the most special moments ever shared in their town. As people lingered around the property, partaking in refreshments, carving their initials into the tree bark and branches, and having their pictures taken at the oak by the professional photographer Annette had hired, Bradley's voice rang out above the chatter once more.

"One last thing." He smiled kindly in Abby's direction. "The inn has arranged to save a large portion of the oak's wood to use as a gift for our town. The city council has contracted a local artist skilled in creating memorial gardens to share her art with us all. Here, at the inn, we'll have a trellis made from the oak to stand in our new reflection garden, which will also be designed by the same talented artist and gardener. If you'd like more information on any of this, please contact Abby Brookshire for details. Thank you."

She smiled back at Bradley, appreciative of all the phone calls and conversations he'd had on her behalf over the last few days regarding a plan for the live oak, and for the new season beginning for them all. Pausing her search for Griffin, who had slipped into the crowd right after the prayer, Abby took note of Annette waiting at the bottom of the stage steps—for Bradley. She handed him a full plate of refreshments, and Abby couldn't help but note the way he touched Annette's elbow in gratitude, or the soft curve it brought to her mouth. Perhaps this new season was full of more beginnings than Abby had dared realize.

She found Griffin observing the crowd and the tree from the border of the property. Her heart warmed at his tender gaze as she approached.

"Thank you for doing this today," he said. "You were right. The town needed this time to reflect on the past so they could plan for a better future."

"Just like us." She reached for his hand. "What you said today—it was perfect, Griff."

"I was honored to have the chance." He squeezed her hand, and Abby twisted to face him fully.

"You've reminded me what hope for tomorrow feels like . . .

and it feels like this. It feels like you." She rose on her tiptoes and pressed a gentle kiss to his lips. "I love you, Griffin Malone. I always have and I always will."

As long as she lived, she would never forget the elation on his face. Griffin wrapped his arms around her middle and lifted her clear off the ground, nuzzling his face in the crook of her neck. "I'm sure glad you feel that way, Bee, since as of August first, I'll be a permanent resident of Oak Springs."

Though they'd discussed his offer to merge Winston's tree company with his storm cleanup business over the next several months, she hadn't heard him specify a date—until now. She pulled his face to hers one more time, kissing him in a way that left no room to question her feelings about this new plan. Or about him.

"I love you, Bee. I always have and I always will." Griffin glanced back at the tree, which might not have long to stand, but whose memory would carry on for a lifetime.

"What do you think? Should we make it official by carving our initials into the bark like the rest of our town is doing?"

"Actually," she said, pressing a hand to the left side of his chest, "I'd rather carve our names into the heartwood."

"Even better."

The End

Acknowledgments

FOR HEARTWOOD BY NICOLE DEESE

God: Above all, always. There is no joy to be found in writing without you.

My hubby, Tim Deese: Thank you for your endless patience when I say at midnight, "Just one more chapter . . ."

My parents, Stan and Lori Thomas: For walking the hardest grief journey imaginable with grace, empathy, encouragement, vulnerability, and love. I'm honored to be your daughter.

My kiddos, Preston, Lincoln, Lucy Mei: I am one blessed mama. I love all three of you dearly.

Coast to Coast Plotting Society Gals—Amy Matayo, Christy Barritt, Connilyn Cossette, Tammy Gray: Thank you for hashing out the plot details of this little novella with me! And, Christy, your idea for the teenagers chained to the tree was one of my favorite scenes to write! Love you all!

Tammy and Conni: Thank you for reading every chapter (multiple times over!!!). You are my not-so-secret weapons.

Early readers—Kacy Gourley, Jessica Wardell, Joanie Schultz, Renee Deese: Your perspective and love for fiction fuels my hardest writing days and makes my good writing days even brighter!

Jessica Kirkland at Kirkland Media Management: Thank you for agenting me well and for loving me even better.

Bethany House Publishers: Thank you for giving me the privilege to be a part of such a fun and memorable novella collection.

Special Thanks:

Joe Deese (certified arborist, tree climbing specialist, and one fantastic brother-in-law!): Thank you so, so, so much for the many questions you answered regarding ALL THINGS TREES and for doing your best to track my many fictional story trails on our phone calls. You're the bestest! PS: Thanks for letting me pay you in burgers. I think I still owe you approximately forty-five more or so. . . .

To the brilliant coauthors in this novella collection, The Kissing Tree—Regina Jennings, Karen Witemeyer, Amanda Dykes: It was such a pleasure to work with you lovely ladies on this project. Thanks for being such a positive group of writers and for sharing your precious stories with our world. Much love to you all!

About the Authors

REGINA JENNINGS is a graduate of Oklahoma Baptist University with a degree in English and a minor in history. She's the winner of the National Readers' Choice Award, a two-time Golden Quill finalist, and a finalist for the Oklahoma Book of the Year Award. Regina has worked at the *Mustang News* and at First Baptist Church of Mustang, along with time at the Oklahoma National Stockyards and various livestock shows. She lives outside of Oklahoma City with her husband and four children and can be found online at www.reginajennings.com.

Christy Award finalist and winner of the ACFW Carol Award, HOLT Medallion, and Inspirational Reader's Choice Award, bestselling author **KAREN WITEMEYER** writes historical romance to give the world more happily-ever-afters. Karen makes her home in Texas, with her husband and three children. Learn more about Karen and her books at www.karenwitemeyer.com.

AMANDA DYKES is a drinker of tea, dweller of redemption, and spinner of hope-filled tales who spends most days chasing wonder and words with her family. She's a former English teacher and the author of *Whose Waves These Are*, a *Booklist* 2019 Top Ten Romance debut, as well as *Set the Stars Alight* and several novellas. Find her online at www.amandadykes.com.

NICOLE DEESE'S (www.nicoledeese.com) humorous, heartfelt, and hope-filled novels include a Carol Award winner and RITA Award and INSPY Award finalists. When she's not working on her next contemporary romance, she can usually be found reading one by a window overlooking the inspiring beauty of the Pacific Northwest. She lives in small-town Idaho with her happily-ever-after hubby, her two wildly inventive and entrepreneurial sons, and her princess daughter with the heart of a warrior.

Sign Up for Authors' Newsletters

Keep up to date with the latest news on book releases and events by signing up for their email lists at:

karenwitemeyer.com

reginajennings.com

amandadykes.com

nicoledeese.com

You May Also Like . . .

This intriguing novella collection crosses the country—from Kansas to Texas, the Grand Canyon to New Mexico—with tales of sweet romance while exploring the fascinating history of the Harvey girls: young women seeking adventure and independence who worked in hotels throughout the country from the early 1880s to the late 1920s.

Serving Up Love by Tracie Peterson, Karen Witemeyer, Regina Jennings, and Jen Turano • traciepeterson.com; karenwitemeyer.com; reginajennings.com; jenturano.com

The path to love is filled with twists and turns in these stories of entangled romance with a touch of humor from four top historical romance novelists! This novella collection includes Karen Witemeyer's "The Love Knot," Mary Connealy's "The Tangled Ties That Bind," Regina Jennings's "Bound and Determined," and Melissa Jagears's "Tied and True."

Hearts Entwined by Karen Witemeyer, Mary Connealy, Regina Jennings, and Melissa Jagears • karenwitemeyer.com; maryconnealy.com; reginajennings.com; melissajagears.com

Ex-cavalry officer Matthew Hanger leads a band of mercenaries who defend the innocent, but when a rustler's bullet leaves one of them at death's door, they seek out help from Dr. Josephine Burkett. When Josephine's brother is abducted and she is caught in the crossfire, Matthew may have to sacrifice everything—even his team—to save her.

At Love's Command by Karen Witemeyer
HANGER'S HORSEMEN #1
karenwitemeyer.com

BETHANY HOUSE

More from the Authors

Assigned to find the kidnapped daughter of a mob boss, Pinkerton operative Calista York is sent to a rowdy mining town in Missouri. But she faces the obstacle of missionary Matthew Cook. He's as determined to stop a local baby raffle as he is the reckless Miss York whose bad judgement consistently seems to be putting her in harm's way.

Courting Misfortune by Regina Jennings
THE JOPLIN CHRONICLES #1
reginajennings.com

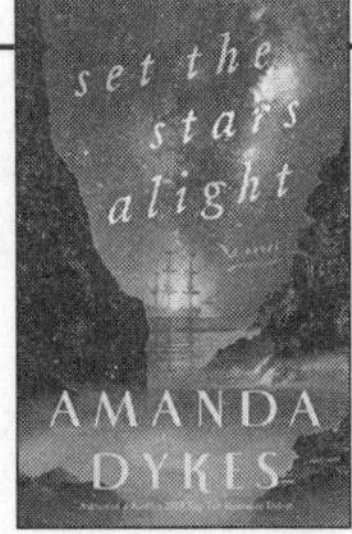

Reeling from the loss of her parents, Lucie Clairmont discovers an artifact under the floorboards of their London flat, leading her to an old seaside estate. Aided by her childhood friend Dashel, a renowned forensic astronomer, they start to unravel a history of heartbreak, sacrifice, and love begun 200 years prior—one that may offer the healing each seeks.

Set the Stars Alight by Amanda Dykes
amandadykes.com

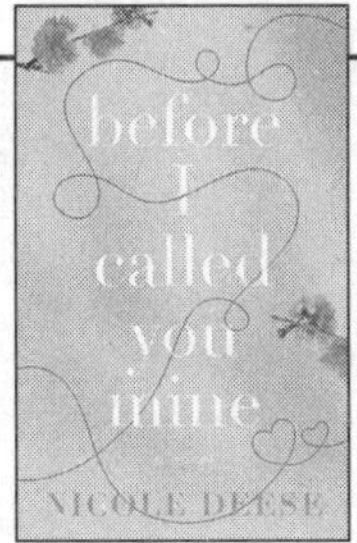

After many matchmaking schemes gone wrong, there's only one goal Lauren is committed to now—the one that will make her a mother. But to satisfy the adoption agency's requirements, she must remain single, which proves to be a problem when Joshua appears. With an impossible decision looming, she will have to choose between the two deepest desires of her heart.

Before I Called You Mine by Nicole Deese
nicoledeese.com

BETHANYHOUSE